D1382136

Let the People Sing

J. B. Priestley was born in 1894 at Bradford, the son of a schoolmaster. He went to school locally and served in the Army throughout the First World War, starting in the ranks and later becoming commissioned. After the war he went to Cambridge, where he read English literature, modern history and political science. Having contributed articles to London and provincial papers since he was sixteen, he moved to London in 1922 and quickly established himself as a reviewer, critic, and essayist, publishing several books a year.

The Good Companions, published on the brink of the 1929 depression, was an immediate success, and has since been filmed twice and dramatised for television. It was Priestley's third novel and made him famous almost overnight. His next novel, *Angel Pavement* was equally popular, as were later novels such as *Bright Day, Festival at Farbridge* and *Lost Empires*. In 1932 Priestley began a new career as a dramatist with *Dangerous Corner*, and went on to become very successful with plays such as *Time and the Conways, An Inspector Calls, Laburnum Grove* and *When We Are Married*. He also became involved in broadcasting, and regularly gave Sunday night radio talks, as well as wartime commentaries during the Second World War. He occasionally wrote for radio and television, but later in life devoted more time to public affairs, representing the UK at two UNESCO conferences. He died in 1984.

By J. B. Priestley

Fiction

Adam in Moonshine
Benighted
The Good Companions
Angel Pavement
Faraway
Wonder Hero
Laburnum Grove
They Walk in the City
The Doomsday Men
Let the People Sing
Blackout in Gretley
Daylight on Saturday
Three Men in New Suits
Bright Day

Jenny Villiers
Festival at Farbridge
The Other Place: short stories
The Magicians
Low Notes on a High Level
Saturn Over the Water
The Thirty-First of June
The Shapes of Sleep
Sir Michael and Sir George
Lost Empires
It's an Old Country
Out of Town (The Image Men – I)
London End (The Image Men – II)
Snoggle

Collected Plays

Volume I
  Dangerous Corner
  Time and the Conways
  Johnson over Jordan
  The Linden Tree
Volume II
  Laburnum Grove
  When we are Married
  The Golden Fleece
  Ever Since Paradise
Volume III
  Cornelius
  They Came to a City
  An Inspector Calls
  Summer Day's Dream

Eden End
I Have Been Here Before
Music at Night

Bees on the Boat Deck
Good Night Children
How are they at Home?

People at Sea
Desert Highway
Home is Tomorrow

Essays and Autobiography

Midnight on the Desert
Rain upon Godshill
Delight
All About Ourselves and other Essays
  (chosen by Eric Gillett)
Thoughts in the Wilderness

Margin Released
The Moments and other pieces
Essays of Five Decades
Over the Long High Wall
Outcries and Asides

Criticism and Miscellaneous

The English Comic Characters
English Journey
Journey Down a Rainbow (with
  Jacquetta Hawkes)
The Art of the Dramatist
Literature and Western Man
Victoria's Heyday

The World of J. B. Priestley (edited
  by Donald G. MacRae)
Trumpets over the Sea
The Prince of Pleasure and his
  Regency
The Edwardians
The English

J. B. PRIESTLEY

Let The People Sing

Mandarin

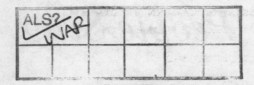

A Mandarin Paperback
LET THE PEOPLE SING

First published in Great Britain 1939
by William Heinemann Ltd
This edition published 1996
by Mandarin Paperbacks
an imprint of Reed International Books Ltd
Michelin House, 81 Fulham Road, London SW3 6RB
and Auckland, Melbourne, Singapore and Toronto

Copyright © J. B. Priestley 1939

A CIP catalogue record for this title
is available from the British Library
ISBN 0 7493 2276 4

Typeset by CentraCet Ltd, Cambridge
in 11 on 13 point Baskerville
Printed and bound in Great Britain
by Cox & Wyman, Reading, Berkshire

CONTENTS

AUTHOR'S NOTE

As a number of episodes from this novel will have
reached the public through their wireless sets before it
is published, a few words of explanation are necessary.
Six months ago the B.B.C. asked me to write a novel
they could serialise over the air before publiction. I had
always refused to allow my novels to be serialised in
newspapers or magazines before they appeared in book
form, but now I agreed to let the B.B.C. have a novel,
partly because I felt we might be at war in the autumn
– when they were going to serialise it – and that
broadcasting would then be extremely valuable to he
public. I stipulated that they should cut and shape such
episodes as they required, and that I should go ahead
and write exactly what I wanted to write and as much as
I liked (I wrote three times as much as the B.B.C.
required), always bearing in mind that the tale must
appeal to an enormous mixed audience. The later –
and, I think, better – chapters were written during the
anxious and darkening days of August, and I broadcast
the first instalment on Sunday, the Third of September,
the very day war was declared.

September, 1939   J. B. P.

CHAPTER I

ASTONISHING ADVENTURE OF AN
OUT-OF-WORK COMEDIAN

ONE MORNING last autumn a little man with a large sad face turned out of Midland Street, Birchester, and climbed the stairs next to the sewing-machine shop. At the top of these stairs are the offices of Silver and Baumber, variety agents and occasional producers of pantomime and touring revues.

The little man told the girl at the *Enquiry* desk that he didn't mind whether he saw Mr Silver or Mr Baumber, and said that he was well-known to both of them. 'No card necessary,' he added, looking hopefully at her. 'Just tell 'em Timmy Tiverton's here.'

'Who?'

'Timmy Tiverton.' He looked less hopeful now.

If the girl's face had put it up in neon lights, it could not have told him more plainly that she had never heard of him. She hesitated. Then a bell rang in one of the two interior rooms, and she went to answer it.

There were five other people in the waiting-room, all huddled together, and looking like the unwanted remains of a concert party. They took no notice of Timmy Tiverton, though he was worth staring at. He looked at a first glance like a prematurely aged youth, but a closer inspection showed him to be in his fifties. One eye looked even older than that, but the other one, in its round blue innocence, had hardly left school. His features, altogether too large for his small slight body, seemed to have been originally poured into a good mould, but they had not been allowed to set properly. His face had lines on it that ran in all directions, and was not unlike a circular railway map. His clothes were shabby but very neat. By the side of his hat, which was round and green and an obvious mistake, was a small worn suitcase. Mr Tiverton contemplated it, and tried over various remarks that might impress Mr Silver or Mr Baumber. He had plenty of time to do this, for more than ten minutes passed before the girl reappeared.

'Well, miss? All right, eh? Mr Silver or Mr Baumber?' Even off the stage, he had the peculiar voice, hoarse but with rusty squeaks in it, of the old-style comedian.

'Neither,' replied the girl in a hard tone. She was carrying some papers and gave the impression that work was being piled upon her. 'They can't see you.'

'Can't see me! Did you give 'em my name? Timmy Tiverton? Sure you got it right?'

She gave him a contemptuous stare. 'Yes, I'm not deaf. They both said they'd nothing for you and were too busy to see you.'

Timmy shook his head. 'I can't understand it. Sounds like a mistake. Now, miss, are you really sure – '

'I've told you,' she cried angrily. She tried to pretend he was no longer there, and put some paper into her typewriter. But there he was, still staring at her, with two eyes that didn't match in the funny big sad face. She had to look up.

'You don't want me to tell you what they said about you, do you?' she asked, with a kind of bitterness, as if life was a bad business and he ought to know better than to want to poke his finger in and stir it up. 'Oh, go on. I can't help it, can I?'

'No. Didn't say you could.' He hesitated a moment, then bravely: 'What did they say about me?'

'Leave it alone. There isn't anything doing, and that's that.'

'I see,' said Timmy, and went to pick up his hat and case. Then he came back to her, just for a parting shot. 'Believe it or not, young woman, but I was topping the bill at the Empire here before you were born.'

'That doesn't surprise me,' she retorted, not even looking at him now.

'I always hated the sight of Birchester. Worse than Bradford,' he added thoughtfully. 'And that's saying something. *Good* morning.'

He made a good exit, and a grand indignation carried him down the stairs. What, a little two-by-four provincial agency like Silver and Baumber giving itself airs now! Bread-and-dripping tours! Why, there'd been a time when these Silvers and Baumbers, playing at being agents up in Birchester, couldn't have got a single week out of him, not if they'd asked for it on their bended knees.

'No, old boy, not on their bended knees.' He said this out loud to a tall fat chap at the foot of the stairs.

'Eh, what's that, old boy?' asked the tall fat chap, in a fruity baritone. He was a certainty for King Rat or Demon Wolf again, opening Christmas Eve, Middlesbrough. 'How *are* things upstairs?'

Timmy could not resist it. He went closer, raised himself on tiptoe, half-closed his eyes, and whispered carefully: 'Looked a bit queer to me. Silver's in his underpants playing himself at darts. Baumber's throwing pound notes out of the window because, he says, it's his sister's birth-day. And somebody's left five performing sea-lions in the waiting-room. The girl up there says it's never been like this on a Monday before. So I said to myself: "Well, old boy, why wait?" But all the best, all the best!'

That was all very well, but by the time he had reached Midland Street, Timmy felt as if he were walking with lead boots on at the bottom of the sea. Silver and Baumber wouldn't even see him now. Nothing left for it but to try the only other agency in Birchester, Packles in Shelving Square. Timmy had never bothered with Packles before. They came at the bottom of any list of agents. If Packles didn't want you, then nobody wanted you.

Shelving Square was a small dirty square not far from the Town Hall, and seemed to be chiefly occupied by moneylenders and agents for corsets. Packles were at the back of one of the larger and dirtier houses in it, and Timmy succeeded at once in seeing young Mr Packles, who had a swollen face.

'It's a gumboil,' he explained gloomily. 'Hurts like hell. Didn't get a wink o' sleep last night.'

'Sorry to hear that.' And Timmy was, very sorry.

Young Mr Packles, who was not very young, grunted. 'Well, I've 'eard of you, of course – '

'Of course,' cried Timmy cheerfully and confidently. 'Top o' the bill – '

'But it's a long time since,' young Mr Packles continued brutally. 'About when I was still at school. If I'd been asked, I'd 'ave said you were dead an' buried.'

'Here, steady!' Timmy stared at him reproachfully. 'I've been in work all the time. Only finished last Saturday. In Warrington. Closed after ten weeks tour. *Warmer and Merrier.*'

Young Mr Packles winced, though whether it was because he had been suddenly reminded of his gumboil or because he had heard of *Warmer and Merrier* before,

Timmy did not know. He hoped that Mr Packles had not heard of *Warmer and Merrier*, which had been a terrible hotchpotch of a touring revue, with no proper book, no proper production, no proper rehearsals, no proper anything. What a show! One old set that seemed to represent the Bay of Naples half eaten by rats; one of those pantomime choruses of bony school-kids; and the other five in the cast all belonging to one family, a family completely devoid of talent, a family that only stopped quarrelling when it decided to turn in a body on him, Timmy Tiverton, just because he did occasionally get a laugh and a hand. No wonder the public preferred ninepenn'orth of pictures. 'Yes,' Timmy continued, pretending not to notice the wincing, '*Warmer and Merrier*. It had the makings of a good little show, but the management didn't know enough.'

'The only report I 'ad on it,' said young Mr Packles, who might have owned the Palladium by the way he talked, 'said it was terrible.'

'Badly managed. Badly booked. You know how it is.' And Timmy gave this talking gumboil his most charming smile, and felt his face cracking with it.

'We like bang-up-to-date acts.' And Mr Packles waved his hand, though at what, Timmy could not imagine. 'B.B.C. turns, specially. I don't think you've been on the air, 'ave you?'

'No,' replied Timmy, who had faced this awkward question before and hated it like poison. 'I like my public to see me.'

'He wants *what*?' This question came in a shout from about twelve inches behind Timmy's right ear. He jumped, then turned indignantly. An elderly man, with a long spreading kind of nose and suspicious little eyes too close together at the top of it, was standing there, bending forward, and holding a black ear-trumpet almost big enough for a gramophone.

'He says, Dad, he likes 'is public to see 'im,' bellowed young Mr Packles.

'What public?' shouted old Mr Packles, moving his trumpet round from his son to Timmy.

'Any public,' roared Timmy, almost inside the trumpet.

Old Mr Packles nodded, as if somehow all this confirmed his worst suspicions, then said quietly to his son: 'I don't catch on to all this, Fred, but if he wants an audition, he can 'ave one.' He turned to Timmy again. 'Comedian, eh?'

'That's right,' Timmy shouted. 'Comedian. Funny man. Make you laugh.'

'You come into this other room, then, an' make us laugh. Eh, Fred? How's your face this morning? Looks a lot worse to me.'

'An' it feels a lot worse,' his son told him gloomily. 'This way, Mr What's-it.'

If the two windows in this other room had been cleaner, they would have framed as good a view of some of Birchester's dirtiest roofs as any man could want. It was not a cheerful room. It contained a number of dusty photographs, an old upright piano, five rickety chairs, and a stack of bottles that had once held So-and-So's Pale Ale. It also contained more than its fair share of Birchester's sooty murk, which makes the whole city seem like one vast railway station. Sitting very close together near the piano, young Mr Packles nursed his swollen face while his father carefully extended the enormous ear-trumpet towards Timmy, who by this time hated the pair of them.

'If you want a pianist,' said young Mr Packles, 'you'll have to wait till this afternoon.'

'I can manage,' said Timmy grimly. 'Of course, you're

not seeing the act under the best conditions. I mean to say – '

'That's all right. We're used to it.'

'We've 'ad some of the best 'ere, the very best,' old Mr Packles shouted in his startling tuneless voice. 'You go on. Make us laugh.'

Timmy nodded, closed his eyes a second, tried to forget he was in a back room on Monday morning in Birchester with this awful pair, then all desperate comic sparkle, he began one of his favourite numbers. 'Now the missis once moved in socie-tee,' he sang, loudly and confidently, but feeling like one of the front rank of the Light Brigade. He did one verse and the chorus, then went into his patter. 'You don't know my wife, do you?' he asked the Packles', who were now looking as if they had never known anybody. 'My wife's a very fine woman, a very fine woman. Very fond of pets. I say, she's very fond of pets. I'll never forget the time she came back with a big bird-cage. "Look at what I've got," she says. "Well, Maria, what 'ave you got?" I asks. "It's a parrot," she says – '

'Half a minute,' young Mr Packles interrupted gloomily. 'Is this the one about the parrot that didn't like cheese?'

'That's right,' replied Timmy, feeling like a burst balloon. 'I always find it gets a big laugh – the way I tell it.'

'We know it. Dad,' he shouted down the trumpet, 'it's the one about the parrot that didn't like the cheese. I'm telling 'im we know it.'

'Quite right,' said his father, in what he mistakenly thought a whisper. 'Doesn't seem to 'ave much go about 'im, this chap, does he? But we'll give 'im another two or three minutes.'

Timmy swallowed hard, told himself to remember that this seemed about his last chance, then plunged into his patter again. 'And then there's my brother. What a man!

I say, what a man! I'll never forget the day he got married. Now we all went along early in the morning – '

It was here that old Mr Packles leaned towards his son and spoke again in what he imagined to be a whisper, completely drowning Timmy. 'I told your mother to stop in bed today,' said old Mr Packles. 'I told her if she didn't rest properly today, with her legs in that state again, she'll 'ave another fortnight of it, an' a nurse into the bargain.' Then he turned, rather startled, towards Timmy. 'What did you say?'

'I said *good morning*,' Timmy shouted at the top of his voice. 'You lot don't want a comic, you want a clinic.'

So now, he thought, as he found his way out of Shelving Square, nobody wanted him. And this was Timmy Tiverton, eccentric comedian, who was topping the bill when he was twenty-four, making his hundred a week. Timmy Tiverton, always a riot! He had about three pounds fifteen shillings left in the world, with a shirt or two in his little case, and a prop basket in the L.M.S. cloakroom at Crewe. He was back in Midland Street, and as it was nearly one o'clock he turned into the 'George' for all the lunch he felt he could afford, a glass of bitter and some bread and cheese. The bar was crowded with big red-faced Birchester business chaps, with their necks swelling over the backs of their collars, all talking about the bad times and swallowing double whiskies. Not a man there, it seemed, was making any money. Everything was a dead loss. The silver they chucked down on the bar every few minutes for more double whiskies must have been wrenched out of the children's money boxes or the gas meter. With these brass-faced giants roaring all round him, Timmy stood at the bar counter, gnawing at cheese that tasted like soap and washing it down with beer that tasted like nothing.

A miserable old man, wearing a placard *Blind*, came

shuffling in, rattling two or three coppers in his tin cup,
Poor old beggar! He might have been specially sent in,
Timmy thought, just to tell him not to be so sorry for
himself when there were so many people a lot worse off.
Timmy found sixpence.

'Now outside – you!' shouted a barmaid fiercely.

'We've told you before not to come in here,' another
barmaid cried.

'That's right,' a fat customer jeered. 'You and your
blind! Hop it!'

And Timmy, angry and disgusted, saw the potman
making his way round the bar to put the old man out.
Typical of Birchester. Hearts like dried peas.

'Here you are,' said Timmy loudly, and instead of giving
him sixpence he made it a shilling, which was certainly
more than he could afford. The next moment the blind
old man was hustled out. And everybody was staring
reproachfully at Timmy, who stared back at them
defiantly.

'What did you want to go and give him something for?'
cried the nearest barmaid. 'That old devil's been told
hundreds of times not to come in here.'

'It's just the same at the "Lion",' said the fat customer.

'That's right, Albert,' said his friend. 'Same at the
"White Hart" and the "Standard", I know for a fact.' He
wagged his head at Timmy. 'You shouldn't encourage
'im.'

'I should think not!' cried the barmaid, regarding
Timmy with contempt.

He faced them boldly. 'I never heard such talk,' he
protested. 'Why shouldn't I give him something? Here's a
poor old – '

'Poor!' And the barmaid almost screamed it. 'He's not
poor. I only wish I made half what he does.'

'Biggest fraud in Birchester, Old Walter is,' said the fat man. 'Famous character round 'ere.'

'I did hear once,' said his friend thoughtfully, 'that Old Walter owns at least half a dozen cottage houses out Bamley way.'

'We like to look after our customers.' And the barmaid looked severely at Timmy. 'Everybody hasn't money to throw away on that old twister, even if you have.'

'Oh – me!' said poor Timmy, making the best of it. 'Money's no object with me. I just don't know what to do with it, that's my trouble.' And he picked up his little case and made as good an exit as he could.

But he had an idea. Tommy Dobson, the manager of the Birchester Palace, was an old acquaintance of his, and it was just barely possible that Tommy might know of something for him. It was worth trying. Anything was worth trying now. It was getting on for two now, but it was Monday and there would have been a band call, and Tommy might still be there.

He went to the front and tried the box-office. A very smart young man was in there, going over the sheet with a girl.

'Good morning, good morning! How's business?' Timmy tried a bright opening.

The smart young man raised his eyebrows, which were very thin and very black and first-class for raising purposes. 'Good morning. Business is just fine. Wanting seats for tonight?'

'Me?' Timmy smiled, and tried to put his thirty-odd years experience of the profession into the smile. 'I'm Timmy Tiverton.'

The eyebrows stayed where they were, pasturing on the upper slopes. Their owner gave a little cough, and that was all. No recognition of the name, no answering smile, nothing.

Timmy had to flounder on. 'And I'm an old friend of Tommy Dobson's, and I didn't want to leave Birchester without having a word with him.'

The young man seemed faintly amused now. 'Where have you been?'

'Been? Just finished a short tour. Why?' Timmy had to edge away a little because a large determined woman had now arrived at the box-office window.

'Because Tommy Dobson's been dead and buried these last six months.' The young man turned away. 'Yes, madam? Two for Thursday? Certainly.'

Timmy walked slowly down the steps, feeling like a ghost. He hadn't known Tommy Dobson very well, hadn't set eyes on him for years, but if poor old Tommy had been his dearest friend it couldn't have been worse. Dead and buried for months. Timmy began to feel that he too was dead, but somehow hadn't been buried.

His one desire now was to find somewhere quiet. He climbed into a trolley-bus, which after a mile or so stopped at a large gateway, and there Timmy got out and wandered into a park. Not far from the entrance was a circular space, with seats all round and in the middle some little fountains and pools, and above them, dominating the scene, a very ugly statue. As Timmy dumped himself and his case on an empty seat, this statue seemed to have its eye on him. It was a statue of Alderman Sir Benjamin Flitwick, in whom Birchester appeared to take a mysterious deep pride. Sir Benjamin had a very long mournful face, with whiskers all round it, a frock-coat that had been much favoured by pigeons, very baggy trousers, and he was holding a sooty scroll. He and Timmy disliked one another at sight. To Timmy, now lighting his last

cigarette but one, Sir Benjamin there represented everything he had always disliked about Birchester. As for Sir
Benjamin, you could almost hear him saying that this park
of his was not intended for out-of-work comedians from
nowhere, but for good respectable Birchester citizens,
several of whom were sitting on neighbouring seats,
yawning, spitting, scratching themselves, reading newspapers folded into six-inch squares of print, and telling
small children to stop it at once. For Birchester, which
has a pall of smoke that never allows the sunlight to come
through, it was a fine afternoon. Quiet too. The hard-
working city was all round you, but out of sight and
muffled. There was a kind of woolly thickness about the
air and it made Timmy feel rather sleepy. But not less
miserable. A little ghost, new to it and not knowing what
to do in Birchester, might easily come here of an
afternoon.

All that happened to Timmy for the next half-hour was
that a young man wearing an old raincoat and carrying a
small worn suitcase came hurrying up, took a quick look
round, then coolly moved Timmy's case to make room
for himself. 'Give me a light, chum, will you?' he said,
almost in a whisper. He had bright blue darting eyes, and
a slight Irish accent. Timmy found a match for him, then
looked away because he was anxious to avoid further talk.
But the young man blew out a cloud of smoke, and then,
to Timmy's relief, was gone.

Timmy leaned back and closed his eyes. He could easily
have wept. He felt old, tired, finished. Not that there was
anything wrong with his act; he was as good now as he
had been when they had paid him a hundred a week; but
people weren't the same and the world wasn't the same,
that was the trouble. All machines now. Films – fun out of
a tin. Wireless – more machines. And now these Hitlers

and Mussolinis with *their* machines. It wasn't properly human any more. Look at all these new acts – all alike, crooning away into mikes, pretending to be Americans; they might all have been turned out by a machine. All the real warm liveliness and fun going out of the world. It was about time he went too.

The sound of voices made him open his eyes. A police inspector and a sergeant were standing between him and the statue, looking round sharply and talking in a quick rumble. Once they took a good look at him. Well, let 'em. He'd done nothing wrong except to try and give people a good laugh for the last thirty years. Perhaps that was a crime now. Even so, he reflected grimly, they'd have to go back a bit for most of their evidence. He watched them go on into the park.

Then he closed his eyes again. He tried to keep his mind on the present, for he had to decide what to do, but it went floating back into the past, when the world was all different. The huge Empires were crowded to the roof again ... the band rattled out his old opening numbers ... he was doing quick changes in the wings once more ... then having his stout and oysters during the long wait ... seeing all the boys and girls on Sunday at Crewe or Doncaster stations ... getting back to London with the next three months booked solid and money to burn and nobody worrying ... and Betty. He hadn't thought much about her for years now. She was one of the prettiest and cleverest little soubrettes on the halls, and everybody had laughed at him and said she'd never have him, but they'd got married, that week in Newcastle, and for three years he'd never known whether he was on his head or his heels, for they'd been so happy and they'd spent money like millionaires, not caring at all because they seemed to make so much between them. Then suddenly, no more

Betty. Out like a light. As he followed her again to the grave, he seemed to follow scores of them, clever boys, merry girls, to the edge of the dark. In some mysterious way he could still see the vast, smoky, coloured caverns of the packed Empires and Palaces and hear the orchestras rapping out the jolly old tunes, while at the same time he could also see the lights of friendly faces going out one by one; some of them, like Betty, asking too much of their frail bodies and suddenly dropping; others dying by inches of drink and despair; and others again – yes, there were plenty of them; he had to face it – not wanting to live on, pulling a trigger, making a hole in the water, knowing they were finished and so going clean out of the bill. And now what was he going to do? For he was finished, too.

He was disturbed again, this time by one of the ugliest little boys he had ever seen, a messy, dribbling pie-faced urchin, who was standing near the seat and staring at him with eyes like sour gooseberries. He shook his head at this solemn visitor, then stared away, trying to think. What was the best way for a sane man, who knew he wasn't wanted, to clear out of the world that didn't want him? No throat-slashing, of course. Drowning? They said it felt all right once you got past the first choking stage, but somehow Timmy didn't fancy trying it. He felt desperate, but not as desperate as all that. What he wanted was a decent back door out, not a jump into a stinking black canal.

'Hey!' cried the ugly little boy.

Tommy shook his head and pulled a face at him. What a time to be bothered with a kid like this!

'Eee, you 'ave got a funny face.'

'I know I have, boy, but just pop off now. Your mother wants you.'

'She doesn't,' cried the little boy triumphantly. 'She's

poorly. Me Uncle Alfred brought me 'ere. That's 'im over there. Look!'

'I don't want to look. Just tell your Uncle Alfred to take you away.'

Now what, Timmy thought, about a gas-oven? Said to be comfortable and not too inconvenient. But that was all right if a chap had his own gas-oven, but it would be a bit thick to take a room specially so that you could put your head in the gas-oven. You couldn't very well say to the woman: 'Well, if you've got a good gas-oven, I'll only want a room for tonight.' What about taking a hundred aspirins? But suppose they just made you sick and silly? Stomach-pump work, and when you come to all your money's gone on aspirin.

'This is 'im,' announced the little boy. 'Me Uncle Alfred.'

Timmy had to look. There was Uncle Alfred standing a few yards away, a sagging oldish man, with a face like a boiled suet pudding that had been wedged into a bowler-hat too small for it. This little boy would grow up to look like that, and was probably only too anxious to get on with it. Not for the first time during these last few years, Timmy now regarded the whole biological process with suspicion. What was the point of it?

'What's in yer bag?' asked the boy.

'Never you mind.' Timmy still looked away.

'Go on. Tell us. What's inside?' The boy had raised his voice now.

This brought Uncle Alfred into the scene. 'Allus the same that lad is,' he observed with some complacency. 'Wants to know, and won't take No for an answer. Ask, ask, ask, that's 'im.'

The little suitcase had apparently been pushed right off the seat by the young fellow who had asked for a light so urgently. Now the little boy lifted it on to the seat again, and for the first time since he had sat down Timmy had a look at it.

'Why, that's not mine,' he cried, looking in bewilderment from the case to the boy and from the boy to Uncle Alfred. 'It's like mine but it isn't mine. It must be that young fellow's. Perhaps he swapped 'em on purpose.'

To all this, Uncle Alfred replied: 'Is that so?' He had a suspicious little eye in that boiled pudding face of his.

'I can open it,' said the boy. 'Look!'

'Now, lad, no touching,' said Uncle Alfred, much too late.

For now the case was open on the seat, and the boy had pushed aside the newspapers that were lying on top. Underneath them was a rum-looking metal canister.

'It's ticking – like our clock. I can 'ear it,' said the little boy, poking it with his fat forefinger.

'Look out!' yelled Timmy, and as the boy jumped back, Timmy grabbed at the bomb – for he was sure it couldn't be anything else – and instinctively hurled it as far as he could away from everybody, straight at the pools and fountains and the statue.

It hit the base of the statue, and then that Birchester park seemed to split into two. When the park jerked itself together again, Sir Benjamin Flitwick suddenly came to life. Above the smoke that still obscured his damaged pedestal, he swayed and lurched, made a protesting sign or two with his scroll, and then despairing of this new state of things he toppled into the water with a magnificent crash and splash. The last thing Timmy noticed was the scroll trying to come to terms with a fountain, which might have been able to turn it into a spouting fish. There was no time to see anything else, beyond the obvious fact that nobody was hurt except Sir Benjamin, because

Timmy was obeying a deep impulse and was now running as he hadn't run for years. It was a silly thing to do, but fortunately he had sense enough to run the right way, not into the park where the police inspector and sergeant had gone, but out of the gate.

CHAPTER II

TWO HUNTED MEN

'HERE, WHO they blowing up in there?' asked the bus-conductor.

'That statue,' Timmy gasped, 'just – fell – down.' He had not run so hard for a long, long time, and now he was fighting for his breath. All the people in the bus were looking curiously at him.

'Old Ben Flitwick in there has just gone bust,' the conductor explained to everybody. Then he turned to Timmy again: 'You were in a hurry to get away, weren't you?'

'Big – noise – always upsets me.' Sinking down, Timmy wished for once he was even smaller. He had no idea where the bus was going to, except that it was going away from the centre of the city. It couldn't go too far away for him. If it had been some other city, he might have risked staying and explaining everything. But not in Birchester. They'd never believe him in Birchester. Uncle Alfred had seen it all, for a start, and Uncle Alfred wouldn't believe he was innocent, because with a face like that, Uncle Alfred wouldn't ever believe anybody was innocent. And you could bet your boots that Birchester would have it in for anybody who tumbled down their Sir Benjamin.

He took a sixpenny ticket and did not ask the conductor any questions. Nor did he ask himself any of those

questions that had been worrying him in the park, those
questions about gas-ovens and large packets of aspirin.
What he wanted to do now was not to get out of this life
altogether but simply out of Birchester. Half an hour later
they were out of Birchester and had arrived at the smaller
but still independent town of Settlefield. You could not
tell where Birchester ended and Settlefield began, for
there was no change in the long dreary road or its dingy
side-streets, its factories and warehouses, its large but
already decaying cinemas, its fish-and-chip shops, its football pool advertisements, its lamp-posts with filthy bits of
paper piling up round them. But Timmy had played in a
melancholy semi-underground music-hall in Settlefield, in
a terrible revue called *Hollywood On The Dole.* (It didn't
mean anything, that title, but it did combine two leading
ideas in the local public's mind, for half of them were on
the dole, and they were nearly all interested in Hollywood.) This gave him his bearings. He nipped off the bus
and hurried round to the railway station. What he needed
now was a good cross-country train, and he was lucky, for
one was due to arrive in a quarter of an hour.

Feeling a hunted man already (though that was better
than feeling an unwanted man), he crept into the refreshment room and had a very strong cup of tea and a large
dull Uncle Alfred sort of bun. He asked for them in a
whisper, carried them into a corner as if they were
dynamite, then ate and drank with his back carefully
turned to everybody in the place, with the result that he
had them all staring at him, asking each other what was
the matter with the funny little man, and storing details
of him up in their memory. When he left for his train,
every eye followed him. It was a grand exit, only not at all
what Timmy, who was unconscious of all this attention,
had intended. It did not even occur to this destroyer of

Sir Benjamin, this criminal already notorious in Birchester, to rid himself of his round green hat.

'Did you say a round green hat?' the Inspector had asked. 'That's right,' Uncle Alfred had replied. 'And one eye's a bit bigger than the other – you can't miss him.' 'He'll have got rid of that hat,' said the Inspector. 'Never ought to ha' bought it,' said Uncle Alfred.

It was a good long corridor train and it had that air of leisure which belongs to all cross-country trains. 'Let-us explore-our-country,' it said in its own puff-chuff fashion. Timmy found an empty compartment almost in the middle of the train, and he made himself very small in a corner of it. Indeed, he made himself so small and looked so old that the magazine boy, a Snow White enthusiast, called to the tea-wagon girl: 'Come and 'ave a look. We got Number Eight in 'ere.' Timmy watched the countryside go zigzagging by with a growing satisfaction. His gas-oven mood had vanished. True, his future seemed even more uncertain now, when it might be complicated by the police, but somehow it didn't seem so desperate. Probably it is better to be wanted by the police than by nobody at all. Moreover, Timmy could not help feeling that for the first time in some barren years he had really accomplished something. He had toppled Birchester's Sir Benjamin clean off his perch and landed him upside-down in a nice pool of water. After chuckling over this for a while, he dozed off, and did not wake up properly again until they arrived at a large station.

The first thing he noticed in this large station was a hastily scrawled newspaper placard on the bookstall: *I.R.A. Outrage at Birchester!* It was almost opposite his carriage and he had plenty of time to stare at it, which he did with some pride. So they thought he was the I.R.A., eh? That explained the bomb, of course, and he saw that the young man who swapped suitcases must have been on the run; but the police would be hard put to it to explain *him*, Timmy Tiverton. But that didn't mean they wouldn't want to catch him. Probably his description had been sent out already. And now he wished that the train would move on again, and kept moving restlessly himself as if to give it a push. Just when it ought to have been going but still wasn't, a man came into the carriage. He was a very neat, very clean, very careful kind of man, with rimless eye-glasses and a brand-new despatch-case; and he looked like a dentist. He sat in the middle of the opposite seat, gave Timmy a severe glance – as if to say: 'I'm afraid we'll have to have that one out,' took out of his case a small file of papers and a nice sharpened pencil, and began to be very busy and important. But even this did not make the train move.

'This train is late,' he said sharply, as if Timmy, an older inhabitant of it, was partly responsible.

'If you ask me,' Timmy replied warmly, rich with fellow feeling, 'it's disgraceful the way they keep us hanging about. Think we've nothing to do but sit in here,' he added, not without a sense of its irony. 'Every time alike. And then they ask,' he went on, as if he and Rimless Eyeglasses were a pair of cabinet ministers, 'for a square deal.'

Instead of making some decent human reply to this, the man merely made a *mmming* sound and stared steadily at Timmy through his rimless eyeglasses. This made Timmy so uncomfortable that he opened the window and looked down the platform, ostensibly to see what was keeping them there. The last thing he expected was that he would see what was delaying them. But he did. Moving steadily down the train with the guard, looking into every com-partment, were two large men, one in plain clothes, the other in police uniform. They were less than twenty yards away. Timmy's head shot back. Some cool tricky criminal work was needed now. He turned quickly: 'Here, does this train go to Liverpool?'

The other man was quite shocked. Such ignorance! 'Certainly not. Another line altogether. Different station.'

'Excuse me!' cried Timmy, and dashed out into the corridor, feeling that he had left that chap with a completely wrong impression without really telling him anything. And now, what next? It was too dangerous to try getting out of the train farther down. A luggage-van? As the train would have to move on very soon, they had probably closed the doors of the luggage-vans. It was worth trying.

In the nearest van there was a good deal of stuff, several trunks, and crates and odd packages, and in one corner where there was a very tall crate and a lot of stuff piled all round it, there seemed to him a grand hiding-place. In the dim light, he groped and climbed over several packages, entangled and disentangled himself from a bicycle that he had not noticed before, then edged himself into the dark corner. There were two quite unexpected features about this corner. First, it was breathing hard. Secondly, as he discovered when he put out a hand to steady himself, it seemed to be wearing a beard.

'*Blub — chuck — crustacuck!*' said the beard.

'Sorry!' said Timmy, releasing the beard, but staying where he was. There was just room for two of them, and there would not be time now to find another hiding-place. Santa Claus must put up with him.

There was a pause. Its silence was distantly broken by a few odd shouts and whistles from the platform.

'What Do You Do Here?' asked the beard, speaking

slowly and very carefully spacing the words. It sounded like a foreigner.

Timmy felt that this demanded a cautious reply. 'Well, what are *you* doing here?'

The beard thought for a moment, then answered in the same careful style: 'I Hide From Police.'

A dark corner of a luggage-van is no place in which to bother about putting over a good line, but when you have been putting them over for more than thirty years, as Timmy had, you do it automatically. So now Timmy heard himself replying, in exactly the same style as his companion: 'I Hide From Police Too.'

'So!' cried the beard.

'Yes, so!' cried Timmy.

They both let it go at that for the time being. There was quite a long pause, during which Timmy waited impatiently for a sign that the train was moving out. Beard cleared his throat and was obviously going to speak again when Timmy gave him a sharp nudge. Somebody was coming into the van. There can never have been a crate that breathed so hard as that tall one in the corner. But nothing happened; the man went out again. The tall crate gave a lurch and hit Timmy on the forehead. But that did not matter because now at last they were off.

By this time Timmy could see a bit. His companion did not look in the least like Santa Claus. He was a very tall, thin, oldish man, with an enormous high forehead, gold-rimmed spectacles, and of course a beard, a grey beard that was long without being bushy, and went down in a leisurely and very foreign fashion to a point. As they crouched together, often bumping as the train shook itself, they were able to exchange a good deal of information about themselves, and they spent the next hour whispering questions and answers. But Timmy got his questions in first, and discovered from them that his companion was called Professor Ernst Kronak, that he was a Czech from Prague, had had to leave his country because of the Nazis, who disliked him very much, that he was in England waiting for permission to go to America, where his son Karl, also a professor, had been for some years and was now expecting him. All that part was straightforward enough, but after that it was hard to understand, because it was all complicated talk about passports and visas, but so far as Timmy could make out, Karl had not been able to arrange yet for his father's entrance into the United States, and in the meantime the Professor's permit to stay in England had expired. This meant that officially the poor Professor now had no right to be anywhere, except in a Nazi concentration camp being beaten up by a gang of German louts; so he had had to dodge out of London; and now here he was, with only a pound or two in his pocket, and a few addresses and letters of introduction from his son's wife, who had been an English girl. Here he was, a harmless old bird if there ever was one, hiding in a luggage van and afraid to look a policeman in the eye. What a world, said Timmy, and what a life.

The Professor, who seemed to be a very learned man, spoke very good English, but you knew he was a foreigner because he talked so slowly and carefully, putting out each word as if it were a pound note. Timmy was not unused to this. He had had a lot to do with foreigners in his time, having been on the same bill with hundreds of them: jugglers, acrobats, conjurors, circus acts. They were all right, foreigners, once you tumbled to their queer little ways. This Professor was all right. A proper big scholar, you could tell that, one who had studied like mad all his life; but at the same time a bit simple. They were getting along fine behind that crate.

'But you too hide from the police,' said the Professor, staring at Timmy with large, mild, spectacled eyes, 'and you do not appear to me a criminal type of man.'

'Me! Least criminal type of man you ever saw, Professor. Just an accident, that's all. But for all that, them police they were searching the train for me.'

'I think you mistake there,' the Professor corrected him gravely. 'The police at the station, they were searching for me.'

'Not them! It was me they were after. The whole damn' lot of 'em's after me this very minute.' He had to shout this because the train was making a tremendous din and all the trunks and packages were clashing and clattering with it.

'To break passport and visa regulations is now a very serious offence,' the Professor shouted. 'It was I those officers were searching for — that I saw at once.'

'Don't you believe it.' And Timmy almost sneered at him. 'What have you done? Just a little — er — well, technical bit o' nonsense. But me — why, I've just blown Alderman Sir Ben Whosit clean off his perch in a park in Birchester — and in sight of all eyes. Yes, Professor — like that — *boom*!'

'So!' The Professor was impressed. 'You are perhaps an anarchist then? That is interesting. I did not know that England has anarchists. In a certain limited sense, all the English may be said to be anarchists. But because of this limited and natural anarchy of the national soul, there is not — '

'Just a minute,' Timmy begged him. 'You're getting it all wrong, Professor. Now just listen and I'll tell you just how it happened.' And out came the story, which lasted a long time, and Timmy had to answer the Professor's numerous questions often at the top of his voice, so that at the end he was hoarse and rather exhausted. It was very cramping in that corner, too.

'At last I understand,' the Professor shouted, as the train jolted them. 'The Irishman knew that he was being followed by officers and so when he saw you were almost asleep he made a change of bags and left you with the bomb. The Irish,' he continued, as if settling down to a lecture, 'are a people outside the main stream of Western European culture, although they are Roman Catholics. Their country was never a part of the Roman Empire. Their island is remote. It is lost in Atlantic mists. Their culture – '

'Hold on, Professor,' cried Timmy, for the first time but only for the first of many many times. 'I know this is going to be good and let's have it later, but just now we ought to be thinking about ourselves and never mind the Irish. If we stick in here till we get to the next big station, we'll be nabbed as sure as eggs is eggs – '

'As what?'

'Eggs is eggs,' Timmy bellowed.

'Eg-ziz-egs,' repeated the Professor thoughtfully. 'Now that is something I have not heard before. Tell me, please – this *Eg-ziz-egs* – is it perhaps a mutilated form of some ancient name – perhaps an old Celtic or Iberian deity – '

'No, it isn't – it's just eggs, things you eat. But the point is, we've got to get off this train at some little station because they'll be watching at all the big stations.'

'This is your own land. You know its customs better than I do,' said the Professor with dignity. 'But you speak as if we should go together. Is that what you wish?'

'Well – ' and Timmy was rather embarrassed – 'that's up to you, Professor. I thought you might like a bit o' company. Though, mind you, it's me they're after and it might be dangerous for you.'

'No, because it is I they search for. I was about to say you might find it dangerous being with me. Otherwise, for me it would be a pleasure, Mr – '

'Tiverton. Timmy Tiverton. Make it Timmy. We can't start mistering on this job. Here, I must stand up or I'll be tied in knots.'

They both stood up now. There seemed to be yards and yards of the Professor. A proper maypole of a chap. From this superior height, he patted Timmy genially on the shoulder. 'It is good, then, Timmy Tiverton. We will go together.'

'Spoken like a man, Professor!' cried Timmy heartily. 'Now the first little stop we make, out we pop, then we can decide afterwards what the next move is. You leave it to me. I'm going out to do a bit of scouting. No good you moving. Everybody'd notice you.'

He climbed over the packages and trunks again, taking care to avoid the bicycle, and just as he was scrambling over the last and largest trunk he discovered that a large railwayman – a guard or ticket inspector – was watching him.

'Are you looking for something?' asked the man, in a deep suspicious voice. He looked rather like Ramsay MacDonald in his prime.

Timmy was up now, dusting himself and thinking quickly. 'That's it. Looking for something and can't find it anywhere.'

'Your own property, I presume?' And he produced this as weightily as if it were the text of a sermon.

'Certainly, certainly. It's a – well – I don't know exactly how to describe it – or what you'd call it – but – a sort of basket. About this size. And – er – it's a bright red.'

'A bright red?' The man didn't seem to like the sound of this at all. Timmy wished he had made it a deep black.

'They have to be a bright red,' Timmy told him, with an air of being suddenly confidential. 'It's a sort of rule. Not that there's anything *dangerous*, y'know – but it's so we can tell 'em easily. As a matter of fact, I can't,' he added, lowering his voice. 'Between you and me, I'm practically colour-blind, an' that's my trouble. I don't let on, of course. Might lose the job. So keep it to yourself. But it *is* a bright red – take that from me.'

'Have you looked in the top van?'

'Not yet. Here, where's the next stop?'

The man looked at his watch. 'In five minutes we'll be pulling up – it's just a halt – at North Bintington Junction. We don't stop again until we – '

'If you're going that way,' Timmy interrupted, anxious now to be rid of him, 'I wish you'd have a look in that top van for my basket. I'll try down here when I've got my breath. I get asthma, y'know, in trains – always did, always will.'

The large solemn railwayman stepped forward and looked as if he were about to give Timmy a final blessing. But what he said, in a tone of the deepest melancholy, was: 'I have a brother-in-law who had to give up the nicest little market-garden round Grantham way all because of asthma. Did you say bright red?'

'Brightest red you ever set eyes on.'

The man suddenly stopped and turned. 'What's inside it?'

'What's inside it? Well – various things – all sorts, really. Depends on – well – the time of year.' Timmy's power of invention seemed to have stopped working. 'Just now – it's – er – chiefly children's money-boxes. It's all a new idea.'

'So long as it teaches them to save,' said the man, nodding his approval. 'I'll see if it's there.'

Timmy sat down on the nearest trunk and breathed hard. Then he called to the Professor, who emerged wearing a high black sombrero and carrying a shiny black bag. He seemed taller than ever, and most fantastically foreign.

'Y'know, Professor, you're going to be about as easy to hide as a giraffe. But what we've got to do is to nip out at this next halt – North Bintington Junction – '

'Where is this? I have a large-scale map here – '

'Oh no, you don't. You can play with that later on. We've only a minute, so come on.'

The train, giving snorts of disgust, halted part of itself alongside the little platform of North Bintington Junction, and Timmy, afraid of being seen by that guard or whatever he was, nipped out like lightning, leaving the Professor to follow him. He kept out of sight in the tiny waiting-room until the train started to move again. Then he joined the Professor on the platform, and together they watched the train gather speed and vanish into the dusk of the late afternoon. It seemed to take with it all signs of activity and life. An immense calm descended upon North Bintington, which appeared to consist entirely of immense fields into the middle of which somebody had carelessly tossed this little railway station. On the platform were two seats, an automatic machine, some milk-cans, an advertisement for cattle cake and a poster saying 'Jugo-Slavia Welcomes You!' Against this background the Professor looked all wrong, and as conspicuous as a gilded elephant. But on the other hand there was nobody there to notice him.

And then, quite suddenly, there was. But he was only a very young porter carrying a mug of tea. He was so young, so pink and round and innocent, that he looked as if he had just been born in the ticket office. And he was even more surprised to see them than they were to see him.

'Did yer come off train?' the porter enquired.

'We did.'

'Ay, well, you've got a bit o' time to wait – you ought to ha' gone on – '

'No, no, my lad, we know what we're doing,' said Timmy, telling himself he only wished they *did* know what they were doing.

'Yer didn't get out 'ere, did yer?' The porter was astonished. This did not seem to have happened before. 'Oh – well – I'll 'ave to take tickets, won't I?'

The Professor handed over his ticket and then sat down and hid himself behind a very large map. The porter opened his eyes still wider and took a quick gulp of tea before risking a look at Timmy's ticket. Finally he shook his head. 'Nay, nay, y'oughter gone straight through. Yer've made a bit of a mess o' this, yer know. Straight through, y'oughter gone.' He returned both tickets to Timmy, and had a good swig of tea this time, coming up for air after it like a diver.

'We changed our minds,' said Timmy, with a certain airy sweep, as if they were a couple of eccentric million-aires. 'Now, my lad, tell me – where *is* this place?'

'This? Oh – it isn't anywhere, properly speakin' – this isn't. Last place God made – that's North Bintington. No use anybody comin' 'ere.'

'You've got a lot of tea-leaves round your mouth, my lad,' Timmy observed rather severely. 'Wipe 'em off; it looks untidy on duty.' But this was really to gain time. He was trying to think what they ought to do next. There was something about this immense rural landscape, with its feeling of remoteness and emptiness, that stopped him thinking. Show him nothing but turnips and he felt like one. He was a man of the cities.

Unexpectedly it was the Professor who now took charge. He called to them both over his map, which he flattened across his knees when they approached him. 'Denberry-Baxter. The Manor. Chilham Moss,' he announced, very slowly and carefully. As they did not reply but only stared, he continued: 'I have a letter to him – Denberry-Baxter. And this Chilham Moss, I think it is not far from here.'

'Never 'eard of it,' said the porter.

The Professor plunged into his map again. 'It is not far from Castle Claydon.'

'Oh well – now yer talkin',' said the porter. 'Castle Claydon – well – it's up that way.' He pointed to some of the largest and dreariest fields in sight. 'Eleven miles – might be twelve – might be thirteen – '

'Might be fourteen,' said Timmy.

'No, it won't be fourteen. Put it at twelve.'

'That is where we shall go,' the Professor announced decisively. 'To present my letter to Denberry-Baxter, The Manor, Chilham Moss. There is a train to Castle Claydon, eh?'

'Ay, yer can get a train. But yer'll 'ave to wait five hours.'

'Five hours! We're not waiting any five hours,' cried Timmy, who had had enough of North Bintington Junction already. 'I'll – I'll walk first.'

The porter thought hard, rubbing the end of his nose with the edge of his tea-mug. 'Now if yer take this road out 'ere, an' go a couple o' miles, yer'll come to a crossroads, where the main road cuts across, and this crossroads is a bus-stop. Bus there'll take yer straight to Castle Claydon. Down there a couple o' miles. Yer can't miss it 'cos there's an eatin' place there called *Annie's Pannie* – '

'Annispanny?' cried the Professor, interested at once. 'Is that an old name? It has some resemblance to a – '

'Leave it, Professor, leave it,' Timmy interrupted hastily. 'I'll have plenty of time to explain all that when we're walking that two miles. Out here, is it?'

The young porter shepherded them out, and then pointed. 'Straight down. An' *Annie's Pannie*'s bus-stop.'

They were about a quarter of a mile down the road before the Professor, who had been quiet and thoughtful, finally spoke aloud. 'Anispanny's bustop? Did you understand that, my friend, or did you pretend to understand. The young man there was a peasant type who might be expected to make use of ancient names and forgotten idioms – '

'The young man,' Timmy began, with some emphasis, 'simply told us that the bus stopped at the place called – and God knows why, except that people get sillier an' sillier – *Annie's Pannie*. Look! There's a woman called Annie. She starts an eating house. So instead of calling it Annie's Pan, she calls it Annie's Pannie. And don't ask me why. I don't know an' I don't care.'

'If we have to wait for this bus, we had better eat with this Annie. I am hungry.'

'Yes, I could do with a bite too.' They trudged on in silence for several minutes. The road was narrow and dull, and nothing but cows seemed to have happened in it for a long time. 'Now who's this Denberry-Baxter, who lives at the Manor, What's-it-Moss?'

'He is one of the old friends of Elizabeth, my son Karl's wife. She gave me some letters, to old friends in different parts of the land, and said that all of them could be trusted to help me if I should need help. Now I do need help,' the Professor observed, with great simplicity, 'and as this Denberry-Baxter lives far away from London and the police, I thought I would see him and perhaps ask for shelter.'

Timmy looked dubious and made an appropriate sound. 'You're not going to ask him to shelter me for a week or two as well, are you?'

'Why not? He is, I believe, rich, with a large house. He will be pleased to shelter us both.'

This seemed to Timmy to be taking a good deal for granted. 'Y'know, where you come from, Professor, it might work out all right. But here in England, especially with chaps with big houses, it mightn't be so good. They're inclined to be a bit pernickety. Don't bank on it. And you'd be better off without me, I fancy.'

The Professor stopped, and looked down sternly at his small companion. 'We are friends, are we not?'

'Prof,' cried Timmy earnestly, 'you're the only friend I have in the world at this minute.'

They shook hands with great solemnity. 'We are both innocent men who have done no wrong,' said the Professor with feeling, 'and already we have helped one another and we must go on helping one another. Let us walk quickly for now I am hungry.' And he set off again at a great pace, so that Timmy had almost to trot to keep up with him. It was now that Timmy had to explain what his occupation had always been, in reply to the Professor's questions. The Professor then told him gravely that he did not share the prejudice of many of his scholarly colleagues against comedians and their like.

'The Comic,' he announced, taking even longer strides, 'has its place beside the Beautiful and the Sublime. In the true Comic there is a large element of the Unconscious. It depends upon a balance – and very subtle it is, this balance – between certain conscious feelings of superiority and the deep de-ee-eep feeling of inferiority in the Unconscious. For what happens when man emerges from the womb – ?'

'I dunno, Professor,' Timmy gasped, as he hurried along. 'It's always been a mystery to me. And I'll tell you frankly, I'm not sorry. I don't fancy all that business.'

'When man emerges from the womb,' the Professor continued, just as if Timmy had not spoken, 'he feels helpless and afraid. He is very small and the world is very big. This feeling he never loses, de-ee-eep in the Unconscious. But some things, such as being safe when others are being hurt, give him definite superiority feelings.'

'Who is this? He sounds a nasty piece o' work to me,' said Timmy.

'All of us. These superiority feelings in themselves are not good – '

'They sound awful,' muttered Timmy.

'But if they come to balance this other deep de-ee-eep inferiority feeling, this is good. There is release, and so we have laughter. Suppose we see an accident, only a little accident, happen to a person – what do we do? Always, always we laugh.'

'That's right. Nearly bust ourselves. I remember, one time, I'd gone – '

'So! Always we laugh.' As he repeated this, the Professor put his foot on some very fresh evidence of cows, and the foot slipped and he shot out his long length and down he came. The queer hat went one way and the shiny black bag another. He ripped out some guttural words that sounded to Timmy, who was all solicitude, very adequate to the occasion. Without a smile and murmuring his sympathy, Timmy recovered the hat and the bag, and then helped the Professor to his feet. From behind he now looked most rural and pastoral.

'Never mind,' said Timmy. 'It'll all brush right off when it's dry. No damage done. Right as ninepence. Well, as I was saying, talking about always laughing at little accidents, I remember one time I'd gone – '

'So, to continue,' said the Professor calmly. 'Always we laugh. But if the incident has been truly comic, we do not laugh at the other's misfortune – though it is that that gives us the conscious feeling of superiority – but we laugh out of a sense of release.'

'I dare say,' Timmy panted. He had given up hope of his own reminiscence. 'But not so quick, Professor I haven't got legs like a racehorse.'

'In essence the Comic is spiritual,' the Professor announced, to the mild surprise of a couple of heifers that were looking over a gate. 'But it belongs not to entirely spiritual beings but to creatures like ourselves who are half-spiritual, between beasts and gods.'

'Well, if that's where we are, you can have it,' muttered Timmy in the rear.

'That is why the Comic is the most truly human of the æsthetic categories. The theory that it is the mechanical pretending to be the vital, this is only part of the truth. You have read Bergson on the Comic, of course?'

'Of course – not,' replied Timmy promptly. 'Never heard of him. But then, I'm ignorant, just plain ignorant. But I've never been much of a one for reading. Papers, of course, an' now and then a magazine or two. But books – no. I'd rather have a nice talk, y'know, compare notes a bit, than bother with a lot of printed stuff. Of course with you it's different, naturally. I expect you 'ave to do a lot o' reading, just to tell these students what reading they ought to do, so they can go away an' tell the kids what *they* ought

to read. I suppose it works out all right,' he concluded
dubiously.

'There is no real life without knowledge,' declared the
Professor, almost as if he were officially opening a university library. 'And there is no good life either, my friend,
without your very human art, the Comic. Both are necessary, both are valuable.'

'Yes,' said Timmy, drawing from that bottomless well of
irony known to all the English poor, 'I expect you're
right, Prof. An' no doubt that's why we're footin' it down
this road – which I've now had quite enough of –
wondering what's to become of us.'

'I see lights not far ahead.'

'That'll be Annie lighting up her Pannie,' said Timmy
cheerfully. 'And bus or no bus, I vote we see what's in it.'

Annie had given the crossroads quite a metropolitan
air, for her establishment had a fine neon sign in bright
red and also a smaller sign, saying *Eats,* that flashed in
and out, to tantalise both the eyesight and the appetite of
the beholder.

But Timmy was disgusted. 'Look at that – *Eats.* What
sort of language is that? American, that's what it is. *Eats!*
Comes of spending all their time at the pictures!'

The place evidently did a brisk business. There were a
good many lorries and cars parked outside, and several
others on the move to and from the main door. There
were two rooms, brightly lit but rather thick with the smell
of food and tobacco smoke, and in the far room the
customers seemed to be busy playing at penny-in-the-slot
games.

'They come here driving machines,' the Professor
observed, as he peered in, 'and soon they will go away
driving those machines. But now that they are having a
little rest, they must play with these machines. Why is it

that they cannot feel either useful or happy without a machine?'

'Professor,' cried Timmy earnestly, 'I've been trying to puzzle out that very thing for years and years. Compared with the people I used to know, all these are barmy. Honest, they are. Barmy! What about ordering the *Ninepenny Special* – steak-and-kidney pudding and peas? And I'll 'ave some tea.'

'And I will have coffee,' the Professor sighed. 'It will be very bad, but I will have it.'

So they stayed in the first room, which was in direct communication with the kitchen, and had a little table to themselves near the door. With his little steak-and-kidney pudding steaming before him, and floating in that steam the amiable spectacled gaze of his new friend, Timmy not only felt better than he had done all that day but better than he had done for weeks and months. A hunted man with no future in his profession, he felt cheerful and expansive, twice the fellow he had been in Birchester that morning. And the pudding was all right too, wonderful value for the money.

The Professor, who had attracted some notice, especially from some loutish lorry-drivers at the next table, but who seemed quite unconscious of the fact, dealt manfully with his pudding, looked about him with his large impersonal curiosity, and insisted upon giving Timmy a lecture on the English.

'Such a place as this,' he observed, without any suggestion that he was grumbling at it, 'would be better in my country or in almost every country I know. The food and the drink would be better, for somebody would care about such things. The service would be better. The place itself would be decorated with more taste. There would be some music. There would be something more gay about the atmosphere. The quality of life would seem better, and yet the people themselves would not be better. There is something in these people, even in this air, that you would not find in Europe. I say in Europe, because to me England is not in Europe. That is an illusion.'

'It's half in America these days, if you ask me,' Timmy muttered. '*Eats at a roadhouse*. That's how they talk now. Get it from the pictures.'

'Apart from what remains of the old feudal world, now the possession of the rich,' the Professor continued, as usual as if Timmy had not spoken, 'the quality of English life is, on the surface, inferior and often disgusting. Yet it has an inner quality, not expressed in outward civilised forms, that is superior. It is deeper than politics though possibly it would not exist now if there had not once been revolutions here. It is not religious, though there is about it a suggestion of religious feeling. It is a kind of deep unspoken poetry that every man here carries about with him, in his own interior world, and that is not expressed in communal and civic life but only in instinctive conduct and in your literature. Perhaps, my friend, all this not clear to you.'

'Prof, I'll be honest with you,' said Timmy, screwing up his droll sad face. 'I can listen for another hour – just keep on if you're feeling like it – but I haven't enough in the upper storey to know what you're talking about. You remind me,' he added thoughtfully, 'of an illusionist – Russian, I think he was – that I was on the same bill with many a time about twenty years ago. He'd go on just the same, for hours. But he was a good turn – illusionist, y'know – making girls and Chinamen disappear – an' all that.'

'So!' And the Professor chuckled, making his long pointed beard wag wonderfully. 'Perhaps I am an illusionist too. Though I cannot make girls and Chinamen disappear – not yet.'

There was an interruption. First, a sound as if the whole evening outside was being torn in two. Then the owner of the motor-cycle hurried in and demanded a cup of tea. Having taken a quick gulp of his tea, the young man turned away from the counter and approached the lorry drivers and our friends. He was an untidy, weather-beaten youth with wide blue eyes and reddish hair. He came forward diffidently, cleared his throat, then enquired shyly if anybody had seen anything of a girl on a motor-cycle.

Timmy and the Professor shook their heads. One of the lorry drivers, a big chap, asked what sort of girl he was looking for. 'I've seen all sorts on motor-bikes in my time,' he added, winking at the others.

This question about the girl, which was not unreasonable though it was not asked in a reasonable and helpful spirit, plunged the youth into the scarlet depths of confusion. He seemed almost girlish as he stood there stammering and twittering.

'She's – she's – well, you couldn't mistake her – she's got – sort of dark curly hair – and – and grey eyes. She's – quite beautiful,' he ended fervently.

'Oh – Cecil!' cried one of the drivers, in mock reproach.

The other, the big loutish fellow, grinned unpleasantly and said he would know what to do with the girl if he did come across her.

'What did you say?' asked the youth, as if he really could not believe his ears.

The big fellow repeated his remark with even more unpleasant emphasis, and Timmy, who was a game little man and who had taken a fancy to the obviously lovelorn young man, told him to shut up.

But now the youth was no longer diffident and confused. His reddish hair was bristling and his eyes blazed with fury. He seemed to leap forward to the table, and instantly he leaned over it and put a hand on each arm of the big fellow and said: 'You'll apologise for that.'

'I won't.' And the big fellow tried to rise and shake himself free of the young man's grasp, but strangely enough he couldn't. And there was something so bristling and menacing about the youth that the big fellow now found it hard to meet his look.

'If you don't take that back,' said the youth quite softly, 'I've a good mind, you big dirty-mouthed suet pudding, to tear the liver and lights out of you.'

''Ere, what d'yer think you're doing?' cried one of the other two drivers, getting up and giving the young man a push.

But the young man, who was as quick as a cat, recovered himself at once, and releasing the big fellow he flashed out a long left at this second driver that sent him over the back of his chair and crashing against the wall. Then the young man, who now looked like a first-class middleweight in action, stepped back a pace, lightly dusted his hands, and waited with dancing eyes for any trouble.

Both the men came from behind the counter and asked what the idea was and what was going on round there. The third driver, who was no fighting man, was suggesting that it was about time they moved on. The big fellow was looking sullen and indecisive. The man who had hit the wall was trying to rise.

'I'm just waiting for this chap to apologise,' the young man explained, a shade of diffidence creeping into his manner again. 'But if I'm a nuisance, I'll take him outside if you like.'

In the old days when he had had the money, Timmy,

like nearly all his kind, had been a patron of the ring. 'You could give him a stone or two,' he observed in a rather detached manner to the big fellow, 'but I fancy he'd make mincemeat out of you with that left of his. Did you notice his timing?'

''Ere, we got to be going,' the big fellow growled, shuffling to his feet. Then, to the young man: 'All right. Sorry I spoke. 'Ere, let's get Joe out.'

The young man helped them to get Joe out, and then returned, at Timmy's invitation, to drink a fresh cup of tea with Timmy and the Professor. He was now once more the shy youth who had first asked the question about the girl, and as he answered their enquiries the blood crept under and flushed his clear skin. It was hard to believe that only a minute or two before he had seemed so menacing. His name was Roger Liss, and when he was at home he lived in North London, but most of his time was spent in travelling about the country on his motor-cycle, trying to sell a device patented by his elder brother. This had something to do with carburettors, but as neither Timmy nor the Professor knew much about carburettors they did not pay much attention to his enthusiastic account of this device. What interested them was not this improvement of the internal combustion engine but his attitude towards and relations with this girl. It was obvious that this youth, at once so shy and yet so fierce, was deeply in love. This he admitted, turning towards them a defiant scarlet face.

'Her name's Hope Ollerton,' he confessed, stammering a little. 'I've only known her about six months, and only really met her eight times – no, nine, counting the first. I got her a motor-bike – a rotten old thing, but it could go all right – because she wanted one to come up here on and try for some job. She wouldn't tell me what the job was – she's had all sorts of jobs – but she won't tell me anything much about herself. Y'know, sort of keeps up a mystery girl business.' He sighed. 'She's really the most extraordinary girl. Quite young, y'know. Only about twenty-two. But she seems to have been all over the place. Can't make her out really – and I'm usually very good about people – y'know, I spot their characters and so on right away. But I get so confused when I'm with her. And I said I'd come up here with her, just to see she got on all right with the bike, but then she gave me the slip. Sometimes I think she likes me, but then at other times she goes on as if she couldn't stand me at any price, so I never know where I am. I'm not usually such a chump – but somehow – well, really this girl is quite extraordinary.'

The Professor smiled as if he were about ten thousand years old. 'I think I have heard such things before. Beautiful young women often behave in this way. You said, I think, she is beautiful, eh?'

'Yes, yes, she is,' said the young man eagerly. 'And I don't mean that I just think so, though of course I do, more than anybody. But she really *is* beautiful. People stare at her all the time. All kinds of chaps,' he added gloomily, 'chase her round. It makes everything very complicated for her. Don't suppose I've got a dog's chance really, but I have to keep on trying. Just can't help it. If you're going to be in this part of the world you might run across her. You can't miss her. She's got one of those – sort of – wide girls' face – with big eyes – greyish – and a lot of dark curly hair, a bit untidy as a rule but the general effect's marvellous. And her name's Hope Ollerton.'

'We have it down in the records,' said Timmy solemnly. 'And if we see her, we'll tell her you're going round asking for her and knocking 'em down like nine-pins if they say a word against her.'

'No, I wouldn't say that,' cried the youth in some alarm.
'I'm sure she'd hate that. And I oughtn't to have lost my
temper with those chaps, but I've had a hell of a day
trying to find her and I was getting fed up. I do quite a bit
of boxing in my spare time,' he concluded, rather
apologetically.

'Has this Miss Hope Ollerton – ' and the Professor
spread out the name carefully – 'ever seen you as you
looked with those men?'

'Oh no! Good lord, she'd probably never speak to me
again. I mean, she's had to knock up and down a bit – no
money, y'know – but she's not that kind of girl at all.'

The Professor merely smiled again, but added another
five thousand years to it. There was the sound of a bus
arriving, and one of the men behind the counter called
that it was their bus.

'If you should run across her,' said the young man
hastily, 'I wish you'd let me know. Send me a wire or
telephone – or something – to this address.' He gave
Timmy a card with an address scribbled on it, then went
outside with them to the bus that would drop them at
Castle Claydon, shook hands solemnly, and saw them off
as if they were old friends.

'A nice lad,' Timmy observed in the bus, 'an' very quick
on his feet and with a lovely left. I'm surprised somebody
didn't persuade him to turn professional. Though he's
better off as he is.'

'He is too quiet and shy with his young woman,' said
the Professor thoughtfully. 'That is all that is wrong. He
will find out. And now, my friend, for Mr Denberry-Baxter
at The Manor, Chilham Moss, near Castle Claydon.
Where, I am sure, we shall be most welcome.' And the
bus, as if it had overheard him and had its own ideas, gave
a deep sceptical hoot.

CHAPTER III

A NIGHT WITH SIR GEORGE

TIMMY GAVE the bell another good pull and from far inside the house they could hear it jangling. But nobody came. And there was no sign of a light anywhere near the great front door. They stood there in almost total darkness, for now it was late – they had had to walk from the bus-stop at Castle Claydon to Chilham Moss and then find this Manor House – and there was no moon. They had walked about half a mile up a drive, and the house looked enormous, a real mansion. Why, the front door was as big as three ordinary front doors.

'Nobody at home,' said Timmy, rather hopefully. He had always been doubtful about this call on Denberry-Baxter, and this mysterious gloomy grandeur did nothing to restore his confidence. He was hoping that they would have to go back to Castle Claydon and settle down for the night in some sensible little pub.

'There is somebody,' the Professor announced. 'I saw a light when we were walking up – it must be somewhere round the corner there – and I thought I heard music. Let us go and see.'

'Well, but if they won't answer the front door –' Timmy protested.

'It is a very large house and if the servants are out, then the others may not hear the bell. This way.' And the

Professor turned to the left, to find his lighted room, and Timmy had to hurry after him. He had been right about the music. They could hear it now. Turning a corner, they found themselves looking through the open French windows of a large lighted room. The music was coming from a wireless cabinet and also from a violin, which was being played in an enthusiastic slapdash style by an immense stout old fellow, who was sitting very close to the wireless cabinet and actually had his music propped against the side of it. Although it was a cool autumn night, the old fellow was not wearing a coat or waistcoat, only a billowing chequered shirt above his vast baggy tweed trousers, and yet even with so little on he was sweating profusely. Timmy stared at him in amazement.

'It is the Schubert Octet in F Major,' said the Professor, stooping towards Timmy's left ear. 'He is playing the first violin part, and just finishing the second movement. He is playing it very badly, but after all it is extraordinary that he should be playing it at all. Let us wait. He will never last through the fourth movement – you will see.'

So they waited on the lawn, just outside the gold bars of light that stretched through the open window. The room was as odd as its occupant. It was crammed with stuff, all higgledy-piggledy, rather like a second-hand shop. The spoils of Empire seemed to have been gathered there. It was a room that held the gorgeous East in fee. There were Burmese gongs, Chinese Buddhas, Indian elephants in brass and ivory, helmets, shields, swords and guns from Arabia and Persia and Afghanistan. Miscellaneous books and solemn quarterly periodicals were piled up everywhere, in every corner, in arm-chairs and settees and on top of the grand piano. It was a mystery how the old fellow, who looked a crimson mountain of a man and had a snowy summit of wild hair, ever moved about that room without bringing down piles of books, impaling himself upon a sword or two, or breaking his shins upon some shining Oriental trophy. And he looked like a mad old emperor, fiddling away there, trying to keep time with the eight invisible musicians in the wireless cabinet.

'Only in England could such a thing be seen,' exclaimed the Professor, during a long passage for the clarinet, when the violinist refreshed himself hastily from a giant tumbler. 'What a people and what a country! One minute it is all cheapness and dreary commerce, and the next minute it is Alice through Wonderland.'

They waited without moving for another five minutes, and then the old fellow, who had been finding it more and more difficult to keep up with the other first violin in the wireless cabinet, suddenly gave it up in despair. 'Damn your eyes, boys, you're taking it too fast for me,' he cried, put down his instrument, took another swig at what looked like a giant-size whisky-and-soda, and put a match to the very largest calabash pipe Timmy had ever seen.

The Professor stepped forward into the light. 'Sir,' he called, 'we have been ringing some time – '

'What's that?' roared the old fellow, struggling to his feet. 'Come in, come in.' He switched off the wireless set. 'Been ringing, eh? Well, Ketley's about somewhere. That's my man – Ketley. Must be in. Come in, come in, come in.'

'Mr Denberry-Baxter?' the Professor began, formally.

'Sir George Denberry-Baxter, as a matter of fact,' said that gentleman, in a large off-hand manner. 'Glad to see you. Rum-looking pair, if you don't mind my saying so, but glad to see you. Sit down. Have a drink.' It was now obvious that Sir George had had many drinks already. His immense face, looking scarlet under its white thatch, was beaded with perspiration. It was a most formidable countenance, with a great nose that looked as if it had been badly broken at some time or other, for it was both dented and twisted; there was a deep angry scar on his right cheek; and he had fierce little bloodshot eyes. But at the moment he beamed hospitality and good cheer, and finding two odd glasses he poured out whiskies-and-sodas for them.

'I have here a letter,' the Professor began again.

'Never mind letters. Too late in the day for letters. Have a drink. Better make it a toast. Schubert!'

'Schubert!' they muttered, and drank with Sir George. The whisky was uncommonly strong.

'I thought they were playing the fourth movement too quickly,' said the Professor, with great tact.

'By thunder, you're right, too. Running away with it. They take everything at a devil of a pace nowadays. I can't keep up with 'em. Can't keep up with anything. Now why did that scoundrel Ketley keep you waiting at the front door? If he's gone out wenching again – he's fifty if he's a day, but the minute I bring him back home he can't keep his hands off 'em – I'll rip the coat off his back. Soon see if he's in, though. Listen!'

And Sir George gave the largest of the Burmese gongs an immense whack, so that the room seemed to shake and the whole night to hum with its unfathomably deep rich tone. A few moments later from somewhere within the house there came an answering note from a similar gong. 'There he is. Make him take that with him at night, wherever he is in the house – it's just an empty warren, this place is – just to prove he hasn't slipped out. You a musician?'

'In a very small amateur way,' the Professor smiled. Then he looked grave and formal again, and insisted upon pronouncing his name slowly.

'Timmy Tiverton's my name,' said that little man, shyly.

Sir George suddenly pointed a finger at him. 'Seen you before somewhere. Never forget faces. Any kind of faces, yellow, brown, black. Used to surprise 'em in the East. And I've seen you before. I'll remember soon, you see if I don't.' He turned to the Professor again, in his odd masterful fashion. 'Play the fiddle?'

'No. I play the piano. Or I did, in happier days.'

'Then, by crumpets, we'll have some music. We'll try one or two of the Mozart sonatas. Open that piano, while I find 'em.' He turned to Timmy now; he seemed to be a great chap for giving orders. 'You're the right size. See if there's a music stand under the piano, and drag it out. And finish your drinks, finish your drinks. It's one of those nights when you need a drink or two to cope with this damnable climate. Now then, gentlemen, a little Mozart.'

He bustled them round, and soon had the Professor, looking very impressive and very foreign, seated at the piano, and himself towering over the music-stand with his violin ready for action again. Timmy sipped his very strong whisky, and wondered what he was doing there, among unpredictable giants in this gigantic dark house. Sir George and the Professor, after some happy discussion, decided which sonata they would tackle, and they were just about to begin, and Sir George had his bow poised above the strings, when they were disturbed by a deep and somehow very significant cough from the lawn just outside the window. All three heard it and turned.

'Now who the devil's this?' growled Sir George. 'Always the same. There's a kind of conspiracy to put something between you and Mozart or whatever it is that makes life worth living. What is it? Who is it?'

A police sergeant stepped into the room.

Timmy went cold. The Professor stiffened and then

slowly rose. Sir George stared angrily, annoyed at the interruption. It was a large police sergeant but he had a rather small head at the end of a long stiff neck, so that he looked not unlike a gigantic wooden doll. He looked hard at all three of them – and put Timmy's heart down into his boots – and then addressed himself to Sir George.

'I beg your pardon, sir – ' he began.

'And I should think you do, marching in here just when we're going to enjoy ourselves! Here we are, miles from anywhere, just settling down to a bit of Mozart, and in comes the police force. And for two pins, sergeant, you'd ask to see a form or two, want to put a rubber stamp on some paper or other, all that sort of thing, eh? Now listen to me, sergeant. I'm Sir George Denberry-Baxter and I've had forty years of that sort of thing. I've governed islands. I've governed peninsulas. I've governed territories the size of England. I've had forty years of seeing that forms were filled in and properly stamped and documents put into the right despatch-boxes, and I've walked miles and miles up and down the ranks of soldiers and policemen, white, yellow, blue and black. And by Christmas!' he roared now, having worked himself up into a gigantic passion, 'I've had my share of it, and I won't have any more of it. I don't want police sergeants. I want Mozart.'

He looked for a moment as if he were about to throw his violin at the sergeant's head, but then he put the instrument down, threw himself down into his enormous camp chair, and swallowed about half a pint of whisky and soda. Then he looked sternly at the sergeant and said: 'Have a drink.'

'Well, sir,' said the sergeant, still apologetically, 'I'm on duty, you know, sir – '

This did him no good at all. 'If you're on duty, my man,' Sir George thundered, 'then don't come in here.

You've no duty that brings you into a gentleman's private house. So either come off duty and have a drink, or stay on duty and clear out.'

The sergeant decided to ignore this. In his wooden style, he looked the irate Sir George in the eye and said, as if submitting a report: 'A few minutes ago, sir, seeing the house all dark from the lane, I heard a loud noise, which might have been a sort o' signal – '

'It was that gong. If you hit it properly, you can hear it three miles.'

'Quite so, sir. Well, as we've had word that there's some very suspicious characters – '

'Suspicious characters!' Sir George, in his contempt, almost blew like a whale. 'I don't believe in your suspicious characters. Is he a suspicious character? Is he a suspicious character?' As he asked this, he pointed first at the Professor and then at Timmy, to their horror. For the sergeant, following the finger, took a careful look at them. 'Am I a suspicious character?'

The sergeant smiled. 'Not exactly, sir.'

'Then you're wrong,' cried Sir George triumphantly. 'I *am* a suspicious character. Have been for years. By thunder, if you knew the half of what goes on in my head, you'd have me handcuffed in no time. Eh? Well, you'd better have a drink.' And Sir George, puffing and blowing and snorting, found another odd glass, and poured out another very stiff whisky, not from a bottle but from a gallon jar. Timmy and the Professor exchanged careful glances.

'My respects, gentlemen,' said the sergeant, with enormous wooden solemnity. He took a tremendous pull at his whisky without blinking an eyelid. Then he felt that he ought to make a little conversation. 'It's these I.R.A. chaps that's giving us so much trouble. All over the place, they are. One of 'em blew up a statue this afternoon in Birchester.'

'Good for him,' cried Sir George, to Timmy's secret delight. 'If I'd my way, I'd blow up the whole of Birchester. Never saw such a damned place! Blow it up, blow 'em all up!'

'So you see, sir, hearing this noise, I just wondered what was going on here,' the sergeant concluded.

'What's going on here is music.' Sir George rose and waved a vast arm at the sergeant. 'So finish that whisky and pop off, sergeant.'

'Certainly, sir.' He emptied his glass, then suddenly looked quite sharply at Timmy, who by this time had relaxed and was now caught off his guard. 'Didn't I see you this morning in Claydon market-place?'

'Yes, I fancy you did,' stammered Timmy. 'Yes, I'm certain I saw you there.'

'Are you?' said the sergeant pleasantly. 'Well, that's odd, because I wasn't within forty miles of Claydon this morning.'

'Well, what of it?' demanded Sir George. 'You fellows look all alike in uniform. Now pop off. I want some music. Good night.'

'Good night, sir,' said the sergeant. Did he – or did he not – take a last quick look at Timmy and the Professor? Off he went, however, and Timmy put a hand to his forehead and discovered that it was cold and damp. He also discovered, the moment after, that the fierce little eye of Sir George was upon him. 'Seen you before somewhere, you know. Don't tell me. I'll remember. Not wanted by the police, are you, by any chance?'

'Me?' Timmy sat up straight. 'No – not really. Here, why should I be?'

'Why should you look as if you are, eh?' Sir George

bellowed with laughter. 'Now then, you don't want Mozart – I can see it in your eye – so just go and find Ketley, tell him the two of you are staying the night, and tell him to bring some sandwiches in about an hour. Ham, and plenty of mustard. Try the billiard-room. Here, take a torch.' He plunged forward with a sweeping gesture to lay a hand on an electric torch, knocked over a bronze idol, a chain helmet and two elephants, blasted the whole room and hurled a curved dagger at the opposite wall, where it stuck quivering, then put the torch into Timmy's hand and almost swept him out of the room.

Timmy went slowly down a long cold corridor, musty and smelling of moth-balls, and all he could hear out there were the rats and mice scampering and scratching behind the woodwork. He had never been in a house this size before, and now in its dark emptiness it seemed to him a crazy terrifying place. At the end of the corridor there were stairs going up and stairs going down, and after a little hesitation he decided that the billiard-room would probably be downstairs, so down he went. At the bottom of a short flight, he had to go along another corridor, which seemed colder and mustier than the one above; and by this time he felt such a long way from anywhere, and everything seemed so completely unreal, that he was ready to bolt through the nearest door back into the outside world. But then he heard the *click-clack* of billiard-balls and saw a band of light under a distant door. He hurried along to this door, and was about to open it when it was suddenly opened from inside, nearly knocking him down; moreover, a monstrous thing was standing there, a thing that had dark trousers and shoes but an upper part, both body and head, that consisted only of a large dark-metal disk; and then this monster let out such a clang that Timmy could feel the sound knocking him back into the corridor. All this turned out to be the man Ketley smacking the other Burmese gong.

He was a cool card, this Ketley, a lean, darkish, old-soldier sort of man, who was wearing a dirty striped house-coat and smoking a black cheroot. He nodded and said: 'Well?'

'He says,' Timmy panted, 'we're staying the night – there's two of us, an' will you bring some sandwiches in about an hour. Ham, and plenty of mustard.'

'There isn't any ham. It'll have to be tongue.' Then Ketley took out his cheroot to make a reproachful sound at the back of his teeth, sent the gong and its stick skimming into a corner, and continued: 'The gov'nor must be good an' bottled, isn't he?'

'I suppose he is – really. I thought at first,' said Timmy carefully, 'he was barmy.'

'He *is* barmy. Sunstroke started it. *And* lifting the elbow. He was well on when I left him. Who's the other fellow with you?'

'He's a sort of foreign professor.' Timmy felt he had to go cautiously here. 'An' his son's wife was an old friend of this Mr Denberry-Baxter and gave him a letter to him, if you see what I mean.'

'Not sure that I do, chum,' said Ketley in his soldierly style. 'But what I'm sure of is this – that isn't the gov'nor – for he's Sir George and has been for twenty years. It's his nephew you want. This is his house, not the gov'nor's. He's in East Africa. If I was you, I'd push off tonight.'

'I never wanted to come here,' Timmy explained. 'But it's a bit late now, y'know, and they seem to be settling down to a musical evening.'

'That's 'cos the gov'nor's bottled.' Ketley sounded very gloomy. 'You wait till tomorrow morning.'

Timmy did not like the sound of this. 'Why, what about tomorrow morning?'

'Never mind. Play you fifty up. Or snooker, if you like.'

Timmy hadn't played billiards for a long time, but he used to play in his earlier days, and he elected for the fifty up. Ketley, who seemed to do himself very well, was drinking bottled beer, and insisted that Timmy should join him. They began playing in an easy careless fashion.

'Isn't there anybody else here but you?' asked Timmy, who had been wondering about this for some time.

'There was. Eight servants when we took over. They all left. Couldn't stand the gov'nor, chum. You'll see what I mean. We've only a deaf old woman who comes in every morning. Place is going to rack an' ruin. There'll be hell to pay when the owner comes back. But the gov'nor doesn't care. When he isn't plain barmy, he's bottled. I've had so much of him now, I'm not so sure I'm all there myself. One of the girls who left was a lovely piece,' continued Ketley, missing an easy cannon. 'Talk about curves! But there's one at the farm here – Ruby – who's as good. Artful little devil too. You ought to have gone for the red there, chum.'

After an hour of this they took a long dark walk to a pantry, where they cut some sandwiches, loaded themselves with more bottled beer, and then set out for the music-room, which apparently was the one room downstairs that Sir George used and into which he had crammed all his own possessions. By this time even the Professor was somewhat flushed and untidy and Sir George was now like a crimson mountain in eruption. He was using an Oriental shawl as a towel.

'And about time, too, Ketley. Music always gives me an appetite. This isn't ham, you blockhead. I said *ham*.'

'That's right, gov'nor,' replied Ketley in a very easy

familiar style. 'But there isn't any, see? You'll have to put up with tongue.'

'I've seen *you* before,' said Sir George, once more pointing straight at Timmy's nose.

'Course you have,' Ketley told him. 'You sent him along to me to tell me about – '

'I don't mean tonight, you wooden numskull,' bellowed Sir George, throwing the damp shawl at his henchman. 'I mean years ago – years and years ago – before we all went off our heads. Now don't tell me.' He stared hard at Timmy, then finally let out a whoop. 'I've got you. A pound to a penny I've got you. On the halls.'

'Quite right,' said Timmy, delighted to be recognised. 'And Timmy Tiverton's the name. Comedian.'

Sir George patted him on the shoulder. It was like being patted by an oil furnace that had been burning whisky. 'Knew I'd get you. Timmy Tiverton, eh? Good man, good man. Why, you used to sing that song about not giving father any shrimps.'

'Cockles,' Ketley corrected him.

'One of these days, Ketley, I shall throw you straight through the window. Don't be so damned impertinent. Though I believe you're right.'

'He is,' said Timmy smiling proudly. 'It was one of my most successful numbers. *You Can't Give Father Any Cockles.*'

'*And you can't give Mother any gin,*' Sir George sang loudly. He turned to the Professor. 'Play "You Can't Give Father Any Cockles," doctor.'

The Professor raised his hands apologetically. 'I am sorry, but I do not know this *Cockles*. Perhaps I pick it up though.'

Sir George had reached over for his fiddle and began humming the tune, with some expert assistance from Timmy. A minute later, Sir George could play the chorus, and two minutes later the Professor, who didn't look that kind of pianist at all, but who nevertheless seemed to have a knack that would have earned him a living in many a public-house singing-room, had contrived a good rousing accompaniment on the piano. Standing among the spoils of Empire, Timmy, doing his act as he had done it nearly thirty years before, doing it well, but feeling like a man in a dream, sang the verse, with the help of a few vamping chords from the Professor, and then went swinging into the refrain, with Sir George not only fiddling variations on the melody but lending his voice to Ketley's as Timmy's chorus. All together, they roared:

> *You can't give Father any cockles;*
> *You can't give Mother any gin;*
> *Auntie's a sport,*
> *But don't give her port,*
> *You never know what she'll begin. . . .*

The words might have been foolish and vulgar, but the tune had a confident jolly swing, which any man in his senses could enjoy. These men did enjoy it. And when they had had enough of that song, Timmy remembered another of his old successes *Roly-Poly For Mrs Moly*, and then a later one, just after the War, *You Know What To Do With Your Rhubarb*. They seemed to sing themselves back into another and happier world. Timmy had not been so happy for a long long time; the years that stood between him and his youth and success now seemed only like the flying soundless years of a dream. The noisy male companionship and the drinking deep into the night made the Professor forget that he was an elderly exile and almost turned him into a rowdy student again. As for Sir George and Ketley, no doubt they too returned in spirit

to an earlier and happier time, and in any event there
had descended upon them the same fine uproarious
mood. At the end of the third song – after many rep-
etitions, with the gigantic glistening Sir George urging
them to make it louder each time – the odd quartet was
like a little band of brothers. Even Ketley, the coolest and
probably the most sober of the four, seemed ready to
swear eternal friendship.

'Sir George,' cried Timmy hoarsely, with his face all
screwed up as if he did not know whether to make it laugh
or cry, 'believe me or believe me not, but you've done
something for me tonight I didn't think any man could
'ave done for me again. Sir George, you've made me
happy. Poor old Timmy Tiverton, Sir George, you've
made him feel like a man again. An' I'll – I'll say to your
back now what I'd never say to your face – Sir George,
you're a great gentleman. You are. An' for God's sake,
put a coat on, you're sweating like a bull.'

'Ketley,' said Sir George, 'you'll have to take the little
man to bed in a minute because he's tired and he's had
too much to drink. And look after him, look after him,
because in his own way – and a very good way it is too –
he's an artist.'

'Very good,' the Professor smiled. 'Quite true. An artist.
And we must cherish our artists.'

'And our scholars, our philosophers, our thinkers,'
added Sir George, almost sternly. 'Among them our friend
here Dr Krudiebacker from Vienna – '

'Thank you very much,' said the Professor modestly,
'although I am really Professor Kronak from Prague.'

'Don't let's have any pedantry, doctor,' cried Sir George
reproachfully. 'Don't imprison the soaring creative
human spirit in a cage of pedantic forms. Remember

Mozart. Remember Schubert. Remember Mrs Moly and her roly-poly. Just hand me those two elephants, Ketley.'

'You're bottled, gov'nor,' Ketley reminded him, as he passed the two bronze elephants.

If his master heard this, which is doubtful, he chose to ignore it, and now, with an elephant in each hand, he drew himself up to his full height and addressed the other three as if there were at least three thousand of them. 'Gentlemen, it is my custom on such felicitous occasions,' he began, in splendid form, but stopped to sneeze and did not trouble to complete this fine opening sentence. 'It is my pleasure to welcome you here under the ancient roof of the Denberry-Baxter family, a family that, with the solitary exception of myself, who have recently retired after a brilliant career in the Colonial Service, a family, I say, that has left no mark whatever in our national history. But – but, gentlemen,' he continued, just as if he were making some superb debating point, 'though you have made no mark whatever, you are just as welcome under this roof as any great minister of state – in fact, a damned sight more welcome. Unless it should be the elder Pitt, the great Lord Chatham. It was said of Chatham, gentlemen, that when he was Minister of War nobody left his presence without feeling a braver man – '

'That is curious,' the Professor put in, 'for the same was said of our own great statesman – '

'But the last thing we wish to do now,' Sir George went on, with a stern glance at the Professor, 'is to explore the morass of political life. We have here with us a scholar, philosopher and musician. I refer to our friend Dr Krudiebacker from Vienna. Also an artist, no other than Tommy Tupperton, late of the Tivoli, Oxford, Empire and Middlesex music-halls. And to celebrate this occasion, though I trust you will be with me for many weeks to come – '

'Hear, hear!' This was from Timmy, who felt at that moment ready to stay for months.

'I present to each of you, as a personal tribute, a bronze elephant of fine design and workmanship. Dr Krudie-backer, your elephant! Tommy Tupperton, your ele-phant! And welcome, a thousand times welcome, to the Manor!' And with a final hospitable wave of the hand, Sir George Denberry-Baxter took a deep breath and then marched straight out into the night.

'Don't worry about him,' said Ketley, who did not seem in the least surprised. 'He's gone to cool off. He's very bottled, fairly plastered. I'll attend to him later. I'd better show you two where you can sleep, though if you take my tip you won't stay.'

'I do not understand this,' said the Professor, smiling dreamily. Indeed, he gave Timmy the impression that he was floating in the air. 'Now, this elephant – ?'

'Oh, just put 'em down anywhere,' said Ketley. 'Come on.' He marched them upstairs, and first disposed of the Professor and then took Timmy into a small bare room on a side landing. 'This used to be the butler's.'

'What became of the butler?' Timmy asked, as he helped Ketley to spread some sheets and blankets.

'He left too. The gov'nor only just missed him with one of them souvenir spears of his. Nasty temper the gov'nor has at times, very nasty. Room all right?'

'It'll do nicely, thanks.' Timmy gave a thoughtful sniff or two. 'Just trying to work out why it should smell of pickled walnuts. Would that be the butler?'

'It might. Here, where's your bag?'

Timmy looked embarrassed. 'I haven't got a bag. It was pinched. But don't worry, I'll be all right.'

Ketley stood in the doorway a moment, looking rather

sinister. 'Watch out in the morning, chum. Take it easy. Good night.'

Timmy did not spend long trying to make out what Ketley had meant. All the fantastic events of the day had to be reviewed. He had to go back to Silver and Baumber's office and start all over again. But actually no sooner had he taken himself back to Birchester again than he fell fast asleep.

When he woke up it was full daylight, with all the chill gold of an autumn morning. It took him a minute or so to remember where he was. His most precious remaining possession was a watch, which Betty had given him. This watch, which could always be trusted, announced that it was forty minutes past nine. He made a sketchy sort of toilet in an immensely high, dripping tank of a bathroom on the main landing – and regretted that he could not have a shave, for he was a very spruce little man – and then cautiously went downstairs. The house did not look quite as enormous now as it had seemed last night, but it was even more imposing in the daylight, in spite of the fact that everything was beginning to need a thoroughly good cleaning. In a place this size there ought to have been a lot of people about, and without them it seemed forlorn and depressing. In the big hall below there was somebody tiptoeing about, rather like a ghost that had mistimed its visit. It was the Professor, and he brightened up at once on catching sight of Timmy.

'My friend Timmy Tiverton,' said the Professor, shaking Timmy's hand, 'I am very pleased to see you.'

'The pleasure's mine, Professor.'

'I tell you, my friend, I have been asking myself many difficult questions, and increasing the headache I have been feeling. It is the old problem of distinguishing between the objective and the subjective.'

'I don't follow you, Professor, but for God's sake don't start a long lecture so early in the morning, when all I want's a cup of tea.'

'No, no,' said the Professor earnestly. 'I do not wish to lecture. But I wish to know whether certain events really happened, that is in the world outside the mental self, or whether they must be classed as subjective phenomena, like the strange events we notice in dreams. And I was dreaming very much last night or this morning. Now I remember very well playing the piano while the large fat man played the violin. That is all right. I have played the piano many times before. But did you sing some comic songs?'

'I did. A few of my old numbers.'

'Ah, that is good.' The Professor's face cleared for a moment then looked doubtful again. 'But – er – roly-poly?'

'That's right. Roly-poly for Mrs Moly.'

'Thank you, my friend. I have been worrying, for I told myself this roly-poly cannot have happened, yet it did not seem subjective. But these elephants now? Please tell me the truth, my friend. Can you remember elephants?'

'Course I can. I wasn't that bad. Sir George gave us an elephant apiece, and then Ketley told us to leave 'em, because the old boy was bottled. It's all straightened out, Prof, and you're not going barmy. Here, come on. I want a cup o' tea or something. Let's try and find what's-his-name – Ketley.'

After exploring for a few minutes they found their way into the kitchen, but Ketley was not there, only a little crab-apple elderly countrywoman. 'Ah, good morning,' cried Timmy, and it was not until she nodded and smiled but made no reply that he remembered that Ketley had told him she was very deaf.

'Where's Ketley?' he roared into her ear.

'Hasn't come down yet,' she replied, nodding and smiling away. She appeared to have just finished her own breakfast, and Timmy decided not to stand on any ceremony but to ask her for something to eat and drink then and there. It took him some time to make the old dame understand that they were only too willing to breakfast in any corner of the big kitchen itself and did not want distant tables laying for them. But she was a friendly old dame, glad to see a couple of new faces even if she could not converse with them, and soon they were helping her to make breakfast. The Professor applied himself with scholarly care and thoroughness to the task of making toast; Timmy, who had often done it before, fried the eggs and bacon; while the dame herself laid the table for them and made the tea. In the end they ate a thundering good breakfast and then smoked a cigarette together, contentedly watching the blue smoke curl and fade above the table in the yellow shaft of sunlight. It was now after half-past ten.

They discussed the situation with an easy confidence born of breakfast. 'If this is not the Denberry-Baxter who was the friend of my daughter-in-law,' said the Professor, 'but, as you say, his uncle, I do not think that will matter. This Sir George, even without troubling to read the letter – for I could not interest him last night in this question – asked us to stay with him. Many weeks, he said – or did I dream this?'

'No, that's right. Many weeks to come. Of course, he was a bit tight, not a doubt about that. But still – it ought to be all right. Do you remember that police sergeant coming? Put the wind up me all right, that did. I thought he had his eye on us, but good old Sir George did it on him all right.' And Timmy chuckled, and added appreciatively: 'He's a character, this Sir George. Been a big pot in his time, too, from what I could make out.'

'One of your English builders of Empire,' said the Professor solemnly. 'An imperial ruling type. Like the Romans, the English have – '

But this was cut short by the sudden and violent entrance of Ketley, who, looking darker and dingier and more sinister than ever, charged in, bellowing: 'Coffee, coffee, coffee, pronto! He's shouting for it like a madman. Come on, come on, where is it?'

'Good morning,' said Timmy and the Professor together, very politely.

But Ketley had no time for them and merely gave them a glance and a wave. He hastily put the coffee things together, including an enormous steaming jug of the beverage itself, and then dashed out with the tray. The other two, feeling that they ought not to linger in the kitchen any longer, followed him along the corridor, but they did not go upstairs but remained in the main hall. Angry noises from upstairs suggested that Sir George was still asking for his coffee. They hung about, feeling a shade less confident than they had done just after breakfast but not at all disturbed. And as it looked as if it might be some time before Sir George came downstairs, they told one another that a stroll round the grounds would do them no harm. They unbolted and opened wide the great front door and stepped out just in time to meet a police constable who was wheeling a bicycle up the drive. They stopped dead, and let the policeman approach them.

'I'm looking for Sir George Denberry-Baxter,' he announced, in a slow stubborn manner. He had the look of a very slow, stubborn young man, a good end man for the local tug-of-war team. 'I 'ave a message for 'im from the sergeant.'

'Would you like to give it to me?' asked Timmy.

'No, I wouldn't.'

'Sir George has not yet come down this morning,' the Professor told him carefully.

The policeman did not like the sound – or the look – of the Professor. He looked hard at Timmy again, then beckoned him to one side. 'He's a foreigner, isn't he?'

Timmy, thinking quickly, took him farther away still, and whispered: 'He's a dentist from America. Came specially from Chicago. But don't say anything.'

'Are you from Chicago as well?' asked the policeman.

'Me! Never been there in my life. I'm a – well if you must know, I have a nice little wholesale sweet business in Bristol. But I'm here – well, I'm *really* up here to have a look at Sir George's collection of Indian elephants – brass ones, y'know. They're a little hobby of mine,' Timmy added modestly. 'It passes the time.'

''Ow?' asked the policeman.

'What d'you mean *'ow?*'

'I mean I can't see 'ow brass elephants is going to pass much time,' said the policeman slowly and stubbornly. 'An' now that you're telling me so much, sir, might I 'ave your name, if you please?'

'Certainly. Thomas Hudson. And my friend is – er – Dr – er – Moly from Chicago.'

'I see. Well, I think I'll go round the back an' wait till I can see Sir George Denberry-Baxter.' And off the policeman went.

Timmy and the Professor walked slowly down the drive. 'I don't like that policeman,' Timmy confessed. 'He'd got a funny suspicious manner. Asked our names, but of course I gave him false ones.'

'And suppose now Sir George tells him our proper names, eh? Then he will know there is something wrong with us.' The Professor shook his head dubiously. 'I think these police officers should not be coming like this. Perhaps we had better explain everything to our friend Sir George.'

'We might chance it,' Timmy agreed. 'He's a bit high-and-mighty and hasty, Sir George is, but he's a good sport.'

'Exactly so. And we will say to him: "Sir George, you are a good sport, and we are both in trouble – " Begin like that, eh?'

They strolled to the end of the drive and back. Sir George was waiting for them at the front door. But he looked quite different. Last night he had been untidy, red-faced, and jolly. Now he was very neat, in a rather old-fashioned style, looked yellow in the face, and appeared to be anything but jolly. These differences were obvious at once, but they pretended to ignore them. Smiling, they gave him a hearty greeting.

All they received in return was a curt nod. Then he looked sharply, out of his fierce, little, bloodshot eyes, from one to the other. 'My man Ketley tells me that one of you has a letter to me. Is that so?'

The Professor produced the letter at once and handed it over. 'It is from my son's wife.'

Sir George gave it one contemptuous glance, then returned it. 'This is addressed to my nephew. He's away – for the whole winter. In East Africa. I'm afraid I can't do anything for you.' He turned and shouted: 'Ketley, bring that bag.'

The Professor stared and did not seem able to speak. Timmy did it for him. 'Just a minute, Sir George,' Timmy began, and though he flinched a little when the large yellow glaring face turned his way, he continued manfully: 'What are you talking to us like that for? What have we done? Why, last night – '

'It isn't last night now, it's this morning,' Sir George rapped out.

'You've said it!' And Timmy produced what he hoped was a hollow laugh. It was hollow enough, he thought, but was it a laugh?

'Fellows swaggering in here from nowhere, arriving unasked in the middle of the night – '

'It wasn't in the middle of the night,' Timmy shouted at him, 'and – you wouldn't *let* us explain.'

'Don't shout at me,' roared Sir George. 'Damned impudence, I call it. Ketley, Ketley!' Ketley appeared, bringing with him the Professor's shiny black bag. 'Ketley, see these fellows out of the grounds. I've some business to attend to.' He went stamping indoors.

The three of them, with Ketley in the middle, looking from one to the other with a sardonic grin on his dark face, went slowly down the drive. Timmy and the Professor moved along as if they were sleep-walkers.

'Don't say I didn't warn you,' said Ketley.

'Never have I been treated in such a way, except by Nazis,' the Professor observed, mournfully rather than angrily. 'This man – he is a democrat in the evening and a Nazi in the morning. I think he is a madman.'

'It's his only excuse,' cried Timmy; and he too spoke more in sorrow than in anger. 'I call it a cruel trick. Lights it all up for you at night – an', bless me, I felt better last night than I've done for years – an' then knocks it all down in the morning. It's enough – enough – to take the 'eart right out of a chap.'

'I told you not to stay,' said Ketley, quickening the pace a little. 'He's barmy when he's bottled, the gov'nor is, but it's a fine free-and-easy barminess. Say anything to him then. You 'eard me last night. But the morning after – well, you've just seen a bit of it. By about six o'clock he'll just be getting human again, and then after that so long as he doesn't get too bottled he won't be bad. He's as nice a chap half-drunk as anybody could wish to see.'

Timmy snorted. 'Him an' his staying for weeks and months an' his brass elephants! I hope the rats get him.'

'I've said worse than that, chum,' Ketley remarked easily. 'But here I am, still on the job.' He stopped. 'I'll leave you here. There's the gate straight in front, and if you turn to the right you'll come to Castle Claydon, and if you go left you'll come on the Pickley road. Oh – Mr Tiverton – before you go, just give me the words of *Roly-Poly for Mrs Moly* again. You see, if the gov'nor gets bottled again tonight, he'll be trying to remember 'em.'

'Will he?' said Timmy. 'Well, if he does, tell him from me to sober up and forget about it – just like he did with us – the two-faced old toss-pot! Come on, Professor.'

The tall man and the little man, the philosopher and the droll, Knowledge and the Comic, trudged on down the drive, moving slowly and in silence into the morning's golden but broken world. Just as they reached the gateway and hesitated a moment, a little country bus came along from the right, and Timmy waved at it.

'We've got to jump on this bus quick, Professor,' he cried.

'But we do not know where it is going or where we want to go,' the Professor objected.

'Oh, don't we? Well, I've just seen that suspicious policeman coming down the drive on his bike, an' I think we want to go anywhere away from here. Hey, bus!'

CHAPTER IV

WE JOIN HASSOCK & CO.

BETWEEN THE road and the edge of the little wood, on
a bit of level turf, a large van was drawn up. It was not
quite as large as a furniture remover's van, but it was a
very roomy and imposing affair. It had been generously
rather than neatly painted, in a manly scheme of crimson
and royal; and on each side there appeared in fine
gamboge letters the name *Hassock's*. The whole thing was
too large and dashing for ordinary commerce, but on the
other hand it was just a shade too much subdued for the
fairground. Its owner appeared to be aiming at some
mysterious target that did not entirely belong either to
tradesmanship or showmanship but combined something
of both. The owner, Mr Hassock, was there, at the back of
the van, holding a frying-pan over a Primus stove. He was,
in fact, frying sausages, and was taking care not to give
them the full fierce heat of the Primus flame. Just behind
him, laying a picnic table for two on top of a box, was an
unusually attractive young woman.

'This mustard in little tubes,' the young woman began,
idly.

'Clever idea!' said Mr Hassock, with the air of a man
who had had a few clever ideas himself in his time. He
was a stocky man in his fifties, bald, bulbous-nosed, with a
leathery-beefy look about him. His suit of green tweeds

might have belonged to an English squire in a French farce.

'It's not clever, because it puts you off,' said the young woman, 'At least it puts me off. Sort of ointment touch about it. Well, I'm ready when you are.'

'I like my sausages very well done. Not burnt, mind you. But crisp, very crisp. Though sausage-skins aren't what they used to be. Sort of cellophane some of 'em seem to use now. You have to take the sausage right out of its skin to eat it, and then, in my opinion, it isn't really a sausage, just a bit of minced meat and bread-crumbs. I think these'll do now.'

The girl, who was really astonishingly good-looking, opened wide her darkly-fringed grey eyes and gazed at the frying-pan, with a hand thrust among her dark curls. She looked as if she was day-dreaming of remote mountain peaks and mysterious islands, but what she actually said was 'I think I'll fry a slice of bread. I adore fried bread, and I'll risk what it does to me. No, you start, Uncle Fred; I'll do it myself, thanks.'

Mr Hassock was not really her uncle but her mother's cousin. Her name was Hope Ollerton, and she was the girl that the young man, Roger Liss, was searching for on his motor-cycle. Her own motor-cycle was not in the van but in a garage miles away, where she had disposed of it, after much argument and what she called 'charm work,' for three pounds fifteen. And she was not here as a guest but had come to work for Mr Hassock. The contents of the van, which included a battered piano, a set of drums, some old theatrical curtains and spotlights, and a great number of packages, gave a clue to the particular mixture of tradesmanship and showmanship that provided Mr Hassock with a not uncomfortable living. For Mr Hassock was a travelling auctioneer of his own goods who first entertained his patrons before conjuring half-crowns out of them. Every autumn he changed his entertainers. Miss Ollerton, who sang a little and danced a little and was, as the astute Mr Hassock knew very well, pretty enough to be forgiven her lack of any real talent, was to be one of these entertainers; and now they were on their way to pick up the other two, a man and wife who would serve as comic singer and as pianist.

'And don't forget,' said Mr Hassock as they ate their lunch, 'that with any luck we don't do so badly out of the sheet music. It's a side line, of course, but in a good town I've known the sheet music pay the rent – and a bit over.'

'Clever, aren't you?' said the girl, half affectionately, half mockingly. A certain suggestion of wistful fragility, which had undone so many romantic youths, was completely absent from her manner of dealing with sausages and fried bread. She might look like a princess in a Celtic fairy tale, but actually she was a level-headed young woman with an excellent appetite and astonishing powers of digestion.

'Up to a point, I *am* clever, very clever,' said Mr Hassock slowly and with an air of detachment. 'But beyond that point, I miss it. Not because I haven't the ideas, but because when I've made a few pounds I like to take it easy and enjoy life. Now if I'd had a bit o' dyspepsia or rheumatism or something, just to keep touching me up and egging me on, I'd have been worth a fortune now. Look at Johnny Wooler – you know – chap that has these holiday camps. Known him for years. Some of these ideas of his he got from talking to me, when he hadn't fifty pounds in the world. I'll trouble you for another cup o' tea, my dear. But Johnny always had headaches, an' couldn't ever settle down to enjoy himself, so he always had to be scheming and planning and working. Now he's worth a tidy fortune, and nearly all I've got in the world is inside that van.'

'But if you enjoy life, I can't see you're missing anything,' said Hope, dividing the last sausage into two equal portions. 'What's the good of having a lot of money if you have headaches and things all the time?'

'But if you've got enough money, you can usually find somebody to cure you. That's what Johnny Wooler's doing now. I don't say I'd change places with him, mind you. I'm not grumbling. I'm just telling you how it often works out. And talking of working out,' he continued, after he had dealt with the last bit of sausage, 'I only hope to goodness this couple we're picking up this afternoon don't lift the elbow too much. That's the trouble with the sort of pro you have to take on this job. They wouldn't want the job if they weren't on the downgrade, and too often, believe me, it's the booze that's done it. Some of 'em that I've had just didn't eat. Couldn't afford to. Just drank and drank. Human sponges – terrible! I expect your mother told you – I never touch it.'

'I do when I get a chance,' said the girl defiantly.

'You won't with me,' said Mr Hassock sternly. 'Cocktails! Muck! It's getting so you can't get into some of these road-houses as they call 'em because they're so jammed up with young women shouting for cocktails. Some of 'em with trousers on.'

'What's wrong with trousers? I nearly put mine on this morning. They're very comfortable.'

'You needn't tell me what trousers are like, girl, when I've been wearing 'em for fifty years. But you needn't try an' make me believe you wear 'em because they're comfortable. A fat lot you girls care for comfort. You wear 'em because you think they make you look like Greta Garbo or somebody.'

'Know it all, don't you, Uncle Fred? You –' But she broke off to stare beyond him, into the little wood. 'What are they playing at? There are two men in that wood, hiding or something.'

Mr Hassock's social criticism seemed to him much more important than two men hiding in the wood; though he did not believe they were hiding in the wood. What she had really seen was probably a couple of fellows messing about with a trap. He waved aside the whole wood, and resumed: 'Don't tell me you get all these fads and fancies because they're natural, because I know better.'

'Well, if you start by calling them fads and fancies, of course, they just can't be natural after that, can they?' And then she stared again, but this time began giggling. 'Look!'

Mr Hassock turned just as a little man with a rather big head finally wriggled through the wire fencing. This little man gave an anxious look round, then approached them cautiously. He had a very droll face. He came quite close.

'Good afternoon,' he whispered, very confidentially. 'Oo, what a lovely smell of sausages!'

'You can't have any,' said the girl. 'We've eaten them all.'

'That's all right. Some other time.' He winked, then suddenly looked anxious again. 'Have you seen any police-men about here?'

'No,' replied Mr Hassock. 'Are the police after you?'

'Yes, I fancy they are,' was the somewhat surprising answer. 'We had to dodge off a bus back there, an' then we cut across some herds. Now don't get it into your head we've done anything wrong, 'cos we haven't. It's all a mistake, really. I never did anybody any harm in my life, and I'm sure the Professor never has.'

'What professor?'

'He's still in the wood. He's so tall and foreign-looking, he'd give us away. He's one of these exiles, an' as nice a chap as you could wish for, even if he does like to lecture you.'

'I've been trying to think who you remind me of,' said Mr Hassock impressively, 'and now I've just remembered. You put me in mind of a comedian who was doing very well on the Empires at one time. Tommy – no, Timmy – that's it, Timmy – Timmy Tittle – no, Tiffy – no – Tilly – '

'Tiverton,' said the little man, who could stand it no longer.

'That's right,' cried Mr Hassock. 'Timmy Tiverton, that's him. You're almost his double. I expect you've been told that before, eh?'

'No, I haven't.' He laughed.

'Well, I'm surprised.'

'Don't be silly,' said Hope. 'He hasn't been told it because he's the same man. I can see it written all over him.'

'Clever girl,' said Timmy, 'clever girl.'

'Timmy Tiverton, eh? Why,' said Mr Hassock reminiscently, 'it must be twenty years since – '

'Why is it always twenty years since anybody ever saw me?' demanded Timmy. 'I'm getting tired of this. You might think I'd been dead and buried. I've been about all the time, doing my best to entertain the public. I've – '

'There's a car coming,' said the girl sharply. 'Get in the van.'

'Steady a minute,' protested Mr Hassock.

But Timmy had popped into the van like a rabbit going home. And only just in time, too, for the girl's intuition had been right. The car was a police car and it stopped.

'Have you seen two men – tall man and a short man – come this way?'

'No, I haven't,' replied Mr Hassock truthfully.

'Wait a minute, Uncle,' cried the girl. 'Was the short man wearing a striped suit and a bright green tie? He was? Well, I saw them then. They passed about half an hour since in an open car, going that way,' and she pointed the way the van had come. 'Yes, I'm positive.' And she gave them a bewitching smile as she watched the car turn round, preparing to go back along the road it came.

'I hope you're not going to tell me as many lies as you just told them,' said Mr Hassock, not altogether approving this lawless conduct. 'And looking as if you'd just been born. T-t-t-t! All right, Mr Tiverton, you can come out now.'

Five minutes later the Professor was being introduced, after which he began a complicated speech that was cut short by Mr Hassock.

'Now listen, I'll tell you what I'll do,' said Mr Hassock. 'I'm going on now to Tetchworth Junction to pick up a couple who're going to work for me. I'll take you as far as there inside the van, and that'll get you out of this district nicely. How's that?'

Timmy and the Professor were delighted. They found themselves more or less comfortable places among the packages. The girl rode with Mr Hassock in front. Off they went.

'And it just shows you,' observed Mr Hassock, who once he struck a vein of social and moral philosophy was inclined not to return to lighter topics, 'it just shows you what can happen. This Timmy Tiverton was top of the bill one time. Must have earned big money. And now look at him. Broke to the wide, I'll be bound, and with the police after him.'

'He hasn't done any harm,' said the girl confidently.

'Not with that funny pathetic sort of face. He just *couldn't*. Was he any good as a comedian?'

'Yes, he was what I'd call good, but whether you'd like it or not I don't know. Most of these turns you youngsters like seem very bad to me. But Timmy Tiverton was all right. He was a bit after the Dan Leno style, though not so good, of course. I've an idea he used to sing a song about roly-poly pudding. I must ask him about it before he goes, just to see if I'm remembering all right. But it's a good illustration of what can happen to a man, slipping down, down, right from the top. And now that I think of it, that little chap married a star, too – Betty – Betty – I'll remember in a minute – she was a pretty little thing – comedienne, you know, they used to call 'em then – and I fancy she died not long after. Perhaps that started him on the downgrade.'

'Poor little mannie! Oh – Uncle Fred – we never asked them to have something to eat. We could have given them sandwiches.'

'They'll manage for an hour or two. We'll be at Tetchworth by half-past three.'

And so they were. As there were no signs of any policemen near the sleepy little station, Timmy and the Professor, all ruffled and covered with bits of straw, came blinking out of the van into the afternoon sunshine. While Mr Hassock went to look for his performers, who were arriving by train, Hope insisted upon presenting her guests with two large sandwiches.

'We have heard of you before, young lady,' the Professor told her gravely. 'We met a young man who was searching for you on his motor-bicycle.'

'Not Roger Liss?' cried the girl, at once surprised and delighted, as if this promised to be the first real piece of talk she had heard that day.

'That's him,' said Timmy. 'A nice lad, too. Came asking about you in *Annie's Pannie.*'

'I don't know what *Annie's Pannie* is, but he'd no business to be going round asking about me,' said Hope loftily. 'Actually, I gave him the slip. I can't *bear* Roger Liss for more than about an hour – he's so spluttery and stammery and yammery – and looking like a sick duck.'

'Well, he didn't look like a sick duck last night,' said Timmy, chuckling. 'He went on more like a Donald Duck.'

'He is a fine young man,' the Professor announced, 'and he loves you truly. There is more than one kind of love. In fact, there are no less than six kinds. First – '

'How do you know he does?' demanded Hope, a pink spot on each cheek. 'He didn't say he did, did he? Gosh, he comes absolutely crawling to me, gasps and stares and chokes and goes on like a sick idiot, and then when I leave him he has the cheek to go round talking about me. You wait until next time I see him! That is,' she added, returning to her loftier note, 'if I ever bother seeing him again. I probably shan't. What cheek though!'

But her indignation, which had all the appearance of having been artificially pumped up, now paled before that of Mr Hassock, who came striding out of the station looking purple-faced and in danger of immediately exploding. He was carrying a telegram.

'Those blithering Panwicks aren't coming,' he shouted to Hope. 'Sent a wire instead. Got a *professional engagement,* they say, instead. There's a fine thing – and typical, just typical! More damned trouble and nonsense over bits of comic singers and piano players than over all the rest of the business put together. Wasting my time! Oh – I'm fed up.' And he leaned against the dropped back-board of the van and blew hard, as if to prevent himself from exploding.

Timmy did not like to intrude upon this vast despair, but he took the girl on one side. 'What's he want comic singers for? Doesn't run a show, does he?'

'Yes, a sort of show,' she whispered. 'That's why I'm here, though I don't mind telling you – I'm terrible. But, you see, he auctions things, and gets people in and keeps them amused by running a little free show. I haven't seen how it works yet, but that's the idea.'

'Well, but – don't you see?' said Timmy, greatly excited. 'I mean to say, what about me and the Professor. I'm an old pro, and better than anything he's ever likely to pick up. And the Professor can play the piano.'

'Can he really?'

'Play you anything, the Professor will. I've heard him. We were at it together only last night. He's a classical player too, the Professor is, proper musician. We'll have to train him a bit for the rough stuff, but he'll be all right. Well, what about it? We'll help you out.'

'Uncle Fred,' she called and ran across with the news. Mr Hassock slowly emerged from his deep ocean of despair. He turned and looked steadily at Timmy and the Professor as if he had never really seen them before. History, it seemed, was about to be made. It was a tremendous moment. Finally, Mr Hassock held up his hand: 'We'll have to have a talk about this, gentlemen. Some questions I want to ask. Now, Hope girl, would you like to stay here and look after the van?'

'No, I shouldn't,' said Hope. 'I hate missing anything.'

'We'll go across to that café,' said Mr Hassock, 'and talk about this over a pot of tea in a corner.'

There was no difficulty about the corner, for this was one of those rather old-fashioned and vaguely Oriental establishments that are all corners and bamboo and beaded curtains. It was only the middle of the afternoon, yet already the whole place seemed damp with tea, as if the patrons had been throwing it at each other instead of quietly drinking it.

'Now,' said Mr Hassock, when they were all settled, 'it's one thing giving chaps a bit of a lift, and it's another thing employing them. So, before we go any further – what's this trouble with the police?'

Timmy and the Professor told their stories, through which their innocence shone like a star.

'Good enough,' said Mr Hassock. 'Well, if you'd like to help me out for a few weeks, I'm your man. I should take that beard off, Professor, because of the police. And you'd better change your appearance a bit, Tiverton. The police haven't your name, of course?'

'You bet your life, they haven't. They're looking for the smallest member of the I.R.A. not for a comedian. In fact, now I think of it,' Timmy continued, shrewdly, 'safest thing me and the Professor can do is to take a job outside the big towns, because it's the chaps who are doing nothing that the police keep an eye on. Am I right, sirs?'

'You sure are, big boy,' said Miss Ollerton, who ever since she was fifteen had been taken to the films by all her male acquaintance.

'And we start right off the beaten track,' said Mr Hassock, looking very cunning, as if he had had all this in mind for months. 'I'm opening this season at Dunbury. Never been there before, but I've had my eye on it for some time. To begin with, it's the right size. You see, my business is no good except in places of a certain size. If they're too small, there isn't enough money about. If they're too big, they've got so many amusements they won't bother with me. What I have to have,' he continued earnestly, 'is one of these towns where half of 'em don't know what to do with themselves of an evening. That's where we come in. We give 'em a bit of a free show, get 'em laughing and singing, and then when they're all in a good humour I sell 'em my goods.'

Timmy looked a bit dubious. 'It's not one of these touches, is it, where you wrap up two fountain pens, three gold rings, a pair of opera glasses and a gold watch, all into one parcel, and then ask who's got the courage to offer you a shilling for the lot?'

Mr Hassock looked offended at the very suggestion. 'No, it certainly isn't.'

'Well, thank God for that,' cried Hope. 'I don't mind telling you now, Uncle Fred, that's what I thought it was. But I didn't like to ask.'

'More fool you, girl! No, that's played out. I sell 'em genuine stuff, better value for money than anything you'll find in the shops. But where I can beat the shops is that I get my customers all together and in a good temper, and there's a bit of competition. And then again a shop, unless it's one of these big stores, has to stick to its own line, but I sell 'em just whatever I've been able to pick up cheap from my wholesalers. You see, nowadays there's always something going dirt cheap – might be crockery, might be cutlery, might be imitation jewellery, might be fancy goods, might be women's stockings or dresses or what not, might be men's shirts and pyjamas and so forth – but, believe me, I've got two wholesalers in London – and they know me and know I'm ready to pay cash on delivery – that for ready money can always find me a few lines at prices to take your breath away. And it's not damaged or faulty stock either – except just now and then – but it's bankrupt stock or mass produced stuff there's been a glut of – '

'From Japan and Germany, I think,' observed the Professor.

'Now and then, but not as often as you'd think,' replied Mr Hassock. 'A lot of it's American. They're always turning out too much of something over there. But that's the idea. And believe me, it isn't doing anybody any harm. Though of course the local shopkeepers don't like it, but by the time they've got together and are asking the local council to stop my licence I've moved on to the next place. The trouble is, I can't get back to some towns. So I have to find new ones of just the right size. This Dunbury's new to me, as I said before. Actually, it's one of these oldish little towns, with a market square and all that, but it's coming on fast because *United Plastics* have their big new works there. I looked it all over a few weeks ago, and I've rented a good room in the market square for the next fortnight, booked some digs and everything.' He looked at Timmy and the Professor. 'Three pounds a week, to start with, and a bit of commission on top if we do well. All evening work – half-past six to half-past ten, roughly. Keep you both going while you want to lie low, eh?'

'I'm on,' said Timmy.

'It is all experience,' said the Professor, 'and I have been most interested in what you have said. I will do it, though I do not want to lose my beard. But no doubt it will help to baffle the police officers. And I will change my name. I must be English, I think. Jeremy Bentham, your Utilitarian philosopher, was very English, so, as a modest tribute, I think I will call myself Professor Bentham. So from now onwards, my friends, please – I am Professor Bentham.'

Hope looked at the three middle-aged men, who were as solemn as owls, and suddenly flung her arms across the table, buried her face in them, and moaned and shook with laughter.

'Now what's the matter with her?' demanded Mr Hassock, staring at the quivering dark curls.

'The whole movement of the feminine mind, like the chemistry of the female body, is quite different from the male,' the Professor began, earnestly. 'It proceeds from an entirely different – '

'Oh, don't,' the girl begged him, 'you'll make me die. Gosh – I've been on some stunts – I've even been Zata, the Roumanian Gipsy Girl who will tell you your destiny – but this looks like being the silliest – '

'Come on,' said Mr Hassock rising. 'It's sixty miles to Dunbury and I'd like to unpack tonight.'

'Dunbury,' said Timmy, 'it is. First stop – Dunbury.'

CHAPTER V

SO THIS IS DUNBURY

DUNBURY IS a very English little town. It is very English not only in its mixture of the old and the new and of the industrial and the gentlemanly traditions, but also in its muddled air of never having properly settled down to be urban. It is built for the most part of red brick that is neither surprisingly clean nor shockingly dirty; it has a market square, a large old parish church, and a bad inn that is given two stars in the Automobile Association's hand-book. At the east end of the town, where the railway runs, *United Plastics* have built an enormous factory so bang up-to-date, so white and glittering in its modernity, that it looks like a compromise between a film studio in California and a gigantic hotel in Algiers, and if only the sun shone brilliantly all day and every day in Dunbury – and the architect will be surprised and sorry to learn that it doesn't – nothing would have been more suitable and attractive. Grouped about the *United Plastics* buildings are various other and smaller industrial concerns. At the west end of the town, between the parish church and the rusting gates of Dunbury Hall, are villas and bungalows and the Dunbury Golf Club and the Dunbury Tennis Club; and out here it is all rather gentlemanly, rather old-fashioned, rather charming, for this is where the people with dividends or pensions, some of them old townsfolk, others strangers attracted by the gentlemanly atmosphere of Dunbury West, all reside for nine or ten months out of every twelve. Between the industry on the east side and the gentlemanly leisure on the west, in a number of very dull little streets running north and south from the market square, are the common people of Dunbury.

The market square itself, of course, represents everybody, and is an odd mixture of the old and the new, the gentlemanly and the plebeian. Some of the shops have been there a long time; others have been dumped into the square almost overnight. Thus, two doors away from the old-established *Family Grocers and Italian Warehousemen* is a branch of a chain-store grocery, with its windows so filled with cut prices and red ink that they seem to be bleeding in the public service. Mr Pelter's father kept the chemist's shop before him; Mr Pelter himself is one of those good old-fashioned chemists who put sealing-wax even on small packets of jujubes and wash their hands every five minutes; but Mr Pelter can peep out, between the two glorious flasks of coloured water in his window, and see across the way the branch of a chain-store druggist's, on the American plan, crammed with cheap cameras, sixpenny detective stories, automatic bridge sets, alarm clocks, with everything in fact except drugs. Then not fifteen yards from one of these sixpenny stores, all in vermilion and gilt like a round-about, where you can help yourself to nails and screws, is Binns and Sons' ironmongery and hardware establishment, which has been there so long and accumulated so much stock that it is nearly dark inside and it takes them twenty minutes to find half a dozen inch nails for you. Again, if you want to eat in the square, you can go to 'The Bull' and have four gloomy watery courses in the Coffee Room, or to the Misses Jackson's *Primrose Tea Rooms*, or to the proletarian *Fish*

Restaurant (with chips) kept by Joe Tile, who is making a very nice thing out of it. And of course Hollywood has its outpost in the square, at the *Elite Picture Theatre*, where you may see its tough guys, who knock fellows down so readily and easily, and its young women with their egg faces and voices like seagulls. Nearly all the girls in the shops around the square try to look like these glamorous beings, with the result that there is hardly a whole young feminine eyebrow left in this part of Dunbury.

Of the various public buildings in the square the most interesting is that plain old one, of weathered brick but with two fine flights of stone steps in front, known as Market Hall. It is two hundred years old, and originally belonged to the Foxfield family, the lords of the manor, now living out at Dunbury Hall on the western edge of the town. A Sir James Foxfield, who had a passion for music, a passion that was shared by nearly all the folk of Dunbury then and for several generations afterwards, bequeathed the Hall to the town so that the musicians among them – and the place was once famous for its music – could have a good solid building to perform in, for the delight of all their fellow-citizens and of the whole community for miles around. The main entrance to the Hall is about twelve feet above the ground level, and is reached by either of the curved flights of steps. With its doorway between these steps, underneath the Market Hall proper, is a much smaller but fair-sized room on the ground floor, used for auctions and small meetings and unambitious exhibitions or sales-of-work and the like; and it is called the Little Market Hall. And this was the room that Mr Hassock had rented from the Town Clerk. It suited him because it was in the middle of the town, where nobody could miss it, because it was just the right size, and because when its two very big doors were wide open the whole room could be seen – and heard – from the square itself. This is what Mr Hassock liked, for he had to catch the idler and the passer-by, and the reason why he preferred towns of this size was that they had a high proportion of people who did not know what to do with themselves of an evening. Sometimes he had to remove the whole front of some empty shop he had rented; but here, once he had arranged his platform, curtains, lighting, and had set his entertainers going, he had only to open those big doors and the people would come drifting in. Once they were inside he knew how to make them stay.

'But what we'll do,' he explained to his three entertainers, after showing them the outside of the Little Market Hall, 'is to drive round and get fixed up at the digs, then have a quick bite to eat, and then unload so that the van can be laid up. Notice the bills.' They announced in dripping red print that *Fred Hassock Will Be Here On Wednesday.*

Timmy and the Professor were dropped at the corner of Pike Street, just behind the market square. The owner of this corner house, their landlady was Mrs Mitterly, a middle-aged widow, a nervous untidy little scrap of womanhood, seven stone of minor ailments, incapable of doing anything really efficiently, but with something in her that could out-battle and out-live ten-ton dinosaurs. She had two children, a girl of twenty-one called Fern, and a boy of nineteen called Raymond, and both were working for *United Plastics*; all this and more came out before she had taken them to the top of the bedroom stairs. She was a very quick little woman. Her hands seemed to dart about like swifts, now tugging at her apron, now straightening her wisps of grey hair, now twisting together; and smiles came and went in a flash, nods and glances and grimaces flickered and were gone; and she never seemed either to start or finish a sentence

'A married couple of course the gentleman said – I mean when booking the room – so I thought a double bed in the front,' she said, in her own peculiar style of half gasping, half rattling on. 'But I think now Fern and me in the front – Fern'll just have to put up with it – you two in the two back rooms – they're smaller but there'll be one each – I know you gentlemen don't like sharing – and Raymond'll have to go back into the front attic – he's not in much these days, anyhow – just a lodger, I tell him – not that I care whether people stay in or go out – but of course with your own boy it's different, isn't it?'

And she showed them two little back bedrooms, sketchily furnished but reasonably clean. 'And if there's anything you want, just ask – I try to do my best – but there's reason in everything, of course, not that I think you gentlemen – that's why I'm glad really it's not a married couple like he said – because I think gentlemen are, well, some women don't care how much trouble they give – just to put you in your place, I always say – '

'I will have to give trouble at once, Mrs Mitterly,' the Professor announced gravely. 'I must have hot water, plenty of hot water, for I am now going to shave off my beard.'

Mrs Mitterly gasped, frowned, nodded, smiled, all within a second. 'Oh – well, of course – if you think you ought – there'll be some in the kettle – but it seems such a funny thing to do – my husband once thought of growing one – '

'My friend Professor – er – Bentham,' said Timmy solemnly, 'has been engaged to play the piano, and we thought it wouldn't look well to do it in a beard. And my name's Timmy Tiverton, and I'm a comic.'

'Yes, I'm sure you must be – I mean, I thought there was *something* – but the first gentleman said it was some kind of theatricals – though they won't like it here – oh, they're very particular here about everything these days – you should hear what my Fern says. Let's see, did you have a bag, Mr Tiverton?'

'No, but I've sent for my basket. It's at Crewe. I'll have to buy a few things, though. I'll do it now, Professor, while you're shaving. Then we'd like something to eat, please.'

They had their late high tea in the front room downstairs, all very grand, but not very comfortable because it appeared to be so full of furniture, including a piano, that it was rather like having a meal inside a fully loaded remover's van. Timmy, who knew all about digs, said that they would soon dodge this uncomfortable grandeur and eat with the family in the large back kitchen-dining-room. The Professor, who kept feeling his newly shaven chin and then making sure that his moustache was still there, looked just as odd and foreign now as he had done before, but on the other hand he certainly looked different.

'I do not feel very happy yet,' he complained. 'It is like being naked. It will demand great courage to sit upon a platform playing these songs about roly-poly feeling so naked. It will also be a great change from lecturing on the history of Western civilisation. Already in my mind I am enlarging that history, for Western civilisation – '

'I'll trouble you for the brown bread, Prof,' said Timmy, who was now able to cut in at exactly the right moment. 'And take my word for it, I'm not going to be too happy trying to do my act in a place like that, no band, no proper stage, nothing. But still, I like this chap Hassock and the kid's grand.'

'Mr Hassock, I think, is an expert on mass psychology,'

said the Professor. 'I will be glad to observe his methods. Is this a good meal we are eating?'

'About what I expected, Professor. Not good, but not too bad. How do you find it?'

The Professor sighed. 'I do not understand how a nation that eats so badly can accomplish so much. Unless it is that the constant irritation of an outraged stomach produces restlessness and a desire for adventure in distant lands. The French, who eat so well, wish always to return to France. But the English will settle anywhere. Perhaps their stomachs remember what it was like at home. And now we must go and help Mr Hassock.'

The van was now standing at a side door of the Little Market Hall, and Mr Hassock, who had found three able-bodied fellows to help, was carefully working out a way of transferring the piano on to the platform. Hope was carrying in the curtains. Timmy and the Professor helped her, and then the three of them began carrying in the parcels and packages of stock. When the piano was safely on the platform, the odd-job men brought in the rest of the stock, while Mr Hassock and his entertainers began to hang the curtains, which were bright red and blue with large silver stars sewn on to them An electrician arrived to install the extra lights that Mr Hassock had brought, and now with these lights and the starry curtains the Little Market Hall began to look very gay. Fred Hassock had arrived.

The van was empty now, and Mr Hassock paid off his men. 'I'll run it round to a garage,' he told the others, 'and then we'll talk about a programme. Just tidy up a bit there, will you?'

'Well, here we are,' said Hope, without any noticeable enthusiasm, 'and here are some of the songs I have to try and sing.' She brought out a pile of sheet music. 'And to sell, because that's part of the racket. Not that anybody'll want to buy a song they've heard *me* sing. Professor, take some of this music.'

Timmy looked at her curiously. 'What have you been doing before this? Just stopping at home?'

'Me! No fear! Look, we'll take one copy of each song, just to practise with, and then we'll put all the rest in separate piles, eh? I haven't stopped at home since I was fifteen. I've tried everything – or nearly everything.'

'Such as?' said Timmy, taking more music from her.

'Well now,' said Hope, looking exquisitely dreamy, 'I started in a chocolate shop in Finsbury Park, then I went to a tobacconist's, then I sold souvenirs at Brighton and nearly ran away with a Roumanian, then I was a manicurist in Bournemouth, then I went to Egypt because I thought I was going to be a sort of hostess but I wasn't so I soon got out of that, then I came back and we buried my father and I didn't do much that year, just a bit of model stuff, photographers' not artists' models, and then I tried being a dance hostess at the *Rat-and-Trap* – did you ever go there? – my golly, that was a dirty hole – but I soon chucked that, and then I was a mannequin but I hadn't really the right figure because I've got hips an' things; and then I did a few bits in films down at Denham, crowd work mostly, but once I had a line – I had to say: "Hello, Charlie, you devil!" – it was in "Mayfair Murderess," but they cut my line right out and I was furious, and so then I went into non-stop variety with a friend of mine and we had to keep coming on wearing nothing but a few Woolworth pearls and diamonds and it was so draughty I had a cold all the time I was there – oh! – and that's not all. I tell you, I've knocked about a bit.'

'So!' said the Professor, carefully straightening fifty copies of a popular new number called *Wiggle Your Ears*

For Walter. 'And all this time while you are trying so many different things, what you really wait for is the right young man.'

'And that's just where you're wrong,' cried the girl, banging down her music. 'And I might as well tell you now, Professor Bentham, that right young man stuff makes me sick. Yes, sick!'

'No,' said the Professor calmly, turning his attention now to another number that promised well, *Hoopy-Toopy-Toots,* 'you are under a mistake there, my child. You are an essentially and deeply feminine type, and the whole inner nature of your being is now orientated towards the love life. As Goethe says – '

'Never mind what he says. It's what Hope Ollerton says about Hope Ollerton that matters. And what I say is: "Keep your love life. And your men, young or old, right or wrong – keep 'em!" I've seen millions of 'em, and I hate that look in their eyes.'

'All right, all right,' said Timmy, grinning, 'but don't be too hard on us. An' we don't all sit about in nightclubs, either. But what is it you *do* want?'

'What I want,' said Hope dreamily, and looking angelic as she raised her face, 'is a little sports car of my own, painted bright red and with red leather upholstery. And I'd just go on and on in it, never stopping anywhere very long, and people would say to each other: "I wonder who that girl was in the red car. She was marvellous." And I'd have gone far, far away – in my lovely little red car.' She sighed deeply, and her eyes were misty with dreams.

The Professor sat down upon a box containing two dozen cases of cutlery, and held up a long forefinger.

'Look out,' whispered Timmy. 'We're in for it.'

'To me this wish of yours is most interesting,' the Professor began, in his most impressive manner. 'It is a symbolic utterance of your generation. It is the new world revealing itself. First, you wish for a piece of mechanism. You wish for it not to come to terms with reality but as a means of escape – as you say, going on and on, never staying long. But not to escape altogether. No, to become a romantic legend. Now I see in this – '

But at this moment there was a great bumping up the steps at the back of the platform, and then a table walked on, arrived in the middle of them, hesitated a second, shifted a few inches this way and that, as if beginning a ritualistic dance, and then finally stopped dead. It puffed and blew for another moment or two, then there crawled from underneath it a very odd chap. He was both large-boned and loose-jointed, had a vague wavering kind of face, and quite remarkable eyes. These eyes, which were a glittering light grey, did not seem altogether human. There was about them a suggestion of some other species. It was not that they merely seemed queer set in the face of this shambling odd-job man. They would have seemed equally queer in any other face. They were not, somehow, our sort of eye.

'Beginning to look nice, isn't it?' cried this newcomer, grinning at them. 'Stars an' suchlike, eh? Piano, eh? I've got the stool for it out there. Brought that and this table on a hand-cart. I'm going to work here, y'know, with you. Candover's the name. I'll get the stool.'

The three of them watched him go out. From the back he still seemed to shamble but at the same time his head jerked sharply as he moved, so that he looked like a marionette.

'Uncle Fred told me he'd engaged a local man to help us,' said Hope, speaking in a low voice. 'What do you think of him? A bit odd, isn't he?'

'Odd!' said Timmy. 'Take my word for it – and I've seen plenty of 'em – he's barmy.'

'His eyes are so funny. Did you notice?'

'Yes,' said the Professor. 'They are set in an unusual way. He is an unbalanced type. Perhaps he has been an epileptic.'

'I was with one of them once,' said Timmy, 'going to Cardiff through the Severn Tunnel. Just as we were going into the tunnel, he started moaning. "Here, steady, old man," I said, but – '

Candover was coming in again, not only carrying one of those old round hard piano-stools but twirling it hard as he came, and chuckling happily. When he drew near, he sat on the stool and whirled himself too.

'Having a grand time, aren't you?' said Hope.

Candover nodded brightly as he went round. He reminded Hope now of Harpo Marx, and she could not help feeling that he would never speak again.

But he did, almost at once. 'Piano-stool,' he announced cheerfully. 'You haven't told me your names. Did you remember mine? Candover.'

Timmy told him their names and then asked him if he had always lived in Dunbury. Candover replied that he had, and was at present living with his old mother and his unmarried brother Bob, who had a very good job in the gas works. 'I can work hard, too,' he continued, smiling vaguely at them, 'but I can't settle, not like Bob. Always changing. But that's not the funny thing about me. Have you heard the funny thing about me?' The queer bright glance travelled from one to the other.

'I have very strange dreams, I have,' Candover continued, very serious now. 'Every night, and not only at night, but any time I shut my eyes for a minute or two. I could have one now – in two minutes.'

Timmy and the girl left this to the Professor. 'No doubt,' said the Professor. 'But we all have dreams, only we do not always remember them. And these dreams often seem very strange to us. The dream – '

'Not like mine. I've had mine always, ever since I can remember. And they're not like anybody else's.' Candover stated this simply, as a fact. 'You see, they've nothing to do with me or with my mother or Bob or anybody I know, or with Dunbury. I'm not in them at all. I just see what's happening, like you do at the pictures. Only they're better than the pictures – I mean, clearer and much more going on. I see armies taking cities and setting them on fire, all kinds of soldiers and cities – you wouldn't believe! And important men making speeches and crowds cheering, people of all sorts of colours in all sorts of clothes and funny places – big white buildings, towers made of metal, gardens with trees and flowers in, that are all different – and big ships fighting on the sea and even up in the air – not like our aeroplanes at all, much bigger – and storms, awful storms, and earthquakes and huge waves coming in from the sea and fire coming out of the ground, and thousands and thousands of people, all kinds of people, running and screaming – '

'Here, stop it,' cried Hope, regarding him severely. 'You're making me go all goosey. Come on, let's finish tidying up all these things.'

They paired off, the Professor taking charge of Candover. The other two could hear them whispering together as they worked. Timmy and Hope did some whispering, too, chiefly to the effect that Candover was obviously barmy and that his talk about his dreams was not to be encouraged. Then Mr Hassock returned, smiling but very brisk and busy, very much the expert and the boss.

'Can't work out some sort of programme tonight,' he said. 'We'll have to do that in the morning. But we can make sure everything's all shipshape here, ready for the morning. That stuff'll have to come farther back. Can't we pull that curtain over a little? That's better.' He looked about him, rubbing his hands. 'Good room this. Just what we want. Now I know you people haven't the least notion what happens, but you leave it all to me. I've been doing this for years. All I want to know from you three is just what you think you can do best. Have you looked through these songs? Have you tried the piano yet, Professor?'

The Professor hadn't, and now he did, first striking a few chords, then trying a few runs, then giving them some fine scraps of Bach, Beethoven and Brahms.

'We might do worse than give 'em two or three minutes of something classy,' said Mr Hassock, who was now in a creative vein.

'Can you play this song?' asked Hope, handing it to him.

The Professor had no difficulty in reading the music, which was easy enough, but he obviously still lacked the touch, the snap, the swing; so Hope stood over him, with Timmy and the grinning Candover in attendance, and marked with clapping hands the kind of crisp rhythm that she wanted. 'Come on, Professor,' she cried, hands and feet tiptapping away, 'you're doing fine. But put some snap into it. Swing it, boy, swing it!'

As soon as they had finished trying to swing it, Timmy heard a spluttering sound coming from the neighbourhood of his left foot. It was being made by a pale young man with nervous blinking eyes.

'Eh?' said Timmy.

'He can't do that,' said the pale young man, blinking harder than ever.

'Well, give him a chance. It's the first time he's run through it. You wait!' And Timmy stared indignantly at this fellow, who could walk in unasked and start criticising.

'No, I don't mean that. I mean, none of you can do it.'

'What's wrong with it?'

'Who is this?' asked Hope, also coming to stare, and immensely enlarging, heightening, deepening, the pale young man's nervousness. 'Go away. We're trying to rehearse a bit.'

'But that's what I'm saying. It's no use.'

'Well, of all the cheek!'

'Young man,' said Timmy severely, 'don't you come barging in here telling us it's no use. When we want your opinion, we'll ask for it. Pop off.'

'I won't pop off,' the young man cried, almost screaming. 'I've been sent here to tell you that you can't sing and play in this building.'

'It's young Orton,' said Candover, coming closer. 'He's a clerk at the Council offices, he is. His father was the best left-hand slow bowler Dunbury Town cricket team ever had, but this chap doesn't do anything much.'

'I've been one of the Dunbury Harriers for two seasons,' cried Orton indignantly.

'That's no reason why you should come harriering in here,' said Timmy. 'Who are you to tell us we can't rehearse?'

'Hey, what's going on down there?' shouted Mr Hassock, who was at the other end of the platform and high above them all, for he was standing upon a chair that he had placed on top of one of his larger cases. He was changing one of the side curtains. 'Uncle Fred, you look out,' Hope warned him. 'You look to me as if you're going to hang yourself with that curtain.'

'You Mr Hassock?' the pale young Orton called, moving

away from the group round the piano. 'Well, I'm in the Town Clerk's office, and I was told to tell you that no singing and playing can be allowed here.'

This was so preposterous that Mr Hassock did not take it seriously. 'Don't be silly. I've rented this room for two weeks, on the understanding that not only do I conduct my auctions here but that we also run an entertainment. They know all about it at your office. There's some mistake.'

Young Orton blinked like mad but he did not retreat. He went a few paces nearer, and raised his voice. 'But the office sent me here,' he shrieked. 'Your agreement says you can run an entertainment so long as the building is licensed for one. But now it isn't licensed for entertainment.'

'What?' Mr Hassock fairly bellowed his astonishment. 'I don't believe it.'

'Steady, Uncle,' Hope cautioned him.

'You leave this to me, girl. I've handled these red-tape merchants before. Now then, young man, what are you trying to tell me?'

'The licence for this room, the Little Market Hall,' the young man shouted, 'is covered by the licence for the big hall upstairs. There's only one entertainment licence for the whole building.'

'Well, that's all right,' Mr Hassock roared. 'The big hall upstairs is a sort of concert hall. They told me that.'

'But the committee hasn't renewed the licence for the Market Hall, so this room isn't licensed either and so you can't do any singing and playing down here.'

This sent Mr Hassock into a purple fury. 'Oh no, you don't,' he stormed from his height. 'You go back and tell 'em they can't do that to me. I've got my agreement – '

Young Orton produced a large folded document that

he waved up at Mr Hassock. 'This is the duplicate. There's a clause that says the room must be licensed – '

'I know, I know. Stop wagging the damn thing. But they said it would be licensed, 'cos it had been for fifty years, a hundred years, thousands and thousands of years. They can't let me come here like this, and then tell me it isn't. They can't do a thing like that to Fred Hassock, young man.' He looked down at his assistants. 'Now don't worry, you people. Some of these town councils are always trying these little games. But they don't come off with me. I've been doing this too long. I'll watch it. Now listen – '

And poor Mr Hassock, forgetting his perilous position, made a sudden movement that sent the chair off the packing-case and sent himself flying into space. He landed clean off the platform, among some chairs that were stacked below, and looked as if he must have broken every bone in his body.

As they bent over him, horrified, he opened his eyes, groaned, muttered: 'They can't do that to Fred Hassock – you'll see,' groaned again, and then fainted.

Half an hour later, after a doctor had been and gone, the unconscious Mr Hassock was removed in an ambulance, accompanied by Hope, to the Dunbury Cottage Hospital. He was a tough healthy man, the doctor had told them all, and was in no real danger, but it looked as if there might be some broken bones.

'And a fine mess you've made of it, young man,' said Timmy severely to young Orton, as they watched the ambulance go. 'Butting in to tell us what we can't do.'

'I couldn't help it,' said the unhappy young man, who had already been shattered by the forked lightning of Miss Ollerton's reproachful glances. 'I had to tell him what I was told to tell him, hadn't I?' And he appealed to the Professor.

'Now that Mr Hassock has been injured,' said the Professor gravely, 'it would be well for you to explain to us exactly what has happened, so that we can understand the situation.'

The young man was only too anxious to do this. It appeared that since Mr Hassock had agreed to rent the Little Market Hall, the music licence for the whole building had not been renewed because the Council had not decided what to do with the Market Hall itself. There was, young Orton told them, and had been for some time, a strong feeling among the most influential people of Dunbury that the Market Hall was no longer being made proper use of and was really a waste of a good building and a fine central site. The people of Dunbury really did not want a communal concert-hall any longer. On the other hand, two sets of very important persons had their own plans for the Hall. *United Plastics* was willing to buy the Hall from the town, in order to rebuild it and then use it as a central showroom for their products and as a town office. They claimed that *United Plastics*, with the various small industrial concerns that chiefly lived on the patronage of the big firm, now kept Dunbury going, and that therefore the best building in the town should be a showroom for their famous products. The other party, representing the leisured residents of West Dunbury and led by Lady Foxfield the rector, and Colonel Hazelhead, wanted the Market Hall to be turned into a museum, for Dunbury, they pointed out, was not one of your recent, jumped-up industrial towns but an ancient borough and market with many charming historical associations. Then why not have a Dunbury Museum? And where could it be better housed than in the Market Hall? Meanwhile, both parties agreeing that it was useless in its old capacity, its music licence had not been renewed, and as the Little

Market Hall had never been separately licensed, there could be no public piano playing and singing and entertaining on that platform from which poor Mr Hassock had taken his high dive. And that, young Orton, blinking solemnly and slowly, told them, was that, and wished them good night.

'And it all sounds a bit fishy to me,' said Timmy, as they walked back to Pike Street. 'Seems to me they've done the dirty on Hassock. On us, too, for that matter.'

'I do not understand it,' said the Professor, rather sadly, as if there was altogether too much now that he could not understand. 'The industrialists want a showroom and offices, to make more money for themselves. The ladies and gentlemen, they would like a museum, so that people may come and see how important they have been in the past. So! But what of all the people who are not industrialists or ladies and gentlemen of old families, the people who were given this fine Hall originally for their music and enjoyment – have they no say in this matter? And if not, where is the democracy?'

'Well,' said Timmy slowly, 'I don't know much about democracy or anything, 'cos I've never bothered much about politics. You don't in the profession, y'know. But it seems to me if they haven't enough about 'em to keep this hall of theirs, they deserve to lose it.'

'My friend,' sighed the Professor, 'never let anyone say you know nothing about politics. You have arrived at once at the heart of this and many, many other matters. What we will not trouble to keep, that we deserve to lose. That is why I am here, still looked for by police officers, without my beard, without my university and my classes, trying to play on a very indifferent instrument *Hoopy-Toopy-Toots*, and about to be forbidden even to do that.'

'I'm not so sure,' said Timmy aggressively. 'I didn't

come here to this one-eyed hole to be mucked about. If Hassock says "Stick it," we stick it.'

As soon as they were inside the house, little Mrs Mitterly darted out at them, smiling, nodding, tidying herself, all at top speed, and cried, as if she had an overwhelming treat in store for them: 'Want you to meet – Raymond, where are you? – my boy and girl – Fern, here a minute – and we'll all have a nice cup of tea – you look tired out – perhaps you wouldn't mind coming into the back – a bit cosier – '

Raymond was a gawky gloomy youth, probably very shy, who stared at Timmy and the Professor as if they might be about to condemn him to death. His sister Fern was plumpish and pale, and meant no harm to anybody; but unfortunately the film star she admired most was one of those exotic and enigmatic creatures who are always seen at the beginning of their films sitting alone in very fashionable restaurants or standing alone on the promenade decks of liners, aloof and mysterious, and who half-close their eyes before replying to any question and then only answer very briefly; and now Fern was working hard with herself on these lines, with the result that she did not appear in the least mysterious and exotic but simply not very well and strange in her manner. Indeed, the Professor so misjudged the eye closing technique that he afterwards told Mrs Mitterly that he thought her daughter's eyes ought to be tested, and was the innocent cause of various arguments, sulks and explosions.

Over the tea, Timmy, who was anything but secretive, told the Mitterly family what had happened about the Little Market Hall. He had an ally in Mrs Mitterly.

'I'm not surprised,' she declared. 'You know that, Raymond. Just what I expected – I mean if one lot doesn't get at you, the other will – Raymond was going on about it only the other day – was it Saturday, Raymond? – no, it can't have been, because we didn't have the chocolate cake until Sunday and I fancy you were eating a piece of chocolate cake at the time – but it's what your uncle always said – I mean your Uncle Harry, Fern – not Wilfred, he'd never bother – too much taken up with his precious pigeons – '

'Here, mother,' growled Raymond, his ears turning bright red, 'stick to the point.'

'You see,' Mrs Mitterly told them, to explain this interruption, 'Raymond knows all about it. Don't you, dear?'

Her son looked very angry at this, being one of those youths who feel that every time their name is mentioned in company some valuable secret is being given away. He muttered something – that he knew a bit about it.

'And how is this then?' asked the Professor.

'Raymond,' said Fern, as if she were a beautiful spy talking to an officer of the Foreign Legion, 'plays the clarinet.'

'So! The clarinet, eh? That is very good.' The Professor nodded and smiled. 'I like the clarinet.'

'The clarinet's all right,' said Timmy. 'Never forget – there used to be a clarinet player at one of the old Empires – might be Newcastle, might be Leeds – it's years ago, anyhow – but this chap was very bald and I could see him when I looked down, and when he played he used to pull the skin about on top of his head in the queerest way, as if sort of ripples were crossing it, tide coming in, y'know. Fascinated me. Couldn't keep my eyes off it.' He looked across at Raymond, now coming out of his deep shame at being revealed as a clarinet-player. 'Where did you play yours?'

Mrs Mitterly, all eagerness, answered for him. 'Oh – in

the Dunbury Band – we used to have a lovely band here – my cousin used to play the big fiddle in it – and Raymond got in just after he left school – didn't you, dear? – and it's such a shame it's finished.'

The Professor looked grave. 'But why is it finished?'

Raymond, not being himself the subject of discussion now, could reply without embarrassment. 'The band wasn't doing so well as it had done, to start with. Then the well-to-do people stopped subscribing, for various reasons. Then we used to get so much from the Town Council, and last year they stopped that. So that finished the band. And now they're going to take the Hall. I believe that's what some of 'em were after all the time.'

'Wouldn't surprise me,' cried Timmy. 'They're trying to do it on you. Don't have it. Start the band going again.'

'Well, I couldn't,' Raymond mumbled. 'I was just nobody – the youngest they had. But, you see, old Ben Drayton had been the conductor for years and years – and he'd run the band – and then he retired because he had to have an operation. That made it worse.'

'And Sir Robert Foxfield – that's the old family at Dunbury Hall – he died a year or two ago,' said Mrs Mitterly. 'And he'd always liked the band – and made all the local nobs subscribe – but his wife this old Lady Foxfield we have now – doesn't care about it – and she won't let her son – he's Sir Reginald now – have anything to do with it – proper old tyrant she is, they say – '

'That lot went off it,' said Raymond, very firmly for him, 'because after old Drayton had to leave, Tom Largs took the band over – and he's a socialist and all that – and of course that West Dunbury lot don't like him – and he spoke out against them – and that just about finished us.'

'Well, I think Jessie Largs is awful,' said Fern, without

any mystery or anything, just straight out. 'You ought to see the way she goes on.'

'What's that got to do with it, chump?' demanded her brother. 'We're talking about the band now, not about the office staff of *United Plastics*.'

The Professor slowly rose to his full height and even without his beard he looked very impressive. 'This band should be organised again. The people should have joy. They should not allow their Market Hall to be taken from them. And Mr Raymond should play his clarinet. Thank you for the nice tea. Good night.' And he bowed right and left and then strode out, making a first-class exit.

Mrs Mitterly looked very pleased, taking these fine manners as a personal tribute. 'Well, I'm sure – your friend's a proper gentleman – even though he might be a bit foreign – '

'I like it,' said Fern dreamily, as if remembering old Vienna and Monte Carlo and goodness knows what else. 'I like that style.'

'He's right, too,' said Timmy, who was now ready to follow the Professor upstairs. 'We put up with too much. You get your clarinet out again, young man.'

Some of his gloom had departed from Raymond. He looked far more purposeful. 'All right, I will, Mr Tiverton.'

'Only,' said Timmy at the door, 'don't start playing it tonight. I've had a long day. Good night, all.'

CHAPTER VI

FIRST APPEARANCE

IT WAS nearly noon next day when the resident doctor at the Cottage Hospital finally came down to tell them about Mr Hassock. They had been waiting in that little room over an hour, and indeed Hope herself had been hanging about the hospital all morning. Outside it was quite a nice morning, with a thick heavy autumn sunshine flattering the brick walls of Dunbury in the foreground and giving the background a kindly haze. But it was not a very nice morning inside that little room, which contained six hard chairs, a lot of cupboards, an unattractive calendar from a firm of surgical instrument makers, and a smell of operations. That room did not stand any animated talk from persons who were not on the staff of the hospital. It soon reduced Hope, Timmy and the Professor to slow whispers, and not long after that it brought them to complete silence. Then the resident doctor marched in. She had cropped grey hair, pink-rimmed spectacles, and tremendous shoulders; and looked like an intellectual blacksmith in a skirt. Her name, as she breezily announced on entering, was Dr Buckie.

'Well now,' she shouted at them, 'you want to know what we think about your friend or whatever he is – eh? What the damage, is, eh? Naturally you're anxious – what?'

They nodded and smiled timidly, feeling like mice.

'Well – ' and here she produced a cigarette-case from some mysterious back pocket, and in no time at all had a cigarette alight and was blowing smoke in their faces – 'he took a toss all right. Might have injured his spine and then where would he be, eh? Touch and go, after a fall like that, whether a chap would ever walk again. Known lots of cases. But your friend or whatever he is – Mr – er – Haddock – Hassock – well, he's been lucky – what? I've gone over him and all I can find is a couple of fractures – I think they're fractures, but I can't be certain yet – and some muscular trouble, of course – he's had a bit of pain. Oh yes, quite a bit of pain,' she added, as if that might do Mr Hassock all the good in the world, 'but there's nothing to worry about. So there you are.'

Hope looked at Timmy, and Timmy looked at the Professor, and the Professor looked at both of them and then back at Dr Buckie. There they were, but where were they?

'He's been fussing away about some business that brought him here,' Dr Buckie continued, in her hearty fashion. 'Something – Sister said – about singing in the Little Market Hall.'

'We were going to,' said Hope, 'and they say they won't let us.' And she explained the situation.

'You'd better go up and see him,' said Dr Buckie. 'Ask Sister upstairs. You'll find him a bit dopy, but he'll probably settle down better after he's seen you – so it's all to the good.' Hope hurried out. Dr Buckie remained to finish her cigarette. 'I'm in favour of anything that'll put life into these people here. Miserable creatures, most of 'em. No guts. I like guts. Can't get on without 'em. I've only been here about six months but already I've had a fight with nearly everybody of any importance in the whole place. Money-grubbers at one end of the town, and snobs at the other, with a lot of poor half-wits in between. That's Dunbury. Perhaps that's England nowadays, but hope not, eh? You're not English,' she said sharply to the Professor, catching him off his guard. 'German?'

'No,' stammered the Professor, 'I am a Czech – but nobody here is supposed to know – so – please – '

'All right to me. Ever know Professor Kolin?'

The Professor lit up at once. 'But yes – for years and years he was colleague – and my friend.'

'I worked under him for six months,' said Dr Buckie proudly. 'Thought I was going to specialise then – but the money ran out. I'll do it yet, though. Well, that's splendid. We'll have to have a talk about Professor Kolin – he was a great man – '

'He was indeed a great man,' the Professor assented.

'Can't imagine what a colleague of his would be doing in this hole,' Dr Buckie went on, in her breezy way, 'but I suppose it's some of this exile misery – '

'I will tell you, because I feel I can trust you.' And the Professor rapidly explained who he was and what he was doing there.

'Well, that's the sort of world it is now,' said Dr Buckie. 'If you get into any trouble here, I'll try and help you out. And if you want to put some life into 'em, then put some life into 'em.'

'Some kind of release is necessary,' said the Professor, dropping into the manner that Timmy had come to know quite well. 'In the modern world, where the emphasis is laid not inside but outside the human consciousness, upon the machine, there is – '

'That's right,' shouted Dr Buckie. 'Absolutely agree with you. You read Alexis Carrel's book, eh? All in there, though a bit too religious for my taste. Think I hear that good-looking girl coming back. She ought to liven 'em up a bit here.'

'Only saw him a minute,' said the breathless Hope. 'But he wants us to carry on, no matter what happens. Says they've done the dirty on him and he won't have it. Not just business, he says, but the principle of the thing. Fight 'em, he says. Though he says you two'll have to be careful, because of – you know.'

'Yes, we know,' said Timmy cautiously.

'But if we can keep it going somehow, it'll be good for business when he does get out, and anyhow, he says, whatever it costs, he's not going to put up with it. But if you two want to go, he says, he'll understand – '

'They don't want to go,' said Dr Buckie. 'They're going to stay here and blow the place up. But I've got to go, because I've a lot of work to do. And I'll do my best to have poor Haddock back with you as soon as it's humanly possible. Can't say better than that, eh? Morning.' And out she marched, leaving the room, which had seemed packed a moment before, now looking comparatively empty.

'It's the Professor that mustn't be caught,' said Timmy, as the three of them left the hospital. 'I don't mean it mightn't be awkward for me – but they mightn't connect me with that funny business over in Birchester, whereas the Professor's done for if he gets into trouble and lands in court. They'll spot him for a foreigner, and then this passport business starts – and then where is he?'

'I think it is not enough to have no beard and call myself Bentham. I think also I must wear dark spectacles. They are very good, these dark spectacles.'

'Unless the police are camping in that hall,' Hope announced, 'we're going to give 'em a little show tonight.

But if the police do come, then you two have got to dive out quick. We must work that out carefully.'

'And we can't possibly let the public in,' said Timmy, a conscientious professional, 'before we've rehearsed.'

'That's true,' Hope sighed. 'I'm terrible. We'll rehearse this afternoon.'

Early in the afternoon they found the side door of the Little Market Hall open, and on the platform, grinning and staring at them with his queer bright restless eyes, their strange assistant, Candover.

'Thank goodness they haven't locked us out,' said Hope, to Candover as well as to the other two.

'They can't do that,' replied Candover, grinning away. 'They can only stop you singing and playing, because of the licence. That young chap came again, not ten minutes since – y'know, that young chap from the Council office – and he said that. You can sell things, he said, but no entertainment.'

'I dare say,' said Hope, 'but that's just the opposite of what we want to do. We can't sell anything because Uncle Fred's laid up, but he wants us to give them a nice free entertainment – for publicity.'

'I could sell things,' cried Candover.

'No, my friend, you dream too much,' said the Professor. 'What dream did you have last night?'

Candover's vague wavering face became still and red, and his eyes glittered.

'Now stop it,' said Hope, and called Timmy away.

'There were thousands and thousands of small brown men with hairy caps,' Candover said, going nearer the Professor, 'and there was a city in a desert, with towers and domes . . .' After that the other two could only hear the murmur of his voice.

'I think,' said the Professor, when he joined them at the

piano, 'that what he saw last night was the great sack of Bagdad by the Mongols under Hulagu, brother of Kublai Khan.'

'Now, steady, Professor,' said Timmy. 'What would he know about all that, whatever it is? He's just barmy.'

'My theory is this,' replied the Professor, with great earnestness. 'By some accident, which we cannot understand, the unconscious dreaming mind of this man reflects the universal mind or world memory. Thus he witnesses great events separated by thousands of miles and, what is more strange, thousands of years perhaps from his waking self. This world memory – '

'Professor, we want to rehearse,' cried Hope. 'And don't go on about his dreams. He frightens me when he begins to talk about them.'

'That I can understand,' said the Professor. 'For then you are not really seeing a man, but all men, or a kind of reflection in one man – just by some accident – or something greater than humanity, that is, a consciousness – '

But the girl banged the piano hard with both fists. Meanwhile the reflection of the world memory was pulling forward the set of drums, and looking very pleased with himself. A little ruffled at being so noisily interrupted, the Professor now sat down at the piano. The rehearsal began. The Professor, of course, played the piano. Hope and Timmy, when not singing, tried their hand at the drums. Timmy ran through the old successful numbers that he had sung for Sir George Denberry-Baxter: *You Can't Give Father Any Cockles* and *Roly-Poly For Mrs Moly* and *You Know What To Do With Your Rhubarb*. He knew that he would be able to persuade any average audience to sing their choruses with him, and that was what people liked, to let themselves go a bit. Hope struggled through *Wiggle Your*

Ears for Walter and *Hoopy-Toopy-Toots* and the rest, with more courage than skill. Her dancing, of the easier tap variety, was better than her singing, but both were amateurish. 'If you'd just a bit more talent, with them looks,' Timmy told her regretfully, 'there'd be no stopping you.'

'You mean – if I'd any talent at all,' cried Hope, who was refreshingly free from any illusions about herself. 'I told you. I'm terrible and I'll always be terrible. I don't even *want* to be good.'

'That is because the whole inner nature of your being,' the Professor started, 'is now turned – '

'Now don't go on again about my love life,' cried Hope, almost angrily, 'because you make me feel sick. We don't have a love life here. At least I don't.'

'The English attitude towards sex – '

'And shut up about sex. I *hate* sex. I wish there weren't any. Let's do *Hoopy-Toopy-Toots* again.'

'If I hate anything,' the Professor sighed, 'it is *Hoopy-Toopy-Toots*.'

'That number,' said Timmy, 'will get 'em.'

And he was right. That same evening, it got 'em. And the old songs, *You Can't Give Father Any Cockles* and *Roly-Poly for Mrs Moly*, got 'em even more. It was just the right sort of evening for this free entertainment, being dark, with a touch of autumnal fog in the air, but fine. The big doors of the Little Market Hall were wide open, so that everybody passing in the square could not fail to see the lighted platform inside, now looking almost like a proper stage. Nineteen people out of twenty stopped at once, and then, if they were not too far away, they caught a glimpse of a very pretty girl indeed, in a fancy costume, and of a little funny man with a red nose and very eccentric coat, waistcoat and trousers. (Timmy had received his basket from Crewe just in time.) They heard the alluring *tinkle-*

tankle of the piano, and occasionally the *brrrrump-clash* of
the drum and cymbals. Then going nearer they heard the
gusts of laughter at the little man's jokes – good old war-
horses all of them – and then, later, the voices of their
townsfolk raised in song.

Yes, in the beginning it all went very well indeed. Mr
Hassock, the day before, had seen to it that his entertainers should start properly. Mr Hassock, whose knowledge
of the English public was very profound, knew that people
in places like Dunbury are very shy, and that the very
people who are willing before the evening is out to buy a
clock or a case of cutlery are the shyest of all, so that he
arranged with Candover that as soon as the entertainment
was ready to begin, a nucleus of an audience, so many
decoy ducks, should be there. People had not to march
into an empty hall. All they had to do was to join the
audience already there. This they did. The first-comers
were mostly youngsters, of course, giggling girls and
guffawing lads, of the kind that spends so many evenings
walking round and round such market-squares, apparently idling but really busy with the time-old biological
task of sexual selection and courtship. It was only to be
expected that these youngsters would come flocking in.
This was Wednesday night, and most of them had already
seen the film at the *Elite*, a stirring patriotic film about the
soldiers of our Empire made in England by a Hungarian
Jew in imitation of a stirring patriotic film about the
soldiers of our Empire made in Hollywood by a Polish
Jew. But after this first rush of youngsters there came solid
townsfolk of both sexes and all ages. After all, as Mr
Hassock had seen at once, there is not much to do on a
dark autumn evening in Dunbury. And here was a free
entertainment.

To many of the youths there the sight of Hope had

raised this above the level of mere entertainment. They
did not know whether she would sing or dance or not
(and ever afterwards listened with impatience to pointed
feminine criticism of that singing and dancing); they
gazed at her in dreamy ecstasy; they rescued her from
fires, from drowning, from homicidal maniacs down mysterious dark roads; they left Dunbury for ever with her in
powerful fast cars, acquired they did not quite know how;
they listened, with more delight than surprise, to her
faltering blushing confession that it was the very first sight
of them, just sitting there in the Little Market Hall that
Wednesday night, that had captured her great wild heart.
But there was more in her appeal to them than this day-
dreaming, with its possessiveness and swagger, would
suggest. She was to them, as she had every right to be, a
figure of pure romance. She was beautiful, transient,
mysterious, the lady from a far country. She brought
them, for a day or two, to life. Most of these lads had lived
twenty years in Dunbury and might live another forty or
fifty years there, but in the greater life, which ours may
serve as the humble kernels of wheat serve us, some of
these lads were born that night and died a few days
afterwards. And of all this, Hope, trying to remember her
words and the few simple dance steps, was not aware.
Only now and then, however, the image of Roger Liss
would cross her mind.

Timmy became a favourite at once, for this was a simple
audience, not bedazzled by American speed, sharpness
and cynicism and blind to the richer English drollery of
character, and as a good experienced comedian he knew
how to handle it. He cracked many of his oldest and most
dependable jokes, but he depended chiefly on the songs,
and he knew that his business was to persuade these
people to sing themselves. So he began working all the

old gags, asking the people at the right-hand side of the
hall to sing against the people on the left, the women
against the men, and so on. They were shy, at first, but
they were pulled out of their shyness not only by Timmy's
old tricks and by Hope's bewitching smiles but also by the
unexpected aid of young Raymond Mitterly. Raymond
had not only come along himself, bringing his clarinet,
but he had also brought two other members of the late
Dunbury Band, a long thin youth who played the oboe
and a little fat middle-aged man who performed on that
little fat middle-aged instrument, the euphonium. These
three, though they had brought their instruments along,
hidden away in their respective cases, had never imagined
that they would have the nerve to climb on to the platform
and extemporise their parts; but the truth is that Raymond
was among the youths who were instantly enslaved by
Hope, and it was he who compelled the other two to join
him on the platform. A piano, played by a foreign scholar
who had hitherto confined himself to classical music,
occasional and inexperienced percussion effects, with a
clarinet, oboe and euphonium all picking up their parts
as they went along, does not make an ideal combination
for popular music, but these allies, if a trifle uncertain,
gave body to the refrains. And what was much more
important they gave confidence to their fellow-citizens,
who felt, when they saw three of their number boldly
mounting the platform, that the least they could do
themselves was to obey the little comic's command to sing
with him. So good quiet townsfolk soon implored each
other, at the top of their voices, not to give Father any
cockles or Mother any gin, and pointed out over and over
again what happened when Auntie was treated to port.
They demanded, as they had never demanded anything
for themselves, that Mrs Moly – who afterwards became a

great legendary character in Dunbury – should have her roly-poly, and they reminded the whole market-square that if Mrs Moly couldn't have it with jam, she would have it with ham, or with bacon and eggs like her Uncle Sam. The Professor, who could not understand why people should be so content to sing such idiotic words when there were so many good songs about the love of one's country or the early deaths of beautiful maidens or the happiness of children in spring, kept glancing down at the rows of shining innocent faces, and wondered all over again why the English were so strange. Hope felt that they were doing Uncle Fred Hassock proud, and looked at Timmy with a new respect. And Timmy was enjoying himself as he had not done for a long time. He forgot what it was all about, forgot Mr Hassock and Dunbury and the nasty business about the licence, and simply lived in the moment, having his fun with the crowd. Of course, it could not last.

They had just come to the end of the third concerted attempt to grapple with Mrs Moly's problem when there was a pushing, a scuffling, a muttering, near the wide open door, and then a gigantic bass voice roared: 'Now, just a minute, everybody!' A large man in blue uniform pushed his way through the audience, which, wondering and curious, was quiet for the moment.

'The police,' Hope whispered to Timmy and the Professor. 'You two be ready to clear out. Don't forget.'

The Inspector was now looking up at her. 'You people were told last night you couldn't give an entertainment in this hall.'

Hope was not in the least afraid of him, although he looked like two or three ordinary policemen rolled into one. He was an enormous chap with an enormous shiny nose and an enormous moustache. He could have dealt with whole race gangs single-handed. But Hope was not a race gang and looked down at him boldly.

'A young man came here last night,' she cried, in a voice that everybody could hear, 'and muttered something about that. But we didn't take any notice of him, because my uncle had rented this hall for a fortnight and it was understood that he could use it for entertaining the people of Dunbury.'

'Quite right!' and 'Hear, hear!' several people shouted from the back.

'We knew that Dunbury wouldn't go back on its word,' cried Timmy, who felt reckless. 'Now then – chorus again –'

And they joined in, too, so that the enormous inspector, now purple in the face, seemed to be bobbing up and down on the waves of sound.

> *If she can't have jam*
> *She'll take it with ham*
> *Or with bacon and eggs like her Uncle Sam –*
> *So –*
> *Roly poly for Mrs Moly –*

And here the Inspector either had to explode or to blow his whistle. He blew his whistle. The blast cut through the Mrs Moly chorus like a knife.

'Professor,' Hope called softly, 'you beat it now. Quick! And you next, Timmy.'

'Now I'll give you one more warning,' said the Inspector.

'What's the matter with you, Mussolini,' asked a plaintive voice at the back. Everybody except the Inspector laughed. This did not help at all.

'This hall isn't licensed for entertainment,' he shouted,

'and these people know it. They're deliberately breaking the law, and if any of you stay here after I've given you fair warning, then you're aiding an' abetting. Now I give you – '

'Cockles,' a shrill young voice yelled at him. This was a cue for the other popular chorus:

> *You can't give Father any cockles;*
> *You can't give Mother any gin;*
> *Auntie's a sport,*
> *But don't give her port,*
> *You never know what she'll begin . . .*

Now the Inspector completely lost his temper. 'Here, you!' he bellowed at a lad who was singing away, and gave him such a clout that the lad let out a sharp cry and then began whimpering. There was an instant silence.

'I've given you all fair warning,' the Inspector began, loudly but a trifle uneasily.

'Now just a minute, Inspector Parkin.' And a broad-shouldered middle-aged man pushed forward from the crowd. 'What do you think you're doing?'

'I'm doing my duty, an' I don't want any speech from you tonight, Mr Largs.'

'Go on, Tom,' and 'Good old Tom!' came from the crowd.

'You might as well understand, friends,' Tom Largs shouted, with the readiness of a man who had often done this before, 'that the reason why they're stopping you enjoying yourselves down here – and breaking their word to the people who've rented this Little Hall – is because they've taken the licence away from the big hall upstairs. Now the Market Hall was left to the people of Dunbury – '

Here the Inspector tried to interrupt but he was drowned by the encouraging shouts of the crowd: 'That's right,' and 'Good for you, Tom,' and 'Go on, Tom, tell 'em off.'

'And now they're taking it away from the people of Dunbury,' Tom Largs roared at them, his voice thickening with passion. 'They haven't decided yet between them what they're going to do with it, but they know what they're not going to do with it – and that is, let the people of Dunbury have it. Another ramp, that's what this is, just another ramp.'

'That's enough,' the Inspector yelled, using his huge shoulders as he pushed his way nearer the speaker. 'Now I've warned you – '

'And now I'm warning you,' cried Tom Largs, 'and the bosses and snobs that sent you here. I'm warning you all. *Let the people sing.*'

'Hurray!' shouted Candover, almost dancing on the platform in his excitement. 'Let the people sing.'

'Hey, you!' and a heavy hand fell on Candover's shoulder. A police sergeant had arrived on the platform and had now taken charge of the trembling Candover.

'Leave him alone,' cried Hope indignantly.

'You pop off an' get some decent clothes on, young woman,' said the sergeant. 'Any more from you an' you'll find yourself in Queer Street.'

'I like Queer Street,' said Hope scornfully. But she hastily looked round. It was all right. The Professor and Timmy had vanished. And the three instrumentalists, Raymond and his two friends, were now melting away.

Tom Largs had disappeared. The Inspector was bustling the people out of the hall. There was at least one policeman near the doorway, hurrying them out into the square. The sergeant remained on the platform, and though he had taken his hand off Candover he was keeping an eye on him that was like a hand. Candover stood there still trembling, either from fear or excitement. There was nothing more for Hope to do at this moment, so she went behind the screen in the far corner, which she had claimed as her little dressing-room.

Meanwhile, Timmy Tiverton, comedian – for of course he was still in his make-up and eccentric costume – was now crouching in the back of a saloon car parked in the square. He had let the Professor slip out of the hall first, and had been wondering whether to take a chance and take off his grease-paint and costume behind the screen when he saw the sergeant arrive and stand squarely in front of the screen. So he decided to dodge out while the sergeant was still watching his superior officer down among the audience. He backed a few steps, with an absent-minded air, then quickly turned and hurried down the few steps at the back of the platform and made for the little door there, which was ajar. A fraction of a second before his hand could pull it open, it was opened by a large policeman, coming in from the square. Instantly Timmy ducked under the policeman's arm, and was out. The policeman, startled, cried 'Hey!' but remained in the doorway.

Now Timmy had noticed among the audience a thick-set, square-faced chap of fifty or so, who had paid him particular attention. This chap did not laugh and sing with the others, did not relax at all, but kept staring at him in a rather stern, thoughtful fashion, which was disconcerting. Moreover, Timmy had an idea that he had seen the chap before somewhere. And now, just as Timmy was moving away from the policeman's 'Hey!', this chap came hurriedly round the corner from the front entrance, moved forward and saw Timmy and called 'Hey!' even

more masterfully than the policeman had done. Bewildered and alarmed by this 'Hey!' business, Timmy turned
sharply and trotted away from the Market Hall towards
the centre of the square, where about twenty cars, close
together in a double row, were parked.

'Hey!' called Frosty-face, louder this time.

'Oh, no, you don't,' muttered Timmy, convinced now
that the chap was a detective. It was starting to rain and
the centre of the square was not well lit, so he felt he had
a sporting chance of escape. He reached the parked cars
and hurried between the two rows, but then saw that a
few yards away, at the far side, two men were talking, one
of them being the attendant of the car park. And then
another and still louder 'Hey!' came from the other side
of the cars, and Timmy felt he was trapped. He then
opened the rear door of the nearest saloon, tumbled in,
and thanked God, as he crouched well below the window
level, that he was a little man.   .

Nothing happened during the next few minutes but the
rain, which now drummed hard on the roof. Having
almost recovered from this very unpleasant 'Hey!' business, which temporarily jangles the nerves of any man
who feels he is wanted by the police, Timmy began to
peep out and wonder whether he had not better make a
dash for it. But just as he was making up his mind to go,
there were hurried steps and voices, the driver's door of
the saloon was flung open, and a man's voice said: 'Slide
in this way, it'll save time. And let's get out, quick.' A man
and a girl settled themselves in front. Timmy crouched
still lower and wedged himself firmly. This wedging was
very necessary, for by this time the car was travelling at a
high speed along a very bumpy road.

'And this,' said the little man with the very red nose

and the eccentric costume, as they roared and skidded and bumped through the spouting night, and he wondered where the extraordinarily strong smell of goloshes was coming from, 'this is a bit of all right.'

CHAPTER VII

TIMMY MEETS AN OLD FRIEND

'YOU'VE BEEN out there before, haven't you?' said the man.

'No, I haven't,' replied the girl. 'I've heard of it, of course, but just as it happens, I've never been there.'

'Oh – it's quite amusing,' he told her, rather loftily. 'Jolly place, really.'

Well, that's something, Timmy told himself. At least they were all going to a jolly place.

'Turned out a filthy night, though,' said the man.

'Yes, it has, hasn't it?' said the girl, who did not seem to be a very brilliant talker.

'Oh – filthy. Car's skidding a bit too.'

'Is it really? I'd hate to have an accident.'

'So would I. Rather awkward for both of us, eh?'

Awkward for all three, Timmy told them. They were now well outside the town, with not a light about, nothing but the rain. Where they were going might be jolly or it might not, but it certainly was a filthy night, and Timmy did not want to be turned out into the middle of it. So he kept as quiet as a mouse. And fortunately it was a fine large saloon car, so that he did not need to intrude upon the pair in front, who had no chance of hearing his occasional tiny movements above the roar of the engine and the rain.

'I suppose,' said the girl, determined to do her best to be entertaining, 'there won't be many people there now it's turned out so wet.'

'Not quite so many as usual, I dare say. But it's all a car trade there, of course, at the "Dog and Bell." New type of road-house, you see. Miles from anywhere, really.'

So they were going to a new type of road-house, were they? Timmy felt rather more cheerful. These two were just running out for a few drinks and a dance or two. They would have to return to Dunbury. He had only to stay where he was and keep quiet; and even if he should be discovered it would not matter much now. He had a shrewd idea that the fellow driving there would not be anxious to call attention to this little jaunt of his. He was obviously much older than the girl, who was probably a typist in his office or something of the sort.

'Must be making money out there at the "Dog and Bell",' said the man, who seemed a dreary fellow.

'Who owns it?' asked the girl.

'Don't know, really. Woman called Daisy something-or-other – noisy little woman – seems to manage it. May own it too, of course. But probably she's been put in just to make it go.'

'A young woman?'

'Good lord – no! Well into middle-age. Used to be on the halls.'

Timmy, who had already changed from crouching to kneeling, now forgot all caution and lifted his head above the back of their seat for fear of missing any of this.

'Yes,' the man continued. 'On the halls for years. I just remember her. Red hair. Daisy – Daisy – ?'

'Not Daisy Barley?' cried Timmy loudly, not a foot from the man's left ear.

The man shouted 'What!', the girl screamed, and the

car, not to be outdone, described upon the road an immense question mark, before coming to a standstill. When the angry driver had switched on the light, the girl screamed again, for now she saw Timmy's face, or rather the red nose and vast arched eyebrows of that eccentric comedian. T. Tiverton. She herself was a watery young blonde, with a nose no bigger than a baby's thumb and foolish goggling eyes. The man was a thin fellow in his thirties, with one of those thin moustaches that must be far more trouble than they are worth. Timmy did not like the look of them any more than they liked the look of him. But they had to be conciliated.

'Now I'm very, very sorry, I really am, to have frightened you like this,' Timmy gabbled away, not knowing what he was about to say next but determined to keep it going. 'It's all been a little accident, one of those things that might happen to anybody, though for some reason or other – and I've never been able to understand it – but they're always happening to *me*. If I'd to tell you *half* the things that have happened to me, you'd die laughing. Honestly, you would. Now this is just a case in point. A funny expression that, I always think, don't you? A case in point? When you come to look at it – '

'What is all this?' the man demanded, unpleasantly. 'What are you doing in my car?'

'I'll tell you. Now, do you know – er – a Mr Montgomery, who lives in Dunbury?'

'No, I don't,' the man replied.

'I do,' said the girl, who just would.

'Mr *Mackenzie* Montgomery?' asked Timmy, with an air of astonishment, as if this particular Montgomery had never been out for twenty years.

'No, the one I know is called Percy. He's quite young. Perhaps the one you know is his father.'

'No, the one I know – Mackenzie – hasn't any children. That's *one* reason,' Timmy continued desperately, 'why I was let in for tonight's business.'

'What business?' this was the man again. He was losing his hair on top, and serve him right too, Timmy decided. But what was tonight's business?

'Well, you see, to begin with, the reason I'm in this queer get-up is that I've just been doing a turn in the Little Market Hall in Dunbury – '

This interested the girl. 'I didn't know there was anything on there.'

'Well, there is – or was. Me. So my friend Montgomery – Mackenzie Montgomery – or Mack as I always call him – Mack asked me to come out and have a bit of supper at his house tonight, and he said his car would be waiting at the parking place in the square, just near the Hall. He described the car – a saloon just like this. So when I'd done my turn, I hurried out – it was just beginning to rain, you see – and I thought this was Mack's car – very natural mistake, after all – '

'But do you mean to tell me you were going to somebody's house dressed like that?' demanded the owner of the car.

'Ah! – now I'm glad you mentioned that,' cried Timmy heroically. 'You see, Mack's got a wife – and you couldn't wish for a nicer woman – who's not allowed to leave the house – got a very bad heart – and he told me she'd asked over and over again, 'cos I've known them for years, if when I came next to Dunbury I wouldn't come out and do my act for her – make-up an' all. So naturally I couldn't refuse, could I? I think this is Mack's car. I hurry in out of the rain – '

'And lie down at the back,' said the man as unpleasantly

as ever. 'Because that's where you must have been when we got in.'

'Of course I was. But then Mack and I had agreed about that. I was to hide at the back until he got home.'

'Why?'

'Why? Why? I never knew such a chap for questions.' And Timmy concentrated on the girl now. 'We'd arranged that I should hide at the back because Mack would have his wife with him in front, and we wanted to give her a surprise – '

'You said his wife couldn't leave the house,' the girl told him.

'That's right, I did. And in the ordinary way she can't, but twice a week he takes her to see the doctor. She can just stand that. He runs her over to the doctor's. That doesn't take much out of her.'

'I see,' said the man.

'Quite simple,' cried Timmy, convinced that the worst was over.

'Is it? But where did you think she was when you found the car empty?' the man asked pointedly. 'You've just said she could hardly move about, and her husband would hardly take her for a walk, would he?'

All this, thought Timmy desperately, comes of selling so many detective stories at sixpence a time. Well, something would have to be done about this wretched woman.

'Now and again,' he said impressively, keeping his temper, 'they meet the doctor in the square, and then the doctor takes Mrs Montgomery off in her car – '

'Whose car?'

'The doctor's.'

'It's a woman doctor, is it?' said the girl.

'Yes, it is.'

'What's her name?'

'Dr – er – Dr Buckie,' cried Timmy triumphantly. 'Looks like a female heavy-weight.'

This made the girl giggle, and as both she and the man had obviously heard of Dr Buckie, the atmosphere cleared a little. 'You see,' Timmy continued, rushing it now, 'this Dr Buckie runs her up to the hospital and has a look at her, while Mack does a bit of shopping or has his hair cut and so on. So it didn't worry me when I saw this car was empty. I crept into the back. And then I must have dropped off. And here I am. Very sorry, of course, though really it's worse for me than for you.'

'Yes, but you gave me an awful fright, though,' said the girl, more friendly now. 'We're miles out of Dunbury.'

'About twelve miles out,' said the man, starting the car again, 'and you'll have to come out to the "Dog and Bell" because I can't turn back now.' And they were off again.

'That's all right to me,' Timmy shouted. 'Did you say the woman there's called Daisy Barley?'

'No,' shouted the driver, 'it's Daisy – but her other name's not a bit like Barley. Can't remember it now.'

This was very disappointing. Timmy felt he had given himself away for nothing. Daisy Barley, with her red curls, her saucy face and pretty legs, had not only been a star comedienne of the old days, sharing with him the best positions on the bill many a time, but she had also been one of his Betty's very best friends. He had not given a thought to Daisy for years, but now, hunched back in the roaring dark, with nothing to see but a glimpse of the lighted wet road in front, he summoned her image from his memory. What became of her? She had married once – wasn't it to a trainer in Newmarket? – and that hadn't worked; then after the War she had begun to drop down the bill; then she brought a big action against her agents, which she lost, and with it most of her savings; then she had gone out to Australia, and he seemed to remember somebody saying she had married again out there and left the profession. Poor Daisy! Poor Timmy! Poor everybody, blast it! How soon the laughter died down, the music stopped, and the lights went out! Daisy had been a little devil at times. Too many drinks after the show and, what was worse, between the houses. Too many trips to race meetings with the boys. Too many tantrums and scenes behind, for Daisy, with a temper that matched the hot copper of her curls, had always been ready to have a row with anybody who didn't seem to her a friend. But what of it? She'd always been full of fire and fun, the first to run and help a pal. Why, she was worth fifty of this dreary little pair in front here, this long-faced suspicious office chap and his watery little office piece, taking a skulking night out. He hoped poor Daisy was still alive and kicking somewhere in Australia. Perhaps he ought to have gone to Australia, for he'd had a good offer once, when there still were good offers. But it had all sounded too far away, a place to make a chap cry with home-sickness. Well, he was still here in England – wasn't he? – yet after remembering Daisy and some of the old times, he felt half ready to cry, with a kind of home-sickness. For his home now wasn't a place but a time, and it was much worse to be sick for that. You've always a chance to find the place again, but how can you go back and find the right time?

And now they had arrived at a wide crossroads and the 'Dog and Bell,' which was blazing with light and surrounded by scores of parked cars. All very jolly, no doubt, as this chap had said it would be; but not for him. This cocktail-bar-dance-band-radio jolliness always left him where it found him.

'Well, here we are,' said the owner of the car, who had

succeeded in parking it fairly close to a side entrance. He turned round, not suspicious now but still vaguely unfriendly, probably because he was rather uneasy about this jaunt. 'What are you going to do?'

'Stay here, if it's all the same to you,' replied Timmy, rather miserably. 'I can't walk in there looking like this, can I?'

Obviously the man did not want his company on the return journey to Dunbury, but obviously too he could not openly say so, not because of Timmy's feelings but because of the girl's. 'Somebody here might be going back to Dunbury quite soon,' he said with a large careless air. 'I'll see. You hang on. All right, Doris.'

Timmy watched them go inside. The man went in with half a swagger and the other half heavy with fear of being seen by his wife's brother. The girl, Doris, pulled herself together, then drew her shoulders up and forward, as women do when they try on fur coats, because they have an idea this makes them look expensive, pampered, delicate. Poor Doris! Thinking she was going to have a good time in there with that chap. She would never have a good time anywhere with that chap. The thing couldn't be done.

It was still raining but Timmy let down the window for a breath of fresh air. There was plenty of noise coming from this 'Dog and Bell,' including the *thud-thudding* of a little dance band. Miles and miles away from anywhere, in the middle of ten thousand wet fields, and yet they could keep a place like this blazing with light and run a dance band in it. Timmy still did not care tuppence about the place, but for all that he couldn't help feeling a bit out of things. He was cold too and damp. The eccentric costume, short black coat with no lapels, a red waistcoat, and baggy light check trousers, had not been chosen to travel round in on wet autumn nights. A stiff whisky and perhaps a bite of something savoury and hot would be more than welcome. If this thin chap had been a human being, he would have brought something out himself. So Timmy shivered, brooded, and cursed in his dark corner of the car. Dunbury, with the Professor and Hope and Mr Hassock and everybody there, seemed to fade right out, and he felt as if this was a direct continuation of his horrible day in Birchester. He was the same unwanted man, and not any more comfortable now because he had landed himself here in full make-up and costume.

'No harm in taking a look,' some woman shouted. Let her shout and take looks. But not at him, he hoped, and bunched himself still smaller.

But the door was opened and an electric torch was flashed full in his face. He turned and made it even fuller in his face. He was startled and annoyed. 'Here, what – ' he began, almost snarling.

'Lord love a purple duck! Either I'm going barmy or it's Timmy – Timmy Tiverton!'

'Well, yes,' he began stammering, half recognising the voice out of the past.

But now the torch was switched off and a plump little woman had hurled herself into the car beside him, was putting her plump little arms round his neck, was kissing him and laughing and gasping and wetting his cheek with tears. 'My God – what a thing to do to a woman, Timmy, turning up like this out of the blue – and dressed and made-up to go straight on! Oh – Christmas! – Timmy – when I suddenly saw you there, just as if you were waiting to go on, just like the old days, I tell you my poor old heart turned right upside down. I'll have indigestion for a fortnight. An' I don't believe you know me yet, you silly ol' comic – '

'Yes, I do, dear. You're Daisy – Daisy Barley.'

'Of course I am,' she cried, hugging him again.

'Then why the hell didn't that chap say so?' cried Timmy, not knowing whether to laugh or cry himself. He had to explain that remark, and then he told her, very simply and quietly, how he'd been thinking and wondering about her, and she clutched his arm tight, and choked and sniffed and damned herself for a silly ol' woman.

'You see, Timmy,' she explained when he had done, 'I married a chap called Fillans out in Australia – he died out there, so then I came back – and here they call me Mrs Fillans. And what we're staying out here for, I don't know – with you shivering away – poor ol' Timmy! Come on – inside.'

'What. Like this?'

'We'll run through the back and straight up to my little sitting-room,' she cried, 'an' I'll have you out o' them things and a drink an' some hot supper in front of you – in a jiffy. You don't know me now, Timmy. Business woman. An' I boss 'em round here like a female Hitler. My goodness me – come on, dear, stir yourself; we're going – but I'm glad I listened when that chap said he'd got a comedian stowed away in his car! If I'd known afterwards you'd been shivering out here – with me in there, just talkin' to those bits of nonsense – I'd have gone out of my head. Now in there, Timmy, an' straight up the stairs. Here,' she shouted to somebody, 'tell Walter I want him upstairs – sharp.'

She rushed him into a cosy little room that was crammed with photographs of the profession and souvenirs and knick-knacks and feminine rubbish. And she never stopped talking. He still felt too dazed and shy to say very much, and deep inside he was much moved, as if there was another Timmy in there who had to cry over this strange meeting. She was sadly changed, of course, after all these years; the red curls were still there but obviously owed a lot now to the hairdresser and the chemist; the saucy little face had filled out and was heavily lined in spite of its rather thick make-up; the pretty legs had vanished with so many other pretty and amusing things; and this plump little middle-aged woman, over-dressed and wearing too much jewellery and a make-up almost as startling and unreal as a clown's, seemed at first sight only a distant connection of the bewitching and saucy Daisy Barley who used to set her curls and heels twinkling at the enraptured boys and had been known to turn even the fellows in the band into her slaves. Yet it was Daisy all right. Her eyes had not aged and tired. In their reckless greeny-hazel depths the fire and fun and devilment still burned. Agents, managers, sulking audi-ences, marriages, Australia, none of them had got her down. She had winked and shouted and danced her way, through God knows what, into this sitting-room, where she now sat kicking her legs excitedly and looking at him as nobody had looked at him for years and years, as if she could eat him, as if she truly loved him.

'Daisy,' he told her, hardly knowing what he was saying, 'you ought to have seen that wet little blonde in that car.'

'What for? Don't tell me you've gone an' fallen for some messy little piece you've just – '

'No, of course I haven't,' he almost shouted at her. 'But I was just comparing you. They don't make 'em like you any more, Daisy. That's what I meant. They're like half-drowned kittens. You're alive – you're – by thunder! – you're wonderful.'

'Now you're talking, dear. I wondered what had come over you. Ah – Walter!' A stout little oldish chap had come in, with the look of an old pro about him. 'Now look who's here!'

'Blimey!' cried Walter, staring at Timmy as if he was a ghost. 'Wait a minute! Don't tell me. It's Timmy Tiverton. You remember me? Walter Shafton – you remember – the Shafton Brothers?'

Timmy, still dazed, found himself shaking this fellow droll warmly by the hand. Shafton Brothers used to be a very good turn indeed. Hadn't heard of them for donkey's years.

'Now, Walter,' cried Daisy briskly, 'I asked you to come up because I want you to take Timmy up to your room and lend him some of your clothes – you're about a size except you're a lot fatter. That's what comes of working for me. I believe the whole dam' lot of you have put on about three stone each since you came here – an' what we'll all look like in a year or two, God only knows. Off you go, Timmy my boy, an' clean up – an' I'll have something waiting for you down here that'll make you feel like a two-year-old.'

A girl put her head round the door. 'Mrs Fillans, Mr Johnson and his friends are asking for you in the cocktail bar.'

'You tell Mr Johnson and his friends, dear, that one of my very oldest and dearest friends has just arrived – so I'm busy. Now pop off. That kid's Lottie Carwell's daughter – you remember poor Lottie? That time we had with her in Liverpool just after the Grand National. Now go on, Walter, don't stand gassing there.'

Walter explained it all upstairs, while Timmy was changing into a suit much too large for him, Walter's best, too, a Harris tweed so gaudy and so hairy that you wondered which Harris had made it. 'Yers,' said Walter, 'there's 'alf a dozen of us 'ere, boy. When Disy gits back from

Austrylia, what 'appens? First thing, she finds a lot of her ol' pals can't get a job. Eh? Right. Next thing, when she tikes this big brand-new boozer, what 'appens? She can't get staff. Eh? Right. So what does she do?'

'She goes round England on a bicycle,' said Timmy.

Walter, like many drolls, was a very solemn fellow in private life and had only a professional sense of humour. 'I'll buy it, ol' boy,' he said anxiously. 'I 'aven't 'eard this one. All right then, why does she go round on a bicycle?' And he put on an expectant look he had used for thirty years as one of the Shafton Brothers.

'Never mind, Walter,' and Timmy patted him on the shoulder. 'Some other time. So Daisy decided to take you all on the staff, eh? And how does it work?'

'A treat. Look at me. I do odd jobs before we open – plenty of odd jobs in a plice this size – an' then help to wite in the smoke-room – or if necessary' – he concluded with a fine flourish – 'elsewhere.' Now he surveyed Timmy with almost paternal pride. 'Suit's a bit big, I don't deny, but the general effec' is classy – classy in what you might call a country style. I'll pop your costume, boy, into this li'l' bag. This wy, Squire.'

A very promising table for two had been laid in Daisy's sitting-room. Daisy herself was not there, but a waiter brought in a loaded tray and a fine smell of roast chicken. He was a real waiter, not an old pro. 'Would you like a gin and It, sir?'

'No, thanks, I don't like gins and Its,' said Timmy, 'but now that you're asking me, I'd like a little whisky, because I feel a bit shivery.'

'An' you're going to have some whisky, dear.' Daisy bounced in. She must have been redecorating herself, and seemed to have added a good deal of bright magenta to her lips and cheeks, and now could not have been put into the shade by a sunset above a Californian flower-show. 'Pop off, Clarence! We'll serve ourselves. You go an' serve the customers.' Out of a well-stocked cupboard she brought a bottle of whisky, and poured out two hefty ones. '*Highland Pride*, this is. It's about as Highland as I am, but it's got a hell of a kick in it, an' that's what we need at our age, eh? Not that I'm anything like as old as you, Timmy.'

'Certainly not, of course,' said Timmy gallantly. 'Why, I'm fifty-five.'

'Doesn't Time fly?' cried Daisy, now attacking the chicken with a very professional-looking carving-knife. 'But of course you're years an' years older than me. I was younger than poor Betty, y'know. I was nothing but a school kid when I first made my name. Fact is, I'm only forty-six now.'

Timmy nodded encouragingly. This was reasonable of Daisy, who must be now about fifty-four. If she took only eight years off, nobody could grumble. 'Daisy, all the best! Why, this is wonderful, meeting you again! Never thought I'd have such luck.'

'It's not been too good, eh, Timmy?' Her fine eyes suddenly misted above the glass she was holding up. 'I thought it hadn't. Asked an' asked about you, my dear, but nobody seemed to know anything. You're going to tell me how you come to be sittin' in the back of a car in your make-up, an' all about it, but not now, not just yet, dear. Just tuck in, first. My God! – but I do like eating, these days. I can remember the time when I'd just peck at this an' try a bit of that – y'know how girls go on, silly little devils – but now I just like to plant my feet under the table an' gobble, gobble, gobble. Little greedy-guts, that's me. Have some more chicken, dear. I'm having some more.'

'Walter Shafton was telling me you've got a lot of old

pros on the staff here,' he remarked, content to give her a cue.

'That's right. Killing two birds with one stone. You'll see some of 'em soon. I told 'em to come up an' have a look at you. They're a bit slow on their pins, some of 'em, an' one or two are inclined to lift the elbow too much an' talk the customers right out of the place. But you can't have everything, can you? This is my show, y'know, Timmy.'

'I wondered. That chap in the car I came in talked as if you just managed it.'

'That's all right. I want most of these chaps to think that, 'cos if I've to put my foot down – y'know, you've got to watch some of these devils, they'd have you standin' there before the Bench in no time – then I blame the owners. "Can't help it, boys," I tell 'em. "It's the owners." You've got to watch out with all these chaps that come to a place like this an' spend money. Got to flatter 'em all the time, while pretending not to. Don't you run away with the idea I don't know what I'm doin', Timmy, just because I used to be a bit wild in the old days – an' believe me, boy, if I'd known what was coming – well – '

'You'd have been a bit more careful,' he prompted her, grinning.

'I'd have been a damn' sight wilder,' she cried, 'just to make sure I got it all in, before I went and landed myself in Woolloomalloowalloo – or whatever the rotten I place was. No, Timmy, I'm not playin' round. I've got all I brought out of Australia sunk in this house. I thought of tryin' a seaside hotel first – gingering it up, of course – but then I was told of this place, which they'd nearly finished building when the fellow who started it went broke. When I first saw it, I said to 'em: "Don't be silly.

It's miles an' miles from anywhere." I couldn't see any-body comin' here.'

'I still can't see it,' said Timmy, who had been wonder-ing about this for the last hour. 'Where do they come from?'

Daisy laughed, and helped herself to trifle that was only a shade less gorgeous than she was. 'If this isn't plastered with good sherry, those perishers downstairs are doin' it on me, for they ask for enough of it.' She took a large spoonful, winked at Timmy, then returned to the main theme. 'You see, the trouble about you, my dear, is you're not up-to-date. Now, are you?'

'No, I'm not,' replied Timmy sturdily. 'I'm clean out o' date, and I don't care who knows it.'

'You little devil!' cried Daisy, regarding him with affec-tion. 'You don't know how glad I am to see you again. Inside – ' and she tapped her opulent bosom – 'I'm with you every time. But you've got to move on. Things change, an' you've got to change with 'em if you don't want to be left in the cart. I learnt a thing or two in Australia, an' when I came back I came through America – stayed about three months in California an' then another month with a cousin of mine in Chicago – an' I saw there which way things were going. What the Yanks did last year, we'll do next year, y'know.'

'I do know,' said Timmy, rather unhappily. 'But I don't see why.'

Daisy had her answer ready. Obviously she had talked on these lines many a time before. 'Because somebody's always in the lead an' setting the fashion. Fifty years ago it was us. Now it's the Americans. You can't get away from it, Timmy. Every new thing you see here nowadays is only a copy of something they've had for years in America. Look at this place. Road-house. Not near a town, but what does that matter? Everybody with money to spend has a car now, an' likes to use it. Here we collect chaps and girls from twenty or thirty towns. Yes, an' people who used to be content with a quiet country life – they come here, too. They can have a bit o' dinner or supper, a few drinks, dance, play some games – darts an' so on, an' we have competitions an' bits of nonsense. I'm putting in a swimming-pool for the next summer. You've got to keep up-to-date, see?'

A very fat, jolly woman, who looked as if she had just come up from the kitchen, now came in and advanced upon Timmy with an outstretched hand and a beaming smile. 'How was the chicken? An' I bet you don't remember me.'

'The chicken was wonderful,' replied Timmy, staring at her. 'Now – just give me a minute. I'll remember.' He meant it, too, for he knew he had seen those eyes before.

'He'll never do it, dear,' said Daisy.

'Isn't it terrible?' sighed the nice fat woman. But then she smiled again at Timmy. She was a fine woman, and not unlike a kind of gigantic roast chicken herself. But Timmy had to shake his head.

'Why, you fathead!' cried Daisy, 'You remember *Little Katie Sacker, the Singer By The Water Mill* – ?'

And of course he did. Back it came out of the past, accompanied by invisible orchestras and cheered by spectral gallery boys, this image of little Katie Sacker, with her sunbonnet and her fair ringlets, with her water-wheel-effect set, trilling sentimental ballads in a swiss-milk-chocolate soprano. And this was little Katie!

'Yes, that water-mill's turned a bit too much since then, hasn't it?' said Katie. 'Lucky for me I'd always fancied myself as a cook. We've often wondered about you, Mr Tiverton. We have a cup of tea in the morning – '

'A cup! You will have quarts, you mean,' cried Daisy. 'Some of your insides must be like ol' brown boots.'

'And we talk about the old times,' Katie continued. 'And we've often wondered about you. I'm so glad to have seen you again. And I know Daisy is. Aren't you, love?'

'Now don't start that, Katie. They made her sing so many of these kiss-me-farewell-by-the-old-mill-stream numbers when she was a kid that they got right into her blood. Talk about sentimental! She'd make a Christmas card look tough. Now go on, dear. You'll see him again. Hello, who's this?'

It was another of her staff, a grave oldish man, who was once the hind legs of a famous comic horse. Then Jimmy Flagg came up, to have a look at Timmy and to give Daisy a message or two from the cocktail-bar, over which he presided. Jimmy had toured for years as *Denga Din* (presumably related to the celebrated Gunga) the *Mystic Hindoo Illusionist*, and even now, in his trim white jacket, there was still a suggestion of the mystic Hindoo about him, and no doubt his cocktails appeared to be mixed and shaken by magic. He fixed his mournful dark eyes, which seemed to be permanently in the Hindoo line, upon Timmy's, and said he was damned glad to see him and had never forgotten, and never would forget, a postman act of Timmy's that had left him nearly prostrated with laughter in the wings. And all this, and more, was said in a sad voice soft that still suggested Bengal and not a back street in Wolverhampton.

'He's a big success in the cocktail bar, Jimmy is,' said Daisy. 'Aren't you, dear? Does a few little tricks now and then, an' they nearly pass out. These people now think they know it all an' think they're hard to please, but really they're money for jam. All right, Jimmy, I'm coming down.'

She took Timmy on a little tour of inspection. Still dazed by the fantastic events of the evening, and especially by this series of encounters with his old pals of the halls, Timmy did not take everything in very well, could not have described afterwards what he saw, but he took in enough to make him regard Daisy with a new respect. Amazing to think she should be running a place this size, and running it so well, too. Big kitchen, white-tiled and full of gadgets; a long dining-room, so determinedly Tudor that you might have been in Stratford-on-Avon, and indeed the head waiter, who had a manner that could turn any fish that Grimsby forwarded into Dover sole, had once toured with Benson; a dance-room that was a bit Spanish, a bit Viennese, and a good deal Metro-Goldwyn-Mayer, with a five-piece dance band consisting of two enthusiastic young men from Birmingham who were trying to look like love-sick Mexicans and three much older men, whom Timmy recognised as the masculine section of the former *Musical Wilsons*, a good act in its day; a cosy, leathery smoke-room in the Old English a-hunting-we-will-go style; and the cocktail bar, which had a vermilion colour scheme and was so hot and dazzling and queer that it made you wonder if you had a temperature; and it was here in the cocktail bar, which had forty or fifty people in it, that Daisy had to attend to business.

'Daisy,' Jimmy Flagg whispered, 'that chap – Mortimer – from Melminster – he's here again with his pal and those two little pieces.'

'I'll have a word with him,' Daisy muttered; adding to Timmy: 'Now you'll see what this game lets you in for.' As Timmy followed her over to the group of four, he saw her detach one of the men, who were at least twenty years older than the girls they were with, and was in time to hear what she said to him.

'All the best!' she began, as he raised his glass. 'Glad to see you here again, Mr Mortimer. Y'know, I was over in Melminster the other day, an' somebody was saying very nice things about Mrs Mortimer to me. Why don't you bring her over an' let us have a look at her one of these nights. What about Saturday, if you've nothing better to do? We're having another Treasure Hunt. Yes, do!'

She watched him go back speculatively, then took Timmy into a corner. 'I've never heard anything about his wife – but I know he's got one – an' I'm tellin' him straight to bring her here instead o' these bits of typists. I know! I can see it in your eye, you little devil! You're thinking this doesn't sound like Daisy. But don't think I've changed. I want everybody to have a bit o' fun, but I don't like these kids being brought here by men old enough to be their fathers. If this Mortimer's wife just won't have a night out – all right, let him find somebody who will, somebody his own weight. But if you ask me, he's never asked her – an' I'll bet twenty to one she's sittin' at home now wondering why he always has to work so late these days – when he's spending his money – hers, too, for that matter – turnin' the head of some kid who ought to be havin' ninepenn'orth of pictures with a boy her own age. I tell you, Timmy, you may think it's no business of mine, but I'm not interferin' for interferin's sake. I want to run this show so's nobody'll curse the day I ever came here – '

She broke off because a middle-aged square man, with a close-cropped moustache and a bitter, bloodshot look, now came over, and greeted her.

'You're not dancing tonight, major. Thought you couldn't keep off that floor. Lost your partner?'

'Oh, no. She's here.' The major also had a close-cropped bitter, bloodshot voice. 'Came over to talk to you about that, Mrs Fillans. Thought you'd better know. We left the floor for a good reason. May not be aware of it, but tonight you've got a gang of dirty little Jews dancing in there.'

Daisy looked at him steadily. 'Now, just a minute, major. What d'you mean by dirty?'

'What I say.'

'Let's have a look. Come on.' She led the way through to the entrance to the dance-room, where about thirty couples were swaying and shuffling. 'Now then, where are these dirty people?'

'Over there – see? Four of 'em. Can't mistake 'em. Jews all right.'

'Yes, I see. Matter of fact, I know them quite well. Nothing dirty about them, major. They're among the nicest people who come here.' And she still surveyed him steadily.

'So you're goin' to take that line, eh?' The major sounded unpleasant.

'Listen, major,' said Daisy earnestly. 'I'm not takin' any lines. You're takin' a line. An' I'll tell you frankly it's a line I don't like – '

'Whether you like it or not,' said the major sharply, 'you'll find more an' more decent people here are taking it.'

'If I thought so,' cried Daisy, angry now, 'I'd leave this country an' never come back. In the meantime the "Dog and Bell" is open to anybody who behaves properly, an' I don't care what shape their noses are, an' if you an' Hitler don't like it, major, I'm sorry, but you'll have to lump it. Good night.'

She swung away, an absurd little figure but now not without dignity, and Timmy joined her. They walked the length of the dance floor in silence. He knew that now she was feeling upset but he did not like to say anything. This was a new Daisy, a long way from the old madcap. 'I want to look in the dining-room again,' she said finally, 'and then we'll go back to my sitting-room so that you can tell me all about yourself.'

As they entered the dining-room, Timmy pulled her up short. For there, in the far corner, unnoticed before but plainly to be seen now, tucking away, was the thick-set, square-faced man who had followed him out of the Hall and cried 'Hey!' There was no mistake. It was undoubtedly the same severe, menacing fellow. At any moment, if he should look up from his plate, he might be crying 'Hey!' again, and before the night was out he might be heying Timmy into the nearest police station.

'Here, Daisy,' he muttered, 'I've got to get out of this – sharp.' And he hurried out, and looked for the stairs up to Daisy's sitting-room.

'I never knew such a rum little devil,' cried Daisy at his elbow, a trifle breathless. 'I believe you've been up to something, though what you could be up to, God only knows. This way, an' then tell Auntie Daisy all about it.'

Back among the photographs and souvenirs of professional life, Timmy began talking about himself, and he could not have had a better audience. When he arrived at the end of his depressing morning in Birchester, which had left him wondering about suicide, Daisy, half in tears, leaned forward and gave him a bright magenta kiss.

'I'm not surprised either,' she cried, dabbing at her eyes. 'I could never get on with 'em in Birchester. My God – how I used to hate that date! There's something *wrong* with 'em there – got dried peas where their hearts ought to be – or something. Poor ol' Timmy! Still,' she added, brightening up, 'you must have got out of it all right 'cos you're here, not buried in Birchester. Go on, go on!'

So he had to tell her then about the Professor and Mr Hassock and the girl Hope and all the doings at Dunbury and how it was by escaping from the thick-set square-faced chap, down in the dining-room, that he came to be at the 'Dog and Bell' at all. 'And that reminds me,' he concluded, 'I've got to get back to Dunbury tonight. Don't forget that.'

'Why have you? Stay here.'

'I'd like to sometime, Daisy, but – '

'Sometime! Sometime my foot! Fancy talking like that! There's plenty of room for you here. You're one of my oldest friends – a real ol' pal – why – '

'You've missed the point, my dear,' said Timmy quietly. 'I can't just walk out on these people at Dunbury. I don't know what they're going to do now, but whatever it is, I've got to see it through with 'em. Now, haven't I?'

'Yes, of course you have, if that's how you feel about it. But, you see, I feel a bit that way about you, Timmy.'

'What do you mean?'

Daisy hesitated. 'Well, you see, Betty said – the very last time I talked to her – when they only let me have a couple o' minutes with her, an' I think she knew it was all up – she asked me then to look after you – '

He stared at her, his mouth wide open. 'She asked *you* – to look after *me* – ?'

'Now that just shows how much sense you think I have,' cried Daisy. Then she was quiet again. 'But you see, dear, she had to ask *somebody* – being a woman – an' she knew that I'd more gumption than I seemed to have – an' that you'd perhaps a bit less than you seemed to have. Yes, I know, I know. But you were always a fool to yourself, Timmy Tiverton. Why, with your talent – you ought to have been still right at the top. No, don't start mutterin' to me about films an' wireless. That's a good enough excuse for most of this lot I'm employin' here. But you're different. You'd something none of them 'ud got. In a different class altogether – like me. But you've just *let* yourself be pushed out, that's what's happened to you, Timmy. An' I believe poor Betty knew. So she asked me, an' I promised. And I didn't keep my promise, being so damn' busy getting married an' unmarried and married again, runnin' round like a little mad hen. An' that's another reason why I've so often wondered about you, an' made so many enquiries since I came back from Australia, an' why I was so glad to see you. An' that's the plain truth – an' – an' – oh, give me another whisky.'

A few moments later they heard a tremendous noise coming from the doorway immediately below the sitting-room window. Daisy put her head out at once, and bawled: 'Sam, you muttonhead, what's going on down there?'

Timmy looked down and saw that in the middle of an excited and noisy group a very large doorman, presumably Sam, was about to have a set-to with a young man much smaller but much more active than himself.

'Now don't be silly, young man,' shouted Daisy. 'Go along home before you get hurt.'

The young man glanced up and it was then that Timmy recognised him. It was the young man who was in love with Hope Ollerton and had been trying to find her, the chap they met in *Annie's Pannie*, young Roger Liss. 'Here, just a minute,' Timmy called, and told Daisy that he knew the young man.

'Sam, you an' that young man come up here to my sitting-room,' Daisy told him, 'an' we'll settle it all quietly. Come on, young man, there's a friend of yours here.'

There was just time for Timmy to tell her hurriedly all that he knew about Roger Liss before that young firebrand marched in, accompanied by the gigantic Sam, whom Timmy now remembered as a partner in a balancing and strong-man act. He remembered Timmy, too.

'And what happened to the act then, Sam?'

'A widow woman in Brighton, who own three shops – very nice – she take a big fancy to Gus,' said Sam, who was not English but did not seem to belong to any specified alien people either, like many of the fellows who originally came from circus life. Lots of these strong men, acrobats, jugglers, seemed to belong to some mysterious race of their own, and talked three or four languages equally badly. 'So Gus get married – finish. I am not so young as before – do not want to start again. So – finish. Gus says: "Sam, you live with us." Mrs Gus say "No." So I do this and that – not very nice – then I am here. Very good – till silly young man make trouble – eh?' And he scowled at Roger Liss, who had been staring at Timmy.

'Yes,' Timmy told the young man, 'you're right. In *Annie's Pannie*, the other night – '

'I wish you wouldn't go on about your Annie's Pannie,' said Daisy severely. 'Sounds rude to me. Well, young man, we might have some good news for you, but you've got to behave first. Can't start chuckin' your weight about here, y'know. Any complaint against Sam?'

'Oh no, rather not,' the young man stammered, his weather-beaten face redder than ever. 'Just doing his job and all that. Don't blame him at all. My fault probably, but I merely asked a civil question – and some lout down there made a stupid remark, and – well – I'm afraid I rather lost my temper.'

'Always doing that, aren't you?' She tried to sound severe, but could not help twinkling at him. This was the kind of young man she liked.

Roger looked embarrassed, and cleared his throat.

'Well – it has – rather turned out like that these last few days. The fact is, I'm worried.' He looked at Timmy and nodded. 'You know why.'

'So do I,' said Daisy. 'All right, Sam. Pop off. An' tell 'em below the fight's cancelled. Here, I'd better come down. Nearly closing time, an' I'd better keep 'em in a good temper.'

As soon as they were alone, Roger strode forward eagerly. 'Have you seen her?'

Timmy explained briefly how he and Miss Hope Ollerton came to be fellow entertainers at Dunbury, while the young man stared at him expectantly.

'Gosh, that's wonderful!' he cried, when Timmy had done. 'Did she – er – say anything about me – I mean, did you mention to her that you'd met me?'

'The Professor and I told her,' said Timmy. 'You've got a friend there in the Professor. Very sympathetic, the Professor is. Talked about it several times.'

'And what did she say?'

Timmy tried to remember and had to admit that he couldn't. 'That is, not exactly. We've had so much to do, y'know. But from what I do remember – well – I'm afraid she seemed to have a bit of a down on you, old boy.'

Roger nodded miserably. 'I thought she might have, though I haven't done anything. Better if I had, really. She just doesn't seem to like me.' He looked wistfully at Timmy, and asked with great solemnity: 'What do you think is wrong with me?'

'Speaking for myself, I can't see anything particularly wrong with you. The Professor told me you're too shy, and that's what irritates her – '

'I've thought that sometimes, and I'm not really a very timid chap – '

'Well,' said Timmy, 'as I've seen you in action – and you

were just going to take on about sixteen stone of ex-professional strong man – I wouldn't call you timid myself. But I know what it is. Somehow they get you on the run. You must try and cope with her next time. I can't tell you where she's lodging because I don't know myself, but her uncle's in the Cottage Hospital, our headquarters are supposed to be the Little Market Hall, and me and the Professor – very clean and comfortable – are at Mrs Mitterly's, corner of Pike Street. And it's nearly time I was getting back there.'

'I can take you on my motor-bike,' said Roger eagerly. 'I'm going to settle one or two bits of business, and then I'll be free, in a day or two, to come to Dunbury myself. Let me take you there. It's not bad on the back of the bike, and I'll have you there in no time. But let's go now, because I've another thirty or forty miles to do beyond Dunbury.'

When Timmy went below, the whole place seemed to be in that final uproar and confusion which belong to all closing times. Daisy was being the cheery hostess in the middle of a group between the dining-room and the cocktail bar, where there was a small lounge near the main entrance. Timmy hung about, not caring to plunge into the group but wanting to say good-bye to Daisy, who did not know yet where he was living in Dunbury. He was still waiting when young Liss popped his head in the main doorway to say that he and his bike were out there, ready to go. And then it came again, from the cocktail bar, but straight at him. 'Hey!' No mistake. The same fellow, and now pushing his way towards him. 'Hey!'

Timmy turned and fled into the night, which was cold and damp but no longer rainy. In another minute this same night was roaring and swaying all round him, with lumpy ribbons of road streaking past. Several miles of it had gone by before he remembered that he was still wearing Walter Shafton's best suit and that his own stage costume still remained at the 'Dog and Bell.' But he would have worried more about all this if he had not been so busy worrying about how to keep his senses, his wits and his manhood intact on the back of that infernal motor-cycle. If Roger Liss could have torn into his love affair as he now tore into the black night, he would be married within a couple of days. When at last they were under the lights of Dunbury and Roger, under Timmy's direction, condescended to drop down to comfortable *chuff-chuffing* progress, Timmy felt like a man suddenly reprieved. After a few false turns and fresh starts, they found the house at the corner of Pike Street. It looked as if it were waiting up for Timmy.

'You don't think,' whispered Roger anxiously, 'she might be in there, do you, waiting for you?'

'No, I don't. She'll be in her own digs, asleep by this time.'

'I wish I knew which house she's in,' the young man sighed. 'Just to have a look at it before I go. However, I'll be back here in a day or two. Do you think it would be better if you told her you'd seen me again or if we kept it as a surprise?'

'Keep it as a surprise,' said Timmy, rather shortly, for it had been perishingly cold at the back of that horrible motor-bike. 'A surprise is best. I was surprised to get here alive. But thanks for bringing me. And don't start any more fights, my lad, and get into trouble. We may need you here before we've done.'

'Do you really believe that?' said Roger eagerly.

'You never know,' was Timmy's final remark, as he turned away, 'not with people like us, here in Dunbury. So long.'

CHAPTER VIII

HOPE ATTENDS A MEETING OF THE BEST PEOPLE

ON THE morning of the following day, Thursday, Sir Reginald Foxfield, Baronet, sat in his study at Dunbury Hall and browsed in a ten-year-old volume of *Wisden*. It was a misty, damp morning, not very cheerful. The room itself was not very much more cheerful than the morning. Like all the rooms in Dunbury Hall it was shockingly under-heated, and its leather chairs seemed nearly as cold and damp as the lawn outside. Then again, like nearly all the other rooms, this study had far too many things in it; too many large and undistinguished pieces of old furniture; too many over-varnished and smudgy pictures; too many sets of volumes that nobody would ever want to read; so that it looked like the back store-room of an unsuccessful antique shop. Sir Reginald was not feeling very cheerful himself. Though it was nearly three hours since he had breakfasted, he had not yet recovered from the tepid, muddy coffee and the under-done bacon; it was a rotten sort of day; and he did not know what to do with himself. It would be more accurate to say that he did not know what to do with himself here at home, for he knew of all manner of delightful things to do away from home, but they would all cost money and just now he had no money.

Sir Reginald was tallish, thinnish, and in his early

thirties. He looked like a handsome man who had had most of his good looks sponged off. He was a not very good water-colour sketch of a handsome man. Or you could say that he had just missed being good-looking. He had just missed nearly everything, a Blue at Oxford, a place in a county cricket team, a rich marriage, a seat in Parliament. People of his class these days either have no manners at all (like his mother, Lady Foxfield, who was the dragon of Dunbury) or very charming manners. Sir Reginald had very charming manners, and an unusually pleasant voice. If he had been lower in the social scale and had had more energy and application, he might have made a fairly good assistant purser in an Atlantic liner, a reception clerk of an American hotel, or a games instructor at a holiday camp. As it was, he suffered from a lack of money, from his fear of his mother, and from persistent undernourishment, for the food had been equally bad at his public school, his Oxford college, and here at Dunbury Hall. So most days he was rather hungry, rather bored, and inwardly dissatisfied.

Having looked up Bingo Bates's figures for the 1929 cricket season, when Bingo's neat little late cut had served him very well indeed, Sir Reginald tossed aside the *Wisden*, yawned, slapped his chest hard several times to keep warm, looked gloomily out at the misty wet lawn, then remembered he had not yet finished *The Poisoned Pigeon Mystery*, which he had borrowed for twopence from a shop in the market square. He had left the book down here, so he lit a cigarette and settled down into the big leather chair again to follow the crafty moves of Inspector Jenks of the C.I.D. He could not help wondering, rather wistfully, if he would not have been better off if he could have joined the police. Not here in Dunbury, of course, where the police were the usual helmet-touching yokels, but there in Scotland Yard.

This chap Inspector Jenks now – why, according to this author, who seemed to know what he was talking about, this chap Inspector Jenks went all over the place and had a wonderful time. He dashed about in fast cars, handed out pound and ten bob tips as if his pocket were stuffed with notes, discussed clues over dashed good dinners and vintage wines, and immediately fascinated all the beautiful women he met. You couldn't imagine one of the local bobbies – that fellow Inspector Parkin, for instance – going on in this style. But this Inspector Jenks had a far, far better time of it than Sir Reginald Foxfield, tenth baronet and lord of the manor of Dunbury. If he said as much to his mother, of course she'd go clean up in the air, pointing on her way up that he was an idiot to believe the rubbish he was always reading. Probably she'd be right too. All made-up stuff, these detective yarns, with their clever criminals and their still cleverer detectives, who never made their final pounce until they had lectured all the suspects in the library. (What would happen if a suspect refused to be lectured in the library, eh?) Life wasn't really like that. It was much duller. And today it looked very dull indeed.

Pulham, the butler, arrived, and first made his usual throat-clearing noise, which suggested that any opening words of his had a long way to come and many obstacles to pass on the way. Pulham was really a lazy, stupid old fellow, who owed his easy life to the fact that he had a most impressive appearance and a tremendous manner. He looked like a militant but intriguing ecclesiastic, Wolsey in modern dress. To be waited upon by such a set of features and such a manner was to have the most flattering notion of one's importance amply confirmed.

'Well, what is it, Pulham?' Sir Reginald did not enquire very hopefully. It would be some bit of dreary nonsense.

Pulham had now finished his word-dredging sounds. 'A young lady is asking to see you, Sir Reginald. The name is Miss Ollerton. On a matter of urgent business.'

'Miss Ollerton? Don't know her, do I?'

'No, Sir Reginald. The young lady admitted that at once.'

'Oh – well – I don't think I can. She's probably one of these awful young women who come round tryin' to sell things. Eh?'

Pulham shook his head. 'Rather younger than those young women, Sir Reginald, and not quite the manner. She says it's something connected with the town.'

Sir Reginald had no great interest in Dunbury himself, but he knew that his mother had, and now it occurred to him that this girl might have something to do with one of Lady Foxfield's schemes. 'What does she look like, Pulham?'

You could not say that Pulham smiled. But what might have been a smile if it had stayed long enough now flitted across these ecclesiastical features. He dredged a little before replying. 'A very attractive young lady, Sir Reginald. And quite young.'

'All right,' and he adopted a grumbling tone now, as if he was compelled to see pretty girls when they called but resented the fact, 'I suppose I'd better see what she wants. Send her in here.'

He marked his place in *The Poisoned Pigeon Mystery* and put the book out of sight, then took a glance at himself in the spotted old mirror that made you look as if you had smallpox, smoothed down his hair and straightened his tie, and waited.

'Miss Ollerton!' Pulham announced, almost fatefully now, as if he knew what a moment this was.

And then there entered Helen of Troy, the Queen of Sheba, Cleopatra, moonlight over the Pacific, sunrise over the Alps, Hollywood, Tahiti, Budapest, Old Vienna, ten augmented dance bands, a lunch basket at Goodwood, fireworks at Cowes, champagne at Maxims, a new Lagonda, the Derby winner, a million dollars, and all those exquisite, tantalising, maddening girls who are always leaving just as you are arriving, the whole lot of them superbly rolled into one. In short, Hope Ollerton walked in, dressed for a lightning war, immediate and ruthless conquest. And as soon as her magnificent calm eyes met the goggling stare of Sir Reginald, she knew that she had not spent a vain hour sorting out and re-combining her wardrobe. Sir Reginald was for it.

In a rich day-dream, with invisible Blue Hungarian bands playing Strauss waltzes, the doomed young man, still goggling and stammering out idiotically inadequate words of welcome, somehow seated this apparition in the best chair, sat down himself not far away, and waited for her lightest command.

She was saying something about coming to Dunbury with her uncle, who had rented the Little Market Hall but had had an accident, and now the police were interfering and saying she could not use the Little Market Hall. He was becoming entangled among enormous fluttering eye-lashes, drowning in the sad depths of those eyes. Take the Little Market Hall, take the big Hall, take the whole town!

This wouldn't do. He must pull himself together. He frowned at her, and immediately she opened her eyes still wider. He took another good pull at himself. Steady, old boy, steady!

'Let – er – me get this clear, if you don't mind,' he said,

trying to be distant, rather stern. 'You rented the Little Market Hall and now they won't let you use it – eh?'

She nodded. 'You see, you've taken away the music licence. My uncle, y'know, sells things – sort of auctions them – but he gives people a free entertainment as well.'

'No, I didn't know.'

'Well, you know now, don't you?' She smiled, for the very first time. It was terrific.

This auction business was a bit puzzling, though. He couldn't connect this glorious girl with such cheap-jack rubbish. Probably some mistake. 'These – er – sort of auctions, as you say – now, do you mean – well – the usual – '

'He buys a lot of cheap stuff,' she told him calmly and clearly, looking him straight in the eye, 'and then when he's got the crowd in a good temper – by amusing them and letting 'em sing – he makes them buy the stuff. I can't tell you any more because I've never seen him do it. I've only just joined him – and of course so far it's been a complete washout. He goes and nearly breaks his neck, and then your lot here have gone back on their word about the Hall. That's why I've come to see you.'

Sir Reginald now found himself in a difficult situation. His first instinct was to tell her that she had come to the wrong man, that even with his mother forever nagging at him to do something he had refused to bother his head about this Market Hall business. But if he did that, probably she would say she had no further time to waste on him and she would walk out, leaving this room and the whole day even drearier than they were before. Unfortunately he was not a quick-witted young man at any time, and just now, with this astonishing girl calmly staring at him, he found it hard to think at all. So he spluttered a bit.

She waved this spluttering away. She was not there to be spluttered at. 'Didn't your great-great-grandfather or whatever he was give the people of Dunbury this Market Hall?'

'Yes, rather,' said Sir Reginald eagerly. 'He was very keen on music, that old boy, and his idea was that the Hall was just the place for the local musicians to show off in, and for a time I believe it worked jolly well.'

'All right then,' said the girl, still looking him straight in the eye, 'why are you trying to take the Hall away from the people? Dirty trick, isn't it?'

'I don't want to take it away from them. I don't care two hoots one way or the other – '

'Then you ought to care two hoots,' she cried indignantly. 'That's why I came to see you.'

'Yes, of course,' he assured her. 'Awfully glad you did – naturally. But I'm not really mixed up in all this. My mother is, because she and her friends want to turn it into a museum – '

'I know. But who wants a museum?'

'Well, they do, you see. Don't particularly want a museum myself. They get me down rather – museums. But that's the idea. After all, the Dunbury people don't really want the Hall now. Not very keen on music now. Band faded out – and all that – '

'I know all about that,' she told him darkly. 'And if you ask me – it's a racket.'

'A racket?' He stared at her, amazed.

'Yes, a racket. Dirty work at the cross-roads. You lot here, wanting a museum, and the other lot – United Thingumpty-jigs – wanting to bag the place for themselves. My uncle – he can't talk much yet, of course, but you ought to hear him when he does talk – says we've got to make a fight of it if it's the last thing we ever do. Are you a what's it – a magistrate?'

'No,' Sir Reginald mumbled, feeling dazed. 'Was going on the bench one time but then I stood for Parliament – by-election – so chucked the bench idea. Know some of 'em, of course – old Colonel Hazelhead and one or two more. Why?'

'Because we had a row with the police last night,' said the astonishing creature, 'and they went and arrested a man who works for us – his name's Candover and I think he's barmy – but so are a lot of people, but that's no reason for locking 'em up, is it?'

'No, rather not. Candover, eh? Think I know that family. I'll see if I can do anything.'

She ought to have smiled at him then, but she didn't. 'I should think so, too. It's about time you took some interest in things, isn't it? What do you do?'

Looked at calmly and coolly this was all just damned impudence, marching in without being asked and ticking him off and wanting to know what he did. The trouble was, you couldn't look at this girl calmly and coolly. She looked at you like that – and where were you? 'Well, I – sort of – look after things here, y'know – estate an' property, what's left of 'em. Then – as I told you – I stood for Parliament. Didn't get in, of course – but it was a very close thing – only just missed it. Then,' he added hopefully, 'I've played a lot of cricket. Used to turn out for the county second eleven sometimes.' That ought to tell her something. A chap didn't want to boast, but she might as well know that he was somebody.

'Did you?' she said indifferently. 'I don't like cricket. I think it's a silly game.'

'Good Lord! Do you really?' But then lots of girls did, of course.

'I met a man who was supposed to be a marvellous cricketer,' she continued. 'Terribly pleased with himself. His name was Ulceby.'

'Hubert Ulceby, it must have been,' cried Sir Reginald, alight at the sound of that great name. 'Oh – a tremendous fellow, of course. I played against him once. Only once. Where did you meet him?'

'At a night-club where I worked at one time. The *Rat-and-Trap*. Do you remember it? Awful hole.'

'I remember. I was there once, just once.'

'You seem to do everything just once, don't you?' said Hope. And now she smiled again, as friendly as anything.

Basking in this sudden radiance, Sir Reginald drew his chair a little closer, tried to make it all seem cosier and more intimate, and said: 'I believe you've had all sorts of adventures. Haven't you?'

'I have,' she replied, rather grimly. 'An' you can keep most of 'em. You can also keep Mr Hubert Ulceby and his pals. They may be all right on the cricket field, but by the time they ended up at the *Rat-and-Trap* they were a nuisance. But that was the trouble with that place. Fellows only turned in there when they were too tight to want to go home. What with that and one or two other places I've worked in, I never want to see any more tight men. If they could only see themselves! Gosh!' She waited a moment, then looked hard at him. 'I shall expect you to keep your promise, y'know – about Candover. And I think you ought to start doing something about this Market Hall racket.'

He was bolder now. 'Look here, I don't think it really is a racket,' he protested. 'Most of the local people who matter are agreed that the place is quite useless as it is now – '

'Who are these local people who matter?' she demanded.

'Well, you know what I mean.' He was bolder still now. After all, it was confounded cheek of this girl to barge in and try to bully him. A fellow had to stand up to them. They thought nothing of you if you didn't. 'And really, y'know, Miss Ollerton – I can't see why you shouldn't leave the local people to manage their own affairs. After all, you and – and – your uncle – is that all?'

'Oh – no. We have a comedian and a professor with us.'

'A comedian and a professor?' He goggled at her.

'That's what I said,' she told him sharply. 'But go on, go on. My uncle and I – '

'Well, you're just roaming about the countryside, I take it – dashed interestin' life, too, I imagine – so if you feel it's all wrong for you here, you can simply move on. No need to stay and try to arrange everything as you'd like it – is there now?'

Had he gone too far? Yes, he had. The girl was on her feet, and the way she looked at him did not suggest that he had suddenly risen in her estimation. He had to stand up, too. This gave him the advantage of superior height, but that didn't appear to worry her. Also, this standing up suggested she was about to go, and he didn't want her to go.

'Mind our own business, eh?' she cried angrily. 'Shut up and move on – humph?'

'I didn't – '

'You did. And let me talk now, Sir Reginald Foxfield. To start with, we are minding our own business, because we have a contract with your rotten town council – '

'It isn't *my town council* – '

'Yes, it is,' she shouted. 'You lot have it in your pocket. And we've an agreement or a contract or whatever it is that your town council won't keep, an' so they send spotty young men an' then fat police inspectors to shout at us just when everybody's having a good time, an' go an' arrest a harmless barmy fellow like this Candover. And you think we're going to put up with it. Well, we're not, see? My uncle says we're not. I say we're not! The comedian and the professor say we're not. You try moving us on, that's all. If there's any more dirty work and we don't get our rights, we'll turn this whole mouldy town upside down. Now then!'

There was a short interval so that she could breathe fire in his direction and look him up and down as if he were a six-foot goggle-eyed worm. Pulham arrived during this interval, and brought with him, along with his usual Wolsey-in-modern-dress effect, a faintly roguish air.

'Luncheon,' said Pulham, almost winking at them, 'is served.'

This both surprised and alarmed Sir Reginald. 'Oh – I say, Pulham, is my mother in?' This was anything but an idle question. He didn't want this girl to go, probably for ever; but he also didn't want her to run into his mother, whose dislike of her would be immediate and shattering.

'Her ladyship is lunching at the rectory.'

He was saved. 'I'd no idea it was so late, Miss Ollerton,' he said, turning on his most charming manner. 'I do hope you can stay to lunch.'

'All right, thanks, I will, if you really want me to.'

'Good! Pulham, there'll be two of us – '

'Yes, Sir Reginald,' said Putham, still roguish, as if he felt it was high time Dunbury Hall had a juicy bit of scandal, 'I've laid for two.'

Miss Ollerton, who was certainly a cool card, made an entrance into the dining-room that suggested she was a visiting princess and that princesses had now been trained to make much better entrances. (You can't be a mannequin and a show girl without learning something.) She gave no sign of being overawed by the size, age, and social grandeur of this room, probably because she was a very handsome, much admired and spirited member of the genuine democracy, now rapidly growing up within the false democracy upon which we are always congratulating ourselves in England. Mr Hassock and Timmy, for example, would have been overawed, almost in spite of themselves, by Dunbury Hall, by Sir Reginald, even by Pulham, but Hope had been born too late and had spent too much time in places where these very people were apt to make fools of themselves. But if Hope had been sitting down to lunch in the cafeteria of the Paramount Studio in Hollywood, she would have been nearly choking with excitement.

They sat at each side of a tiny isthmus of lunch in a great sea of mahogany. Everything in the room was very large. The table, the sideboards, the portraits on the walls, the candlesticks and other silver ware, all were gigantic. It was about as cosy and intimate as the Victoria and Albert Museum. The only thing that was small there was the lunch itself. It was a terrible little lunch: some cutlets that had more than their fair share of bone and less than their fair share of meat; mashed potatoes and watery cabbage; some thick slices of bread that had neither been toasted nor let alone; a rice pudding that appeared to have been made without milk; and some cheese of the Mesozoic Age. Pulham, assisted by an elderly parlourmaid in a maroon uniform, served this grim fare as if it had been ten courses beginning with turtle soup. There was almost a kind of irony about him. After the melancholy rice pudding had appeared, Sir Reginald, who looked very miserable, sharply ordered Pulham and the elderly parlourmaid out of the room.

'Sorry about the lunch,' he whispered to Hope as the

servants went. 'I know it's no good. Look at this rice pudding. Cook can make quite a decent treacle pudding, and I'd hoped we might be having one. Jolly good stuff and fills you up. But no luck.'

'But if you don't like the food they give you, why don't you change it?' asked Hope.

'Rather difficult, you know. I mean, I do grumble, of course – who wouldn't? – but it doesn't seem to make any difference. That was one reason why I'd hoped to get into the House. I could have lived in town, and done myself really well.'

Hope took a packet of chocolate out of her bag. 'It's got nuts and raisins in. Do you like that kind?'

'Yes, I do, awfully good.' He brightened up at once. 'But could you spare all that? Oh – I say – that's very decent of you.' He accepted rather more than half the slab of chocolate. 'Good idea, this! I must get some in. I can always slip into the study and eat it there. Jolly, crunching into the nuts, isn't it? How do you like the family portraits?'

Hope looked round at them. 'All right. But a bit dull, aren't they?'

'Yes, they are, really. But these are just some of the old boys. The women are upstairs, all along the landing. That's where our best stuff is. Tons of it, y'know. Nobody ever gets rid of anything. Rooms and rooms full of stuff. Wretched servants spend hours turning it out and cleaning things. No time for anything else, really. I've sometimes wondered,' he added wistfully, 'if it wouldn't be better if they attended to us a bit more – y'know, gave us better food and made things look a bit cheerful – instead of bothering so much with the old ancestors. Would you like to have a look round? We won't wait for coffee. It's awful stuff.'

He led the way up a rather dark staircase at the back of the house that brought them to a broad landing, where there were still more portraits, and pieces of armour, and swords and old pistols and daggers, and shredding, moth-eaten lengths of tapestry, and carved old furniture. They explored this landing, with Sir Reginald acting as an apologetic guide, and then climbed again, and did some more exploring and museum work. Both were on their very best behaviour, Sir Reginald, who thought this was easily the most stunning girl who had ever set foot in the house, was anxious to create a good impression now, for he felt he had gone too far just before lunch. Hope felt that she had also gone too far, not because she cared tuppence about this young man but because she had come to try and make an ally of him and could not help feeling that she had lost her temper much too soon. Besides, it was quite amusing to look at this old stuff with the now very attentive Sir Reginald acting as guide. So nothing was said about the town's affairs. Sir Reginald chattered away, and she stared and listened, and now and again rewarded him with a smile that set him goggling again.

All this took time. They had now worked their way to the top of the house, and Sir Reginald proposed that they should go out to the flat roof of the little tower at the back, which would give them a fine view of the country-side. It was still damp and rather cheerless, but it was not actually raining and the mists of the morning had van-ished, so out they went. Hope preferred this to suits of armour and swords and the general mustiness below, and she took some deep breaths and stared about her with genuine pleasure.

'It's lovely up here,' she told him. 'This is where I

should come if I lived here. All that old junk gets me down, but this is fine.'

'Isn't it?' But he looked at her and not at the view. Up here she looked terrific. What a girl! And he had to say something. 'I say – if you don't mind my saying so – you do look absolutely stunning up here.'

'No, I don't mind you saying so.' She gave him a heady look. Then a smile, the very best so far, a clean knock-out. And of course she took immediate advantage of the situation. 'And now you're going to be sensible and decent, aren't you?'

'Well, yes – I hope so,' he stammered. 'But what about?'

'What about? What do you think? About the Market Hall and everything. You're going to stick up for us and for all the ordinary people here, and not let anybody get away with any dirty trick.' She gazed at him earnestly, then threw in another smile for good measure. 'Let's go down.'

'Yes, rather,' he exclaimed eagerly. 'You haven't seen everything in the house yet, not by a long chalk, and we'll go down by the front way. I'll show you.'

It was while they were going down the main staircase between the second and first floors that they heard voices. They arrived at a landing even broader and richer with antiquity than the first landing, and this ran above the fine large hall to which twin curved staircases descended. The voices came from this hall. About twenty people were sitting there and several more were being shown in by Pulham. Hope and Sir Reginald, standing there between two large erect suits of armour, could see without being seen themselves, for there was not much light on the landing.

'Good Lord, I'd forgotten,' he whispered, in alarm. 'It's the museum committee meeting. That's why my mother was lunching with the rector today. Come on, we'll slip out down the other stairs.'

'Oh no, we won't,' Hope told him, softly but very firmly. 'I'm staying here.'

'Oh – really, y'know – you can't do that.' The terrible unscrupulousness of women.

'I can. And I am. Be quiet, they're starting.'

The rector took the chair. He was a large, pink, very clean gentleman with a booming voice, which made him sound as if he were broadcasting himself. He was full of congratulations. He congratulated the ladies and gentlemen of the committee on turning up in such numbers, on their being able to meet in this historic Dunbury Hall, and on their having as a fellow member no less a person than Lady Foxfield herself, upon whom he would call first.

Lady Foxfield was quite unlike her son in appearance. She was a soldierly-looking woman with big craggy features that had been heavily powdered, so that she looked not unlike a whitewashed sergeant-major. She had a hoarse and masterful voice. A frightening woman. 'Now you all know why you're heah,' she told them, looking about her scornfully. 'We've already decided that the town should have a museum. We've had estimates and we know it wouldn't cost very much to make the necessary alterations to the Market Hall to turn it into the right kind of building. We also have a promise of some contributions. Dunbury,' she went on, as if the others there had only just arrived in the place and would want to know something about it, 'is a very ancient and historic borough. All of us heah are proud of its – er – historical – er – associations. We wish to show othahs that we are proud of our – er – ancient history. I understand that there has been some talk in the town about selling the Market Hall to – er – a commercial – er – enterprise. Disgraceful talk, in my opinion. It's not to be thought of.' She looked about her sternly, daring one of them to think of it then and there. 'I needn't remind any of you heah that the Market Hall originally belonged to the Foxfield family, who made a very generous gift of it to the townspeople on the condition – on the condition, please remembah – that the townspeople made a propah use of it. As we all know, the townspeople have shown themselves unfit to use it properly, and the sensible membahs of the council have already agreed that the Hall should be turned into a museum. I have promised to loan such a museum some Foxfield family heirlooms of great historical interest.' She graciously allowed the applause to subside. 'In addition, I am able to announce that the Lord-Lieutenant has expressed great interest in our scheme. Also, that our friend Mr Finningley has promised a very handsome donation to the Museum Fund.' More applause, in the middle of which a little man with a long moustache popped up and bowed. Lady Foxfield now held up her hand and looked very stern indeed, as if about to give the whole battalion an extra half-hour's drill. 'We must all stand togethah, not only for the sake of our ancient borough but also in ordah to preserve the great traditions of our country. A museum will show the people what those traditions are. It will prove a bulwark against danger-ous tendencies. It will tell the people that our motto is still what it always was – For King and Country.'

To enthusiastic applause Lady Foxfield sat down and immediately closed her eyes, giving the impression that in her opinion the real meeting was now over. The rector warmly thanked Lady Foxfield for her public-spirited and inspiring speech, and called upon Colonel Hazelhead, their treasurer to address them.

A very tall, thin man, who looked like some kind of bird that had found its way inside a tweed suit much too large for it, shot up in the front row. It was difficult to catch what the colonel said, for not only was he very staccato but he seemed to swallow half his words, so that only a brief précis of the speech that was somewhere in his head, which was much too small for the rest of him, reached his audience.

'*Um-yah* Chairman . . . *um-yah* Lady Foxfield . . . *um-yah* great pleasure . . . *um-yah* considerable progress . . . *um-yah* some opposition . . . *um-yah* commercial people . . . newcomers to town . . . *um-yah* no real stake in town . . . out for what they could get *um-yah* . . . understand some new trouble last night . . . *bolshie* fellows . . . *um-yah* prompt action by police . . . quite agree with Lady Foxfield . . . *um-yah* bulwark against subversive tendencies . . . glorious history . . . *um-yah* gone out from Dunbury to ends of earth . . . cause of Empire . . . wished to present as own contribution valuable Indian and Burmese objects and *um-yah* . . . prove education in itself . . . *um-yah* patriotism . . . museum fund small but rich in promises . . . *um-yah* friend Mr Finningley . . . final remarks . . . stand no nonsense . . . police to be relied upon . . . *um-yah* stiff sentences . . . *um-yah* . . . *um-yah* . . . *um-yah* . . . listening so patiently thank *um-yah* . . .'

The rector, now sounding more like a national broadcasting station than ever after the colonel's vague barking, boomed his thanks and asked if anybody would like to ask the colonel a question. Mrs Hathersage? Yes, Mrs Hathersage?

The woman who rose in the second row wore a floppy hat that seemed to rest on the bridge of her nose, which was enormous and really all that could be seen of her. Her voice was monstrously out of proportion to her nose, and she might have been a mouse squeaking behind the wainscoting. 'Tweedle,' said Mrs Hathersage, 'tweedle-eedle-eedle-eedle-eedle – tweedle – ?'

The colonel replied to this with three *um-yahs*, which appeared to satisfy Mrs Hathersage and everybody else down there. Meanwhile, Hope and Sir Reginald were still standing between the two suits of armour, invisible in the dusk that was gathering in the upper part of the hall.

The rector now broadcast that Lady Shepshed, who although not a Dunbury resident, had shown such interest in their project that she had been co-opted, would give them her views. 'Lady Shepshed,' he concluded, smiling and beckoning and looking quite idiotic, 'please come to the front so that everybody can hear you.' And somebody – ten to one it was little Mr Finningley – cried very earnestly: 'Hear, hear!'

Lady Shepshed coming to the front was not unlike a revival of the old-fashioned May Day processions with prizes for the best cart-horses. She was not really a very large woman; actually she was short though very broad; but she was wearing so many coats and scarves and was so hung about with furs and jangling chains and took up so much room and made such a commotion, that it was just as if a procession were coming into the place, accompanied by sleigh bells and a drum and fife band. As a speaker, however, she was not noisy and imposing. Her line was the ultra-feminine, the arch and coy line, as if at one time she had played heroines in the old-fashioned musical comedies. She tilted her head, she smiled and pouted, she closed her eyes and then opened them very wide, and at the end of every sentence seemed to wait for the orchestra to give her the note for the big waltz song. Hope enjoyed Lady Shepshed, who was a really good turn.

'Thank you so very much,' she cooed at them all. 'So

very sweet of you to allow me to be one of your committee. As your dear rector has told you – ' and here she gave him a look that invited him to drink champagne out of her slipper at midnight – 'although I don't live in this part of the county, I like to think of dear Dunbury as my town too – *so* many friends here – ' she opened her eyes very wide now, and implored every man present to join her in the second act in Monte Carlo by moonlight – '*such* a dear little town if we don't allow it to be spoilt – and there the museum – *such* a splendid idea – will help enormously. *Such* a pleasure to be with you. Lady Foxfield *so* right in saying it will preserve the great traditions of our country. I do *feel* that the people must be taught to respect those traditions. And now such a delightful surprise. Mr Churton Talley, the great art critic and expert and everything, who knows *all* about museums, has been doing some work down here and is now staying with me, and I've explained *everything* about our museum plan to him, and he's *most* kindly come along to tell us what an *expert* feels about it all.' She waited for the round of applause, then led it herself. Then she threw an enormous smile clean over six rows, crooked her forefinger and beckoned with it in a manner that suggested unmentionable things, and said: 'Mr Churton Talley, come along.'

The rector, to show that the meeting had not been taken out of his hands, rose to his full height and boomed: 'I know we shall all be delighted to hear what Mr Churton Talley has to say.'

Mr Churton Talley proved to be a slender, wavy-haired youth of about fifty-five, with enamelled pink cheeks, a cherry lip, and the eye of a dead codfish. He was wearing a delicious confection of pale blue. He came mincing forward, almost swooned at the sight of those staring faces but bravely recovered himself, and then began delicately hissing at them like an outraged serpent. He was very difficult to hear from above, where half the time, with those long drawn-out sibilants of his, he merely sounded like an escape of gas. Hope began giggling at him and nearly gave away her presence on the landing. He said something about being sure they were working on the right lines, and something about 'plenning for æsthetic es well es hissstorical sssignificance,' and something about the importance of getting really expert advice when the time came to choose the exhibits (he was trying to touch for a job), and went on yammering and hissing for quite a time. He did not go down too well. In fact, as Hope whispered to Sir Reginald, Mr Churton Talley was a flop.

Not so Mr Finningley, the little man with the long moustache, who was known to have promised a fat cheque for the fund. It was clear that Mr Finningley was socially on the make. ('Awful little squirt,' whispered Sir Reginald. 'Only recently settled here. Made a pile in Borneo or Africa or one of those places.') But his very eagerness to please, supported as it was by real money, gave him a good audience. He was, as he said, no speaker. But not only did he want to please, but he was himself, as he said many times, very pleased. Yes, he was very pleased to be there at the meeting, very pleased to be called upon to say a few words, very pleased to be allowed to contribute towards the museum fund, very pleased to hear such good speeches, especially from *the ladies* (he was one of those men who insist upon referring to the ladies in italics), very pleased to know that the Market Hall was to be put to proper use at last, very pleased with the progress that was being made; and he gave the impression that he would have been equally very pleased to have blacked the boots of anybody present. At the end it was evident that his fellow members thought well of Mr Finningley, who might now expect social promotion at any moment.

The rector enquired if anybody had a question, some points that ought – as is the strange habit of points at meetings – to be raised. Someone had. A large lady in purple had a question, and gave the impression she was about to make a contralto solo of it. 'Several of us,' she sang, 'are not very clear as to the exact position at present. Have we received a definite promise from the Borough Council that when the – er – various legal matters are settled – we shall be given the exclusive use of the Market Hall? If not, what is the position at present? I am sure we should all know.' She took a low *A flat* for her final note, and received a murmur of approval.

Major Shiptonthorpe, who was also a solicitor in the gentlemanly interests, was called upon to reply to that question, and to show that he was not trifling with them he unfolded some eyeglasses and put them halfway down his nose, and then looked gravely at the meeting over the top of them. He was glad to have this opportunity of explaining the exact position with regard to the Market Hall. The property was held in trust, and the trust was of an unusual kind. The first step, that of refusing to grant any further licence to the Hall, had been simple enough. ('And I bet you've been doing some wangling,' Hope told him under her breath.) There would be no great difficulty, though certain legal complications would have to be unravelled, in the town turning the Hall into a museum, so long as there was no opposition. But unfortunately there was considerable opposition, for some members of the council, for reasons best known to themselves, wished to accept the offer that *United Plastics* were making for the property, and there were even a few – whose political views encouraged them to make as much trouble as possible – who declared that the Hall should be kept for its original purpose, overlooking the fact that the people were no longer interested in that purpose. 'Now, ladies and gentlemen,' Major Shiptonthorpe continued, removing his eyeglasses and sawing the air with them, 'no decision of the council can be legal, according to the terms of the trust, unless three-quarters of the members at least are in favour of that decision. Thus, at the moment there is a deadlock. Yes, Mr Chairman,' he added, as if the rector would find this a special treat, 'a complete deadlock.' He put his eyeglasses back, turned himself from a major into a solicitor again, and waited for another question and presumably another fee before replying to it.

The rector played up manfully. 'Well, Major Shiptonthorpe,' he boomed, 'we all feel this is an impossible state of affairs. What happens if this deadlock continues?'

Lady Foxfield was plainly heard to snort and mutter 'Preposterous! Time these people had a sharp lesson!'

'I quite agree with Lady Foxfield,' said Major Shiptonthorpe. 'Fortunately, I've made some enquiries – I was up in London yesterday and the day before – and the position is not as bad as it would first appear. Unless the *United Plastics* people have something up their sleeve. There's a meeting of the council tomorrow – and if it's still impossible to obtain this three-quarter majority and the deadlock continues, then we can ask for government arbitration. An arbitrator – somebody, of course, of recognised position and authority – will be appointed, and then the decision will rest with him. I may add – again, I must point out, unless *United Plastics* steal a march on us – that I have reason to believe that any such arbitrator, if only by reason of his background and training, would favour our side of the question.'

There was a murmur of approval and self-congratulation. Hope had a strong desire to throw something at them. They sat there like a lot of enormous stuffed frogs. If there had to be a museum, then these creatures ought to go in it, all in glass cases. But there wasn't going to be a museum. She had promised Uncle Fred that much. And even if she hadn't, she'd want to take a hand now, if only to stop Major Shiptonthorpe and company being so pleased with themselves. Just quietly pinching a large hall, that's what they were doing!

There was a stir below. Somebody had arrived. The rector looked across and nodded: 'Ah! – Commander Spofforth. Well, better late than never, eh, commander? And I'm sure we'd like to hear the commander's views.'

'Certainly,' said Lady Foxfield loudly. Evidently the commander, a burly dark fellow, was one of her favourites. And it was soon obvious why he should be.

'Tough guy, huh?' whispered Hope.

In his bluff sailorlike fashion, Commander Spofforth said he didn't understand why so much hanky-panky was going on. Didn't care a great deal about museums himself, and didn't pretend to, but if the best people in the town wanted the Market Hall as a museum, as they obviously did, then the sooner they took it the better. Inspector Parkin had just told him there was some sort of hanky-panky in the Little Hall last night, with that fellow Largs mixed up in it, as usual. Fellow Largs was an agitator, and probably well paid for it. Latest trick was to bring in a bunch of Reds to take possession of the Hall. Soon put a stop to that sort of thing. Guarantee to do it himself in a jiffy.

'Quite so,' said Lady Foxfield in a loud approving tone.

'Thanks, Lady Foxfield,' the commander continued. 'So let's have no more shilly-shallying, I say, but set to work, take what we want, and incidentally clean up the town a bit. Could do with it – what? So could the old country. Too much arguin' an' beefin', majority an' minority nonsense, talkin' shop stuff. What we want's a bit of direct action – a few people to give orders an' the rest to obey 'em – eh?'

'Heil Hitler!' cried Hope, who found the commander so exasperating that she could keep silent no longer. At the same time she made a sudden impatient movement, sent a suit of armour toppling against the rail, which brought it up with such a jerk that the headpiece flew off and fell with a startling clang into the hall below, only just missing the large lady in purple. Everybody jumped up.

'Now who's that?' cried Lady Foxfield, in a fury.

'Me,' called Hope cheerfully, hurrying towards the staircase. 'Sorry about the helmet. Just an accident.' Having arrived at the stairs, she slackened her pace and descended demurely. Lady Foxfield was waiting for her.

'I've never heard of such a thing,' cried Lady Foxfield, not very sensibly. 'Who are you? I don't know you. What are you doing here?'

'Well,' said Hope, braving it out but not feeling very comfortable now, 'I happened to be here –'

'Just a minute,' said Commander Spofforth. Then he called, in the direction of the front door: 'Inspector Parkin. Inspector Parkin.'

The inspector must have been waiting just outside, for now he entered very briskly. As soon as he set eyes on Hope, he pointed an accusing finger. 'That's one of 'em. From last night. Couldn't mistake 'er.'

'Doesn't surprise me,' said the commander, with the air of a man who has unmasked a vast espionage system. 'Doesn't surprise me in the least. All a put-up job.'

'What *is* all this?' cried Lady Foxfield with justifiable

irritation. After all it was her house. 'I can't imagine what you're all talking about. Reginald!' she now added, with horror. For Sir Reginald was coming down the stairs, slowly, hesitantly, but coming down, like a man, to face the music.

'Sorry, mother. I can explain.'

'Why? Do you know this – er – young woman?'

'Yes. She – came to see me.'

A kind of stir or gigantic shiver ran through the whole committee. Here were goings on. They had all been wrong about Sir Reginald. He was not under his mother's thumb, after all. He spent his time secretly entertaining very attractive and bold young women. Well, well, well!

Inspector Parkin didn't know what to do. He had been ready to march the girl off, and Lady Foxfield might easily have preferred a charge against her – 'found on enclosed premises' or something of the sort – but now it appeared that Sir Reginald knew her. So he did nothing, and as nobody was taking the least notice of him, it didn't matter.

'It's my fault,' said Hope, who felt that the young man, who was obviously afraid of his mother, had now done his share. 'I came about some business – '

'What business?' demanded Lady Foxfield, in an awful tone.

'My business,' the girl retorted.

'Now, now, now,' said Inspector Parkin, feeling that this maintained his authority without committing him to anything.

'What are you now-nowing at?' The girl stared at him, then turned to Lady Foxfield, whose heavily powdered face was almost lilac with anger. 'I came on business and stayed to lunch, and then he showed me the house and then – well, I was just going.'

'Indeed!' From Lady Foxfield, of course, and terrible in its irony. 'Indeed!'

'That's right, mother. Miss Ollerton came to see me, and happened to stay on, and – that's that. Nothin' to get excited about.' Sir Reginald tried to finesse now. 'Hello, Colonel Hazelhead, how are you?'

'I'm not very bright,' replied the colonel. 'Too damp for me. Always the same.'

'Pulham,' shouted Lady Foxfield. 'Ah! – there you are. Show this – er – Miss – er – '

'Thank you,' said Hope, when Pulham had opened the door very wide for her, as if she was going to ride out on an elephant. Then she turned and faced the company, very much in earnest and very young: 'I heard what you all said,' she told them. 'I suppose I oughtn't to have listened, but it didn't seem very private. Well I think you ought to be ashamed of yourselves – '

'Will you leave this house at once,' cried Lady Foxfield, in a tremendous rage. 'Inspector!'

'All right, I'm going,' she shouted, all in a great hurry. 'But don't think you'll collar that Hall because you won't. We're going to wake people up here. You can't do as you like. You wait.' And as the inspector moved towards her, she had just time for a parting shot at him and at them all: 'Let the people sing.'

CHAPTER IX

TWO VISITORS FOR 'UNITED PLASTICS'

AT THE east side of Dunbury, the industrial end, where the railway runs, *United Plastics* had established their chief English works. (The parent company was in New Jersey, U.S.A. and there were several European branches of the industry.) Here they performed one of the astonishing conjuring tricks of our ingenious age. At the back, far from the main entrance, in the queer smelly sheds between the railway and the canal, casein and formaldehyde and phenol, to say nothing of sawdust and a lot of other stuff that nobody particularly wanted, were turned into a witches' brew. The new substances that emerged were passed on to the pressing and moulding departments. Then in the great new building in front, which was so white and glassy and ultra-modern that it hardly seemed to be in England at all, from morning until night there was a tremendous finishing-off, sorting, packing, and invoicing of bowls, cups, plates, ashtrays, combs, manicure sets, cigarette holders, beads, buttons, or whatever the market fancied. At one end, then, a mass of rubbishly stuff that was no good to anybody; and at the other end a river of useful articles, as gaily-coloured as a child's picture-book, and all cheap, durable, non-inflammable, the very things that make the modern world seem so new and strange. They seem oddly artificial and a trifle inhuman, these things, of course, but then so did pottery itself once upon a time.

Raymond and Fern Mitterly worked in that big new factory, along with hundreds of other young Dunburyans, all knowing exactly what to do, busier than bees and much better organised than ants. The system had been originally worked out and blue-printed in New Jersey, but it worked just as well in Dunbury, or for that matter in France or Central Europe. It was a wonderful system. No energy wasted; no fuss, no shouting; reasonable hours; wages well up to the local standard; air conditioning; light and heating perfectly adjusted; and free medical service. No worker could want more – that is, as a worker. The *United Plastics* executives – their own term for themselves – were so enthusiastic about their system that it was surprising their own daughters were not safely at work in one of the factories, instead of fooling about with horses and fast cars miles away. But though these girls kept away, thousands of others were only too eager to be blue-printed, numbered and air-conditioned. So far wherever *United Plastics* manufactured its useful products, so cheap, durable, non-inflammable, there had been the necessary steady supply of workers, also cheap, durable, and non-inflammable.

These executives, like most of their kind, were not only first-class organisers but also bold and cunning advertisers with a touch of the showman about them. (That is why they were after the Market Hall.) Thus, every Friday afternoon, parties of visitors, if they had received the necessary permits, were shown round the main factory building, so that they could admire the system and then become unpaid salesmen for the firm. That is how Timmy and the Professor came to be there. Young Raymond had suggested it, and had arranged for them to have admittance cards. But they were not going merely as sightseers.

They were making another – though very tentative – move in the Hassock campaign, just as Hope had done the day before, when she went to call on Sir Reginald. Mr Hassock, still groaning and grumbling in his bed at the Cottage Hospital, had implored them to make a fight of it, if only for his sake, for he had taken this business of the Market Hall very badly, blaming his very accident upon it and declaring that he had never been so scurvily treated before and that he would not be Fred Hassock, or what was left of him, if he submitted to such tyranny. Not that Timmy or the Professor needed any encouragement, for by this time they were full of fight.

The evening before, Hope had called at Mrs Mitterly's to tell them what had happened that afternoon and to give them the latest news of Mr Hassock. She found Timmy and the Professor sitting cosily with the family, for they had nothing to do this evening as it had been decided to postpone the next attempt to open the Little Market Hall until Saturday. So there they were, all very friendly and cosy. Although Fern's warmest admirer (and she had a few admirers) would not have called her an intellectual, she was oddly fascinated by the Professor, perhaps because his immensely tall, thin, very foreign figure seemed to her to belong to that enchanting world she discovered twice a week at the *Elite Picture Theatre*. Looking more like an open-mouthed unsophisticated girl than a glamorous foreign spy or jewel thief, she would listen to him for hours, which just suited the Professor, who always needed a patient listener. Then Mrs Mitterly enjoyed chatting away with Timmy, a homely little man, full of fun and anecdote, and just her style. Raymond listened idly to both pairs, and occasionally put in a rather shy and gloomy word, but he was haunted all the time now by a vague tantalising image of Hope. And when his mother brought the girl in, so unexpectedly, poor Raymond turned scarlet and for the rest of the evening looked as if he had a temperature.

Hope described her afternoon at Dunbury Hall and what she overheard at the meeting. 'And there they sat like a lot of stuffed frogs,' she concluded, 'just plotting to grab that building for themselves and not caring tuppence about anybody else. I was furious. "All right," I told 'em, "just you wait!" I was livid. Still am.'

Mrs Mitterly, who had followed the narrative with more changes of expression flitting across her face than Lady Foxfield could achieve in a year, now asked: 'What about Sir Reginald? He's not like that – I mean, being still a young man – and I've seen him about – he didn't seem –'.

'No harm in him,' said Hope decisively. 'Not a bad chap really. But feeble. Nobody who wasn't feeble would put up with the ghastly food they have there. And he's terrified of his mother, the old war horse. No, he's feeble. Still,' she added coolly, remembering the infatuated look in his eye, 'we might be able to make some use of him.'

'I'll tell you what,' stammered Raymond, looking about a foot above Hope's head. 'I'd better tell Tom Largs about all this.'

'That's the man who spoke up for us last night, isn't it?' cried Hope. She caught Raymond's eye, smiled at him, and sent him up to about a hundred and five. 'Yes, do. That's the stuff.'

'They don't like Tom Largs,' said Mrs Mitterly, frowning for them, defying them for Largs, smiling for herself, all in half a second. 'He was going to conduct the band – but they – or some of them on the council – he used to be a councillor himself – I don't know why he still isn't – he –'

'He is, mother,' said Raymond. 'He's still a councillor.

Only the others won't back him up. You know what they're like.'

'This man Largs who spoke last night I noticed,' the Professor began, in his most ample style. 'It is a good type of man. There is, first, he who rebels always from a sense of inferiority. It is his revenge upon the world. It is not that type. This man, I think, is inspired by compassion and his own fullness of life. Now this type – '

'We're thinking of paying a visit to the other end of the town,' said Timmy to Hope, having given the Professor his usual allowance of speech.

'Go on,' said Fern to the Professor. 'Never mind them. You tell me about these types.'

'It can't do any harm,' Hope told Timmy, 'and there'll be nothing else to do tomorrow. Uncle Fred says we must wait till Saturday night and then we must have another crack at starting that business even if we all get run in. You see what these *United Plastics* think they're trying to do.'

'Oh – but – you won't be able to see any of the heads y'know,' cried Raymond. 'You only just go round as a visitor. They do it every week. It's nothing, really.'

'Leave it to us, boy,' said Timmy with an easy confidence based on nothing at all. 'You don't know what we can do, once we get started.'

This alarmed Mrs Mitterly. 'Oh – but – Mr Tiverton – I know you don't – but – you won't get Raymond or Fern into any – I mean, there might be trouble – '

'No, there won't, Mother,' her son told her. 'Anyhow I'll risk it.'

Timmy nodded and smiled at her. 'Don't you worry. I don't get other people into trouble, though I'm famous for doing it to myself. But then – look at me – I've got personality. That makes the difference.'

Hope frowned now. 'But we've landed that chap Candover into a mess. And Uncle Fred's worried. So am I. *And* angry.' She looked sternly at Mrs Mitterly, who replied by looking fifty different things back at her. 'You know what's the matter with this town, Mrs Mitterly?'

'Oh – yes – I do.' Mrs Mitterly was all in a flutter. 'For one thing – rates – I mean, just look at 'em – and then – '

'What's the matter with this town,' the girl continued severely, with a certain suggestion of Mr Hassock in the background, 'is that it's feeble. It's all gone wonky and soft. It's half dead. It can't stand up for itself. You go on like this, an' they'll take everything away from you. Lady Foxfield and Major Shipton-what's-it and Commander Tough-Guy-Heil-Hitler, with Inspector Fat Face and his cops pretending to keep order, they'll take one good half of what's going, and the people at the other end of the town'll take the rest. That is, if you let 'em. Or,' she added grandly, 'if we let you let 'em. Because here we are, full of devilment, and our back's up. And either we wake this town up or they'll have to cart us away in a police van. So there you are, Timmy – and you, Professor, though I know you have to be careful – go to it, boys.'

'Well, I must say,' cried Mrs Mitterly, not dubiously but in open admiration.

Even Fern was impressed, though all she said was: 'How do you get your hair to stay like that?'

While Hope now gave Fern a careful examination, first visual and then oral, with all the authority of one who had spent much of her time with professional beauties in the metropolis, and the two girls went into a huddle, Raymond explained to Timmy and the Professor what time they would have to present themselves at the works the following afternoon and what they might expect to see when they were admitted; and Mrs Mitterly, who was a little woman as hospitable as she was spirited, went out to make some tea and find some cake and a bun or two, for a grand conspiratorial snack. 'And dear me,' she said to herself in the pantry, 'I hope nobody gets into trouble, but I must say, so far I'm enjoying this. Makes a nice change.'

So now, on Friday afternoon, Timmy and the Professor were among the twenty-or-so visitors to the *United Plastics* factory. And they were certainly the oddest-looking members of the group. Timmy was still wearing the very hairy and fuzzy Harris tweed coat that he had borrowed from Walter Shafton out at Daisy's place, but he was not wearing Walter's trousers too but a pair of his own, also tweed but a greyish-green colour. This startling costume was crowned by a bright brown hat considerably too small for the wearer. One dab of red on his nose, and he could have gone straight on to any stage to do his eccentric comedian act. The Professor, who was very solemn about this visit to *United Plastics* was wearing his best suit, a dark alien affair cut in a pre-War style, and it made him look taller, thinner, more foreign than ever. Also he had discovered for the occasion a larger and stronger pair of spectacles, which made his eyes look enormous, like those of some super-intelligent octopus-like being from Mars. He had the air of a man who proposed to lecture somebody that afternoon no matter what happened afterwards. These two could not have stood out much more from the ordinary visitors if they had arrived there stark naked playing trombones. Yet the guide, a bustling little woman from the welfare department, allowed them to detach themselves from the party. Perhaps she never noticed when they went or again perhaps she was glad to be rid of them. What is certain is that once they were away from the party, nobody thought of questioning them because nobody could believe that such rum-looking chaps, wandering around alone, could be mere visitors.

The Professor vanished first. One minute he was there, listening gravely to the little welfare woman's prattle, and the next minute he was gone. This would not do at all. Timmy stared up and down the long room, where a lot of girl clerks were working away with adding machines and the like, but there was no Professor. There was a door over on the right, so Timmy popped through that way, climbed a few steps and turned to find himself in the presence of a very large, complicated and important machine. This machine was busy making boxes and then filling the boxes with ashtrays and bowls and saucers and the necessary amount of packing. After that it carefully closed and sealed the boxes and sent them travelling down into another department. There was something at once fascinating and frightening about this machine. Timmy stared at it with his mouth open. For two pins, he felt, it would take him and square him up into a box and fill him full of ashtrays and bowls. If the monster once broke loose it would box and pack and seal up everything and everybody for miles.

There were two fellows in blue overalls in attendance upon this machine, one of them seeing that it had plenty of box material, the other one watching over the steady stream of ashtrays and bowls and saucers, which came swirling down a chute from an upper floor. The ashtray man was nearer and looked more friendly so Timmy went across to him.

'How do?' said the man.

'How do?' said Timmy. 'You haven't seen a tall foreign-looking chap in here, have you?'

'Not this afternoon,' replied the man, still keeping his

eye on the ashtrays and bowls. There was a short silence, then he added: 'But we get all sorts in here.'

'I'll bet you do,' said Timmy, always ready for a friendly chat.

'Yes, all sorts,' the man continued, talking out of the side of his mouth as if this were all very secret. 'And why?'

Timmy began to feel as if he had involved himself in a slow-motion cross-talk act. 'Well, why?'

'Because it's out of the ordredary this place is.'

'Out of the what?' Timmy kept the act going.

'The ordredary.'

'Ah, yes.' A little flood of bright yellow saucers came hurrying down the chute, and Timmy watched the man give them a poke or two, just to show them he was still in attendance.

'Mass production, Yankee style, this is,' said the man, extending his mouth still farther to one side so that the yellow saucers shouldn't overhear him.

'Wonderful organisation, eh?' cried Timmy, as a procession of small purple tumblers now arrived.

'Everything 'ere's been worked out to a fine point. We all know just what we have to do, en' we keep on doing it. Every man, every girl in this place,' he continued, in an irritatingly complacent manner, 'knows just what to do from the minute he – or she – and mostly she – clocks in to the time when he – or she – clocks out. That's system, that is.' He paused for Timmy to admire it.

But Timmy didn't feel like admiring it now. 'Well, I suppose it's all right,' he remarked casually. 'But it wouldn't suit me.'

'It isn't 'ere to suit you,' said the man heavily, steering a gross of dark brown bowls into the machine. 'Or me, for that matter. Though I'm not grumbling, mind you. But you have to keep bang up to date or you're done for nowadays, and all this is the latest thing. Same as making cars an' airyplanes. Everything worked out to a fine point. Look at this machine. Here's something worth coming to see. If you'd told me a few years since there was such a machine I wouldn't have believed you.'

'And I wouldn't have believed it myself if I'd told you,' said Timmy flippantly.

The man didn't like this. 'Don't scoff. Nothing to scoff at 'ere. Anybody who scoffs,' he went on severely, 'just shows he can't keep up with the times. When we get a system like this going everywhere, with machines like this for everything, why – we'll – we'll – '

'We'll all have a hundred purple tooth glasses each,' said Timmy. Then, fearing he had gone too far, he asked hastily: 'What do you like to do when you've done your work here? Watch football?'

'Ah!' cried the man, looking up for the first time, 'now you're talking! That's the one thing – an' the only thing – I don't like about coming here to Dunbury and doing this job. I can't watch the Villa like I used to. Not every other Saturday, that is. I do run over when I can manage it.'

'Aston Villa's your team, is it?' Timmy, like most variety artistes, knew something about professional football himself.

'I followed the Villa for years,' said the man, rather pompously.

'Well, they don't look like getting anywhere,' said Timmy mischievously.

The man stared at him in horror. 'How d'you mean – they don't look like getting anywhere?'

'I mean what I say. Look at the way they shaped last season.'

'Now wait a minute, wait a minute! What was the matter with 'em last season, eh?'

'Well, to start with – '

'There isn't any starting with,' cried the man angrily, advancing a step. 'Before you begin casting aspersions just listen to somebody that knows – '

'I'm only saying – '

'I know what you're only saying 'cos I've heard it before. But let me tell you a thing or two about the Villa.' And now he began tapping the top button of Timmy's waistcoat. 'What some of you chaps who start casting aspersions don't seem to know is that there's luck in football the same as in everything else. You can't make it all scientific, try as hard as you like. There's luck – good luck and bad luck. That's not the players' fault, is it? I'm asking you a question,' he repeated with great and quite unnecessary emphasis. 'Is that the players' fault?'

'No, I don't say it is,' said Timmy, stepping back to avoid the incessant tapping on his waistcoat.

'All right, all right,' cried the man aggressively, coming forward to do more tapping. 'You've admitted it. Don't try and wriggle out of it. You've admitted it. There's good luck and bad luck. Take the management. Who appoints the manager? The trainer? Who appoints them? Do the players? Now let's talk a bit of sense instead of casting aspersions – '

'This is our boxing and packing machine,' cried a voice. It was the little woman who was acting as a guide. 'Now this wonderful machine – '

'I say the Villa just struck a patch of bad luck, that's all,' shouted the man, too far gone now to care about the guide and her party or his machine. 'And I'll prove it. I'll prove to you – '

'Here, look out!' cried Timmy.

But it was too late. There was a sudden crunching and grinding sound, as if the machine had decided to start eating the products instead of boxing and packing them, and then, the chute being hopelessly jammed, there was a shower of brightly coloured ashtrays and bowls and cups and saucers. It rained useful and durable articles. The guide and her sightseers were bombarded with inexpensive and non-inflammable objects. The machine, baulked of its prey, rattled and roared its disgust. The system was in ruins.

'Flaming Moses!' yelled the man, pulling levers. 'Look what you've done now!' And even as he tried to put things right, a cascade of combs and cigarette holders descended upon him. 'Hey, you!'

But Timmy wasn't staying. And as he felt a couple of small tooth tumblers crack under his shoes, he had time to wonder what was happening to the Professor.

At that moment, strange as it may seem, the Professor was sitting in the best armchair in the manager's private office, enjoying an excellent cigar. In polite attendance upon him, ready if necessary to listen to any lecture he chose to give them, were the manager himself, the two assistant managers, and the head of the sales department, all four youngish middle-aged men, very spruce, very keen, not quite English, not quite American, and not quite human, as if they too had been produced by some *United Plastics* process. The Professor was enjoying himself too much and was too deeply concerned at the moment with some of mankind's gravest problems to wonder why he was being treated with such respect. As for the four shrewd alert men of business facing him, they were behaving so strangely simply because they had not the least idea that this tall, odd-looking foreigner was an exile who had arrived in the town to play *Hoopy-Toopy-Toots* in the Little Market Hall, but imagined, because he had been found wandering below and had instantly been brought up here by a secretary, that he was the important visitor they had been expecting, Dr Bentika of the Jugo-Slavian government. So at the moment everybody was happy.

They had been explaining, enthusiastically and almost in chorus, their great conjuring trick, casein, into cup, and had given in some detail an account of their wonderful system, with its extraordinary machines and its minute sub-division of human labour. It looked as if they saw shining before them a new golden age, crammed with cheap and durable products. And to all this the commercial representative of the Jugo-Slavian government had listened with deep attention.

'So!' he began when they had finished and waited for his applause. 'It is, as you say, most ingenious. But one thing I do not understand. You speak as if all this activity – this making and selling and buying and possessing of useful articles – were an end in itself and not merely a means to an end. It is good that we should all have as many bowls and ashtrays as we need. But it is not of the highest importance. It is not important at all.'

'Can't say I agree with you there, Doctor,' said the manager. 'Can't have a civilisation without continually raising the standard of living. Can't raise the standard of living without increasing production and consumption of goods. Seems all very simple to me.'

'But not so simple to me,' the Professor objected, beaming upon them through a little cloud of cigar smoke. 'Civilisation is something more than producing and owning *things*. The things may help us to control our environment, that is true.'

'You can't get away from it,' said the head of the sales department. 'Why, we'd be lost without our inventions.'

'It may be that we shall also be lost *with* our inventions.

I have an ashtray. Good! I have four ashtrays. Still better, for my friends may come to see me. But do I want fifty ashtrays? No. And above all I do not want fifty ashtrays and *no* friends, eh?' The Professor paused, glanced round at his listeners, saw they were about to reply, and continued: 'We must be certain what civilisation is. To me it seems an affair of the mind and the spirit. Where the mind is growing in knowledge and wisdom and the spirit is like a clear flame, there is civilisation. Man is certainly a maker and user of things, but if he is no more than that he is still only man and not yet civilised man. So we must ask ourselves if all this activity and ingenuity of yours is helping the mind to grow in wisdom and the spirit to burn like a clear flame. And here I may remind you, my friends,' he added, beaming upon them again, 'that the social insects, the bees and ants and termites whose communities have existed unchanged for more than a hundred million years, we are told, appear to have solved their problems of production and consumption and have nothing to learn from our economists. We do not know how existence appears to an ant or a termite, which may enjoy ecstasies quite unknown to us, but we cannot help feeling that their failure, as a species, is complete, that the world spirit lost interest in them millions and millions of years ago, whereas there is still a chance, just a chance, for ourselves.'

The four exchanged hasty glances. Even Jugo-Slavia, a state for which some allowance could be made, need not have sent them such an odd representative. However, they had been told to see that the fellow was handsomely received, and so they had better humour him. Their eyes, which were not remarkably expressive, contrived in this second to say all this and more.

The Professor, delighted to find such an audience, now

reminded himself that he had really gone there on behalf of the people of Dunbury. 'If we spent so much time collecting pots and pans for the kitchen that we had no time left for eating anything that was cooked in that kitchen, we should be behaving foolishly.'

'I don't see your point,' said the manager, with an awkward little smile.

'I have not arrived at it yet,' the Professor told him, pulling at his cigar. He paused a moment. 'Now among the ends, which seem to us to justify our lower activities, are the creation and the appreciation of music, to which the making and selling of bowls and ashtrays, no matter how ingeniously produced, must serve merely as a means. Music,' he cried warmly, 'nourishes the mind and the spirit. It is the expression of the struggling deity within us. Bach, Mozart, Beethoven, Schubert,' he shouted, 'Wagner, Brahms – '

'Quite so,' the manager interrupted, rather sharply, as if to suggest this had gone on long enough. 'But I'm afraid I don't know much about music.'

'You are quite right to be afraid,' the Professor told him solemnly, 'unless of course it happens that you have no ear. Many men of the highest culture – even some of the great poets – have had no ear for music, but that is simply a natural affliction, and they have taken care to exercise the mind and purify the spirit with other forms of art or a deep and prolonged study of philosophy.' He looked enquiringly at the manager, who muttered something about being content to enjoy an occasional round of golf and rubber or two of bridge.

'Now here in this town,' the Professor continued, ignoring the manager's nonsense about golf and bridge, 'the people are fortunate enough to possess a large and well-constructed hall of their own, where they can create and enjoy the noble art of music. But I have been told that you wish to take this hall away from them, to use it as a means of selling more bowls and ashtrays. If that is true, then civilisation here in Dunbury is not moving forward but going backward, returning to a new kind of barbarism, filled with machines and swift transport, synthetic bowls and ashtrays, but nevertheless a barbarism.'

'Now just a minute, Doctor,' cried the head of the sales department, who felt more responsible than any of the other three because this acquisition of the Market Hall was originally his idea. 'To start with, the people have stopped using the Hall. They're not as keen on music as they used to be.'

'But why?' asked the Professor, holding up his cigar as if it were a glowing *Stop* signal. 'Because your world, with its clamorous and exacting machines and its organisation of mechanical little tasks, is draining away their spirit of initiative, making them passive in their leisure instead of active and creative. They drift from the work factory to the amusement factory. Instead of music there is now the strange horrible sound of the cinema organ or the barbaric din of the jazz bands, both of which play on the nerves and do nothing for the heart, the mind, the spirit.'

'You may be right, I don't know,' said the manager, in a tone that suggested that neither did he care. 'But it seems to me to miss the point. We're here to manufacture and sell *United Plastics* products. We've brought a lot of money into this one-eyed town. We're easily the largest employers of labour here – *and* we're good employers, believe me – we ought to have some say. It's better for everybody that that old hall should be advertising our goods, serving a useful purpose, than that it should be there doing nothing or – for there's some talk of it – be a museum for a set of West Dunbury snobs.'

'There is nothing wrong with museums in their place,' said the Professor carefully. 'But no museum is necessary here. Too much of England, I think, is a museum. A life divided between museums and factories is not good.'

'But anyhow, Doctor, I can't see that what is or isn't a good life – as you call it – is any business of ours.' This was from one of the assistant managers, who felt he had been quiet long enough.

'It is the only real business we can have, this creation of the good life,' said the Professor. 'Anything else is either mere folly or criminality.'

The four exchanged quick glances again. Really, this was a bit steep.

The Professor now noticed the glances and the eyebrows raised above them, and clean forgetting where he was and who his listeners were, he promptly stopped beaming upon them and frowned as if he saw before him four wilfully obtuse students. 'Mere folly or criminality,' he repeated sharply. 'At the best – like kittens chasing their tails. At the worst – like robbers and murderers. To make bowls and ashtrays, that is good, so long as the mind and spirit are being served. But to take away from the mind and the spirit – as you propose to do in this matter of the Hall – in order to sell more bowls and ashtrays, this is to act either like a foolish child or like a criminal.'

'Now look here,' cried the chief salesman, 'it's nothing to do with us what these people do in their spare time.'

'There is not time and then spare time,' said the Professor, raising his voice to meet the other's tone. 'There is only time.'

'And we seem to be wasting some of it,' one of the four murmured.

But the Professor, though often so absent-minded, had

sharp ears. Now he was annoyed. He put down his cigar and rose to his full height. 'I am sorry to learn that I am wasting your time, gentlemen, but it will do you no harm to spend a few more minutes learning the truth.' He glared at them as he had always glared at the few students who had refused to listen to him properly, and his manner suggested such authority that they did not interrupt him. 'At the back of your minds is the old economic heresy, the idea that men are primarily producers and consumers, and are only real human beings in what you call their spare time. You do not believe that of everybody. Nobody ever did. You believe it of those you employ but not of those who employ you. The great, the privileged, the wealthy have never seen themselves as part of economic man. That is why so many of them cling to medieval trappings, to show that they still move in the feudal, pre-economic world. They insist upon living on another level. First to some extent in America and now in Russia, they thought to bring justice and equality into the world by removing this class, by making all men the economic man of the theorists. But this is equity in the wrong direction. It is bolting the door on the outside. We should aim at making all men great, privileged, and wealthy, raising them all to the level – '

But this was going too far, and two of them promptly told him so. It contradicted itself, they said, for clearly all men couldn't be great, privileged, and wealthy. But he resumed at once, and with even more emphasis.

'You are still thinking in terms of goods and services, of economic man,' he told them. 'But I am thinking of the inward style of life, of how a man thinks of himself. I am not only putting the smokers before the ashtrays in importance, but I am thinking of what it is that brings the smokers together. And in the world of the mind and the spirit it is possible for all to be great, privileged, and wealthy. If *you* enjoy a Beethoven symphony you do not take away from but add to *my* enjoyment of it. And life on this level is not something to be tolerated if there happens to be time for it after the serious business of the world has been done. It *is* the serious business of the world – this life of beauty, wisdom and love – and we only make things and buy and sell them in order to sustain that real life. All men know this deep in their hearts. The coarsest sailor, hurrying ashore to get drunk in the lowest brothel, is still hungering for beauty, wisdom and love. All men know this deep in their hearts, and when those who refuse to listen to what is deep in their hearts, those with busy metallic little brains tell them it is not so, then men cannot help feeling frustrated and in despair, and in their frustration and despair they become violent and cruel. And that is why the world you have made,' he shouted at them, pointing a very long accusing finger, 'is horrible now with violence and cruelty.'

By the time the Professor had reached this climax, Timmy, three floors below, was still lingering near a tiny room that had just been explained to him and the other visitors by the guide. This tiny room was the centre of the *United Plastics* internal broadcasting system. Throughout the works there were loud-speakers, and if an announcement had to be made to all the employees, for fire or air-raid drill, for example, it was a very simple matter to switch on the amplification and from that tiny room issue commands simultaneously to everybody. In her enthusiasm the little woman from the welfare department was good enough to show Timmy and the others exactly how it all worked. The others were not deeply interested and moved away when she did. But Timmy lingered on, still wistfully eyeing the switches.

'Yes, sirs, that is the world you have made,' the Professor thundered, with his large spectacles flashing the necessary lightning. 'Its roots are frustration and despair. Its fruits are violence, cruelty and anguish. And the bowls and cups you sell – the bowls and cups for whose sake you would destroy music and the liberty and happiness of the common people – may soon be running with blood and tears.'

There was a moment's silence, at the end of which the head of the sales department could be heard muttering: 'I don't see what all this has got to do with the Jugo-Slavian government.'

The Professor stared at him. 'It has nothing to do with the Jugo-Slavian government.'

'No, but you have.'

'Certainly not,' replied the Professor with dignity. 'I have no connection with the Jugo-Slavian government.'

'What?' They all stared. Two of them rose to their feet. The Professor regarded them calmly.

'Doctor Bentika from Belgrade,' a secretary announced, holding the door open very wide, as if a bull were about to charge into the private office.

In rushed a round, furry, sweaty sort of man, mopping his forehead with a green silk handkerchief that reeked of eau-de-Cologne, and talking rapidly and unintelligibly as he came. Before anybody could understand a single word he was saying, he had bowed several times, mopped furiously and sent out fresh waves of eau-de-Cologne, and had dashed round and shaken everybody's hand.

'You're Doctor Bentika?' cried the manager, astounded.

'Yais, yais, yais,' he gabbled. 'Doctor Bentika – yais, yais, yais! Pliss – pliss excoosa! Since two day I try see United Plastics – eh? Yais, yais, pliss!'

'Well, glad you're here at last,' said the manager

politely. 'Just sit down a moment, please, Doctor Bentika. There's something here I don't understand.' He looked ominously at the Professor. 'If this is Doctor Bentika, who on earth are you?'

'I am the voice of wisdom,' replied the Professor, doing himself proud, 'and I am now without a home.'

As not one of them had an instant reply to this astonishing statement, the Professor was about to turn and stalk out when he was arrested by a tremendous crackling and spluttering from the loudspeaker above the door. Everybody stared at it.

'Now you people,' cried a voice from the speaker that the Professor recognised at once as his friend Timmy's, 'just you remember they're trying to take that hall away from you, an' if you let 'em get away with this, then before long they'll be taking the milk out of your tea. Don't put up with it, boys and girls. They're trying it on. Take this lying down an' before long they'll be making ashtrays out of you.'

'Here, what the – ' and the manager started up in a fury.

'You know what the motto is – an' if you don't, then come to the Little Market Hall tomorrow night an' see some fun – but anyhow I'll tell you – the motto is *Let the People Sing!*' And these final words fairly exploded from the loudspeaker.

'And that,' said the Professor, who had an excellent sense of the dramatic, 'is the other voice, the voice of the Comic, of Humour, of the English People, and that also is now without a home. Good afternoon, gentlemen.' And this time he did stalk out, and nobody tried to stop him. The manager and the chief salesman were trying to answer the real Doctor Bentika's bewildered questions, and the two assistant managers were angrily ringing bells and shouting down telephones.

As both embarrassing visitors hurried out at the same time, it was not surprising that they met outside and could walk back together to Mrs Mitterly's.

'I think I've started something in there,' said Timmy, chuckling. 'Looked for you all over, Professor. How did you get on?'

'I had a very enjoyable afternoon,' said the Professor.

'You've been lecturin' 'em, eh?'

'No, no. Of course not. But we had some conversation. Something was said about the good life, which they said was no business of theirs. So I pointed out – '

'I know,' said Timmy cheerfully. 'You've been lecturin' 'em. Saw it in your eye. Well, that's not so dusty. We've shaken 'em all up a bit, an' ten to one we've started something.' And humming his roly-poly song, he trotted happily along to keep pace with the Professor's raking stride. 'And we mustn't forget to tell Mrs Mitterly that we didn't get her two kids into trouble. Never set eyes on 'em myself, an' I'll bet you didn't – eh? No, I thought not. Well, that's all right, an' though the battle doesn't begin again till tomorrow night, the afternoon's not been wasted. An' there's a nice piece of haddock for tea. I know 'cos I saw it this morning.'

CHAPTER X

LOTS OF THINGS HAPPEN ON SATURDAY

IT WAS very pleasant that Saturday afternoon in Dunbury. The day had the heavy-gold, coolish sunlight of a fine autumn, and it was windless, calm, just right for tasting a pipe out of doors. Which is what many Dunbury citizens were doing, in their gardens, on the bowling greens, in the ground of Dunbury Rovers A.F.C., or round about the market square, to which they had probably been taken by their wives. On Saturday the market square was crowded with stalls, some of them within the usual ruts of commerce, selling beef and bacon, cheese, fruit and vegetables, clothing and shoes, and others belonging to all manner of cheapjacks, who would fill in a Saturday at Dunbury between two fairs. On this afternoon, which followed the afternoon when Timmy and the Professor visited *United Plastics*, there were in addition to the usual stalls a fortune-teller or two, a man selling a cure for rheumatism, another selling herbs that would cure everything, and the usual swollen-faced, brassy-lunged fellows who offered a confusing mixture of auctioneering and what they called 'a sporting chance.' Between these rows of stalls, under the mild sun, wandered the folk of Dunbury, buying something good and cheap for the week-end and also hoping for a bit of magic to happen. That is why the men from the fairs dropped into town, for though they appeared for the most part seedy fellows with oddly angry voices, as if sick and tired of telling people that there were still miracles, you had only to listen and try to believe a little and then they seemed wizards, curing everything with sixpenny packets of herbs, peering into your future, or flinging away gold rings and watches out of a passionate and aggressive sportsmanship. And the people, most of them rather squat, middle-aged couples, walked rustily and blinking a little as if they had only just been allowed to come above ground, wandered here and there, stayed to listen, stared out of eyes strangely innocent among their wrinkles, and waited for their bit of magic.

Through this Saturday afternoon crowd went Timmy and the Professor and Raymond Mitterly carrying his clarinet case. But Raymond left them at the entrance of the Little Market Hall, which they had to tidy up and prepare for that night's session, and then carried his clarinet out of the market square altogether and through several side-streets to the north of it until he reached a small brick hall that served as an annexe to the Dunbury Labour Club. There he met the long thin youth who had played the oboe and the little fat middle-aged man who had played the euphonium on the platform on Wednesday night, and there were other instrumentalists there, too, for this was the first rehearsal of the newly resurrected Dunbury Band. Enquiries had to be made after old members who were missing, a few new members were introduced all round; there was a good deal of chaffing and back-slapping; and meanwhile they were all putting together and trying out their instruments. Beneath the tootles and gurgles and *pom-pom-poms* of these preliminary flourishes, beneath the chat and laughter, was an undercurrent of excitement. Not only was the band to be brought to life again, but it seemed already as if it were brought to another kind of life. The bit of magic appeared to be just round the corner.

Tom Largs came in, carrying a pile of music sheets. 'Now then, boys,' he shouted, 'sort yourselves out, and let's get started. Clarinets this side. The other wood wind opposite. Brasses at the back. Is Harry here?'

'All present an' correct, sergeant,' cried Harry, who had been bending down arranging his drums and cymbals. He was a gigantic fellow, who had a job in a little iron foundry by the canal and had once been a regular soldier. To prove that he was really there in his proper capacity he gave his big drum a tremendous thump and then clashed his cymbals. A cheer, half serious, half ironic, went up from the rest of the band. Largs gave them one of his infrequent but disarming broad grins, which suddenly turned him into an over-size small boy out for a lark. Meanwhile, steady old George Reynolds, the chief clarinet player who acted as leader, for this was a military band and had no strings, was giving out the sheets of music that Largs had brought with him.

'Now, boys, just give me your attention,' cried Largs, very much in earnest now. 'First, I want to tell you how things stand with regard to the Market Hall. We had a council meeting about it yesterday. What happened was exactly what I told some of you would happen. Some of our worthy councillors who want to keep well in with the West Dunbury snobs, including of course some of our respected tradesmen, tried to rush through the museum scheme. Alderman Shincliffe and his gang, who want to keep in with *United Plastics* for various good reasons, opposed it, of course, and tried to rush through the *United Plastics* offer. After a lot of talk I'd got three brave fellow-councillors to stand by me and say that the people's Hall shouldn't be given to either the nobs or the bosses to play with. Just four of us. If the other two parties could have agreed, as they did quick enough when they took our music licence away, we'd have been swamped, of course, but this time naturally they couldn't agree. So it was a deadlock. Then the West Dunbury lot, who'd been put up to it by Shiptonthorpe, said we'd have to have arbitration, put it to the vote, that another council meeting would simply be a waste of time and we might as well have arbitration as soon as possible, and carried it. As far as I can see, we'll have an arbitrator sent here next week.'

'Is that going to be any good to us, Tom?' cried one of them.

'You bet it isn't. Unless United Plastics can pull a few strings quickly, that arbitrator will turn out to be an old friend of the Foxfields or Colonel Hazelhead, he'll be dined and wined at Dunbury Hall, and he'll do whatever they tell him to do for the sake of the old school tie. That's why they don't mind arbitration. Fairest thing for everybody! It's the old game, the way that nearly every-thing's managed in this country.'

'If that's the case, Tom, I don't see where we come in,' said George Reynolds, rather sadly.

'We come in as the Dunbury Band, and we haven't to ask anybody's permission to organise ourselves into a band, have we? And what's the use of saying the people of Dunbury should have their music as they used to do, if the same people of Dunbury can't even keep their band going? See? And another thing. We'll try and play some sense and guts into the people. We'll waken 'em up – with music. And don't forget this, boys,' he continued, raising his voice, 'we've got to stand by this chap Hassock, the auctioneer who's rented the Little Market Hall. It's in his agreement that he can give his free entertainment there, and when the licence was taken away they forgot to tell him and to offer to cancel his agreement. They're on their high horse about this – sending the police along to stop his entertainment – but all the right's on his side. I had a word with him this morning – he's in the Cottage Hospital just now – and the chap's blazing wild and full of fight. I promised we'd help 'em – and it's the least we can do, because this Hassock's broken agreement is a kind of spearhead for us – and after the rehearsal, boys, I'll explain what I think we can do. In the meantime, before we try anything ambitious and get back to our old form, I've got here a little marching song that Bob Francis and I knocked off last night, and I want to practise it because I fancy it's going to be useful during the next few days. It's called *Let the People Sing!*

'That's the stuff, Tom!' shouted one of the trombone players.

'I know it is, Jack. And now I'll just sing the refrain to give you an idea how it goes, for though you've all got proper parts in front of you, I know very well half of you really can't read music and are only pretending you can – '

Deep groans from the boys.

' – so I'd better give you some idea of it. The chorus then,' said Tom, and then, in a fair baritone, he sang:

> *Let the people sing,*
> *And freedom bring*
> *An end to a sad old story;*
> *When the people sing,*
> *Their voices ring*
> *In the dawn of the people's glory.*

The words may have been the usual conventional stuff, but they neatly fitted a fine marching tune. Soon they were all hard at it. George Reynolds and his clarinets were giving out the air in the first half of the chorus, with the bassoons and heavy brass supporting them with a quiet but sturdy *pom-po-po-po-pom*; and then in the second half all the brass came crashing in with the refrain, while the wood wind trilled and gurgled above them, and Harry rolled his drums and triumphantly clashed his cymbals.

'That's all right for a mere start, boys,' cried Tom, who had now taken his coat off and was mopping his broad shining face. 'But now that you've got a vague idea of what it's about, I want to hear something worth listening to. We're marching into a new life, boys. Civilisation's just beginning at last. The last tyrant's dead. All the chains are off. The darkness has gone, and the people – you and I and our wives and kids and all our pals and their wives and kids and so on and so on and so on, all over the world, everywhere – are coming out into the sunshine. That's the idea. And I want to *hear* it. Come on, now – straight into it, you clarinets, a clean clear-cut melody – and hold back, you brasses, until I give you the signal to go, and then let her have it – ready? One, two, three, four – *Let the people sing* – '

And now they swung into it, and the tune came alive, and people of all colours and customs seemed to come out of their dungeons and mud huts and slums and ghettos and stifling workshops and dark factories and wharfs and fields and mines, and they marched out of cities and across deserts and mountains, singing in a triumph that was the only real triumph the world had yet seen, for it was not the victory of some cunning megalomaniac over tyrants less cunning, it did not celebrate the ascendance of one state above its neighbours, but it was a triumph of Man himself who had found at last a way to live and now came into his inheritance of the fruitful globe. The little hall shook with soaring and thundering sound. Men left the billiard tables and dartboards in the club next door, and came in to listen and stare and finally to sing. In the mean street outside men and women stopped to listen and to hum the tune, while the children, like tiny conquerors, strutted and swaggered up and down to its lilt. Here at least something was happening in Dunbury. Perhaps a bit of magic.

Over in the Cottage Hospital, a little later that afternoon, Hope and Dr Buckie were taking tea with Mr Hassock in the nice private room that Mr Hassock now occupied. Unless her patients were dangerous and complicated cases, Dr Buckie soon became bored with them and with the whole hospital. Mr Hassock was not a dangerous and complicated case, but on the other hand he was a racy and robust character, with much experience of the world, and as the large and strangely masculine Dr Buckie was herself another racy and robust character, with an equally rich experience, she liked his company. She had taken a fancy, too, to Hope, chiefly because she liked the girl's mixture of extreme good looks and direct simplicity. But though both his visitors were enjoying themselves, and tucking into the tea provided for them, Mr Hassock was far from happy. True, he was bandaged nearly as stiffly as a mummy, but though that was a nuisance it was not worrying him at this moment.

'What a man, what a man!' he groaned. 'What do I go an' do?'

'Talk too much,' said Dr Buckie severely. 'Why do they say that women are always gassing? Some of you men are worse than any women. You, for instance. Never had such a gasbag in the hospital.'

'I say, what do I go an' do? I bring 'em here, find I've been done in the eye – me, Fred Hassock, who's as wide as the Blackpool promenade — and then go an' land myself in this bed so that this kid and them two babes in the wood — the comedian and the Professor — have to do it all. Oh — Christmas — I could kick myself.'

'You couldn't,' said Dr Buckie promptly. 'You try. If you can, I'll have something to say to that day sister who bandaged you this morning. By the way, how d'you like your nurses? Fancying any of 'em yet? You men usually do.'

'My mind,' said Mr Hassock, with great dignity, 'is occupied with other things — chiefly the way I've been diddled in this town — an' I've no time to be fancying nurses. But if you want to know, I don't fancy nurses. Never did.'

'I'm surprised. That uniform,' said Hope dreamily, 'is a gift. Why, with an outfit like that — '

'Let's have a little serious conversation, for Pete's sake,' cried Mr Hassock, giving a low groan as he slightly changed his position. 'Now you're going to try an' sell a few things tonight, aren't you? Right!'

'You're not going to tell me you're as hard up as all that,' said Dr Buckie. 'After all your boasting! Making 'em do your work for you for fear you'd be missing a pound or two.'

Mr Hassock nearly burst all his bandages. He went purple. 'Now stop that silly talk,' he shouted. 'You're only showing your ignorance. I don't care about the money. If I didn't sell another thing this year — or next year — or the year after that — I could still manage very comfortably.'

'Well, manage then, and leave it alone.'

'I won't. Haven't you got any idea of principle?'

'No,' replied Dr Buckie cheerfully. 'And when other people tell me it's the principle of the thing that they're concerned about, I get suspicious. That's me.'

'And I don't believe you. But anyhow it's not me. Not Fred Hassock's style at all. And we came here to do something – we've a right to do it – I can show you my agreement with your precious town council – '

'Don't call 'em *my* precious town council,' cried Dr Buckie. 'I've been fighting 'em ever since my first week here. Snobs, cowards, half-wits, and not half a dozen real men among them. No guts. No backbone. Short of calcium. If they paid me a thousand a year, I'd run this town myself, and make it fit to live in. Half of it wants pulling down right away. The other half wants livening up.'

'We're going to do that,' said Hope. 'Aren't we, Uncle Fred?'

'If I could get a word in edgeways,' said Mr Hassock rather bitterly, 'I'd finish what I was going to say. We came here to do something – and either we do it or we tear the place in two. And it's not money,' he added pointedly to the grinning Dr Buckie, 'but the principle of the thing – an' put that in your thermometer an' suck it.'

'Here, steady!' cried Hope, shaking her head at him. 'You're getting very rude and insulting and probably giving yourself a temperature.'

'A lot of doctors would agree with you, my dear,' said Dr Buckie cheerfully and complacently, 'but I don't. As long as he doesn't burst, he's doing himself more good than harm.' She stared at him through her horrible pink-rimmed spectacles as if he were merely a gigantic test-tube. 'His chemistry's working at full blast – glands functioning well – so he's helping to mend himself. Only don't burst, Mr Hassock.'

'Burst! I can't breathe.' He tried a few rather deep breaths, winced and muttered, and then apparently decided to do without breathing. 'Fact is, you're a fraud,

Dr Buckie. Way you've gone on about this town and me, an' now we're going to do something about it, you're beginning to rat on us.'

'She isn't,' cried Hope. 'Are you, Dr Buckie?'

Dr Buckie shrugged her tremendous shoulders, but at the same time winked gigantically at Hope. 'I don't believe you can do anything,' she told Mr Hassock.

'That's all you know. I had that chap Largs in to see me this morning, and he's no fool an' he's plenty of fight in him. A chap like that could make something of this town if he once wakened the people up.'

'I'm beginning to think,' said Dr Buckie, in earnest now, 'you can't waken the English up. They're getting worse, not better. Oh – yes – they can spend money building battleships and making aeroplanes. And if it comes to a push, there are plenty of nice lads ready to go and be killed in those battleships and aeroplanes. But all that's being ready to die, not being ready to live. We're like one of the big dinosaurs, putting thicker and thicker armour on itself until it could hardly move and daren't come out of the slush, and all the time its species was dying because it hadn't enough brains and sensitiveness and enterprise to live. What we've got isn't half good enough, and nobody seems to want anything much better than what we've got. We sit about admiring a lot of people who sit about admiring their great-grandfathers. Where's that take us to, eh? Hello, who's this?'

This was Timmy and he was followed into the room by the Professor. Dr Buckie suddenly began laughing, and the next moment Hope began laughing, too, and then the two oddly-contrasted females laughed and laughed until the tears ran down their cheeks, while the three men stared at them in astonishment.

'What's up?' enquired Timmy, completely bewildered.

'Oh – you know what they are,' said Mr Hassock in disgust.

'We do not sufficiently realise,' said the Professor gravely, 'that the whole nature of woman is profoundly different from that of the male. Beginning with the very chemistry of the body, these differences – '

'No, no, no!' cried Dr Buckie, helplessly, her vast bulk heaving and shaking.

'But surely, doctor, these elementary truths – ' the Professor began earnestly.

'No, no, don't! I'm not contradicting you,' she gurgled. 'I'm just asking you – for God's sake – not to make me worse.'

'But what have we done?' asked Timmy.

'Nothing,' Hope told him, dabbing at her eyes. 'It was just the sight of you two coming in – you looked so – oh – I don't know – I can't explain – '

'Then don't try, girl, and shut up,' said Mr Hassock, with the air of a man who had had quite enough nonsense for one afternoon. 'Let's get to business. And we don't want to keep Dr Buckie. I've no doubt she's a lot to do.'

'Just throwing me out, eh? Suppose I say that you've had quite enough excitement for today – '

'You've just said it was doing me good.'

'Well, I can change my mind, can't I? What about taking your temperature?'

'Oh – for the sake of merry Christmas bells, drop it!' cried Mr Hassock in great disgust.

'Uncle Fred, she ought to stay a minute – just to decide,' said Hope.

'To decide what?' asked Dr Buckie.

'Who's to sell the stuff tonight,' said Hope, turning from one to the other. 'We can't all do it – it would look silly – and we can't decide which.'

'We could toss for it,' Timmy suggested.

Nobody else was in favour of chance deciding who should be tonight's auctioneer.

'I suppose I couldn't decide,' said Mr Hassock, with all the terrible irony of an expert who happens to be lying in bed wrapped round like a mummy, 'only having had twenty years experience of the game.'

'But you mightn't like to hurt anybody's feelings,' said Hope, departing from her usual sound realism. 'That's why I suggested Dr Buckie. Now then!'

The Professor was allowed to put forward his claim first. 'I know nothing of this way of selling, but I have a strong clear voice and no doubt I could address the people on many – '

'You're out. Sorry,' said Dr Buckie, without any hesitation whatever. 'I can't imagine anybody more unsuitable. Sportsman to suggest it, though. Next!'

'Now I don't say I've done it before, because I haven't,' Timmy began, with an air of great frankness. 'But I could do it on my head. Sell 'em anything. Why? 'Cos I'm used to appearing in front of the public an' know how to handle 'em. Watch my chorus work. There you see how to handle 'em. The fact is, not only have I had long an' valuable experience but also I've got personality.'

'It's the wrong kind of personality,' Dr Buckie told him. 'They'll laugh all right when you want them to, but they won't buy anything from you. They won't take you seriously.'

'She's right,' cried Mr Hassock, 'I hate to say it, but she's dead right. Tried out one of my comics last winter and it was terrible. If I hadn't stopped it, they'd have been selling *us* something – it was as bad as that.'

'I'm the one,' Hope told them all. 'And it was quite obvious from the start who's the one. I'm not frightened of them. They'll take me seriously. I can eat it. I'm the one.'

'I believe you are,' said Dr Buckie. 'I can see you selling them something they don't want for three times as much as it's worth. That's the business, isn't it?' she added, turning to Mr Hassock.

'Thank you very much and good afternoon, doctor,' said Mr Hassock. 'In other words, push off.'

When Dr Buckie opened the door two men were discovered standing outside, very close together and looking very anxious.

'Mr Fred Hassock?' one of them enquired, hoarsely.

'All right, come in for a minute, boys,' cried Mr Hassock, who had caught a glimpse of them through the doorway.

They came in and Dr Buckie departed. They had very red and roughened faces, none too clean, and they were dressed in striped suits considerably too small for them, so that they seemed to be bursting out of them. They sounded as if they had been misusing their vocal apparatus for the last ten years. Their manner was at once awkward and confidential. Mr Hassock introduced them to his three assistants as his old acquaintances and occasional late employees, Micky Barnet and Knocker Sullivan.

'Bin workin' a fly pitch in the Sat-day gaff,' said Micky Barnet. ''Eard you was 'ere, Mr 'Assock, so me an' Knocker come along.'

'Thanks, Micky, an' I'm getting along fine. What are you doing round here, Knocker?'

'Workin' the spread again, Mr 'Assock,' replied Knocker, in a deep croaking voice. 'Charlie joined the run-out boys from Brum, so I did a bit o'gazin' – worked the muzzel in the Smoke an' down at Brighton – then tried the spread again. But I'm terrible as a crocus.'

'I keep tellin' Knocker it's a shice,' said Micky earnestly. 'It's not a bad tober – but what's 'is bunce? Tell 'im, Knocker.'

Knocker brought out some money and examined it. 'Not much bottle. A nicker, half a bar, a caser an' a hole. 'Aven't made a flim in one day since Bank 'Oliday.'

Hope and Timmy and the Professor stared at this incomprehensible pair and then glanced enquiringly at each other. Mr Hassock asked further questions, which were answered in the same fantastic fashion as if these two had dropped in from the moon.

'Well, boys, I'm glad to see you again,' said Mr Hassock, 'and if you'd like to make a change, I could drop a line to Billy Fitt, who was telling me he could do with a few old hands as barkers. Or you could go and see him and tell him I sent you.'

'Not for me, Mr 'Assock, thanks,' said Micky. 'I've worked out a good flash for the windbag, an' I'm off to Newcastle. That's a good monkery these days, plenty of smash up there.'

'You can 'ave it,' said Knocker. 'I'll take your tip, Mr 'Assock. Me for the rattler to the Smoke tomorrer, an' I'll see Billy Fitt, with me titfer in me 'and. 'Ere, Micky, we better be scarpin'. See if we can't take another spraser or two from the punters. So long, Mr 'Assock.'

'An' mind the rozzers tonight,' said Micky earnestly, addressing all of them. 'We 'eard something this afternoon in the gaff. But you're wide, Mr 'Assock. All the best!' And out they went.

The Professor stared after them like a man in a dream. 'Nothing, nothing, did I understand,' he said blankly. 'They came and they have gone, and while they were here they seemed to speak of many different things. But in what language?'

Mr Hassock laughed. 'I thought that would stump you. It's all fairground slang. Romany, Yiddish, rhyming slang, and I suppose some of it must be old thieves' slang.'

'But what were they saying, Uncle Fred?' asked Hope, as bewildered as the Professor.

'Well, Knocker said he was here selling herbs – quack doctor stuff. He told me his old partner, Charlie, had left him to join the run-out boys from Brum – that is, the gang from Birmingham running a fake auction – and, by the way, if anybody wants to see me lose my temper just let 'em talk as if I was on the run-out game – though I won't say I've never tried my hand at it. The game is to make people think they're getting something for nothing – and really it serves the greedy mugs right. Then Knocker told me he'd been hawking lucky charms in London – the Smoke – and Brighton, but had now gone back to selling herbs again – the spread, because they spread 'em out. Micky told him it was no good, and said this wasn't a bad market here, but what had Knocker made?'

'Then Knocker took his money out,' cried Hope.

'Yes. He'd thirty-six bob. And he said he hadn't made a fiver in one day since Bank Holiday. Then Micky said he didn't want to go round with Billy Fitt's fair because he'd just got a good display for his mystery packets and he was going up to Newcastle, which is a good district these days because there's plenty of loose money about up there. But Knocker, who's not quite so smart as Micky, said he'd take the train up to London and see Billy Fitt, with his hat in his hand. Then he said they'd better be scarping – that is, hurrying off – to try and make a sixpence or two from the punters, the customers.'

'And now you two had better be scarping,' said Hope.

'Just take your titfers down the apples and pairs, because Uncle Fred is going to tell me how to make the punters bid up tonight.'

Timmy and the Professor made for the door, but Timmy hesitated before going. 'I understood the last thing that was said. He told us to mind the rozzers – that's the police. He'd heard something, so it sounds as if they're all ready for us.'

'Yes, I heard him,' said Mr Hassock solemnly. 'And I only wish to God I could get up and run the show myself, police or no police. But I didn't ask you two to join me to run into trouble of this sort, so I shan't blame you if you want to back out.'

'I shall,' cried Hope instantly. 'But I know they won't.'

'Shut up, girl!' said Mr Hassock.

'I have seen my country destroyed,' said the Professor slowly. 'So this is only a little thing. Whether the people of Dunbury wake up or go to sleep, does that matter? Yes, I think it matters very much. Because now everything matters very much. When all the little things are put together they are a very big thing. That is what we have to remember. Therefore, apart from any personal loyalty, there can be no backing out.'

'And I'm with the Prof. I don't always know what he's talking about,' said Timmy, producing a professional grimace, 'and I doubt if he does. But I'm with him. Also, body and heart and soul with the good old firm of Hassock, with which – man and boy – I have had the honour to be associated these many, many years. Thanking all friends present for the charming gift of the silver fish-knives and the testimonial from the Mayor and Corporation – yours gratefully – T. Tiverton. An' we'll be down at the Hall in good time tonight, ready for anything.

214 LET THE PEOPLE SING

An' just behave yourself with Dr Buckie, Mr Hassock. Remember she has her work to do.'

Outside the Cottage Hospital was a large, elderly saloon car that had once been painted a horrible green. Leaning familiarly against this monster was a weatherbeaten youth with wide blue eyes. Roger Liss again.

'Is she in there?' he asked.

They said she was, and would be there for some little time yet.

'I wonder if I ought to wait,' he mumbled, looking appealingly from Timmy to the Professor. 'You see, I don't want to catch her at the wrong time or in the wrong place. I think I told you, she suddenly buzzed off, leaving me clean up in the air, just as if she'd absolutely finished with me – and I don't want to spoil it now.'

'Doesn't seem a lot to spoil, when you come to look at it, does there?' said Timmy.

'No – I see what you mean – but seeing I've taken a hell of a deal of trouble trying to find her – well, I don't want to spoil it. But I've not much to do these next few days and I've fixed myself up here. Do you mind telling me – what's happening to you people?'

'Young man,' said the Professor, slowly and solemnly, 'we are about to tear the town wide apart. Whatever that means.'

'That's the stuff,' cried the young man, lighting up at once. 'But what's Hope going to do – I mean, tonight?'

'Tonight, we try again,' said Timmy, 'an' if you're in the Little Market Hall, which is underneath the big one, you'll have the pleasure of seeing Miss Hope Ollerton trying to do a bit of auctioneering, that is, if the police let her. In short, there might be trouble.'

'Is there any chance of Hope walking into some sort of shindy?'

'There might easily be.'

'I'll be there,' cried Roger. 'I might come in handy. And I'll have *Green Hell* here outside. What d'you think of her? What a bus! The bike's being patched up so I borrowed this from the back of a garage we do business with. *Green Hell*, I call her, and you'd know why if you had her to drive. You can feel the old engine curling up and trying to snap at your feet. The hand-brake hits you on the knee when it thinks you're not looking. When you throw in your clutch you think the whole dam' thing's coming in half. I'd run you down,' he added with that sudden lack of confidence which warned them he was thinking about the girl again, 'but I think I'd better hang on and have a word with her. I hope she won't be angry when she sees I've turned up again.'

'If she is angry,' the Professor told him, 'then you be more angry and shake her a little and then tell her she is a beautiful girl and embrace her tenderly.'

'Here I say! I couldn't possibly. You don't know her. I tell you, she can be fierce.'

'But you can be fiercer, for I have seen you.' The Professor paused, then added softly: 'That is just what I did, with another beautiful girl, a long time ago, in another world. Yes, and perhaps it is another world we see when we are young and happy in love.'

'It seemed like that to me once, Professor,' said Timmy wistfully. 'I'll swear the very stage doorkeepers were different, and even bottled stout didn't taste the same. I can remember, silly as I look. Here, come on, Prof, an' leave the lad to it.'

The lad did not appear to enjoy being left to it. He looked rather hopelessly at the backs of the pair now marching down the hill. He lit a cigarette, pulled at it furiously, then clean forgot about it and when he still found it in his mouth, at the moment when he was about to greet a perfectly strange young woman emerging from the hospital, he hastily flung down the miserable end of the thing and stamped upon it. Then he sat and brooded, for what appeared to be several weeks, slumped on the running-board of the car. There were several more false alarms. Finally, having decided that a girl he did not look at but knew was there, hurrying out, must be Hope, he did not move forward this time but determined to be casual, saying Hello at the last possible moment. This he did, only to find that the girl was not Hope at all, that she replied cheerfully and encouragingly: 'Hello yourself!' and waited for more, that his stammered apology sounded both idiotic and very ungallant, and that the girl had hardly swung away before Hope herself was standing there in front of him, as cool as he was hot and bothered.

'What's the matter, Roger? Won't she have anything to do with you?'

Now Roger had imagined this scene many times, deciding to play it this way or that, to greet her warmly or to be cold and casual, but it had never begun like this. He was at a disadvantage right from the start. He would be. Always the same when he was with Hope.

'I thought it was you,' he muttered.

This did him no good. She raised her eyebrows and gave him a wide reproachful stare, then as she spoke she began to move slowly away, so that he had to tag along after her. 'Surely I don't look like that! You must have a very queer idea of me, to think I look like that.'

'I wasn't looking at her properly.' And they walked on in silence for a few moments. He did not dare to break it to tell her that he was leaving a car behind.

She decided to change tactics now. 'I didn't know you

were in Dunbury, Roger,' she remarked in a vaguely kind tone, rather like an absent-minded great-aunt.

There were several dashing replies that he might have made to this, but somehow they did not occur to him in time, and he merely mumbled, drearily: 'Well, I am.'

'So I see.' She smiled graciously as she half-turned, as if she were royalty in its Daimler. 'And how's business? And your motor-bike?'

'It's being overhauled. How's yours?'

'Also bust. That thing never was any good. How you could think it was, I can't imagine, Roger. Seems to me you owe me an apology.'

Seeing that she had been delighted when he had found the motor-cycle for her, had been pleased, to say the least of it, when he had offered to escort her down from London, and had then coolly given him the slip, without a word of explanation, any apologies ought to come from her. If he had told her so very firmly, she might have respected him. If he had ignored her faulty conduct and pretended to have been sorry for his own, he would have pleased her. But being young and foolish and in love, he did neither but went blundering into the danger zone between them. 'Well, I don't see that,' he muttered. 'The idea was I should come along and see it was all right. Only you dodged off – didn't you?' he ended feebly.

'And you went charging all over the place,' she cried indignantly. 'Asking people and talking about me in public. And I call that the limit – by gosh – I do, the absolute limit. When I heard that, I was furious. Still am. Yes, furious.' She quickened her pace, holding her head very high.

'I only wanted to make sure you were all right,' he said, with his uncanny instinct for saying the wrong thing.

'All right! Why shouldn't I be all right? Good Lord –

here am I, who've been knocking about for ages, earning my own living, having all sorts of adventures and tough times, and just because you go round to a few garages trying to sell them something they don't want, you talk about making sure I'm all right! Gosh!'

Once again feeling miserable and guilty though not quite sure about what, Roger could only mumble that he was sorry.

This only annoyed her still more. She couldn't very well make another direct attack upon him when he was so abject, so that it spoilt her fun, and what was more important she was annoyed because once again he was so abject. So there had to be another change of tactics. Now she was detached, lofty. 'We're having a most amusing time here accept for poor Uncle Fred landing himself in that hospital – because the local nobs aren't behaving very well, and tried to break our agreement, so now we're starting a revolution, more or less. Do you know Sir Reginald Foxfield?' she enquired graciously. 'He gave me lunch the other day. He's rather nice, though of course we're against him.'

'You wouldn't like some tea or anything?' asked the young man, feeling all over again that she hadn't the least interest in him and that he was like a kind of worm trying to attract her attention.

'No, thank you, Roger. I've had some. But probably you're hungry – are you?' She stopped and turned, giving him a smile so artificial and irritating that it asked to be slapped straight off her face. He looked at her mournfully. 'Well, hurry off and get something. I know how you hate missing meals.'

'No, honestly, Hope, it doesn't matter.' And if there is a hangdog voice as well as a hangdog look, then he produced it now.

'Well, if it doesn't matter to you it certainly doesn't matter to me. But I turn down here, and as I'm going to be very busy I must fly. Are you staying here long?'

'I – well – I don't know,' he stammered miserably.

'Really? Well, good-bye, Roger.' This time there was no possible chance for him to follow her, and he was left standing awkward, rather open-mouthed, and wretched. 'Idiot!' she said to herself as she hurried away, and now really was annoyed with him for making her behave so badly. Nobody had ever made her behave so badly as this ridiculous Roger Liss. What was the matter with him? Or, for that matter, with her?

As for Roger, he went striding back to the hospital to retrieve *Green Hell*, bewildered, frustrated, and as was usual with him at such times, though he was not really an aggressive fellow, full of fight. Clearly she had no use for him, and if he had any sense, he told himself, he would push off as fast as *Green Hell* would take him. But having tried this before, he knew that although the mysterious tormenting girl would give him no happiness here in Dunbury, she had the power of turning all other places into dreary wastes where a chap didn't know how to pass the time. To go out into this disenchantment – and on a Saturday evening, too – was simply too much to expect a chap to do, however badly he was being treated. All he could hope now, and he did hope it like mad for the next two hours, was that these strange doings in the Little Market Hall might at the best give him a chance to win her favour and even at the worst enable him to let off a little steam. A real rumpus and barney now, eh? Why, that would be grand. So in good time he parked *Green Hell* as near the Market Hall as possible. He waited half an hour – and it was now after seven – for the doors to open. There were fifty or sixty other people waiting for them to open, too. Finally, at the risk of being seen and immediately snubbed by Hope, he went round to the side entrance and entered the smaller hall to discover what was wrong.

He caught a glimpse of Hope, but she was busy unpacking a lot of stuff on the platform, and he did not dare to disturb her. But at the far end of the hall, behind the main doors, he found a very worried Timmy.

'See what the artful devils have done,' said Timmy, pointing. 'They've gone and padlocked these doors and taken the key away. And of course the caretaker's gone off for the day. The idea is that we'll give it up as a bad job. An' that's just what we won't do. But we can't even make a start if these doors won't open. Me an' the Professor have had a good try, but we can't shift this padlock.'

Roger had a look at it. He was just in the mood to stand no nonsense from padlocks. 'I'll have these doors open in two minutes. Now what we want are a hammer and a chisel.'

'I don't seem to have mine on me,' said Timmy, with a fine irony that was clean wasted.

'I'll get 'em,' cried Roger as he hurried away. He was the kind of young man who could establish friendly relations at once with any sort of mechanic or workman, for he stood high in the great modern brotherhood of the mechanical-minded; and so it was not long before he returned from the nearest garage with a hefty hammer and a broad hard chisel. This time Hope noticed him.

'If you'd really like to do something useful, Roger,' she called out, in a very easy friendly style, 'you'll go and get those doors open.'

'I'm going to,' he shouted, and felt now that if necessary he would tear them apart with his bare hands. With a formidable cold fury he attacked the chain of the padlock, and soon had cut it through. Triumphantly he and Timmy swung back the two big doors. The hall was open to the market square. The people who had been waiting came trooping in, and soon they were followed by a hundred others, many of whom, of course, had attended the session on Wednesday. After another ten minutes the hall itself was filled, and as before there was a crowd packed into the wide entrance and extending well back into the square itself. And already, before anything had happened on the platform, they were offering in chorus the famous Mrs Moly her roly-poly.

'Come on, chaps,' said Hope, in a state of great excitement and wickedness, to Timmy and the Professor. 'They started it – we didn't. But we can give 'em an accompaniment.'

So the Professor thumped the piano again, while Hope and Timmy banged away happily at the drums and effects. The people roared and thundered that Mrs Moly should have her roly-poly, that Father mustn't be given any cockles, and then fell upon the more recent but equally lilting idiocy of *Hoopy-Toopy-Toots*. They could be heard all over the market square.

This time it was not Inspector Parkin but his sergeant who first appeared. He arrived by the side entrance at the back, and was on the platform before anybody had realised he was in the building.

'Now then!' he bellowed, holding up his hand as if stopping the traffic. The chorus died down, though there were a few catcalls from the back.

'Now you three, drop it,' he said very sternly. 'If you touch them instruments again, you'll be under arrest. And this is the last warning.' Then he addressed the crowd. 'You've all been told once, but I'll tell you again –

for the last time. This 'ere her-hall 'as no licence for singing an' suchlike. It's illegal on these premises. So them who doesn't want to get into trouble 'ad better go quietly 'ome – '

'Oo, I daren't go 'ome,' a mocking voice called from the back. And another said plaintively: 'Kiss me, sergeant!'

'An' we'll 'ave none o' that,' shouted the sergeant angrily. 'Or I'll be taking names in a minute. Now just drop it an' get off quietly 'ome.'

'Just a minute, ladies and gentlemen,' Hope shouted, rather grandly.

The crowd clapped and cheered her. Shouts of encouragement came from the back.

'Now you be careful, young woman,' said the sergeant.

'The sergeant says I've to be careful,' Hope went on at the top of her voice. 'What about, I don't know.'

An impudent and amorous youth in front sounded as if he were about to tell her, but was told to shut up, very fiercely, by Roger Liss, who was sitting very close to him and was quite ready to wring his neck.

'But I want to explain,' she continued, enjoying herself now, 'that my uncle – who's had an accident – took this hall from your town council, and paid a deposit for his fortnight's rent, to give you a free show and to hold his famous auction sales – which he's held all over the country – and we've a perfect right to be here. We're not doing anything wrong. And you want us here, don't you?'

They roared their assent to this artful question.

'Now I warn you,' the sergeant began again.

'And I warn you,' cried the spirited young woman. 'We took this hall to sell our goods, and now I'm going to start selling them, and if you try and stop me – we'll – we'll bring an action for damages.'

The audience applauded this, too. 'I can't stop you

selling your goods,' said the sergeant. 'Not this minute, that is. But if it's likely to lead to a breach o' the peace, I can – an' I will. So just be careful.' And he stepped back a pace or two, to watch the proceedings.

And now Hope showed that she must have been carefully coached by the experienced Mr Hassock. 'I'll tell you why I'm going to ask you to buy some of our things. First, for the principle of the thing. We came here to do business, and we're not going to be diddled or bullied out of it.' More applause. 'And the other reason is, though we can't expect to make any money here in Dunbury – because your town council has behaved so badly to us – we're not millionaires, we have all this stuff here, and my uncle has a contract to take so much stuff every few weeks, so we can't afford to take it all away with us. Now I'm not an auctioneer or anything like that – I've never done this before – but I can tell you that just because we don't want this Dunbury trip to be a dead loss, I'll let you have everything at cost price, less than you'd get it in any shop. Honestly I will.' She smiled at them, so that about twenty youths hurriedly fingered their money and were ready for bankruptcy. 'I wonder if a few of you gentlemen in the front would help me by coming forward and passing down some of the things?'

Along with a few others the impudent and amorous youth darted forward but he was not the first to arrive at the edge of the platform. Roger was there first, and it was Roger who took charge of these volunteers, who offered no resistance to that wild look in his eye. And in the next twenty minutes these young men had handed over and received the money for two dozen gents' shirts, three dozen gents' ties, ten dressing-gowns, four dozen pairs of silk stockings, and eight imitation pearl necklaces. The things were really cheap; the crowd was sympathetic;

Hope proved a good saleswoman; and behind her both Timmy and the Professor were hard at work opening fresh packages. They were now starting on cutlery, for a change.

'And this is just to give you nice, settled-down, married people a chance,' shouted Timmy, who felt it was time he gave his famous personality an airing. 'A bit of useful stuff now, mother.'

'And my uncle, Mr Fred Hassock,' cried Hope, in her loudest and brightest tones, 'told me this afternoon that this was the very best bargain he'd had this year. They're all stainless steel, Sheffield's best. We got hold of them because a big order for Shanghai had to be cancelled. They came to us as a bargain, and they're coming to you as a bargain. Now here's a sample case – eight of each, knives, forks, spoons, and carvers – cost you four or five pounds anywhere else. What am I offered?'

They started at ten shillings and then the bidding went up briskly.

'Where's that sergeant?' Timmy whispered to the Professor. 'Did you see him go?' And of course the Professor, who had done his fair share of unpacking, but as usual had been meditating gravely on the state of the world, had not seen the sergeant go.

'But he has gone, so it does not matter,' the Professor concluded.

'I'll bet it does,' said Timmy uneasily. 'I'll bet he's up to something. You just see.'

And they hadn't half a minute to wait. The first case of cutlery had been sold, to a stout woman who told everybody in her part of the hall that her niece would be married next week; and they were beginning to bid up briskly for the second one, when there was a swirling of folk at the back, some cries of protest, and then there came charging in, like three indigo bulls, the sergeant followed by two constables.

'Oh!' cried a disgusted and very youthful voice, 'blue-bottles!'

And now who should come stamping in by the side entrance and clump his way on to the platform but – Inspector Parkin. And he was not alone. With him were two important-looking personages in dinner-jackets. One was very tall and thin and bird-like, and the other was burly, dark and scowling. Hope recognised them at once as Colonel Hazelhead and Commander Spofforth.

'What you goin' to sing for us?' asked a voice from the back of this solemn trio.

'Just keep order down there, sergeant,' roared Inspector Parkin.

The sergeant stared round fiercely and finally fixed a terrible accusing gaze on two mild young girls who were busy sorting out toffees from a joint packet. A few voices were heard demanding roly-poly for Mrs Moly. One of the constables, zealous with the eye of the inspector upon him, tried to push his way to this roly-poly group but had to give it up because he trod on a fierce little woman's foot and she threatened him with an umbrella.

'Now anybody who doesn't keep quiet,' bellowed Inspector Parkin, who appeared to be in danger of apoplexy, 'is going to find 'imself in very serious trouble. Now, sergeant, keep order down there.' He wheeled round and glared at Timmy. 'And *you* keep quiet.'

'What, me?' cried Timmy indignantly.

'You 'eard me. Yes, you!'

'Why, what are you picking on me for?' demanded Timmy, quite forgetting that he was a hunted man. 'I didn't make a sound.'

'Well, just see that you don't, that's all,' said Commander Spofforth severely, butting in without shame.

This annoyed Hope. 'You leave him alone,' she said fiercely.

It also annoyed Timmy, who was not to be bullied like this. 'I haven't made a noise,' he announced deliberately, 'but now I will, just to show there's no ill-feeling.' And he stepped forward to the drums and carefully beat upon them the familiar and comforting *tom-tiddly-om-pom* and then used the cymbals to bring out the final satisfying POM-POM.

'Hurray!' cried the people, and gave Timmy a tremendous round, which he acknowledged in a neat professional manner. For the next few minutes there was great confusion. Colonel Hazelhead stopped Inspector Parkin from exploding by making peculiar noises at him. Commander Spofforth was shouting and shaking his fist at Timmy, and Hope was shouting angrily and shaking both her fists at Commander Spofforth. Roger Liss, his eyes dancing now, was sitting on the edge of the platform, watching Hope and this unpleasant burly fellow and ready at any second to bound forward and do terrible execution. Down in the audience the sergeant was trying to lay a hand on a very cheeky lad but was being held up by a pugnacious man with a drooping black moustache. One constable was still trying to rid himself of the fierce little woman, and the other was engaged in a shoving match with three hobbledehoys and a fat man. The roly-poly group were accompanying these activities with a curiously derisive version of their own favourite chorus.

Inspector Parkin and Colonel Hazelhead came to the very edge of the platform, and then the crowd became quiet out of sheer curiosity.

'Colonel Hazelhead, who's a Justice of the Peace, will say a few words,' the Inspector announced grimly.

Another type of orator might have made a serious impression upon the crowd at this moment, but unfortunately Colonel Hazelhead, with his very staccato style and queer swallowing noises and his unintelligible patronising gentility, was dead wrong. He seemed to the simple folk in front to be a comic turn.

'*Um-yah* Inspector Parkin . . . as magistrate *um-yah* . . . *um-yah* very serious situation . . . may have to exercise *um-yah* . . . *um-yah* discretionary powers . . . stand no bolshie nonsense . . . *um-yah* . . . *um-yah* last warning . . .'

The crowd, some of whom had been tittering and giggling from the start, now burst into a tremendous roar of laughter. It was as if a comic midget had been squeaking angrily at a good-humoured giant, who had now suddenly caught sight of the droll little creature. There was nothing mean or directly antagonistic about this laughter. It had been evoked by the instinctive common feeling that this long thin pompous chap, with his bleating and yammering, was a comic turn.

And now, just as the great wave of laughter was eddying down and the puce Colonel was protesting and the purple Inspector Parkin was yelling and stamping, the newly-formed Dunbury Band produced its carefully rehearsed effect. Playing lustily, they marched in single file through the side entrance up to and across the platform. Carried away by the music and the dramatic appearance, the crowd rose at them, cheering like mad. For half a minute the Inspector and the others were too surprised to do anything but stare. Then they sprang into activity, and old chaos came again. Down in the hall, the sergeant, who had been reinforced by two more policemen, was the centre of an immense scrimmage, out of which shouts and screams were rocketing. On the platform it was worse. Colonel Hazelhead had rushed, shrieking with fury, at Tom Largs, who was standing there beating time, and Largs had coolly pushed him off, with the result that he got jammed between two circulating clarinet players. Inspector Parkin had charged a couple of cornets, only to receive an accidental bang on the head from the euphonium of the bandsman next to them. Maddened by this he had charged again, this time arriving at the rear of the band, where the gigantic Harry was pounding his big drum, and Harry had cheerfully missed a beat in order to thump the Inspector over the head with his drum-stick. Behind the band, which was still marching and playing after a fashion, crossing the platform and then re-crossing it, were Timmy, Hope and Commander Spofforth, who tried to vent his rage on Timmy, but was stopped by the girl, and now in a black fury he seized her arm and twisted it so that she let out a shriek. This was the moment for which Roger Liss had been waiting all evening, indeed for months, and in three seconds he had rushed through the tail end of the band, had pulled Hope away from the commander, and had completed the whole movement by letting that gentleman have a perfect right on the point of the jaw, so that for a long time afterwards he had the strangest notions of how that evening ended. And now police whistles were being blown; the scrimmage had become a gigantic free fight; and the whole place, from the back of the platform to the entrance, appeared to be shouting and screaming and rocking.

Warned by a shout from Roger to follow him, Timmy had seized Hope by the hand and was hurrying her out of the side entrance, with the Professor only a step or two in front. They cut through the curious idlers and the emerging bandsmen at the entrance, Timmy still leading Hope and following the unmistakable tall figure of the Professor. The night was moonless and heavy with cloud and seemed very dark after the lighted hall. Hope was still shaken and rather dazed, for violent adventures of this kind are more humorous in the remembering and telling than they are at close hand, so she did not know what was happening. But she knew that Timmy was right in insisting that they must clear out, and she made no protest when they arrived at a large car and the long arm of the Professor shot out of it and pulled her into the back seat beside him. Timmy climbed into the front, with the driver. The car then sounded as if somebody had shot it twice; it whined and growled; it was shot again; it roared and quivered; then it shook itself very hard and went bouncing out of the square.

'Here I say, where are we going?' Hope cried, after a minute or two. It looked as if they were leaving the town.

Timmy turned round. 'Hadn't time to tell you. But didn't you hear what young Mitterly said when he came in with the band?'

'I didn't even notice him,' said Hope.

'Well, he said the police had called at our digs,' said Timmy. 'So they probably went to yours, too. Only thing to do, then, is to clear out for the week-end. Save a lot o' trouble.'

'It is certainly much the wisest course of action,' murmured the Professor. 'Though where we can go, I do not know.'

'Neither do I,' said the girl, not very cheerfully.

'Ah, that's where I come in,' cried Timmy triumphantly. 'I've got an old friend who runs a big new pub – one of these fancy road-houses it is – not far from here. She'll look after us. It's where I went the other night.'

'Quite a one, aren't you,' she told him, recovering now.

'Well I suppose I can ring up Uncle Fred in the morning, and tell him all about it.'

They were now outside the town, rattling and wheezing along a straight main road, which could only just be seen in the fitful illumination of the two ancient lamps. Every now and then other and newer cars went shooting past, with a quick snort of contempt. Hope stared hard at the humped back of the driver, who was leaning well forward, all intent, as he had every excuse to be with such a rum old car, on his driving and the road.

'Who's that?' she whispered to the Professor.

'It is a friend of mine,' he replied softly, with a chuckle or two. 'He offered to take us away in this motor-car of his. Do not worry.'

'I'm not worrying,' said Hope, now raising her voice. 'I say, Timmy, I was in such agony when that beastly Commander twisted my arm, I didn't really see what happened. Was it – was it – Roger Liss who knocked him out?'

'It was,' said Timmy, almost smacking his lips. 'And I never saw a prettier knock-out. It was even better than the one he handed to that driver in *Annie's Pannie*. I tell you, that boy's got a wonderful action. What a middle-weight he'd have made if he'd settled down to it!'

'I shouldn't have thought he had it in him,' said Hope coolly. 'You surprise me. Where is he now? Ran away, I suppose?'

'Why – ' Timmy began, but got no further.

'Yes, I think he went away then,' said the Professor loudly and cheerfully. 'Perhaps he does not like to be treated so badly. Perhaps he is proud, that young man.'

The girl made a vague snorting sort of noise. 'The subject doesn't interest me.'

'No, it is very boring,' said the Professor. 'Let us talk of other things.'

'Let's not talk at all. Golly, what a night!' And she settled back, leaning trustfully against the Professor, who smiled rather sadly in the darkness and returned in memory to a lost happy world.

Nothing more was said until they arrived at the 'Dog and Bell,' which was blazing with light and besieged by half the cars in the county. 'Gosh!' cried Hope, peering out, all curiosity now. 'What a place! Looks like a big night here. Perhaps they won't want us.'

'It'll be all right,' said Timmy confidently. 'I remember Daisy telling me – they're having a treasure hunt tonight. Just wait. I'll find her.'

When he returned there was an excited plump little red-haired woman with him, and she almost pulled them out of the car. 'Come on in, come on in,' she cried. 'Daisy Barley's the name, dear, though I suppose it's before your time. My God – what a looker! Where do you find 'em, Timmy? How d'you do? – pleased to meet you, Professor. Yes, I've heard all about you. From my dearest old friend, Timmy here, my favourite man. Come on, we'll fix you up. I wish I could have been with you tonight, but it's Saturday, an' business is business, silly as I look. Oh – an' here's the boy that fights 'em all. Oh, of course, this is the girl. Well, now I understand.'

'Hello, Roger! Thanks for the ride,' said Hope, being very cool though a shade trembly in the voice. 'I knew it was you. At least, I guessed.'

'Did you?' And he was not merely cool but downright frozen. He had never spoken to her in such a tone before. 'Well, glad you're all fixed up. Good night, all.'

'But – Roger – '

He did not reply, did not even look at her again, but climbed back into the car, furiously raced the old engine, then went rattling into the night. She stared blankly.

'Wouldn't stay, eh? Never mind, duckie, you go in an' take it easy.' And Daisy waved a hand at the nearest side door. 'He'll be coming back tomorrow, you can bet your boots, an' you'll be looking like ten million dollars by then an' you can larn him to go off like that, nearly making you cry.'

'Making me cry! D'you think I'd cry for that idiot? I never cry, anyhow. And as for him, why, I've absolutely no use for him – and he knows it.' And Hope gave a last contemptuous stare at that part of the night that had swallowed Roger and his car, then turned sharply, put her chin in the air, and stalked haughtily towards the inn. Only certain vague gulping and sniffing sounds indicated that she might possibly be a trifle disturbed.

'Well, you chaps can say what you like,' said Daisy, steering Timmy and the Professor after the girl, 'but there's something to be said for not still being young – and silly. And here we are – an' the very first thing is to have a nice stiff drink – an' then just make yourselves at home.' She gave a careless nod to indicate the glittering bedlam, now threatening to overwhelm them. 'If it doesn't seem like home yet, it soon will.'

CHAPTER XI

NOT QUITE A TYPICAL ENGLISH SUNDAY

AT FIRST this Sunday morning in Dunbury was like all
the others, so quiet that the sun might have suddenly
bounced up the sky in the middle of the night and caught
everybody napping. It was a nice fine morning, with a bit
of mist round its edges. Not many people came out to
enjoy it. Some whole streets were so empty that they were
like theatrical sets waiting for a harlequinade. At a few
places in or near the market square the startling placards
of the Sunday newspapers had been set out in a row,
together with piles of the papers themselves, in which
important journalists emphatically affirmed what they had
equally emphatically denied two or three Sundays before,
members of the peerage described their beautiful women
friends, and the smallest piece of gossip from Hollywood
was given far larger type and far more space than the
combined arts and sciences and philosophy of Great
Britain. For those who preferred the spoken to the printed
word, the enterprising young minister of the Norfolk
Road Congregational Chapel was preaching on 'Traffic
Signals on the Spiritual Road'; and the Rev. S. A. Philips,
B.A., of the North Dunbury Wesleyan Church had arrived
at 'Your Problem and the Bible: 3'; and our friend the
rector from West Dunbury was allowing his curate, a keen
sound young fellow who had bowled a very useful off-

break all summer for the Dunbury second eleven, to try his hand at 'St Paul and Appeasement.'

Here and there were the usual solitary men, standing at corners, smoking short pipes, and ruminating. What thoughts are theirs, as they survey these empty Sunday streets, nobody knows; they may be meditating upon doomsday, or wondering whether to make it a glass of mild at the 'Lion' or half a pint of bitter at the 'Bull.' A few pairs of sedate elderly men walked out of town to look at the yellow autumn fields and the golden mists and to discuss cottage property and the retail coal trade. A few packs of small boys, returning from Sunday School, jeered at each other, kicked stones to ruin their best shoes, and pointed and shouted at every passing car. But there was not much traffic: a bus or two, with a leisurely Sunday air about them; a few of those overcrowded little family cars wobbling and wandering uncertainly towards the country; and now and then an impatient fast car, thick with the dust of some distant county, knowing and caring nothing about Dunbury, but roaring on to some mysterious remote destination, and leaving behind it a deeper quiet and emptiness that had some hint of irony.

Even after half-past twelve, when church- and chapel-goers were about the streets, and groups of young men, like football teams in mufti, appeared from nowhere, and pairs of girls, either very solemn or giggling, flitted by, and solid citizens massively emerged to enjoy a pint before tackling the roast-beef-and-Yorkshire, even then, at the peak of morning, the town was still quiet and empty. There seemed hardly any life in it. But of course you could not see all the housewives, with wisps of hair falling over and tickling their hot shiny faces, who were having their weekly wrestle with kitchen stoves or gas-ovens, to produce that roast-beef-and-Yorkshire and a nice apple pie to follow. Plenty of activity among them, of course, and, indeed, Nature can show us few creatures more active, cracking and sparking with a more furious energy, than women who have spent a warmish morning in an undersized kitchen cooking a dinner they do not particularly want to eat themselves. Sheer exasperation seems to give them a higher voltage. It is at these times when husbands and children, who now seem like so many idiotic passengers who have suddenly invaded the engine-room, are apt to hear something unpleasant about themselves. Barbed words come whizzing out of the kitchen. Vast edifices of masculine sham now crumble at a blow. Mines that were set in position weeks before are now exploded, in a flash, between setting down the gravy and picking up the custard. If you want a revolution to begin among the English lower-middle class, you have only to call out all the women at about ten minutes to one on any Sunday. Anything left standing after they had done would most certainly be destroyed by the crowd of hungry and embittered husbands.

This explains why this Sunday quietness of Dunbury has deceived so many historians, who have failed to understand how the seeds of rebellion came to be sown during that week-end. On Saturday afternoon, nobody in Dunbury but our friends and the members of the band was ready to rebel, and the people still seemed to have no will of their own. By Monday afternoon, as we shall see, the whole temper of the place had changed. Sunday then was really the critical day. But Sunday, as we know, was apparently as quiet as usual. The mistake, of course, is to search for evidence in the streets and to forget that in England it is what happens behind walls, curtains, closed doors, that counts. Because it was a fine and rather warm morning, and likely to be one of the last of them, the women were hotter and more exasperated and irritable than usual. Kitchens seemed smaller and stoves more devilish than ever. But that is not all. We know now, on the evidence of Edward Mills and Robert Stevens, wholesale butchers long established in Dunbury, that the consignment of frozen carcases from the Argentine that had been delivered to the retailers on the previous Thursday, chopped up by them on Friday, and on Saturday sold as Sunday joints, was an unusually faulty consignment, for which the shippers at Birkenhead had subsequently apologised. The truth is, the refrigeration on S.S. *Panavo* had misbehaved itself during this last voyage; the plant had pretended to be freezing its carcases to the usual temperature when all the time it had really been taking them down to a much lower temperature, penetrating every tissue with its icy breath; with the result that the whole consignment of beef was tough and all the joints that came from it could not be properly roasted with the usual allowance of time. Then, what happened? Why, many families had to wait nearly an extra half-hour; others did not wait so long but found their beef horribly tough; and some others again both waited and then had tough meat at the end of their vigil. This meant that tempers were lost all round.

We shall never know the details, of course, but it is clear that at most of these dinner-tables something was said, probably by a husband or older child anxious to try and make a hot and irritable mother forget her grievances, about the town's affairs and that queer rumpus last night in the market square; and that these innocent remarks only roused that devilish marksman in the exasperated feminine mind, so that good safe men were accused of being so many sheep, all manner of people were bitterly attacked for their arrogant disregard of the people's rights and grievances were no longer minimised for the sake of peace and quiet. The afternoon, which should have been passed in sleep or in slow companionable strolls that were almost like sleep-walking, was now spent, by a husband downstairs on the sofa, by a wife upstairs on the bed, in a heated and bitter stock-taking; quarrels were in the air; tough meat hastily swallowed in an unfriendly atmosphere was refusing to be digested and was turning itself into hot discomfort and downright pain; and so what should have been the Sabbath calm of a golden autumn day was rapidly assuming the aspect of that leaden quiet which comes before a thunderstorm.

In the evening, when the men went round to their clubs or pubs and the women entertained each other, when one married couple called upon another for talk and a bit of cold supper, the fires of resentment were not put out but were eagerly stoked. 'Now here's an instance,' they cried. 'And I'll give you another example,' they shouted. 'And just listen to what happened to me,' they demanded sternly. Husbands who had been accused by their wives, that dinner-time, of being willing to put up with anything, of having no backbone, now showed that they were men of very different mettle. Wives who had vehemently denounced the borough council, the West Dunbury snobs, the *United Plastics* slave-drivers, at about half-past one that day could do no less than reiterate their views eight hours later, and tended to declare that they had been feeling and thinking like this for months. A common mood sustained them all. Not only were they, on the conscious level, infecting each other, but from another direction they were being controlled by a profound change in the feeling of a collective unconscious Dunburyan, who did not live in this street or that, who could not be seen or heard, but who nevertheless determined what should be the spirit of the town. Thus, the Dunbury that went to bed, considerably later than usual, on this Sunday night was not the Dunbury that our friends had known, and indeed was not the Dunbury that anybody had known for a hundred years.

But the very persons who had done more than any others to bring about this change knew nothing about it, for they were all well outside the town, still at the 'Dog and Bell.' One of them at least, Timmy was having a very good day. To be trotting about behind the scenes in this large, prosperous road-house, with its bustle of prep-aration, the cheerful coming and going of customers, was grand fun. It was the nearest thing he had known for years to the big successful variety theatres of the old days. Daisy was here, there and everywhere, now chaffing some of the patrons in the dining-room, the cocktail bar, or near the front entrance, now harrying her odd staff, now having a quick gossip with Timmy in the nearest corner. And then Timmy had an opportunity to have a crack with these old friends of the profession now so strangely disguised as cooks, barmen, and what not. Furthermore that very Sunday night they were to have a 'Grand Variety Concert' instead of the usual dancing. The band, includ-ing what was left of the Musical Wilsons, was to be there. Walter Shafton and one of the dining-room waiters had worked out a good little double turn. Jimmy Flagg would come in from the cocktail bar and do some of his old Denga Din tricks. Katie Sacker would be brought in from the kitchen to sing some of her old numbers. Lottie Carwell's daughter could play most of her mother's suc-cesses on the piano-accordion. There were one or two other local acts too. But not Daisy herself, for these days she could not be persuaded to sing a note in public. 'No, duckie, very nice of you an' all that,' she would say, 'but when Daisy says she's through, she *is* through.' However, she acted as mistress of the ceremonies at these Sunday concerts of hers, and was regarded as one of the best turns there. And now, of course, although there had not been time to announce him, among the contributing artistes was that famous eccentric comedian, T. Tiverton.

During the slack period in the afternoon they had a rehearsal in the dance-room, with Daisy bustling them about and making out her programme and notes, after much pencil-licking. Hope and the Professor were there, but only as audience. Hope said she wasn't good enough, and the Professor pointed out that the professional pianist was much better than he was. Both Hope and the Professor were rather subdued, not quite their customary selves, but Timmy was too busy and excited to ask them why. And after all they could not be expected to enjoy the old pro atmosphere as he was doing. Ever since Daisy had insisted that he should give them a quarter of an hour or so at the concert, Timmy had been thinking about his material and working out a suitable act. To do his stuff again in front of Daisy and some of these old hands, after all these years of cheap halls and bad touring shows, was a bit of an ordeal, as he pointed out to the Professor. 'An' I tell you, Prof,' he concluded, 'it takes me back thirty-five years an' more, back to when I was doin' little trial turns. Honestly, I don't even feel any better than I used to then. Nervous as a kitten.'

'That is as it should be. But I think you are not simply frightened and nothing more,' said the Professor, who had the great virtue of giving any subject presented to him a full weighty consideration. He did not, as lesser-minded persons do, shrug away a topic. He brought all his mind to bear on what was set before it.

'No, you're right there,' replied Timmy thoughtfully.

'I'm in a way all excited and warm and happy about it. Queer mixture, eh? Bit barmy.'

'You are an artist, a true artist,' said the Professor slowly, 'and your natural responses are always those of an artist.' He had to raise his voice now, for the rehearsal was still going on, and the remnant of the Musical Wilsons was working up to a fine *fortissimo*. 'To be an artist is to be more alive than ordinary men but to feel more incomplete than they do, so that the artist feels that he is nothing, or worse than nothing, a kind of criminal, unless he is practising – and successfully practising his particular art. It is a mistake,' he shouted, for now the Musical Wilsons had suddenly and surprisingly arrived at the finale to the *William Tell* overture, 'it is a mistake to suppose – as we Europeans so often do – that the English are rarely artists. The official tradition in England is hostile to art, and so I think is the social tradition based upon the prejudices of a ruling landed class, the feudal England. But a great many of the English, because they are dominated by what lies in the unconscious, are genuine if only half-developed artists. In this they are the opposite of the French, who are controlled by their conscious minds, and appear to be more deeply artistic than they really are. If England were to be conquered, were suddenly to lose nearly all its wealth and power,' he ended at the top of his voice, 'I think the English would soon be famous throughout the world as a race of poets, painters, and actors, and life on this strange misty island, which is essentially romantic in its atmosphere, would seem to the Americans, Russians, Chinese, who by that time would do the world's manufacturing, to be a fairy tale of art and dreams.'

'That's right,' said Timmy cheerfully, and then gave the Musical Wilsons an encouraging hand.

'We're goin' to have a good little show tonight,' cried

Daisy, triumphantly bearing down upon them. 'An' don't think I do it for the money, because I don't. I'd make more without the show 'cos I don't charge 'em anything for it an' they'd drink more if they'd nothing else to do but lift their elbows. I do it 'cos I like it, an' it makes me feel I'm still in the profession an' not just a landlady. There's a cup of tea waitin' for us up in my sitting-room. Come on, duckie,' she shouted to Hope, and then waited a moment to watch that young woman drag herself rather reluctantly out of a deep chair. 'My God, boys, if I'd ever had looks like that kid, I'd have been the Queen o' Sheba or somebody by this time. Look what I've done with what I have got! An' yet I'll bet ten to one this kid does nothing but get herself married to some rate collector or gas inspector or the chap that cuts the butter and cheese in the nearest grocer's, an' then settles in one o' them damned mingy bungalows you see all round London, with a pram taking up all the room in the hall, an' a fumed oak bedroom suite, an' ten days at Cromer if you're lucky – '

'You're out there, Daisy,' said Timmy, as they went upstairs. 'She says that what she'd like is to have a bright red sports car and go roaming around on her own.'

'That's what she told you. Tell you anything, girls will. Don't know what they're saying, half the time. Read some bit o' rubbish in a magazine – an' believe it's what they'd like. Girls! Haven't I been one? Off their chump! They get to know ten chaps, we'll say, and there isn't a pin to choose between these chaps. But a girl will go an' treat the first nine as if they were muck, an' then, just when you're wonderin' how she's come to be as tough as that, she goes crawlin' to number ten and begs him to wipe his boots on her. Isn't that so, Professor? You're a doctor, you know.'

'At a certain period there is a curious balance in the feminine psyche,' the Professor began, 'a balance that – '

'That's just what I've said many a time,' cried Daisy, now entering her sitting-room. 'An' by the way, seeing you are a doctor, you might see if this kid's all right. She seems to think she isn't very well.'

'But I am not a doctor of medicine,' said the Professor, rather startled. 'My subjects are history, philosophy, and, to a lesser extent, psychology, and – '

'That ought to be good enough for her,' replied Daisy carelessly. 'After all, I don't suppose she needs any medicine. Now let's have a nice cosy cup o' tea. Come in, duckie – and cheer up.'

'Come an' sit by me,' said Timmy, making a little fuss of her, for the girl didn't look half her usual self. 'What's up? Your uncle's all right, isn't he? Did you phone him?'

'Yes, and he's all right. Getting on very well. I told him all about last night, and he didn't seem to mind at all. I mean, about us not selling so much stuff because of the bust up. He says that everybody in the town's heard about it and is talking about it. By the way,' she added, looking at Daisy, 'I forgot to tell you. Uncle Fred's sending the doctor at the hospital, a woman called Dr Buckie, out to dinner and to the show here tonight – he's standing treat for her – so can I arrange with you – '

'She can sit at my table with the rest of you,' said Daisy rather fiercely. 'And if she's a doctor, you'd better tell her what's the matter with you, hadn't you?'

'There isn't anything the matter with me,' said Hope, falteringly, weakly, not like her usual spirited self at all.

'Well then, if there isn't,' Daisy continued in the same rather fierce and contemptuous tone, 'why are you behavin' as if you were a sick kitten or something?'

'Here, Daisy, steady on!' Timmy protested.

Two days ago, if anybody had spoken to the girl like that, she would have flared up at once, but now, to the dismay of the two men, she merely drooped, and her mouth fell open and great piteous tears gathered in her eyes.

The impetuous Daisy flung herself across and hugged the girl, exclaiming that she hadn't meant anything unfriendly but had only been trying to buck her up a bit. There, there, there! And now the girl really wept in a wild sort of way, and Daisy comforted her in vague general terms, and Timmy and the Professor, who didn't like to go on steadily with their tea and on the other hand didn't want to look as if they'd deliberately stopped going on with their tea, nibbled and sipped and stared at the photographs on the wall and tried to give the impression that they were not really and solidly there in the room at all.

'I know I'm being silly,' said Hope, when she had recovered and the tea party was in progress, 'and I apologise. I'm not usually like this. In fact, I've never been like this before. It all started this morning. I was all right last night, just a bit tired, that's all. But today I feel quite peculiar. I can't take any real interest in anything and half the time I don't feel I'm really here at all.'

'It might be tummy,' said Daisy earnestly. 'Lobster does that to me. "For God's sake, boys," I've said many a time, "don't let me see it on the table. I can't resist a go, an' I'll be sorry tomorrow." What have you been eating, duckie?'

'No, it's not that sort of feeling at all. Quite different. I don't feel upset in that kind of way.'

'No,' said the Professor, who had been staring at her very solemnly, 'I think it is mental not physical. It is – '

'Please, Professor, don't begin about the feminine soul again and Goethe and stuff, because, honestly, today I couldn't bear it.' She turned to Daisy again. 'It's really peculiar. I can't take the least interest in anything, feel everything's far away, and yet at the same time I feel something terribly exciting's going to happen soon. But of course I haven't the least idea what it is. And I feel – sort of – oh – all vague and misty – as if I hadn't quite wakened up. Yet I don't feel sleepy in the ordinary way. And I can't bother talking to people – I don't really want to tell you all this, but you've been so jolly kind and I don't want you to think I'm ungrateful or just a fool. I've never been like this before, honestly.'

'No, that's right,' Timmy assured her. 'As lively a girl as I've ever seen, up to now.'

'Yes. Well, what's wrong?'

The Professor thoughtfully consumed his piece of walnut cake, brushed his moustache with a large blue silk handkerchief, then cleared his throat and began: 'Conflict. Although people will not often admit it, the fact is that the *idea* of conflict is not unwelcome to our minds. It appears to offer release. In these days – '

'Just a minute, Professor! What is this?' enquired Timmy anxiously. 'We don't want to get clean off the subject.'

'I am about to offer an explanation of Hope's present state of mind. The basis of my theory – which comes, of course, from remembering our affair at the hall last night – is the sharp contrast between the *idea* and the *reality* of conflict. Now if – '

But this time he was interrupted by a scream of laughter from Daisy, who leaned back, kicking her little heels into the carpet, almost drumming with them, while she laughed helplessly until the tears ran down her cheeks, carrying with them streaks of eye-black and ruining her rouge. 'Oh dear, oh dear, oh dear!' she gasped. 'God knows what kind of a piebald mess I'm going to look after this, but I can't help it.'

Timmy laughed with her out of sheer sympathy, but Hope looked bewildered and the Professor still looked grave. 'No doubt this contrast between the *idea* and the *reality* of conflict may seem laughable – '

'No, it isn't that. I wouldn't laugh at that in a thousand years, couldn't squeeze one single giggle out of it, an' don't really know what you're talking about.' Daisy sat up, and now produced a compact. As she tried to repair the damage, she said with a finely dramatic air of the cool and casual: 'But I know what's wrong with her now.'

'What then, Daisy?' asked Timmy hurriedly. 'Never mind the face. It'll keep.'

Daisy pointed triumphantly with her powder-puff. 'She's in love.'

'Oh gosh!' cried Hope in dismay. 'No, I'm not. I can't be. It must be something else.'

''Course it isn't. Written all over you. Why I didn't spot it right away, I don't know, 'cos I've had it badly enough myself. You're in love. You've gone an' fallen, head over heels. You're done for, duckie, clean done for. Sunk!'

'I believe Daisy's right,' said Timmy slowly. And the Professor nodded his agreement.

'Right?' shouted Daisy, as if she had been insulted. 'Of course I'm right. I ought to know, the packets I've had. No mistake at all, dear. What's wrong with you is that you've suddenly gone an' fallen in love.'

'But – but – who with?' stammered the girl, staring helplessly. 'I mean – it doesn't make sense to me. I'm not *thinking* about anybody.'

'That'll come later,' said Daisy grimly. 'This is the first mushy stage. You'll do plenty of thinking later on.'

'But who is it? How can I be in love if I don't even know who it is?'

'Oh – well – ' and Daisy waved a hand carelessly – 'it might be anybody. Probably that boy with the red face and the bright blue eyes – '

'Roger Liss! But I don't like him,' Hope wailed.

'That's nothing. I don't think I ever liked any of mine,' said Daisy thoughtfully. 'Liking doesn't seem to have much to do with it. If it's liking you're talking about – why then, Timmy here's my chap. Always liked him. Didn't I, you little devil? But I never went all goosey and mushy about you, did I?'

'I'm *not* goosey and mushy,' shouted Hope, scarlet and defiant. Daisy grinned; Timmy looked vaguely sympathetic; and the Professor examined her carefully through his spectacles. The tide of scarlet rose, but the defiance went ebbing out, and the girl fled.

With her the fun of it went. Now the little tea-party suddenly became almost tragic. They did not speak; they remembered; and it was as if they sat by the great river of time.

'Professor, you know all about everything,' said Daisy, after this long silent interval. 'Tell me, what is this falling in love business? Is it just sex having its fling?'

'That is the accepted explanation,' replied the Professor, smiling a little. 'But it seems to me to miss the essential point. Romantic love, which does not come to all persons – and indeed some whole races seem to know nothing of it – cannot be explained merely as part of our sexual life. We who have known this falling in love, as you call it here, realise this. Many of those who theorise write without real knowledge because they have never fallen in love themselves, have never been in that state of mind which our young friend is just beginning to experience.

The ancient philosophers, who wished above all things to be in complete control of themselves, called it a kind of madness.'

'And they weren't far out either,' said Daisy, who for the first time in her life found herself in agreement with the ancient philosophers.

'They were nearer the truth, I think, than our modern sexual theorists. It is a form of possession. It is as if something superhuman, a wandering god, took possession of the mind, using it temporarily for some purpose far beyond our knowledge, as a man keeping bees in his garden might take their honey and use it for some purpose, let us say as a birthday present, that they could not hope to understand. And though there can be pain and sorrow in this state of mind, now and then while we are so possessed there are moments when the god lends us his vision, and we see the world transformed and illuminated. And that is why, my friends,' he concluded, smiling at them, 'we were so sad a few moments ago. We were remembering that transformed and illuminated world.'

Daisy stared at him in open admiration, and then nodded at Timmy as if in confirmation. 'You're right, Timmy. He really is a one. Like a – like a – talking book.'

'What did I tell you?' Timmy was the triumphant showman.

'Well, boys,' she cried, getting up and somehow starting to bustle about before she had really done anything at all, 'you must excuse me. There's a hell of a lot to do, an' if Daisy doesn't see they do it, nobody will. An' I've a feeling – an' I'm ready to have a small bet on it – that the "Dog and Bell" is in for a very good night.'

During the next two hours all the signs pointed that way. The evening itself was on her side, for it was calm, spacious, but a trifle melancholy, and it whispered to people all over the county that they could hardly do better than take a run in the car to the 'Dog and Bell,' first to enjoy the journey there and then to rid themselves of any melancholy influence, any autumnal Sunday-night brooding, by enjoying whatever Daisy had to offer in the way of refreshment and entertainment. Cars came rolling up from all directions. Very soon both the cocktail bar and the smoke-room were well filled. The men being bluff, hearty, baronial; shouting to each other: 'You're dead right, ol' boy.' The women were dividing themselves into two classes; those who had decided to be smart, bold, sophisticated, demanding exotic and potent cocktails, crying 'Cheers!' before they gulped them down, and for ever daubing on more lipstick to replace that which they had left on the rims of glasses and the ends of cigarettes; and those who had decided to be shrinking, ladylike, fluttery, and to insist upon 'only just a sip' because anything more would be disastrous to a creature so delicate, so winsomely fragile. And the men whom Jimmy Flagg, who had a very good memory, loudly recognised by name, nearly choked with pride, and immediately ordered rounds of the most expensive cocktails he could mix, and gave him a large tip. And everybody was having a very good time, which means that perhaps two or three out of them all were happy and the rest were noisy, unnatural, extravagant and foolish.

By quarter to eight there was not a single free table in the dining-room. A few tables were not yet occupied, but they had all been reserved. Daisy herself was entertaining her own guests there tonight, at a round table in the middle of the room. And very odd they looked, too. First, there was Daisy herself, in the very brightest green you can imagine, fairly loaded down with jewellery and trink-

ets, and with a make-up that made the ruddiest good
health look like the final stages of anæmia. Then there
was Hope, who was still abstracted and dreamy but who
now was so lovely that a great many women there were
crossly asking their men why they were staring in that silly
way: 'She's a very good-looking girl, no doubt,' they said,
'but that's no reason to go on staring like an idiot, with
your eyes bulging out of your head.' Then there was Dr
Buckie, who had left off her pink-rimmed spectacles and
was wearing tweeds, and no longer looked like an intellectual blacksmith in a skirt but had moved up the social
scale and now looked more like a vast gentleman farmer
trying to amuse a children's party with a little mild female
impersonation. She was in excellent form, however, and
drank, in one swigging, smacking gulp, everything offered
to her. And of course there were Timmy and the Professor, who sat there looking rather worried, as if they
expected at any moment to be slapped on the back by Dr
Buckie and sent crashing into the cutlery and glassware.

'Tell you what, Mrs Fillans,' shouted Dr Buckie, who
had been staring round the room, 'you're makin' a
damned good thing out of this. Why didn't I think of it,
instead of sweating away at medicine, eh?'

'I don't do so bad,' replied Daisy, a trifle overawed by
this tremendous female doctor. 'But it's not so easy as it
looks, dear, believe me. It's quite a responsibility.'

'Dare say. Lots of snags, no doubt. But you're not
wakened up at three in the morning by a perforating
appendix. Try that for a responsibility. I could do with a
bit of this, just for a change.' She stared round the room
again. 'Hello, isn't this young Foxfield? What's his name –
Sir Reginald, eh? Dodgin' his mother for once and after a
square meal, eh? Don't blame him.'

Sir Reginald, who was alone, had gone across to a table

for one, but now the waiter was shaking his head, obviously explaining that the table was already booked. As the young man was turning away, he caught sight of Hope, and brightened at once. Looking a little confused, he came over and greeted her. Somewhat confused herself, she introduced him to Daisy.

'Well, if there isn't a table for you, there isn't,' said Daisy. 'I don't know who's booked that table you wanted, but you can bet your life *somebody's* booked it.'

'I know,' replied Sir Reginald, rather gloomily. 'Waiter chap said a fellow had booked it over the telephone.'

'You sit down here with us,' said Daisy firmly. 'Here, George – lay another place here. We can squeeze you in all right, dear,' she continued, to Sir Reginald, 'and look what you've got sitting next to you – eh?'

'By jove – yes,' said the young man, goggling at Hope, who was nothing like as cool now as she had been the other day at Dunbury Hall. 'Awfully glad to see you again, Miss Ollerton. Been thinkin' about you a lot. Reg'lar shindy after you went, the other afternoon.'

'There'll be some more shindies soon,' Dr Buckie shouted at him across the table. 'There was one last night. Hear about it?'

Sir Reginald blinked and then grinned. 'Yes, rather. Spofforth got knocked out, I hear. Been askin' for it for a long time – howlin' cad.'

'Well, from what I hear,' Dr Buckie went on, complacently, 'there'll be more shindies. So look out! As for me, I'm all for it. Time the place came to life a bit. And you want to tell some of your West Dunbury friends on the Hospital Committee that I said so, you're welcome to, my boy.'

'Oh – quite – but wouldn't dream of it, though,' said Sir Reginald. And then, over the soup, he whispered to

Hope: 'Terrifyin' woman that, eh? My mother's on that Hospital Committee, and when the two of 'em get goin', I believe it's terrific. Wonderful to see you again. Great surprise too. Just dodged out here for a decent feed – you know what it's like at home – terrible – an' worse than ever on Sunday nights. Hello – I say – what's the matter?' For the girl was suddenly doing some astonishing colour changes, first from pink to white, then from white to blushing red. He looked round to see if anything had happened that might account for these startling changes of colour, but all he noticed was that the small table he had tried to claim was now occupied by a red-faced young man who was staring in their direction. 'Do you know that chap?' he enquired. 'I mean that fellow who's just come in. Not a nuisance or anything, is he? I mean, could I do anything, eh? Tell him not to stare?'

'No, no, it doesn't matter,' said the girl, and now gave him much more of her attention and smiled at him a good deal. After several minutes of this, she was annoyed to discover that Roger was no longer busy staring at her but was actually enjoying his dinner. Just as if, like Sir Reginald, he had gone there only to dine; though ironically enough, Sir Reginald, overwhelmed by her unexpected nods and smiles, was hardly noticing what he was eating.

The only person who watched and savoured this comedy was the Professor. Daisy and Dr Buckie were exchanging noisy observations and reminiscences across the table. And Timmy was beginning to rehearse his act to himself, and, like the conscientious performer he was, he was also conserving his energy, giving as little of himself as possible before the moment arrived when he would have to give them everything he had.

When everybody had settled down at the little tables in

the dance-room, where they could have their drinks while the show was going on, Timmy went round to the back of the improvised stage and stayed there. He hadn't felt so nervous for years. For a long time now he'd been telling himself regularly that he was as good as ever (if not a bit better), but how did he know he was? 'I can't prove it from my engagements,' he told himself. 'On paper I'm a dead flop.' And it was some time since he'd had a real audience, who knew the difference between the real thing and mere routine clowning. Now this might be an improvised sort of show, but there was nothing cheap and scratched up about the audience, which represented a fair cross-section of the people you had to be able to amuse when you were bang at the top. If this lot didn't think he was good, then he wasn't good any more, and might as well be dead and done with. What had the Professor said? An artist feels he is nothing – or worse than nothing, a sort of crook – unless he's successfully practising his art. 'That's me all right, Prof,' he murmured, giving himself a last look in the mirror.

'All right, Timmy?' Daisy looked in while the audience was still applauding Katie Sacker. 'Let 'em have it, boy. This is my best night since I came back from Australia – an' don't think I'm tight 'cos I'm not – I'm just happy. Now if you're ready, I'll say my piece. God's truth, doesn't this take you back, eh? I don't know whether to laugh or cry.' Out she went.

'Ladies an' gentlemen *and* friends,' she began, in a very easy effective style, 'I've just been saying at the back I don't know whether to laugh or cry. No, that's not a joke, but have a laugh if you want to. The reason I'm feeling like this is that I can't help bein' reminded of good old happy days, for there turned up here last night one of my oldest an' dearest friends – one of the finest little comedians that ever trod the boards – who as a great personal favour has kindly consented to help us with the show tonight – so that I now have the privilege an' pleasure of introducin' – Timmy Tiverton!'

It was a grand build-up, and though only the older people there – and probably not all of them – could have remembered him as a star, they all took their cue from Daisy, who led the applause as she stepped off the platform and then backed to her seat, and they gave him a tremendous welcome. He was wearing a dress suit that he had borrowed from two fellows on the staff, a much too large coat and waistcoat from one and some baggy trousers from the other, and he wore these things with a hopeless and rather pathetic attempt at dignity. He had on just sufficient make-up to emphasize his own features, to throw into relief that large, droll, sad face. He came blinking on, pulling his suit together, so to speak, and then smirking and bowing with a ridiculous air of importance.

'Oh – ladies, ladies an' gentlemen,' he cried, in his character as an eager, fussy, futile little chap, 'thank you very much – very, *very*, very much. Decent of you! Yes, decent. I – er.'

And here he stopped, not because they were laughing, although they were, but because he had just seen, there, sitting by himself at a little table, not more than five yards away, that thick-set, square-faced chap who had cried 'Hey!' at him the other night, both here and in the market square. There he was, and as grim and watchful as ever, not even smiling. At any moment he might cry 'Hey!' again, bring a heavy hand down on Timmy's shoulder and probably say: 'Tiverton, you're under arrest.' Thinking that Timmy had stopped to let them have their laugh out, the audience immediately obliged him, but while he grimaced and made more fussy little bows, he was saying to himself: 'Steady, Timmy my boy, steady! He won't dare to start anything until the act's over, and that gives you still a chance to slip away. An' make him laugh, for God's sake!'

From now on there was a kind of despair in Timmy's clowning, or rather there was more despair than usual, for no good clowning is without it. The clown is even more eager and anxious than the rest of us are; he wants to show off, to be triumphant and soaring, just as we all do; and like us he finds terrible obstacles in the way, but his obstacles, which include the strange malice of apparently inanimate objects, are more obvious than ours, and we feel that we could easily overcome them. The clown knows, however, that he will be defeated by the hostile world, is already wincing even at his first eager appearance, but is also telling himself that this time, just for once, perhaps everything will be all right – 'though,' you can almost hear him adding in despair, 'I doubt it.' All this was, of course, with Timmy as with most drolls, purely intuitive: what he understood, to the finest of fine shades, was the relation between him and his audience; he wanted to produce a certain kind of laughter and he knew instinctively how to set about it with any reasonable sort of audience; and now, with this new despair added, he gave them everything he knew. He was less broadly eccentric than usual and more of a character. This character he played was suggested at once by his appearance and first entrance: the eager, fussy, half-witted entertainer, very anxious beneath his superficial air of self-importance, who cannot go on with any part of his entertainment because something always goes wrong; he cannot remember the words, the necessary props have been forgotten, there is no music or the band is mysteriously hostile, and so forth. Instead of singing his chorus songs, Timmy merely began them and then became confused. Instead of rattling off some of his funny stories, he singled out the oldest of them, the ones nearly everybody knew, and then would start telling one, would not remember how to go on, would start another, then recollect what he had forgotten of the first, jump to the second again, and land himself in an awful maze of comic anecdotes. The senior member of the Musical Wilsons was in charge of the little band, and to him Timmy appealed for more and better co-operation, and whispered to him certain suspicions he had about the double-bass player. Mixed with all this, so that it kept popping out at odd times, was a fragmentary recitation about a race-horse; and finally, to make the confusion worse confounded, he kept returning to one of those hopelessly involved and senseless political arguments, the like of which you may hear in many a taproom, in which the speaker, growing more forceful and angry the less he has to say, cries: 'All right, then! Take Baldwin. Just take Baldwin. What did Baldwin say about the working man? You don't know. But I know. And I'll tell you what Baldwin said about the working man. Or Winston Churchill. Take him. Go on, just take him!'

At the end of twenty-five minutes, shining and drenched with sweat, his collar and front a sodden wreck, the suit almost back to front by this time, still wildly hoping against hope that something worthy of the audience's attention would come out of this dreadful confusion, this litter of half-remembered songs and stories, of broken recitations and idiotic argument, still appealing for the tiniest measure of co-operation from the jeering band, still demanding a moment's patience from the ladies and gentlemen in front, this little man that Timmy played now suddenly looked stern and noble, wiped his brow, held up an impressive hand, and cried: 'Ladies and gentlemen, my friends if I may so call you – there is one thing – ' And here the band played a very noisy triumphant march, through which the little man went on orating, quite inaudibly, but making more and more triumphant gestures, until he had apparently said all that there was to say on this mysterious subject, and then folding his suit round him, almost as if it were a toga, he stalked off triumphantly, with the band playing louder than ever. And the audience, almost exhausted by laughter by this time, stamped and roared and shrieked for him to come back. When he did come back, smiling and shaking his head, the man himself now and not the character he had played, he was startled by the shout that went up and the storm of applause. He had heard nothing like it for years and years, and had felt, deep in his heart, that he would never hear anything like it again. And when finally they let him go, this weary little middle-aged man dropped into a chair, and wept.

Daisy, so radiant that she looked like a tiny set-piece in a firework display, found him like that, his head buried in his hands, his shoulders shaking, and the shrieks of praise died in her throat, and she put her arms round him and talked to him for a minute as if he were a tired child and the hour too late and the world too big and strange. During that minute there was no show, no 'Dog and Bell,' no years that were gone for ever, and Betty and some others they had both known and loved were neither alive nor dead, and time was a dream.

'Why, you little devil,' cried Daisy, when all that was over, 'you're ten times better than ever. You wrecked me – and the rest of 'em. Why, there's a fellow there in front – '

Yes, there was, Timmy suddenly remembered, in a panic. There certainly was a fellow there in front, and any moment now he might be crying 'Hey!' So he interrupted Daisy at once: 'Thanks, Daisy, it's been grand. But I've got to change – quick.'

''Course you have,' she told him, pulling him out of the chair. 'You're wet through. Run upstairs – you know the way round the back. We'll be through with the show in about half an hour, though after that act of yours, it's really over now. See you later, dear.'

But she didn't. He couldn't be found anywhere. Half a dozen of them, to say nothing of the 'Hey!' man who was most persistent, combed the whole rambling place for him – but no Timmy. Daisy was nearly frantic, and almost threw some of her patrons out in her anxiety to be rid of them, in the hope that when they had all gone Timmy would emerge from some mysterious hiding place. But when at last they all did go, and it was quiet below, and she sat upstairs having a drink and a sandwich, still there was no news of Timmy.

Hope came in, looking tired and wan. 'Here,' Daisy told her sharply, 'give yourself a drink an' a bite, dear, an' don't look like that.'

The girl said that she didn't want anything and sat down and looked as if she wanted everything, including a fair slice of the moon. 'Have you seen the Professor?' she asked, rather mournfully. 'I've been looking for him – I want to talk to him about something rather special – and he hasn't gone up to bed and I can't find him anywhere.'

'The Professor?' Daisy stated at her.

'Yes. Do you know where he is?'

'I'd forgotten all about him,' cried Daisy. 'My God! – has he disappeared too? You know that Timmy's vanished

– absolutely clean gone, the tormenting little devil – and not a soul knows when and where.'

Hope shook her head sadly. 'No, I didn't know.'

'You didn't know! Where have you been then? I've been pulling this damned house down tryin' to find Timmy. An' now you say the Professor's disappeared, too. I'm goin' barmy. An' stop looking like that.'

'I can't help it,' said Hope, almost tearfully. She waited a moment, then lowered her voice: 'You see, I hung about, hoping he'd come up and speak to me. And I got rid of Sir Reginald, who'd just bored me stiff all night. But I thought that might make him come up and speak to me. And he didn't. He just disappeared.'

'Who did?' shouted Daisy. 'I feel I'm going off my chump. Who wouldn't come and speak to you and then disappeared?'

'Why, Roger,' and Hope looked quite surprised that she should have to answer such an obvious question.

'Oh! – you mean that fighting boy who's gone on you?'

'He isn't any more. He can't be – or he wouldn't have just gone away like that. And I know it serves me right,' she wailed, the tears gathering now, 'but I've only just found it out tonight. He must be the one I've gone and fallen in love with, and I seem to have started – just – just when – he's stopped.'

Daisy looked at her in dismay. 'I don't know who's the sillier – us or them. Men! They come charging into your life like mad bulls – must have this, must have that – makin' your life a misery – an' then ten to one the minute you're beginning to fancy 'em they begin doin' their vanishing tricks.'

'What are we goin' to do?' asked Hope, who under this sudden stress of love appeared to have lost all initiative.

'We're goin' to have another drink an' another sand-

wich, an' then we're goin' to bed, duckie, that's what
we're goin' to do. And if you ask me, those three went off
together — which might explain why your boy friend
popped off without a word — but why in God's name they
had to go off, I don't know an' perhaps never will.'

She might have continued in this vein for some time
but there came a knock and following it – the Professor.

'You're back then,' cried Daisy, opening her eyes very
wide. 'Is Timmy with you?'

The Professor was surprised. 'No. I have not seen him
since he performed in the concert. After it was over I went
for a walk, to be quiet in the open air. What has happened
to Timmy?' He listened to Daisy's story and then to
Hope's. He was comforting. 'Do not worry,' he told them,
'for I know it will all come right. Timmy will return as
soon as he can, because he is very happy here and is very
fond of you.' Then he smiled at Hope. 'You will see the
young man tomorrow. Tonight perhaps he was jealous.
Now he is saying to himself somewhere that he will not try
to see you tomorrow, but he will – or if not tomorrow,
then the next day. But this next time you must be kind to
him – eh?'

'Golly, yes!' cried the girl, with enthusiasm.

'Now I call you a comfort,' Daisy told him. 'Any news
on the road outside?'

'But yes,' replied the Professor, twinkling at them. 'I
met a man who had been spending the evening in
Dunbury, and he told me that the townspeople are
becoming quite excited and rebellious.'

'And that man of ours, Candover,' said Hope, coming
to life again, 'will be in court tomorrow. Dr Buckie told
me.'

'Now it's high time,' said Daisy, raising her glass, 'I
looked into all this. Anybody wanting little Daisy

tomorrow needn't call at the "Dog and Bell" because she'll be in Dunbury, seein' if any fur's flying an' lookin' for her Timmy. An' just let anybody lay a finger on that crazy little devil,' she added, immensely defiant, 'an' I'll – I'll – *slaughter* 'em. All right – go on – have a good laugh – but you haven't seen me yet with my monkey up. I tell you, I'm fierce.'

'That I can believe,' said the Professor. 'In the grip of certain emotions, the feminine psyche – '

'An' that'll do from you at this time o' night, Professor. Give yourself a drink, an' then toddle off to bed.'

CHAPTER XII

DUNBURY LOSES ITS TEMPER

It was one of those drizzling and hopeless Mondays. A couple of months might have elapsed during the night, for yesterday had twinkled with the gold and faint mists of early autumn, but now it seemed winter. Though it was no longer warm, it was not yet healthily cold; though there was no sun, there was also no clean spatter of rain; there was only an oozing, drizzling greyness everywhere. It was also a Mondayish greyness. And this was one of those Mondays that seem to be the entrance to an immensely elongated week, as if all Siberia will have to be crossed before Thursday afternoon. It arrived like a little doomsday. By bus, bicycle and on foot, Dunbury wage-earners went off to work like people going into exile. Men who had stayed up late the night before, discussing their grievances, felt worse than ever this morning. Housewives who had lost their temper on a fine Sunday were not going to recover them on such a Monday as this, designed to make the weekly washing a misery. After Sunday's rebellious mood, it only needed a Monday like this, a damp, grey, ticket-of-leave Monday, to bring the whole town nearer to downright revolt. If all the persons in authority there had had a glimmer of tact, they would have gone about their business very carefully indeed, turning orders into requests, distributing a few compliments and smiles, hinting at early prospects of promotion, whispering here and there that this day was really a little ordeal, a kind of sporting test of industrial or civic goodfellowship; but most of these persons in authority had no tact at all, overlooked the supreme fact that we share a common human nature, and of course were feeling Mondayish themselves. So now we can see that probably it was all inevitable. Even the atmospheric pressures over Iceland and east of the Azores were doing their share.

The whole morning, then, all over the town, there were sudden little explosions. Considered separately, they were of no great importance. But we know that they cannot be considered separately. These were not isolated explosions but the splutterings of an enormous lighted fuse. At the Paxton Street School, Mr Crowle, taking a class of forty in English History, suddenly laid down his book and announced that in his opinion our Hanoverian Georges had been just a 'blithering nuisance'. The waiter at 'The Bull' marched into the kitchen himself and told the cook that it was time she gave her gravy soup a six months' rest. Fat Joe Tile startled his wife and daughter in the *Fish Restaurant* by declaring without any word of warning: "Ere, Mother, Doris, d'you know what I think? An' just put that bucket down an' listen. I think we've 'ad enough o' this bloody place.' Four girls at the North Dunbury County School, brought before the headmistress for not having done their homework, told her that it was no use her writing to their parents because their parents had said they didn't see why there should be all this homework. At the *Parisian* hairdressing establishment, next door but one to the *Elite* picture theatre, Elsie Hatfield and Violet Ashby told Miss Wornum that they were sick and tired of her grumbling and that if she didn't like their work she could go and get two girls whose work she did like, because they had had enough. At the *Elite* itself, the manager, Mr Porson, had a very nasty argument with young Gregory of the film-renting company. The manager of Barclays Bank made the mistake of choosing this particular morning to go round to the *Central Garage* in the market square to make a fuss about his car, with the result that a very dirty young mechanic told him to his face that he didn't know anything about cars and that until he did he should keep his temper to himself. 'I don't come into your bank, showing my ignorance, do I?' cried the mechanic, and walked off whistling. The solitary boy employed at the sixpenny bazaar, when reprimanded by the manageress, kicked over a pile of newly arrived boxes, containing toys, and told her he would join the navy; and not ten minutes after this, the girl at the *Toilet Requisites* suddenly burst into tears and insisted upon going home, taking a head-ache and her friend from the *Music and Magazines* with her. And at this very same moment, three old employees of *Birch & Son, Builders & Contractors*, told Mr Birch himself that if he thought he could do that North Dunbury Baths job better, he could go and do it, and see how he liked it.

All this, of course, was a mere beginning. Or so many straws in the wind. Out at the *United Plastics* works, there was some real trouble. Here again, tact was lacking. In the parent company's vast works in New Jersey, USA, the great system had been speeded up yet once more, and details of these improvements had been sent across the Atlantic with a peremptory demand that Dunbury should adopt the new methods at the earliest possible moment, thus, as these American experts said, 'still further eliminating middle-processing operatives' time-energy wastage,' for that is how they talked and wrote, and made a very good thing out of it too. And this, of all mornings, was the time chosen to put these new methods into practice. One of the two assistant managers, with his secretary, and a couple of departmental works managers, all marched into one of the huge rooms, called a halt, and then began to explain why they were there.

'Now I'll show one of you girls exactly what you have to do,' said the assistant manager. 'It's quite simple really. You'll soon pick it up.'

'A nice bright girl now,' a departmental manager called out. On some days this would have raised a laugh. But this morning it didn't, not even a smile. This sinister circumstance passed unnoticed, however, for these managers were worrying more about distant Americans, who could write about 'eliminating middle-processing operatives' time-energy wastage,' than they were worrying about these people here in Dunbury. Really, what happened served them right.

A girl was pushed forward. She was still plumpish and pale but did not at this moment strikingly resemble the exotic and enigmatic creature of the film stories. Yes, it was Fern Mitterly; and this was her hour, and because she did not fail it her fame spread throughout the works and then throughout the town, so that for a time she was quite a little celebrity and attracted the favourable notice, among many others, of a brisk and rising young manager in the Dunbury Co-operative Society, who afterwards married her and then became a buyer for the Co-operative Wholesale Society in Manchester and provided her with a nice little bungalow out Knutsford way, where Mrs Mitterly now goes to stay and admires the shining radio-gramophone and helps with the baby clothes; and all because Fern was the one to be pushed forward that morning and when the test came did not fail it, but discovered an unexpected store of self-respect and courage.

'And what's your name?' asked the assistant manager, whose own name was Muir.

'Fern Mitterly, sir,' she replied in a whisper.

'Yes, of course,' said Muir, rather fancying himself now in this part. 'Well now, Fern, we're going to show you exactly what you'll have to do in future. Just a few changes, that's all.'

It was the departmental manager, who had been carefully coached after the employees had gone on the Saturday before, who now actually showed her what the new movements were.

'Come closer, everybody,' shouted Muir. 'I want you all to see what's happening.' They came, in silence, without the usual whispers and giggling, and watched. 'Now then, Fern,' he said, when the demonstration was over, 'do you think you can do that?'

Fern nodded, and then went and did exactly what the departmental manager had done, only hesitating once or twice. But because she had hesitated, she went through the movements all over again, this time without any hesitation.

'There!' cried Muir, pleased with himself and with her too. 'Nothing in it. You could show any of the others how to do it in less than five minutes, couldn't you?'

'Yes, I could, sir,' said Fern, looking queer about the eyes and mouth. 'But – '

'But what?' he asked, in a kind, loud voice, meant to reassure any doubters present.

'But I'm not going to,' said Fern, all in a rush. 'It isn't – it isn't – right.'

There was a murmur of approval from all the girls looking on.

'I don't understand you,' said Muir, very grand and distant now, the assistant manager with a secretary and a private office upstairs.

Miss Mitterly's reply to this was to burst into tears. There were more and louder murmurs from the other girls.

'Now what on earth's all this?'

The girl stopped crying as suddenly as she had begun. 'It's all right doing that once or twice, just for show, but – but how would you like to do it all day?'

'It's exactly what they've been doing for the last month in our American works.'

'I don't know anything about American works,' the girl retorted, really defiant now, 'but I do know it's not right to expect us to do it like that for nearly eight hours a day, not even if you paid us more – '

'There's no question of anybody being paid any more,' said Muir sharply. 'You can put that idea right out of your head.'

'What about putting this other idea right out of *your* head?' called a voice from the crowd. And this time there was a general laugh.

This annoyed Mr Muir, who glared round and then angrily demanded if Fern had anything more to say.

'Yes, I have. The way we have to handle that stuff all day is tiring enough as it is, and I don't see why we should just go and wear ourselves out to suit somebody in America – or anywhere else. It isn't right, sir.' And more general sounds of approval.

'Don't keep telling me what's right and isn't right,' cried Muir, longing to shake the wretched girl. 'And if you don't want to work the way we ask you to work, then you'd better go somewhere else. Now listen, you girls – '

'We're not going to listen,' cried a fierce dark girl,

darting forward. 'We're going to stand by Fern. Aren't we, girls?'

The girls shouted that they were. Muir told his secretary to take a message to the manager himself, while he took the two departmental managers into a corner and held a conference. The girls crowded round Fern, now a pale proud heroine, and the fierce dark one urged them to stand together. Several men and youths, their own work held up by this stoppage, came in to ask what was happening. When they were told, they stayed on, to see what would happen next.

The manager, convinced that young Muir had made a mess of things, happened next. He joined the conference in the corner, then came striding out of it, holding up his hand, as if the silence was still not silent enough for him. 'Six girls will be shown once again how to work this new method,' he announced, taking their consent for granted, 'and then those six will demonstrate it to the rest of you. I'll give you ten minutes. Except you,' he turned to Fern Mitterly, sharply, 'and you're dismissed. If you hand your card in upstairs, they'll give you a week's money. Now then – six girls – this way.'

The only girl who moved was Fern, who slowly walked out of the room, no longer a glamorous and exotic type, but a pure and noble working girl. The others watched her go in silence, but immediately afterwards all began talking excitedly and angrily.

'Now let's have no more of this nonsense,' shouted the manager, a thoroughly bad judge of a situation. 'We can't afford to waste any more time. We've all got work to do.'

'Well, go and do it, then,' somebody shouted.

'Who said that?'

'I did.' And a snub nose and a lot of freckles emerged from the crowd. It was young Reynolds, son of George

Reynolds, leading clarinet of the Dunbury Band. He was one of Fern's admirers, and had kissed her twice, once at a party and again at the end of the annual outing. 'And I'm not going to say I'm sorry neither. You'd no right to sack her like that. She only said what she thought.'

A dozen of the girls, led by the fierce dark one, loudly agreed with him. The manager was about to make another angry speech when Jessie Largs, one of the office staff, came hurrying in from upstairs. She was a sturdy determined girl, a feminine and younger version of her father, Tom Largs, and she enjoyed making provocative speeches even more than he did. This was a chance not to be missed.

'Now listen, everybody,' she began, breathlessly but with plenty of voice still left, 'that girl, Fern Mitterly, is being victimised. She was only speaking up for all of you – '

'You be quiet!' roared the manager.

'I won't. And don't let 'em treat you like this. You earn more than you get already and they're only trying to drive you harder. Come on, we'll all walk out.'

'Anybody who leaves this room will be instantly dismissed,' the manager bellowed at them.

'Don't take any notice of him, girls,' she told them.

'Come on, boys,' shouted young Reynolds. 'All stand together.'

'If we all stand together, we'll be all right,' yelled Jessie.

'Now I warn you all.' The manager pointed to Jessie. 'And you can take yourself out now. Whatever happens, you're not coming back here, I can tell you that.'

'I don't want to come back here,' she shouted, enjoying herself now. 'And you can just go and tell your American bosses that we're men and women hère and not robots. They can't come and machine-gun us when we go on strike. Come on, girls. Come on, boys. Let's leave 'em to think it over quietly, and tell their American bosses to keep their slave-driving systems where they belong. Come on, everybody, outside! We'll show them they can't treat us like dirt.'

And out they went, marching through one department after another, collecting everybody except a timid handful, and within half an hour not only were the new methods not in operation but the old ones had come to a complete standstill, and the wonderful system existed only in the blue-prints and files in the offices upstairs, where the manager and his assistants were now holding a most desperate conference. In another half an hour it was all over the town that at least half the *United Plastics* employees were out on strike.

A youth named Edward, employed in *Binns and Sons'* ironmongery and hardware shop, that old-established firm, heard the lightning rumour, which was of more importance to him than mere town gossip because he was walking out with one of the girls there. Also, he too was under the influence of this terrible Monday morning, and at present was hating the sight – the uncommonly dark and gloomy and congested sight – of *Binns and Sons'* ironmongery and hardware. Perhaps it was unfortunate for all concerned, though typical of this fateful day, that a few minutes after the news arrived there entered Mr Finningley, whom we saw, all smiles and bows, at the museum meeting, and with him Major Shiptonthorpe. Just as Mr Finningley had been determined to be impressively amiable and gentlemanly at Lady Foxfield's, so here, with Major Shiptonthorpe's eye upon him, he was equally determined to be stern and gentlemanly, standing no nonsense from the lower orders. And he could not have chosen a worse moment, for Edward, the assistant from whom he would stand no nonsense, disliked Mr Finningley at any time and now hated the very sight of his short figure and long moustache.

'Now look here,' he began, tapping on the counter.

'Yes, sir, what is it?' asked Edward, almost meekly. After all you can't be rude to well-to-do customers just because you're feeling annoyed with everything.

'I don't expect much intelligence from you people,' said Mr Finningley in a clipped, curt style that he hoped would impress Major Shiptonthorpe. 'But really – '

'Why don't you expect much intelligence from us?' asked Edward, cutting in calmly.

'Well, wouldn't be here, wrapping up pennyworths of tintacks, I suppose, if you – '

But Edward cut in again. 'I don't wrap up pennyworths of tintacks. I sell them in boxes for tuppence.'

'I haven't come here to argue, I've come to make a complaint – and a pretty strong one, young fellow – and if you don't choose to listen, though I believe you made the mistake, I'll have a talk to your employer.'

'Quite!' said Major Shiptonthorpe.

Edward, who was quietly coming to the boil, gave the major a surprised look. 'What do you mean by *Quite*?'

'Are you talking to me?' He was staggered.

'Of course I'm talking to you. You said *Quite*, and I'm asking you what it meant, because I don't see any sense in it.'

'Stop that,' shouted Mr Finningley, 'and listen to me. My gardener, who's nearly as big a fool – '

'As me?'

'Yes, as you, if you insist upon knowing. I say, my man came here with a very important order, nearly a week ago – '

'And we sent the goods on to your house an hour ago,'

said Edward calmly, 'and we didn't send them before because several of the fittings had to be specially ordered.'

'Humph! Hope you haven't made a mess of the order,' said Mr Finningley.

'No, I don't think we have,' remarked Edward quietly, almost dreamily, 'but I think it would serve you right, Mr Finningley, if we'd made a howling mess of it. Why should you come in here shouting about our intelligence and calling us fools? Where are your manners?'

Mr Finningley had no reply ready. But Major Shipton-thorpe took charge of the situation for him. 'Did I really hear you ask this gentleman where his manners are?'

'Quite!' replied Edward.

'You'll hear more about this,' said Mr Finningley.

'And if I hadn't an important engagement – but I'll write a very stiff letter to your employer.'

'For all I care,' Edward told him, quite rudely now, 'you can write a letter so stiff that it won't go into a letter-box. And now – I've some work to do even if you haven't.' And he banged down on the counter, very close to Mr Finningley's right hand, a half-opened parcel of cheap scouts' knives, several of which sprang out at Mr Finningley, who hastily drew back, and the next moment was gone, taking his Shiptonthorpe with him.

This was bad enough but there was worse to follow, and before lunch and in that very market square. The setting for this terrible scene was the far corner of *Pembrey & Co's* drapery and haberdashery shop. There in that corner was the awe-inspiring figure of Lady Foxfield, wearing a hat that suggested she was about to play charades, and tweeds so ill-cut and dingy that they established at once her social eminence. Now although Lady Foxfield had such big craggy features and such a stern, martial appearance, she had a genuine feminine passion for the arts of the needle, and worked away at tapestry, *gros- and petit-point*. As a rule her material came down from London, but it happened that this morning found her both out of wool and patience, and so, before going on to Mrs Hathersage's villa, where she was lunching, she had decided with some misgivings to see what Pembreys – 'the wretched Pembreys,' as she always called the shop – could do for her. So here she was, and at the other side of the counter was the latest addition to Pembreys' staff, a girl called Bessy Swinton, a girl with red hair and far too much lipstick and a detestably common bold look about her, a girl who had not been in Dunbury very long and had lately announced, to various young men in the back seats at the *Elite*, that she did not intend to stay there very much longer. And the other assistants were being very busy as far away from that corner as they could possibly contrive to be. But now and again they gave it a quick startled glance.

Lady Foxfield was behaving in the way she always behaved when she condescended to enter Pembreys', rather as if she had been called upon to ransack a dustbin. She picked things up very gingerly and then hurled them away from her, at the same time screwing up her face apparently to lessen the risk of infection. Now the coloured wools were flying out of her hands in every direction. She might have been trying to juggle with them. Also, she made little snorting sounds, and now and again closed her eyes, which presumably demanded an occasional rest from the disgusting spectacle of the wool, the assistant, the shop itself. At first, Bessy Swinton had been too busy bringing out more and more wool to notice how this customer was behaving, but when all the coloured wool they had was there on the counter, for this extraordinary woman to chuck about, Bessy had now time to observe her, first with astonishment and then with growing indignation.

'Oh! – no, no, no, no,' muttered Lady Foxfield, as if she were right down at the bottom of the dustbin now. More wool went flying.

'Can't you find anything you want?' asked Bessy, quite politely, though there was a dangerous glint in her eye. She disliked this drizzling Monday as much as anybody else.

Lady Foxfield did not answer this question, which seemed to her quite unnecessary. She was making it quite plain that so far she had not been able to match her wool from this wretched stock. As the counter was now covered with wools, she gave an impatient little push and sent a couple of loosely wrapped parcels clean overboard.

'I say,' said Bessy, after waiting a reasonable time for a reply to her question, 'you needn't throw everything about like that, y'know.'

Lady Foxfield stared at her in amazement. 'What did you say?'

'I said: "You needn't throw everything about like that." You're making an awful mess.'

'Do you know who I am?'

'No, I don't,' replied Bessy, 'but that isn't the point. I don't mind showing you all the wool we have in stock, but that's no reason why – just because you can't find what you want – you should throw it about. It'll take me at least half an hour to tidy – '

'I'm Lady Foxfield – of Dunbury Hall.' This was not announced with any heat, nor with any great emphasis; it was merely announced without any possibility of mistake. The girl was addressing Lady Foxfield of Dunbury Hall.

'I don't see what that's got to do with it.' And the girl did not look away or show any sign of confusion but continued to answer Lady Foxfield's stare with a steady young impudent stare of her own.

'Ask Mr Pembrey to come heah at once.' And now Lady Foxfield closed her eyes and looked as if she would not open them again until Mr Pembrey stood bowing before her.

'Mr Pembrey's away. He went to London this morning.'

Lady Foxfield now raised her voice so that it dominated the whole shop. 'Who's in charge heah?' she demanded.

Little Mr Tomlin had just slipped out to lunch, so Miss Fawcett, the senior assistant, tall, thin, spectacled, reluctantly approached them.

Lady Foxfield announced herself again although this time it was not necessary, and then said: 'I wish to make a very serious complaint. This young woman has been impertinent – most impertinent. Behavin' in the most extraordinary mannah.'

'What's impertinent and extraordinary about it, I'd like to know?' cried Bessy, much angrier now than she had been before. 'You come in here, looking as if we'd all got the smallpox or something, and I do my best to serve you – and then when I ask you not to throw everything about and make work for us – '

'Now, Miss Swinton,' said Miss Fawcett feebly.

Lady Foxfield made a noise like an irritated horse. 'What on earth is the use of bleatin' at the girl in that mannah? I demand an instant apology.'

'Well, you won't get one from me,' shouted Bessy. 'With your *Do you know who I am?* Whoever you are, you've no manners or consideration for anybody.'

'Miss Swinton, please, please,' cried Miss Fawcett, in distress. 'Perhaps I can find what you want, Lady Foxfield.'

'I want an apology. Besides – there's nothin' heah. Rubbish!' And she swept some more wool off the counter.

This was too much for Bessy's last straining thread of self-control. 'Leave the stuff alone, can't you – you – you pompous old frog!' she blazed. And as Lady Foxfield stepped back a pace and appeared to swell up with outraged dignity, Bessy grabbed half a dozen balls of wool and hurled them straight at her and then followed them up with a dozen more. She then cried loudly: 'Oh – blast!' ran upstairs and locked herself in the ladies' washroom, wept a time, carefully made-up her face again, swept out of Pembreys' and Dunbury altogether and was last heard of in a milliner's in Nottingham.

To form any adequate idea of the talk there was that day round Mrs Hathersage's lunch-table, you have to go back to the French and Russian revolutions. Mr Finningley arrived early with his story. Mrs Hathersage complained about two plumbers who had taken possession of half her villa; they hadn't exactly *said* anything, but their manner had been most peculiar. Colonel Hazelhead was there, and gave it as his opinion, between *um-yahs*, that subversive agents were at work in the town. Lady Shepshed, so hung about with things that she was like an agitated Christmas tree, told a confused story about her chauffeur, who had been most rude to Mr Churton Talley, so that apparently that exquisite being had been compelled to return, faintly hissing and half-swooning, to London. The rector came booming in, and as usual shook hands with the company as if they had just been brought off a shipwreck, and announced that as he had just heard most disturbing rumours, he had told his curate to spend the afternoon investigating them. 'We must all do what we can,' he pointed out. Then Lady Foxfield arrived, still blinking and outraged, and now you could almost hear the tumbrils rattling down West Dunbury Avenue. 'Never – *never* – been so insulted in all my life,' she declared, not three seconds after entering. 'What *are* these wretched people coming to? Will somebody tell me what's goin' on heah in Dunbury?' And so, although the very foundations of the social system seemed to be cracking, it was a very successful lunch-party indeed, with everybody talking at once and hardly noticing what they were eating.

This could not be said of another and much smaller lunch-party in the gloomy Coffee Room of 'The Bull'. Daisy was hostess, and Hope the solitary guest; and though they talked a great deal, they certainly noticed what they were eating and took a great dislike to it. So far they had not enjoyed this day in Dunbury. The Professor had been left behind at the 'Dog and Bell' because they were all agreed that he would be safer there. No word had come from Timmy. And not a sign of Roger Liss. They had visited Mr Hassock and renewed acquaintance with Dr Buckie, which had been very pleasant and had neatly disposed of the latter part of the morning; and now they had to stay on because Candover did not appear before the Bench until the middle of the afternoon. Both were secretly disappointed because Timmy and Roger had not suddenly and miraculously appeared. 'The Bull', which was not cheerful even on a fine Saturday and simply gave up all hope on a drizzling Monday, had done nothing to cheer them. 'They can say what they like, duckie,' said Daisy, looking about her with distaste, 'but I like to have a man or two about. They haven't much sense but somehow they liven things up. I've heard of this place. But it's even worse than I thought. It's gettin' me down, dear.'

The Coffee Room appeared to have been originally designed and furnished for a deeply melancholy giant. Everything in it was gloomy and on a gigantic scale. The engravings were the largest ever seen; the sideboard went on and on and on; the smallest round table, at which

DUNBURY LOSES ITS TEMPER

Daisy and Hope were lunching, would seat ten; the cruet looked as if it weighed half a hundredweight; and the knives and forks suggested that roast elephant was some-times on the menu. The lunch was terrible. It was served by the same waiter who had challenged the cook, quite unsuccessfully, on the subject of gravy soup, which duly made its appearance. The waiter still carried about with him an air of unsuccessful protest. He kept bringing, from distant tables or the vast sideboard, various half-empty bottles of sauce, to which he gave a medicinal shake or two before placing them in the shadow of the gigantic cruet. After the soup came a few fish-bones and skin embedded in a congealing white paste; then some very pale boiled mutton and tasteless vegetables; then some green jelly and thin custard; and finally a cheese that was too hard and some biscuits that were too soft.

'Now,' said Daisy, pushing away her cheese and biscuits and finishing her glass of stout, 'I'm not one to complain, not as a rule. An' I'm in the business myself an' know what you can do an' what you can't do. But this,' beckon-ing the waiter, 'is just a bit too too.' They had the room to themselves, as well they might.

'Yes, madam? The bill?'

'The bill, certainly. Now you haven't asked us how we've enjoyed our lunch.'

'No, I haven't asked you, madam,' said the waiter, an oldish and melancholy man, 'because I noticed you weren't enjoying your lunch. And I'm very sorry.'

'Well, that's something. D'you think you'd enjoy a lunch like that?'

The waiter leaned forward and slowly shook his head. 'To tell you the truth, ladies, I'm ashamed of it. Believe me, I've worked in good hotels in my time, and it's no pleasure to me to serve food like that. But I can't do anything. I've tried.'

'Well, I'll try now,' said Daisy briskly. 'Who's the manager – or proprietor – and is he in?'

'Mr Jurby's the proprietor, and I know he's in.' There was a sudden gleam, perhaps the last before resigned old age set in, lighting up the waiter's questioning glance. 'Would you really like to speak to him?'

'You just pop down an' tell him so.' And then, as the waiter went, she turned to Hope: 'Might as well start letting steam off. I've got plenty. What are you lookin' so mournful about? Can't you stop thinking about that boy?'

'I wasn't thinking about him.' Hope struggled with her thought. 'I was just wondering. Daisy, is life really awful? Sometimes I think it's marvellous. Then suddenly – like just now – it seems awful – a sort of dreariness and misery and everybody getting older and older – like that waiter – '

'We ought to have the Professor here for this,' said Daisy. 'But I've seen plenty in my time, dear, an' my opinion is – life's pretty bloody awful if you just let it run on of its own accord – it'll go an' do you in – but if you make an effort an' stand up to it an' don't weaken – well, it's not so bad. An' that's the honest truth, dear, as I see it. Here's his lordship.'

Mr Jurby was a big paunchy man who wore riding breeches, thick khaki stockings and heavy boots. 'Ah – morning! Wanted to see me, eh? Anything I can do for you?' There was a breezy condescension about Mr Jurby.

'Are you the manager?' asked Daisy, with dangerous meekness.

'Manager? Good lord – no! Proprietor. Bought the place a year or two ago. Wanted to settle down in the old country. Out East before that. Twenty years of it. Gentleman's life up to the last two or three years. No good now. Well, anything I can do for you? Don't usually come into the Coffee Room this time of day, y'know.'

'Pity you don't.'

'What's that?' And Mr Jurby left his moustache to grow by itself.

'If you ask me, it's a pity you don't come in here more,' cried Daisy, who had now taken a strong dislike to Mr Jurby. 'This lunch of yours is the worst I've had for years. I wouldn't give it away, let alone charge four-and-six for it. Muck!'

'Now, look here,' said Mr Jurby belligerently, 'just keep calm before you say something you'll be sorry for. Can't please everybody, y'know. Monday too. Worst day of the week. People like you don't realise the difficulties of – '

But Daisy could not possibly pass this. 'Difficulties? I know all about the difficulties. Don't try to kid me. I'm in the business.'

'Oh indeed! Where?'

'The "Dog and Bell".'

'Oh! So you're that woman?' cried Mr Jurby, who had some good financial reasons for disliking the 'Dog and Bell'.

Daisy bristled at once. 'What d'you mean – that woman?'

But Mr Jurby didn't explain. His manner, however, became increasingly unpleasant. 'If I'd known it wasn't a guest who wanted to see me, I wouldn't have come charging up here. Don't come out to your – er – road-house or night-club or whatever the place is and start making a fuss, and don't expect you to come here – to a very old-established hotel with a good reputation all over the county, asking for me and then shouting out nonsense about your lunch. Eh?' he added, this time to Hope, who was, he now noticed, an uncommonly good-looking girl.

Hope, who knew all these tricks, merely stared hard at him and slightly raised her eyebrows, thus taking him down several score pegs.

'I'll tell you what's the matter with you,' said Daisy, calmly but with considerable emphasis, 'an' I've met your kind before, runnin' these bad hotels. You seem to think a hotel's a sort of arm-chair you can just flop into. You're so pleased with yourselves that you've no time to attend to your business an' look after people properly. Look at this room! Enough to give you the creeps! And then the lunch – my God! If you ate that lunch yourself, then you don't know the difference between good food and stinkin' bad food an' so shouldn't be runnin' an hotel. If you didn't eat it yourself, then you've got a dam' sauce puttin' the rubbish in front of us an' expectin' us to pay good money for it.'

'These people paid their bill?' asked Mr Jurby of the waiter, who was hovering in the background with that gleam still in his eye.

'Not yet, sir. Do you want me to – ?'

'Certainly not. No intention of letting them off. Old trick that! Give them their bill, see you're paid properly, an' then see they go without making any more disturbance.' And Mr Jurby went clomping to the door, in his best tea-plantation-manager style, but did not go out at once but turned there, pulling at his moustache and giving Daisy a last haughty stare.

'Disturbance!' she cried, not missing the opportunity. 'Why, man, can't you see I'm tryin' to give you a last chance of dodging the bankruptcy court? Your business is nearly dead now, I can tell that, an' you've only got to go swaggering round like an overweight gentleman jockey, too pleased with yourself to look after your customers, for another six months, an' you're done for. People won't stand for it nowadays. You're a fool to yourself.'

But only the bang of the door answered her. The waiter came forward, to be paid, wearing a melancholy smile and slowly shaking his head. 'I've tried to say it,' he whispered, as he picked up the money, 'but it's no use.' He hesitated a moment. 'I've heard great things of your place out there, madam. Wonderful business you're doing. I suppose – there mightn't be a chance for me – not very young, of course – but a lot of experience – and willing, very willing – ?'

It was Daisy's turn now to shake her head slowly. 'I'm sorry, but I'm afraid not. Completely full up. Sorry!'

'I suppose you are full up, too, aren't you?' said Hope, as they left the gloomy hotel. 'But I couldn't help feeling terribly sorry for that old waiter. I caught a despairing sort of look on his face just as we went out.'

'I know, dear, I know,' cried Daisy, 'and it wasn't quite true, not with our business goin' up all the time the way it is. But it was the kindest thing to say. Fact is, he's been too long in these good old-fashioned, old-established, well-known-to-the-county indoor cemeteries, an' he'll never get that resigned we'll-all-have-to-make-the-best-of-this-menu look off his poor old face. So I just couldn't do with him, an' I'm sorry. And you're quite right about this town, duckie. It's just about time it began to sit up an' take notice. Saving its life, that's what you lot are doin'. Now we'd better find out where this chap of yours is on trial. Haven't been in a police court for years.'

At the back of the Town Hall, in a yellow-pine room smelling of furniture polish, they found the Petty Sessions in full swing. They looked down upon the proceedings from a balcony, having had the choice of going up there or sitting at the back of the ground floor. ('Let's go upstairs, I always prefer it,' Daisy had said, as if they were going to the pictures.) It was not much of a balcony, only four rows of wooden benches, but Daisy pushed them both down into the front row, where they had a fine view. There were five magistrates and two of them Hope had seen before, at the museum meeting, one being Colonel Hazelhead and the other the large lady in purple (she was still in purple) who had sung her speech in a deep contralto. Two of the others were middle-aged men of a commonplace appearance, but the fifth, the chairman, whose name, they discovered, was Sir Frederick Ettlety, was by no means commonplace, for he was short, bent, very wrinkled, very deaf, and appeared to be about a hundred years old. At regular intervals he made a whinnying sound that ended with a very noisy throat clearing. It was as if he were winding himself up to go another two or three minutes. The first few times he did it, Daisy could not be persuaded that the little old man in the middle was making all that noise. After that, she watched him, fascinated by this trick. 'Gives the place a bit o' life, doesn't it?' she whispered appreciatively.

It was all very dull at first. After an errand-boy, who, to the delight of the public, blushingly bore the name of Clarence, was fined five shillings for riding his bicycle without a light, the court plunged into a dreary morass of a case about a lorry and a bus, one of which – and neither Daisy nor Hope troubled to discover which one it was – had reversed into the other. After twenty minutes of it, Daisy noticed that Hope was staring hard at somebody on one of the public benches below, where there was quite a crowd. 'Who you staring at, duckie?' she asked, anxious for any diversion.

'That man there – look – nearly at the end. Wait until he looks up again.'

He was a small man, and he was wearing dark glasses and a bushy greyish moustache. There was something all wrong about him. He did not hang together as a real person. Once you had definitely noticed him, you could not quite believe in him any longer. Daisy stared and stared.

'What is it about him that's – I dunno, but – that's queer?' asked Hope.

Daisy began shaking and gasping and then would have shocked the whole court by an explosion of laughter if at that moment Sir Frederick had not decided to wind himself up again. 'Don't you see?' Daisy gurgled, right into Hope's left ear, at the same time squeezing her left arm very hard. 'It's that daft little devil. I recognise the top of his head an' the coat he's wearing. It's Timmy, an' God knows what he thinks he looks like! It's a wonder they don't arrest him right off – with those specs an' that bogus moustache. Looks just like a little murderer to me. I can't help it – I'm old enough to know better – but I tell you, dear, I love that little man.'

'Why don't you marry him?' whispered Hope.

'Now that's an idea, duckie, an' I never thought of it. Why, for two pins – '

'Silence!' shouted the usher.

'So I seen this bus turning,' a witness continued, very solemn and with his eyes closed, 'and I says to my friend who's with me, I says: "If one o' them two isn't careful," I says – '

'*Whinny – whinny – whinny – whinny – whinny – kerracha – crush-oiks*,' went Sir Frederick; and then, all wound up again, cried peevishly: 'What's he say? Speak up, man! Can't hear you.'

'There used to be one of them old Karno sketches, just like this,' Daisy whispered. 'Only better – of course.'

After another five minutes, during which they spent most of their time leaning over the rail to try and attract Timmy's attention, the bus-and-lorry case was adjourned. And now James Candover was called.

'This is it,' said Daisy, at once excited. 'Here – why aren't you giving evidence – or whatever they do?'

'I wanted to. But Uncle Fred said No. He and that Mr Largs have arranged everything. Here's that inspector I told you about.'

'And a nasty piece of work, too,' Daisy observed severely.

Inspector Parkin, explaining why the man Candover had been charged with conduct likely to lead to a breach of the peace, said that on Wednesday evening last, after having received certain information from the Town Clerk's office, he had proceeded, along with Sergeant Pegswood, to the Little Market Hall, where he found a noisy public entertainment in progress, contrary to licensing regulations, the said music licence having been taken away from the premises, so he carefully warned everybody concerned that the law was being broken –

'Yes, an' 'it Willy Jackson over the 'ead, you did,' a very shrill woman shouted from the back.

'Order there!'

Colonel Hazelhead was heard to say, in the tiny lull that followed, that he was inclined *um-yah* important case *um-yah* state of public feeling. Jealous of these *um-yahs*, perhaps, Sir Frederick did a magnificent whinnying and winding. After that, the Inspector concluded by saying that a serious disturbance was threatened and as the man Candover's conduct was especially noisy and impudent and calculated to lead to a serious breach of the peace, an example was made of him and he was taken into custody by Sergeant Pegswood. Sergeant Pegswood?

'On the evenin' in question,' Sergeant Pegswood began, after consulting his notebook, 'I was on duty with Inspector Parkin, the Inspector bein' down below an' me goin' round the back an' on to the platform of the said 'all. When I arrived, Councillor Largs was makin' one of his speeches, sayin' it was a ramp, just another ramp.'

'An' so it is!' came a cry, and there was some laughter and cheering at the back. All five justices sat up, the clerk looked stern, the usher shouted, and Inspector Parkin stared hard and menacingly.

'Inspector Parkin warned Councillor Largs,' Sergeant Pegswood continued, very slowly and solemnly. 'Then Councillor Largs said he warned him, the Inspector, and then said: "Let the people sing." On which, Candover, who was in an excited state of mind an' jigging about, shouted very loud: "Hurray! Let the people sing." So I took 'im into custody.'

'What did the man shout, Sergeant?' asked Sir Frederick, who looked very bewildered.

'He shouted: "Hurray! Let the people sing".'

'That's right,' cried a voice from the public benches. 'Let the people sing. Altogether, boys!' And now there came quite a chorus from the back: 'Let the people sing.'

After order had been restored, Sir Frederick looked at his fellow-magistrates in complete bewilderment, started to whinny, actually checked it, then said in a high quavering voice: 'Must say I don't understand this at all. Everybody shouting about singing. No sense in it at all.' Here Colonel Hazelhead leaned towards him and whispered into the ancient ear. 'Really? You astonish me. Don't know what we're coming to. Well, is that all, Sergeant Pegswood?'

The sergeant said it was.

The large lady in purple, stimulated by all this talk of singing, now sang a question. Was this man Candover one of the entertainers on the platform?

'No, your wor – ma'am,' replied Sergeant Pegswood. 'Not exactly, he wasn't. Not dressed up or anything. But he was helping, an' in this very excited condition – '

'Drunk, do you think?' asked the magistrate at the far end, speaking for the first time.

No, the man wasn't drunk. 'But knowing 'im to be a bit of a queer character – '

'What d'you say? Queer character?' Sir Frederick quavered, leaning forward and curving a hand over one ear. 'What sort of queer character? What's wrong with the man, eh?'

'Well, your worship,' replied the sergeant, 'I do 'ear 'e 'as dreams, an' that's well-known about 'im in the town.'

'Dreams, eh?' cried Colonel Hazelhead, as if he had suspected it from the first. 'Unbalanced type – *um yah* – '

'Well, we all have dreams,' said the one at the far end.

Sergeant Pegswood, who knew that this particular magistrate was new to the job and not of much consequence, replied rather shortly that these dreams of Candover's were different, being peculiar.

'So are mine, often. Aren't yours?'

'What's this?' cried Sir Frederick, who was losing his bearings again. He appealed now to the clerk, whose voice had a familiar pitch.

'This man Candover has peculiar dreams, Sir Frederick,' the clerk explained, 'and it's just been remarked by the Bench that our dreams are often peculiar.'

'Oh – fiddle-faddle! Must get on, must get on,' cried Sir Frederick, 'otherwise, be here all day. Can't bother about beams here, peculiar or not. Anybody representing this man?'

Up popped a young man in a dark blue shirt, who had been sitting next to Tom Largs, to whose daughter Jessie, now at the Labour Club, organising her strike, he was engaged.

'Just one or two questions, Sergeant Pegswood,' said this young man, who was a cool hand, in spite of his youth and dark blue shirt. 'Now I suggest that Candover was only repeating what had already been said – as a sort of slogan – Let the people sing.'

'He shouted Hurray first.'

'Well, don't you ever shout Hurray?'

'No, I don't,' replied Sergeant Pegswood emphatically.

'You wouldn't!' yelled the woman who knew about Willy Jackson.

'Well, Candover apparently does, being an excitable sort of chap who has peculiar dreams – '

'Has what?' asked Sir Frederick, peering over.

'Peculiar dreams,' the clerk told him.

'What again? I won't have our time wasted – ' But here the old gentleman had to wind himself up again, and at the end of his winding had to be given a glass of water. When he finally recovered he glanced round with contempt at Candover and the police witnesses and the young solicitor, appeared to have forgotten what the case was all about, turned to his fellow justices and said in a voice audible to everybody present: 'Can't waste any more time on obvious drunk and disorderly case of this kind. I suggest thirty shillings and costs – eh, gentlemen?'

They might all have been on a string that the old gentleman had just pulled. The clerk shot up from his desk and made urgent sibilant sounds. Colonel Hazelhead's neck grew longer and longer, as he tried to explain and expostulate, until he looked like one of the tree-top-eating dinosaurs. The large lady in purple, no doubt feeling clean left out of it after that 'Eh, gentlemen?' began a contralto aria of protest. The other two magistrates talked to one another across the other three, rather like the two corner men in a minstrel troupe. Inspector Parkin whispered in the bright red ear of Sergeant Pegswood. The young solicitor in the dark blue shirt flapped his arms and made angry sounds, as if he had suddenly decided to be Donald Duck. There were some derisive calls and whistles from the public. And Timmy Tiverton, under the impression that he was completely unrecognisable, was now staring up at Daisy and Hope and grinning in the shadow of that bushy false moustache. 'I wouldn't have missed this for anything,' cried Daisy, taking it all in. 'An' a wet Monday matinee, too. Hello, they're startin' again.'

The clerk, who was anxious to make an end of this case, had persuaded Sir Frederick to allow the young solicitor to make a statement, after which the man Candover himself, who had somehow been overlooked in all this turmoil, could be questioned. The young solicitor declared emphatically that here was no case at all. 'I submit,' he said, with a grand professional air, 'that this man was arrested simply because the police, who had been good-humouredly chaffed by the crowd, lost their temper. Candover was only repeating what other people had been shouting. He did not deliberately do or say anything calculated to lead to a breach of the peace. And he is an inoffensive man who has already been put to much inconvenience and some mental strain by the unwarrantable action of Sergeant Pegswood, who no doubt was only trying to do his duty but in this instance has clearly been over-zealous.'

Candover did not show any more signs of mental strain than he had done on the platform of the Little Market Hall. He was just the same odd, shambling, grinning fellow. But when he turned those glittering eyes of his towards the Bench and finally fixed his gaze on Sir Frederick, that old gentleman was so fascinated that he put on an extra pair of spectacles through which to return the stare.

'Most extraordinary fella,' Sir Frederick could be heard muttering. Then he shouted: 'You been in front of me before?'

Candover shook his head, and then remarked: 'But one time I dreamt all this.'

'You what? Speak up, man.'

The clerk popped up and shouted: 'He says he dreamt all this.'

Sir Frederick looked with horror from the clerk to Candover. 'What's all this stuff about dreaming, eh? An' speak up, speak up, man, don't mumble your replies.'

'Please, sir,' said Candover in an astonishingly loud clear tone, 'I've the most peculiar dreams, always have had, all the time – ask anybody that knows me. Very, very strange dreams – like what you see at the pictures, only much better – clearer and more goin' on. Fleets o' ships sinkin', an' cities all on fire, an' hundreds an' thousands o' people running about an' screaming an' then dropping down dead – '

'That'll do,' yelled Sir Frederick, and then gave himself a thoroughly good winding up. 'Any more of this and we shan't know where we are. Place like a madhouse. Peculiar dreams!' he snorted. 'Can't understand police bringin' case of this kind. Doesn't make sense. Dreams!'

Here both the clerk and Colonel Hazelhead tried to explain that the charge was something quite different, but the old gentleman waved them away and told them angrily they could not teach him, at this late date, how to conduct himself as Chairman of the Bench. 'Wasting time, too. Can't go on with this nonsense all day. Case dismissed. And in future,' he added, pointing a trembling finger at Candover, 'keep your dreams to yourself, my man. Can't expect the police to listen to your rubbish about dreams. Something else to do. Don't let me see you here again, you and your dreams. Go along now. Next case.'

Outside, in the drizzle, Daisy and Hope found the little man with dark spectacles and the bushy moustache hanging about, and marched straight up to him.

'Excuse us,' said Daisy, 'but I wonder if you'd mind telling us something. We're strangers here.'

'Oh, yais, please, yais,' replied the bushy moustache, in the voice of a foreign spy in a music-hall sketch.

'Thanks very much,' Daisy continued hurriedly. 'Well, we're lookin' for a friend of ours who disappeared last night, God knows why, and who's been seen round here this afternoon looking like nothing on earth and wearing some Woolworth goggles and a bit of hearthrug. And come on, you silly little chump, or we're all goin' to get wet. I've a car in the square.'

'When did you recognise me?' asked Timmy, as they walked through to the square.

'Just as soon as we saw you,' replied Daisy sharply. 'And then we spent a long time wonderin' why you thought you ought to come here lookin' like a half-blind sea-lion.'

'Disguise,' said Timmy. 'I've to be careful, y'know, Daisy.'

'If that's your idea of being careful, it isn't mine. It's just as if I'd turned up at that police court in tights. An' what became of you last night? You had us all lookin' everywhere for you?'

'I'm sorry, Daisy, but I hadn't time to explain. It was that chap I told you about – I'm sure he's a detective of some sort – the chap who shouted "Hey!" at me here, last week. Had to dodge him. He was sitting bang in front at the show. So I got young Roger to give me a lift and put me up for the night.'

'So that's why Roger disappeared,' cried Hope happily. 'But where is he now?'

'He dropped me here, and then went to do a bit of business. Us chaps have to live, y'know, which is something you girls always seem to forget.'

'You get in here,' said Daisy, opening the door of her little car, 'an' squeeze yourself in at the back an' stop talking nonsense. And pull that bit of hearth-rug off your face, I don't want it tickling the back of my neck when you lean forward an' tell us some more about us girls. Now then, all ready? I shan't hurry 'cos I'm a terrible driver an' have to be careful. So don't start one of your silly arguments. Just talk quietly and sensibly, both of you, while I keep an eye on this greasy, slippery, damnable road.'

After a journey that was really quite unadventurous and yet had about it the air of a desperate enterprise, they were sitting costly up in Daisy's sitting-room, trying their hands at impersonations of Sir Frederick, when the Professor marched in, showing unusual signs of excitement.

'Professor,' cried Daisy, who liked the first word as well as the last, 'you missed it. Candover was let off, after one of the best comedy sketches I've ever seen. Now what's the matter with you? Anything happened here?'

'But yes, most certainly,' replied the Professor, beaming upon them all. 'That young man arrived once more.'

'What – Roger?' This from Hope, of course, and Hope all on fire.

'No, no, that other young man who admires you so much – Sir Reginald Foxfield.'

'Oh – him!' This was, it seemed, the end of Sir Reginald, who was now obliterated.

'Yes, but it is most important. For after he had enquired for you, and I told him you were not here, he gave me some important news – important for the town of Dunbury, and important for us because we wish to help the people of the town. Now tomorrow afternoon, as you may have learned, there is to be an arbitration about the Market Hall, by Government order or suggestion, I do not know which. Each party will state its case, and the arbitrator will then decide what is to happen to the Hall. Good! Well, this Sir Reginald tells me the arbitrator has been appointed, and tomorrow this young man, commanded by his mother, will go to bring this arbitrator to the town. So!' And the Professor looked at them triumphantly.

Timmy spoke up for them. 'Well, that's all right, Professor, but I can't see where the excitement comes in. What of it?'

'If those Foxfields have him in tow,' said Hope, 'then it's just what Mr Largs said would happen. That's why the West Dunbury snobs didn't mind a what's-it – arbitrator, because they knew he'd be one of their lot. I heard them say that at the meeting.'

'You know too perhaps there is much trouble today in the town,' said the Professor, 'A big strike at *United Plastics* and much unrest everywhere – '

'Includin' "The Bull" hotel this lunch-time,' Daisy chuckled.

'The arbitrator,' the Professor began, just as if this were to be another of his lectures.

'What happened at "The Bull," Daisy?' asked Timmy, who did not feel that this was the time for a lecture.

'The arbitrator who has been appointed,' the Professor began again.

'Oh – I wish you'd been there, Timmy,' Daisy continued. 'We had a terrible lunch – '

'I insist upon speaking,' the Professor thundered, and looked so fierce that there was now a dead silence. Immediately he became apologetic. 'I am sorry. That was bad manners.'

'No, go on, Professor,' Daisy told him. 'Get it off your chest.'

'This arbitrator who comes tomorrow,' said the Professor, very impressively, turning to Timmy, 'is our friend – Sir George Denberry-Baxter.'

Timmy whistled. 'Somebody's in for a rough house, then,' he said, and whistled again. 'He'll take their Market Hall away from 'em all right, that terrible old codger will. Remember how he threw us out.'

'Yes, yes, but remember also how he was the night before – eccentric perhaps, but full of warm human feelings.'

'I know, but he was plastered then. He's one o' them queer birds that aren't human until they're properly pickled.'

'I've met 'em,' said Daisy, who had met all kinds. 'Though I don't really know what you're talking about.'

'You see, Professor,' continued Timmy, 'if they'd only have this arbitration late at night, when he's well plastered, he'd think nothing of giving away the whole town, but there's no chance of that. Pity! As it is, he'll be murder.'

'Not so,' said the Professor calmly. 'You forget that the young man, Sir Reginald, is driving him over here, for he is acquainted with the mother and will stay the night at Dunbury Hall. Now Sir Reginald, who is a simple young man, tells me that the food and drink are of very poor quality at Dunbury Hall.'

'He's right too,' said Hope, shuddering.

'Very well. So I told him,' the Professor continued, 'that he must bring Sir George here to lunch tomorrow, before the arbitration meeting. It is on their way. They would be given, I said, a splendid lunch. And Sir Reginald said he would do that.'

'Professor,' cried Timmy, 'you're on to something there. Could we do it, d'you think? Daisy, we've just a chance, if you'll join in.'

'Boys, you're up to some devilment, I can see it in your eyes,' said Daisy. 'And certainly I'll join in.'

'Can you telephone Roger?' asked Hope, rather wistfully. 'Wouldn't he be useful?'

'That's not what you mean, girl,' Timmy told her. 'But for all that, he might be useful, an' I was going to ring him up tonight anyhow.'

'I'm not quite on to your little game yet,' said Daisy. 'Where do we start?'

'Down in that bar of yours,' said Timmy thoughtfully, 'is Jimmy Flagg, late Denga Din, the great Indian illusionist. Is he as good with the mixed drinks as he used to be with the sword-and-basket trick?'

'He's better,' replied Daisy, promptly and proudly. 'Give Jimmy a free hand mixing 'em, and after three or four you'd think he was doing the Indian rope trick. Do we start with him?'

Timmy exchanged glances with the Professor, then nodded. 'I think we start with him. An' you might as well be practising "Welcome, Sir George – it's a great honour," because tomorrow you've got to be very good. If you are, and if Jimmy's as good as you say he is, and Katie and company in the kitchen make everything on the menu nice, tasty and salty, we've a sporting chance, an' Dunbury's going to have some fun.'

CHAPTER XIII

SIR GEORGE LUNCHES AND ARBITRATES

ALL TUESDAY morning it rained hard, and at lunch time they were unusually quiet at the 'Dog and Bell.' Timmy and the Professor, who had decided to keep out of Sir George's sight until after lunch, had posted themselves at a first-floor window to watch for his arrival. Just after one o'clock, when they were beginning to feel rather anxious, a muddy saloon car drew up and there, framed in its window, looking as if it had been moulded out of Cheddar cheese, was the vast dubious face of Sir George Denberry-Baxter. 'And as sober an' sour as the devil,' observed Timmy. They passed the word below.

'Humph! So this is the place, eh?' said Sir George, not yet stirring from the car. 'Hardly my style y'know, Foxfield – brand-new, Americanised, lower-middle-class-on-the-spree, sort of thing.'

'It's really quite good, sir,' Sir Reginald told him, 'and it'll be quiet now. You'd hate our lunch at Dunbury Hall.'

'Yes, seem to remember it wasn't very good. Couldn't have a look at the cold sideboard at your club, eh?'

'I haven't one in Dunbury, sir. Really, I promise you won't find this place at all bad.'

'All right. What a place! What a day! What a country!' And grumbling and growling he heaved himself out and made for the entrance. He was sorry now he'd accepted this silly little job, though he'd been glad enough when it was first proposed to him, for it gave him something to do for a day or so and at least a temporary shadow of his old authority. Dunbury was a miserable little town; young Foxfield was a bore; Lady Foxfield was a woman entirely without wit or charm; and there would be a very bad dinner and some dreary local gentry waiting for him tonight at Dunbury Hall. He'd have been just as well off at home, yawning over a book and cursing Ketley.

'Oh! – I say – how d'you do?' cried Sir Reginald, seeing Daisy and Hope, who had suddenly arrived where they could not help being seen and had taken great care to be worth seeing.

'Oh! – how d'you do? Are you lunching here?' cried Daisy, all surprised and lady-like and fluttering.

Sir Reginald had to introduce them to Sir George Denberry-Baxter, who was rather grand and grumpy with them, though he looked sharply several times at Daisy, for he felt he had seen her before somewhere, and regarded the extremely good-looking girl with some satisfaction.

'We feel this is a very great honour to have Sir George Denberry-Baxter calling here,' said Daisy very carefully. 'I must show you our cocktail bar, and perhaps you'll have a drink before lunch. It's such a miserably cold day, isn't it?' And then she bustled them into the bar, which they had to themselves. 'Now we're very proud of Jimmy here, our barman,' Daisy continued, doing her stuff. 'Jimmy, I want Sir George Denberry-Baxter to try one of our Specials. Will you, Sir George?'

'Well, if you insist. Good stiff short drink, is it?'

'We think it's wonderful, don't we, Jimmy?'

Jimmy nodded and smiled, showing his excellent false teeth. He did a little Denga Din work at the back of the bar, and then put before them his pale foaming Specials.

A close observer might have noticed that the Specials given to the gentlemen were not only larger but also slightly different in colour from the ladies' cocktails.

'Oh! – I say,' Sir Reginald gasped. 'Got a wollop, hasn't it?'

'Humph – pretty good short drink,' said Sir George, having downed his Special without a quiver of an eyelash. He smacked his lips. 'Vodka in it, among other things – eh?'

'Ah you need more than one even to start guessing,' Jimmy told him, and at the same time, in true Denga Din style, produced another Special. Sir George swallowed half of it, made a tasting noise, frowned, muttered 'Bacardi perhaps,' swallowed the other half and said: 'No, perhaps not.'

Daisy saw that this was the line to take, at least until Sir George had had a few and became human. The analytical chemist line. Scientific research, not mere boozing. 'Nobody ever guesses even the main things in it,' she said to him, 'though I must say you're doin' better than anybody so far.'

'Oh, I'll get it,' replied Sir George, picking up the third Special. 'Excellent short drink, by the way. Now then!'

Altogether he had six of these depth charges, and both Daisy and her barman regarded him with respect, for here was no ordinary man. Sir Reginald had only had three, but these had left him with a definite tendency towards sweeping gestures and a horrible goggly-squinting look that he directed at Hope. But Sir George was merely becoming amiable. His vast face was pink now instead of yellow. His eye was brightening. And he seemed about half as large again as the disgruntled old fellow who first entered the bar.

'Well, bite of lunch now – eh? Ready, Foxfield? But I

say – think we ought to insist on the ladies joining us, eh? What d'you say, ladies? Can't leave us now, eh?'

The ladies, who wanted to giggle when he was not looking but found themselves almost hypnotised by the bright fierce glance when that vast face hung over them like a moon, demurely expressed their pleasure and led the way to the dining-room. There were only two or three nondescript travellers bunched together at one end, and Daisy marched her party up to the other end.

'I hope you like oysters, Sir George?'

'Oysters? Madame, I've been waiting for months, stuck there in a ramshackle country house miles from anywhere, just waiting for September and civilisation and oysters. You remember the Walrus and the Carpenter? Well, I'm both of 'em. Oysters? Splendid! Oysters by all means.'

'I ordered them specially from Colchester,' said Daisy with some pride.

'You're an extremely sensible woman, and I knew it the moment I set eyes on you. I can lunch like a king on oysters.'

'Oh – but I've ordered a lot of other nice things as well.'

'You have, eh?' roared Sir George. 'Well, you won't find 'em wasted on me. I've been living the most extraordinary existence, in a house miles from anywhere that belongs to a nephew. Servants all walked out – God knows why – and I've nobody to look after me but my man, Ketley, and a deaf old woman, and I've been living for weeks on tinned tongue, boiled eggs and whisky – a barbarous existence. A-ha! These oysters look good. And I'll trouble you for the brown bread, Foxfield.'

'I'm very anxious for you to tell me what you think of some champagne I have here, Sir George,' said Daisy, all very ladylike and artful. 'A lot of people complain it's too dry – and it *is* dry, I'll admit – '

'Can't be too dry for me,' said Sir George promptly. 'But glad to tell you what I think of it. Very sensible of you to suggest it. Excellent idea of yours, Foxfield, coming here. Quite right about it. Didn't trust your judgment, but I was wrong. Always admit when I'm wrong,' he told them all, 'and I've admitted I was wrong all over the place – East Africa, Burma, Borneo and Fiji – I was damnably wrong in Fiji and remind me to tell you about it after lunch if we've time. Is this the champagne you're worried about?'

'Yes, is it all right?' asked Daisy, putting on a sort of helpless-little-woman anxiety. Actually it was the best wine she had in the place. 'Not too dry?'

'Certainly not. Dead right. Mind you,' he continued, after emptying his glass, 'I don't think it's a lady's wine. Or a boy's' – and he looked sternly at Sir Reginald, as if to forbid him touching a drop. 'And no doubt this uncommonly pretty gal here would prefer something sweeter. But for a civilised English adult male taste, it's perfect.' He reached out for his glass again, and found that it had been filled, for the waiter had been carefully instructed that morning by Daisy.

After the oysters, there was an excellent dish of kidneys with a burnt wine sauce, and then a cheese soufflé; and Sir George had two helpings of everything, never stopped talking, never stopped drinking the first-rate champagne; and by the time they were ready for coffee he was in tremendous form.

'I've one or two liqueur brandies I wish you'd try,' said Daisy, still using the same technique, though now, with Sir George all rosy and ripe, it was hardly necessary.

'My palate,' said the great connoisseur, 'is entirely at

your disposal. You'd have to go a long way to find a man with a nicer appreciation of good brandy than George Denberry-Baxter. And don't imagine that a good cigar will blunt my palate – though I know some of 'em tell you that – because it won't. Oh – cigars here, eh? Good! Now then, this is brandy number one, is it? Now don't tell me what it is. Let me just give you my impression of it.' He took a prodigious helping, sniffed a bit, then poured in a capacious mouthful, rolled it round and chewed it and slowly swallowed it, closing his eyes. When he opened them again, he stared across the table at Sir Reginald, who had also closed his eyes. 'Foxfield's bottled, isn't he?' Sir George whispered to Daisy. 'Can't hold it, eh? Pity! Wake up, young Foxfield!'

Sir Reginald slowly opened one eye, and said dreamily: 'Did my mother ask you to dinner tonight?'

'She did. Why?'

'Don't go,' said Sir Reginald, wagging his head. 'It'll be ghastly – ab-so-lutely ghastly, ol' boy.'

'Yes, a trifle bottled, I think, though he's quite right about the dinner and I think "ghastly" is *le mot juste*.' He swallowed the rest of the brandy. 'Nothing wrong with this. Capital stuff. Don't let 'em talk you out of it!'

'But is the other better, that's the point,' said Daisy, winking at Hope, who suddenly began giggling.

'What are you laughing at?' demanded Sir George, with mock fierceness. 'Me?'

'Yes,' replied Hope boldly. 'I think you're a wonderful turn.'

'And you're quite right – so I am. Explain why, after-wards. But must settle this brandy question. Least I can do, after the excellent lunch you've given me. Now then.' He tackled an even more prodigious helping of the second brandy. Then he looked up and frowned. 'Turn? Turn?'

'Sorry,' said Hope. 'I wasn't being rude.'

'No, no, no, wasn't thinking of that. Turn, turn?' He wheeled round and pointed an enormous forefinger straight at Daisy's little nose. 'Been trying and trying and trying to remember where I've seen you before. Now I've got it. Turn! You were on the halls, weren't you? Little soubrette with red hair. Saucy little puss. Daisy – Daisy – Daisy – '

'Daisy Barley,' she prompted him delighted with this recognition.

'That's it. Daisy Barley. And you're Daisy Barley, little Daisy Barley. Daisy – for you must allow me the privilege as a very old and fervent admirer – Daisy – your health!' And that finished his glass of the second brandy. 'Nothing wrong with that brandy. A shade sharper than the first, perhaps, not quite so smooth. I don't know, though. Mustn't do Number Two an injustice by flattering Number One. Better try One again – least I can do.'

While he was busy with the bottle, Daisy winked at Hope, who murmured an excuse and hurried away.

'Yes, very fond of the old halls,' said Sir George, pulling away at his big cigar, reminiscent and mellow now, 'and spent a lot of time in 'em when I was in town on leave. Bachelor, y'know. Used to be able to fiddle and sing dozens and dozens of the old songs, catchy bits of nonsense. Which reminds me of a most extraordinary business we had over at my place, one day last week. Had a wonderful evening – some good music and then some of these catchy old music-hall songs – with a Dr Krudiebacker from Vienna and a little comic I hadn't seen for years, Tommy Tupperton – and we were all getting along like a house on fire when I popped out to get a breath of air, because playing and singing made me devilish warm, and then when I went back they'd clean gone. It was late and I was tired, so I didn't bother much, and then in the morning I forgot about 'em because I was bothered by a couple of fellows turning up with an obviously faked letter of introduction, sort of thing that's liable to happen to a man like me, long public service in all parts of the Empire and that sort of thing, and then a policeman came asking a lot of idiotic questions, and what with one thing and another I didn't remember about these other nice fellows, Krudiebacker and Tupperton, until evening. I tried to make some sense out of my man's yarn, but Ketley's a fool – runs after the local girls all the time and drinks on the sly – and just talked nonsense. So there you are. Might have dreamt it, of course – often dream like the devil – nothing else to do in that manor miles from anywhere – often feel like a ghost haunting it. Ketley said I hadn't dreamt it, but then he's such a liar, and such a confused and inconsistent sort of liar, I never believe a word he says. In fact, he's only to say a thing for me to believe the opposite, which is nearly as good as if he told the truth, when you come to think of it – hello, hello, hello! Now who the blazes are these two?'

The Professor arrived first, and held out his hand smiling. 'You remember me, Sir George?'

'Remember you? Certainly, certainly, I do. Schubert, Mozart, eh? Dr Krudiebacker from Vienna. By gad, Ketley was telling the truth for once. Just shows how damned inconsistent he is. Deceives you every time. And Tommy Tupperton!'

'Timmy Tiverton,' said that little man, whose professional pride compelled him to correct this mistake.

'That's it. Timmy Tiverton. Of course, of course. No cockles for Father, but plenty of roly-poly for Mrs Moly, eh? Come on, sit down, and have a drink. What are you doing here?'

'We are here on a mission, Sir George,' replied the Professor gravely. 'We are trying to rescue the town of Dunbury. It is a good little town but its people are fallen asleep. For instance, they have an old hall that was given to them to play music in, and now it may be taken away from them. You have heard of that?'

'Heard of it? I'm here to hold an enquiry about it, though I didn't know anything about the musical part of it. Have to be getting along soon, too, though how, I don't know. Young Foxfield, who was to drive me in, looks bottled to me. Can't hold his drink apparently.' And to show that he could, Sir George helped himself again. He was now in exactly the same ripe state in which they had first seen him. He was, of course, much more formally dressed, having got himself up in a morning coat and striped trousers for his arbitrating; but now his thick white thatch of hair was wildly untidy, he was beginning to perspire, the scar on his right cheek looked angry again, and his fierce little eyes glittered like tiny slivers of glass. Gigantically he rose to his feet, swallowing more brandy on the way, bowed to Daisy and thanked her most warmly for his splendid lunch, and now took charge of the situation, as if he was governor-general again and this was a day of crisis in some mysterious colony. 'Young Foxfield must be put to bed. Take him away, gentlemen. I must have some sort of conveyance to take me to Dunbury, where I don't propose to stand any nonsense from anybody. And having settled this little matter, I propose to return here in time for dinner. And I'll trouble you, Dr Krudiebacker, to pass those excellent cigars. And now – a final nip of brandy just for the road, eh? And we're all going to Dunbury, y'know. Must keep together. Yes, by crumpets, there must be no separating now or God knows where we'll be.'

One of them muttered a doubt about the police.

Sir George was horrified. 'Police! Don't bother your heads about the police. Lot of numskulls. Haven't spent half my life inspecting rows of 'em, all over the Empire, to worry about police now. Any policeman who lays a finger on any member of my party in Dunbury can say good-bye to his uniform. Now, let's be moving.'

From now on it was as if they followed him, perhaps just as they walked down the dining-room, through some invisible door, some magical entrance, into another world, which looked like this one, had the same backgrounds and furnishings, but behaved very differently and was quite fantastic. From this moment to the very end of the day, all of them, Timmy and the Professor, Daisy, Hope and, as we shall see, even Roger Liss, felt they were moving in this other fantastic world, which had somehow been made visible and audible to them by Sir George, who in his turn could only find the key to it when he was gloriously ripe – for you could not say, coldly, that he was drunk – with good liquor. He created a whole atmosphere, all by himself, and afterwards it was hard to believe in it or him or in anything that happened under his spell. Yet it did all happen, and there are sober reports to prove it happened.

At the entrance, after Sir Reginald had been left in Timmy's room, where he fell fast asleep, they reassembled at the entrance. Roger was there with *Green Hell*, which Sir George did not object to at all, but even praised. 'Much better than young Foxfield's muddy little rattletrap,' he cried. 'It has dignity. It has style. It has vintage. Does it go?'

'More or less,' replied Roger, grinning. 'Better sit in the back though and hold tight.'

So Sir George and the Professor sat in the back, where they plunged almost at once into an involved argument about the Hittites; Timmy sat in front with Roger; while Daisy drove Hope in her little car. The world was wet and silvery but the rain had ceased. There was very little talk between the two on the front seat of *Green Hell* because Roger was busy all the time coaxing the ancient monster along the road. In the back, between the rumbles and explosions of the engine, the Hittites were discussed.

'Where do we go now?' shouted Roger, as they drove into Dunbury.

'Anywhere you like, my boy,' replied Sir George amiably.

'He means – where's this arbitration business going on?' cried Timmy, turning round.

'Oh – that! By thunder, I'd clean forgotten about that. Glad you reminded me, Tupperton. So busy arguing with Dr Krudiebacker here. Now let me see. Got it somewhere. Yes – here it is – the Guildhall. Devil of a lot of people hanging about, aren't there? What's the matter with 'em?'

'Perhaps they have decided to change their habits,' said the Professor. 'Perhaps they are waking out of a long sleep.'

'Some of 'em's on strike,' Timmy told them.

There was quite a little crowd outside the entrance to the Guildhall, which was a fairly old but not very imposing building, just off the market square. At the door were two policemen.

'Tell you one thing,' said Sir George, as he climbed out. 'I'm going to be devilish thirsty. Feel it coming on now, and this affair may last hours – though not if I can help it. Ought to have brought something with me.'

'It's here,' cried Daisy, appearing as if by magic at that moment. 'Take it.'

'Thoughtful of you, very thoughtful indeed. Many thanks.' Sir George glanced down at the paper-covered bottle he was now holding. 'What is it?'

'Good old malt whisky. Looks nearly like water. But it's thirty years old.'

'By Christmas, what a woman!' roared Sir George, to the delight of the whole crowd. 'You're a little miracle. Well now, in we go.'

'Beg pardon, sir, 'as all your party got business inside?' asked one of the policemen.

'Yes, officer,' replied Sir George, with immense dignity. 'They are all with me, Sir George Denberry-Baxter.'

'Yes, yes, that's all right. This way, please, Sir George. Everything's ready. Everybody's waiting.' This was from little Mr Orton, from the Town Clerk's office and late of the Dunbury Harriers. He was in his best suit and a great state of fuss.

'And that's where you're wrong, young man,' said Sir George severely. 'Everything is *not* ready and everybody is *not* waiting. I am not ready and I am not waiting. Now, lead on.'

The rest of them followed him in, hardly noticed in his shadow. The hall was not very large; it had a narrow gallery running round three sides, about twenty rows of little cane-bottomed chairs on the ground floor, and a rather high platform; and it was nearly full, not with ordinary townsfolk but with councillors, privileged persons, members of the groups that were claiming the Market Hall. Hope noticed nearly all the people she had seen at the museum committee meeting at Lady Foxfield's. And Tom Largs was there, with his daughter and the young solicitor, still wearing the same dark blue shirt.

While the five from the 'Dog and Bell' found seats for themselves in one of the middle rows, Sir George, still carrying his bottle, rolled gigantically towards the platform, where the mayor, two senior aldermen and the town clerk were already installed behind a long table. Young Orton, pale and damp with anxiety, appeared to be acting as something between a master of ceremonies and an usher. There was a round of applause as Sir George, who now looked a most picturesque and imposing figure, settled himself in an immense high-backed chair in the middle of this platform group. He acknowledged the applause by a nod and a wave of the hand, and then busied himself with arranging the decanter of water, the glass, and his bottle of pale old whisky, within easy reach. The mayor, the two aldermen and the town clerk all looked terrified, as if a cat had suddenly arrived to take the chair at a meeting of mice. Young Orton laid some documents in front of the great man, who now produced a giant-size pair of folding *pince-nez*, and clapped them on the end of his nose at an odd angle. He looked now like a scholarly pirate.

The mayor, a thin earnest man in the furniture trade, opened the proceedings. He seemed to have learnt his speech by heart, and spoke it as if he were a foreigner who could produce the sounds but did not really know what the words meant. 'We Are Met Here,' he told them, 'To Decide The Future Of Our Old Market Hall As We Have Not In Accordance With The Law Been Able To Secure The Necessary Majority In Our Borough Council Meetings Therefore In Accordance With The Law We Are Met Here To Decide By Arbitration The Decision Of The Arbitrator To Be Final Such Arbitrator Having Been Appointed By His Majesty's Government Namely Sir George Denberry-Baxter.' Then he added, dropping into ordinary Dunbury speech: 'And I 'ope that you will all keep good order as there's been enough trouble in the town already.' And this was received with a few gentlemanly *hear-hears* and some mild applause.

The town clerk now rose to explain how the Market Hall came to be in the possession of the town, but he had a squeaky little voice, read his speech very rapidly, and only told his audience what nearly all of them knew already, so nobody took any notice of him. Sir George regarded him with some astonishment, as if he were a talking insect, helped himself to whisky and water in an extremely dignified manner, and then only partly stifled a vast yawn.

'He's 'as bottled now,' whispered Timmy to the Professor, 'as when we first met him. You'll see.'

The *United Plastics* people were to present their case first. The manager, the two assistant managers, the head of the sales department, with a secretary or two, were there, looking extremely worried, as well they might, for they had a strike on their hands, neither the new system nor the old one was working at all, and cables that became more and more intelligible, the angrier they were, had been arriving from New Jersey at all hours. They were not presenting their case themselves, however, but had imported a haughty young barrister from the Middle Temple, who now came forward, coughed twice, made a little bow to Sir George, coughed again, then began: 'On behalf of my clients, *United Plastics* – '

Sir George stopped him. 'What are they?'

'I was about to explain, sir. *United Plastics* is a very prosperous company, of American origin, that has its English factory here in Dunbury, and it is easily the largest employer of labour in the district. On behalf – '

'What is this stuff they manufacture?' asked Sir George,

breaking in again. 'Is it the stuff they make these little coloured ashtrays and bowls out of?'

'Yes, sir, it – '

'Loathe the stuff. Never did like it, never shall. But, of course, I'm old-fashioned, clean out-of-date – eh? Anyhow, lot of other people do like it, I suppose, eh? Firm makes money, eh?'

'Yes, sir. I have here the figures of the annual expenditure of the company in wages – '

'Keep 'em. Don't want figures. No use addling our wits with a lot of nonsensical figures.' He took another pull at his whisky and water. 'Go on. What do these people want to do?'

'It is their desire, sir, to acquire the Market Hall and use it as a showroom for their products and, of course, as a central warehouse, offices, and so forth. They are willing to pay a good price to the town for the purchase of the building, considerably more, in fact, than it could command in the ordinary way.'

'Why? What's the point of it?'

'Er – I should like to consult my clients before I answer that question, sir.' And he went into a huddle with the manager, the two assistant managers, the head of the sales department, while Sir George helped himself to more whisky and then mopped his brow.

'It seems, sir, that the policy of the parent company in America has always been to try and associate its products in the public mind with places or buildings of historical or strongly æsthetic interest. Thus, the parent company has recently acquired the birthplace of a well-known public figure, Senator Jenks, and is using it as a showroom – '

'What, a whole town?' roared Sir George. 'Oh! – I see – one house. So their game is somehow to persuade the

idiotic public that their plastic stuff is very new and yet
very old all at the same time. Cowardly, I call it. If you're
new, *be* new, I say. Not new myself, don't pretend to be.
Almost an anachronism, I am. But I'd respect these people
a bit more if they didn't go and pretend to be Senator
Jenks's grandmother. Not that I care who Senator Jenks's
grandmother is, because I never heard of the fella.'

'Quite, sir,' said the young barrister very smoothly.
'That was merely an example of the policy. But what I
should like to emphasise is that my clients are ready to
pay a handsome sum to the town for a building that is no
longer useful – '

'What's the town going to do with the money?' asked
Sir George, staring about him masterfully. 'Anybody
know? Not decided yet, eh? What do you say?' This to the
unfortunate town clerk, blushing and squeaking. 'Can't
hear you. Never mind, let it pass.'

'By establishing their factory here, my clients have
brought a great deal of money into the town – and – '

'And made a very nice thing out of it, I'll bet my boots.
And if they hadn't, they wouldn't still be here. No, don't
think much of that argument – never did. It's a little
shopkeeper's point of view, that. Won't pass it. Eh?' he
added, to the mayor, who was saying something. 'Speak
up, Mr Mayor, speak up, and let us all hear you.' There
was some applause at this.

'I just wanted to say,' said the mayor, who clearly did
not know what to make of Sir George, 'that some of us –
who've been for many, many years in the service of the
Borough, senior members of the Council, and so forth –
feel that this offer by *United Plastics* should be given very
serious consideration.'

'Ah!' Sir George made this sound very significant. 'Ah!
You do, eh? Senior members of the Council, eh? Well,

well, well!' He shook his head, looking like a distressed red-and-white lion, refreshed himself again, and then stared down in surprise at the place where the young barrister had been standing a minute before. The man there now seemed to be a different size and shape. 'What,' enquired Sir George slowly, 'is the idea of this?'

'I'm the manager of the sales department of *United Plastics*,' he began, in an ingratiating tone, 'and I feel that our counsel hasn't perhaps put forward our claim as it – '

'Sit down, sir,' Sir George thundered. 'Let's have none of your sales department tricks here. No salesmanship! No pedlar's artfulness! Just a quiet, straightforward discussion of this little problem. So sit down, sir,' he bellowed.

The mayor and the two aldermen, who had been exchanging timid and bewildered glances, now trotted off the platform, and received a scattered round of applause, led by T. Tiverton. Sir George completely ignored this sudden retreat, but looked very fiercely at the little town clerk, who, perhaps because he was feeling lonely and afraid, beckoned to young Orton. Sir George did not like this, glared at the town clerk, waved young Orton towards him and said loudly: 'Come along, young man, don't stand dithering there. Who are the next claimants?'

Young Orton scampered round like a rabbit to the museum group, from which Major Shiptonthorpe emerged, a legal man but also a gentleman representing the gentlemanly interests, and as he came forward he took off his eyeglasses so that he would be ready to saw the air with them at any moment. Major Shiptonthorpe's manner said very plainly: 'These commercial people having got what they deserved, you will now see how we do the trick, all in a neat, gentlemanly fashion.' All the museum party watched him with a proud confidence. The arbitrator himself did not observe this approach, being busy mixing more whisky and water.

'Sir George, I represent the Dunbury Museum Committee – Major Shiptonthorpe – and – '

Sir George stopped him. 'Any relation to Tubby Shiptonthorpe who used to be out in Johore?'

Major Shiptonthorpe smiled. 'My cousin.'

'You know he came a nasty cropper, poor old Tubby,' said Sir George, striking a rich vein of reminiscence. 'No brains, of course, not a glimmer of 'em. But I didn't mind him. The last time I saw poor Tubby – it was in a filthy little rest house during the rains – he'd got the idea in his muddled head that there was a whole secret society of Malays after him. All nonsense, of course. Wouldn't leave the little brown girls alone, that was Tubby's trouble. You fellas,' he added sternly, 'think you can do what you like out there, and it doesn't work, y'know, Shiptonthorpe, it doesn't work. Well, glad to have had a word with you Shiptonthorpe. Never forget poor old Tubby. Now let's get on.'

Major Shiptonthorpe smiled again, but this time very faintly. 'As I said, Sir George – '

'Look here, Shiptonthorpe,' said Sir George severely, 'I've a good deal to do, y'know. Can't gossip here all the afternoon. Some other time, if you please. Now then, who's representing these people who want a museum?'

'I am,' shouted Major Shiptonthorpe, losing his temper. 'I've said so already.'

'Don't take that tone with me, my dear sir,' and Sir George, purple with fury, thumped the table and set all the papers dancing. 'Coming up here, chattering about your cousin! Now then, sir, what have you to say?'

'A number of – er – influential residents, headed by Lady Foxfield, have formed a Museum Committee, and the proposal of this Committee is that the Market Hall, which is no longer needed for its original purpose, should be placed at the disposal of the Committee in order that it should be turned into a museum – '

'Yes, yes, yes,' said Sir George irritably. 'You sound to me as if you're going round and round in a circle. What sort of museum?'

'With your permission, sir, I should like to call upon Lady Foxfield to answer that question. Lady Foxfield!'

The lady came forward in a grim purposeful manner. She nodded to Sir George. 'How d'you do?'

'How d'you do?' he replied glumly, staring down at her with some distaste. He decided to refresh himself before listening to what this grim-looking female had to say.

Lady Foxfield, who had a strong rather than a fertile mind, began the same speech she had made at the meeting at her house. 'Dunbury is a very ancient and historic borough. All of us heah are proud of its – er – historical associations. We wish to show othahs that we are proud of our ancient history – '

'Why?' asked Sir George, rather quietly for him.

'Why?' she repeated, looking at him as if she could hardly believe either her ears or her eyes. 'Surely it's important to preserve the great traditions of our country?' And her friends applauded this and one or two of them, including Mr Finningley, cried 'Hear, hear!' Which was unwise of them, for Sir George glared in their direction and then when he returned to contemplate Lady Foxfield again, he looked at her with more distaste than ever. But he did not reply at once, and now Lady Foxfield rashly assumed that she had the moral superiority and began to hector him. 'There is no need to point out to one who has served his King and Empire in many parts of the world, that these traditions must be preserved, that a museum will show the people what those traditions are, and that – er – therefore – it will prove a bulwark against dangerous tendencies.' And the whole museum group clapped hard and Mr Finningley cried 'Hear, hear! Bravo!'

'Quiet!' shouted Sir George angrily. He was now very ripe indeed. As he half-rose to his feet and leaned over the table, he swayed slowly, and his enormous face shone with sweat. Then, to everybody's astonishment, he suddenly cried: 'Is my friend Dr Krudiebacker, late of Vienna, still here? If he is, I now ask him to step forward.'

The Professor, more astounded than anybody else, discovered that he was being propelled out of his seat and along the row by Timmy. He did not go right down to the platform, however, but stood against the wall at the side, where his height made him immediately conspicuous.

'Ah, there you are,' shouted Sir George, still leaning on the table and swaying. 'Now, Dr Krudiebacker, you're a man of intellect and learning, a foreigner but one who knows something about this country – so I want you to tell us – very simply, very clearly – what you think are the great traditions of this country. Now listen, everybody, listen carefully – especially that fella down there who keeps shouting 'Hear, hear!' like an idiot. Dr Krudiebacker?'

'The great traditions of this country,' cried the Professor in a loud clear voice, 'are these. First, the liberty of the individual. So long as they do no harm to others, men must be allowed to develop in their own way. Second, that which goes with liberty – toleration. Third, voluntary public service. Fourth, a very deep love, a poetical love, rooted deep down in the unconscious, of England and the English way of life, of the fields and woods, flowers and birds, of pastimes, of the poets and story-tellers. Fifth, which you find everywhere among the common people, humour and irony and along with these a profound depth of sentiment. You may say some of these are characteristics and not traditions, but here in England, where everything is hazy, nothing clearly defined, characteristics of the people and traditions of the race melt into one another and cannot be separated. That is all, I think – except to say, as a foreigner, that I love these traditions very much and that the world would be much poorer without them.' And the Professor gave the company a short stiff bow, then marched back to his seat.

Sir George shook his white mane. 'Thank you, Dr Krudiebacker,' he roared. 'And now, at last, you've heard something worth listening to, after all this drivel about selling ashtrays and Senator Jenks and Tubby Shipton-thorpe and museums that are bulwarks against dangerous tendencies. I like dangerous tendencies, and I hate bulwarks.'

'One moment, please!' called Lady Foxfield sharply.

'Certainly not, madam, you've had your moment, and told me I didn't want to preserve the great traditions of our country. And with all due respect to you, madam – and with none at all to your idiotic friend down there who keeps shouting "Hear, hear!" – I say you're talking a lot of nonsense. And bad nonsense too. I love our traditions. I want the English to be more English every year, so that Dr Krudiebacker keeps coming back to admire us more every year. And I can't see that a public building taken over by fellas who shout "Hear, hear!" like idiots and all manner of old busybodies, who stuff the place full of warming-pans and broken old horse pistols and moth-eaten bonnets and shawls and a lot of other junk – '

'Really!' shouted Lady Foxfield, in a fury. 'Really, this is quite – '

'Don't try to bully me, madam. Either resume your seat or leave the building.' Sir George stood erect now, though still swaying dangerously, and waved her away. As she went, he took a tremendous drink, gasped for air, then returned to his discourse, which was wilder and louder than ever. 'Museums? Nothing wrong with 'em in their place. Sent lots o' things to museums myself, wonderful stuff. Still got plenty left. But this little town doesn't need a museum. Ridiculous idea! Only persons who could seriously entertain such an idea ought to be in museums themselves. Put them in a museum, and then let the other people wake up. I believe you people here,' he added, with some dim recollection of what the Professor said to him at the 'Dog and Bell', 'are all going to sleep. Music now? Where does music come in? Comes in somewhere, I know.' He stopped at this point because he found that the little town clerk, who was desperate, was tugging at his sleeve. 'Don't do that, man. Detestable habit. If you've anything to say – say it.'

'I'm afraid,' stammered the town clerk, 'that is – I really think – we ought to adjourn – as you're not feeling well – '

'Not feeling well?' roared Sir George, glaring at him. 'Never felt better in my life. Must be the air. Half a mind to come and live here. As for adjourning – that is a most improper suggestion, my dear sir – '

Here Major Shiptonthorpe, who was still standing near the platform, took courage. 'I agree with the town clerk. Under the circumstances, we cannot possibly accept the arbitration – '

Sir George thumped the table again. 'I'll reply to you when you've answered three questions. What are these circumstances you talk about? Who are you – apart from being Tubby Shiptonthorpe's brother – and we know what that's worth? And how can you refuse to accept an arbitration award when it hasn't yet been offered to you? And another question. Is it necessary to stand there flapping your eyeglasses about like that? If not, then go and do it somewhere else. Now we'd arrived at music. Why? Where did music come into this? It didn't, I suppose.'

'Really preposterous!' This came, quite clearly, from Mr Finningley.

'Put him out,' thundered Sir George to young Orton. 'Fella who's been making nuisance of himself all afternoon — with his "hear, hear!" — getting worse now — put him out.'

Young Orton moved slowly in the direction of the museum group, from which came cries of protest. Mr Finningley, was standing in the middle of them crying: 'No, no, no, no, no!' Several of them were for leaving in a body, as a protest against these monstrous proceedings, but Lady Foxfield, having now returned to her seat, shouted grimly that she didn't propose to leave it when nothing had been settled. Young Orton somehow never arrived at Mr Finningley, but that did not matter now because Sir George's attention was elsewhere.

Tom Largs had decided that it was their turn. 'You see,' he told Sir George, 'this Market Hall they're trying to take away from us was given to the people in the first place as a kind of musical headquarters. They used to be famous for their music round here.'

'They did, eh? Well, why aren't they still famous for their music?'

'Oh — they let it go,' replied Largs. 'Even the town band winked up a few months ago — I think some of these people you've heard helped to kill it so that they could

say that nobody wanted the Hall for music any more – but
now I've just revived it.'

'You have? You the conductor, eh?'

'Yes. Try to be.'

'Come up here, my dear fella,' roared Sir George with
the most astonishing enthusiasm, 'and let me shake you
by the hand. Now we're getting to something, after all this
Jenks and Tubby Shiptonthorpe and warming-pan nonsense. What's your name? Largs, eh?' They were shaking
hands now, and there was considerable applause from the
back seats and the little gallery. 'What is it you've got – an
orchestra?'

'No, not yet. Just the military combination – brass and
wood-wind.'

'Ah! – pity about that. If you'd had strings now, by
thunder! – I'd have played for you myself. Think – think
into what a heaven you can wander, with a full orchestra!
Bach, Mozart, Haydn,' shouted Sir George ecstatically,
'Beethoven, Schubert, Brahms. But what,' he continued,
coming down to earth again, 'can you do with a military
band?'

'You'd be surprised,' said Largs, settling down beside
him.

'Have a drink?' Sir George took a good pull himself.

'No, thanks,' said Largs. 'But nearly everything's
arranged for this combination nowadays. It's not the same
thing, of course, without the string tones, but you'd be
surprised what we can do. We've a rehearsal at half-past
six today, you ought to come and hear us, so long as you
realise we're only just beginning again. Now what about
this Market Hall of ours, which was given to the people of
Dunbury for their music?'

'It's yours,' declared Sir George, with passionate emphasis, 'and, so far as I'm concerned, it stays yours.' He turned

to the crowd. 'My decision is – that the Market Hall is not to be used as a show-room or a museum or for any other nonsense. It must remain the property of the people of Dunbury so that they can play in it and sing in it – '

'Let the people sing!' cried a tremendous voice in the gallery.

'And a damned good idea!' roared Sir George. 'The best I've heard for months. Let the people sing!' There was some cheering at the back, and several cries of protest from the front rows. Sir George now turned to the town clerk. 'If the Hall is open for the people to sing in, then keep it open. But if it isn't open, then see that it's opened at once.'

'Do nothing of the kind,' cried Major Shiptonthorpe.

'The Hall is closed,' said the town clerk, screwing up his courage and his face with it, 'and I shall take care that it remains closed. I cannot possibly accept this decision.'

'You're quite right,' Lady Foxfield called out. 'Whole thing's preposterous.'

'Hear, Hear!' from Mr Finningley.

Feeling that he had the best people with him, the town clerk grew bolder, looked Sir George in the face, and said loudly: 'We cannot accept this arbitration.'

Instead of exploding, Sir George was now surprisingly calm, though it was not a reasonable and sober calm, but one that might be found in some moon-haunted stratosphere of lunatic high spirits. He did not address himself to the little protesting group near him, but to the whole audience. His manner had immense dignity; all his words were quite clearly pronounced, as they had been throughout the afternoon; he swayed a little and his gestures were perhaps a trifle florid; but there was not much outward evidence to suggest that Sir George Denberry-Baxter was now governor-general of some distant dominion of Cloud-Cuckoodom.

'No doubt you have heard,' he began, in the broad oratorical style with its frequent grave pauses, 'that my arbitration in this matter of the Market Hall has been refused. I came here to do my duty to you people of Dunbury, without prejudice, with no desire but to see that justice should be done. A man of ripe experience in government, grown old in the service of the Colonial Office of His Majesty's Government, I was invited, I accepted the invitation, I came. And here I am.'

This statement was loudly applauded, and, muttering something about 'an old throat trouble,' Sir George seized the opportunity and had another large whisky. He emerged from this whisky more dignified than ever, almost regal, although there was now a very wild glitter in his eye. 'I have listened – I trust with reasonable patience – to some of the most astounding rubbish that has ever afflicted my ears. I need only mention ashtrays, salesmen, Senator Jenks, Tubby Shiptonthorpe, warming-pans and bulwarks, to refresh your memories of these incredible speeches.' He now stared with great severity at Mr Finningley. 'The fact, too, that we have here several little men with long moustaches who cry "Hear, hear!" at every fresh piece of idiocy, has not made things easier. Whether these same little men, with the noisy women they have brought with them, many of whom, to their shame, bear old and not entirely undistinguished names – though if the Foxfields ever did anything of any importance, it's the first I've heard of it – I say, whether these men and women have plotted and intrigued to deprive the citizens of this borough of their music, for which, let me remind you, though I didn't know it myself – damn it, a fella can't know everything! – I say, for which they were once famous, and could be famous again, though I have no hesitation in saying that my friend here is completely wrong in simply using a woodwind and brass combination, because the string tone – so clear, so vibrant, capable of such exquisite modulation – is essential. You must have strings,' he told them, with great earnestness. 'First and second violins, violas – a difficult but very beautiful instrument, cellos and double-basses. Without them your band can make a loud and cheerful noise – excellent, excellent, I've no objection to it in its place – but it will never achieve the true singing tone – '

'Let the people sing,' cried a man in the gallery, probably because he had had enough of this bewildering oration.

Sir George accepted it as a cue. 'Certainly let the people sing, my friend. Not only that. By thunder, the people are going to sing – and in that Hall too – before I leave this town. Neither the freemen of Dunbury, the singing freemen of Dunbury, nor George Denberry-Baxter can be dictated to by a lot of drivelling solicitors and clerks and salesmen and retired shopwalkers with over-grown whiskers. It can't be done. Follow me,' he shouted, rolling along the platform, then turning and pointing at Tom Largs, who was still on the platform: 'Come along – oh! – and bring that bottle with you, it's not quite empty yet.' He descended gigantically to the floor level and came rolling forward, shouting: 'Dr Krudiebacker, Tommy Tupperton, all my party there, rally yourselves, rally yourselves, and prepare for action – '

One of the policemen had come in to see what was happening. 'Now then, sir,' he called out, with an attempt at severity, 'we can't have all this noise.'

'My good man, this isn't a noise,' said Sir George, smiling wickedly upon him. 'These are merely a few observations and high-spirited exclamations. The *noise* hasn't begun yet. But it will – it will.'

'And remind me, duckie,' said Daisy in Hope's ear, as they followed in the surging wake, 'to ring them up at the "Dog and Bell" to say I shan't be back for some time. It looks to me as if we're going to be busy here, what with one thing and another, for the rest of the evening. An' if there's one who's not going to miss anything it's little Daisy.'

CHAPTER XIV

THE PEOPLE SING

DAISY SPOKE too soon when she said she was not going to miss anything. Within an hour, she felt she was missing everything, including her friends. They had all vanished. Timmy and the Professor had disappeared, presumably with Sir George, in the crowd between the Guildhall and the market square. It was quite a large crowd, too, for now two-thirds of the *United Plastics* employees were out on strike, many other persons had been told to stay away from their work or had stayed away without being told, and a few hundred housewives who normally would have been at home at this hour were wandering about in twos and threes, in or near the market square. Dunbury really was waking up. 'But it needn't go an' swallow everybody I know,' Daisy muttered to herself. For not only had Timmy and the Professor disappeared into the crowd, but the young man Roger had vanished too, to the distress of Hope, who was still waiting for him to say something; and now, just as Daisy had discovered that her little car was still safely parked in the square, Hope, whom she had thought was following on, had melted away too. Daisy looked everywhere among the chattering folk hanging about the square, but the girl was not there. They had agreed that as soon as they knew the car was still safely there – and on a normal day in Dunbury neither of them would have bothered about the car, but this was clearly not a normal day – they would have tea, leaving the men, wherever they might be, to get on with their antics. So now Daisy went to look for the girl in all the tea-shops and cafés round the square, and as there were five of these, including the back room at the confectioner's, and they were well filled, this took some time and about as much patience as Daisy had at her disposal. Muttering 'Blast the kid!' she gave up the search at the last tea-shop, the *Geisha*, and after a short scrimmage with a stout woman, two children, and four awkward parcels, managed to find a place for herself and ordered a pot of really nice, fresh, strong, hot tea. At first she told both herself and the waitress that she didn't want anything to eat, but then she discovered that it was nearly six o'clock, immediately weakened, and suggested rather than ordered a bit of toast and perhaps some brown bread and a cake or two.

It was after she had eaten all the toast and the brown bread and was just finishing her second cake and third cup of tea that she remembered that she had the address of Timmy's digs in her bag. After all, Timmy was her man or as near to being her man as any fellow would ever be these days, and if she was going to spend any more time looking for anybody it had better be for him and not for the girl, who was nice enough but now so love-sick she was half out of her senses. Besides, it was all right waking the town up, having a bit of devilment with that crazy Sir George, and all that, but Timmy needed somebody to look after him or he'd easily walk into more trouble. And so, refreshed and purposeful, Daisy set out for Mrs Mitterly's in Pike Street, which she found after a few enquiries and a bit more than she wanted of that 'straight across, then bear right, first left and second to the right' nonsense.

Mrs Mitterly answered the door. She was so excited that the most widely different expressions – of delight, suspicion, fear, bewilderment, doubt, contentment – flitted across her face at a fantastic speed, so that she was like an express view of one of the old silent films. Except that she wasn't silent. 'Yes, of course,' she twittered. 'I've heard Mr Tiverton speak of – yes, do come in – we're all rather upset here – you know about the strike – and then my boy's just gone out to play with the band – no, Mr Tiverton's not in – haven't seen him since – but the other one's in – yes, the Professor – and so pleased – yes, this way – '

There in the sitting-room was the Professor, looking very pleased indeed, and talking to a pale, plumpish girl who'd been mistakenly messing about with her hair and eyebrows. Mrs Mitterly's Fern, it appeared. 'The one who started the strike, really,' the proud mother explained, almost gasping under the pressure of all these goings-on. 'Well, you did, Fern. Everybody says – '

'Yes, all right, Mother, but you needn't go on about it.' This was the Fern who was now on her way, though as yet she did not know it, to meet the young manager in the Dunbury Co-operative Society and to find herself very soon in the nice little bungalow out Knutsford way turning on and off the immense radio-gramophone. She had been listening, for the last time, to the oddly fascinating talk of this tall thin elderly foreigner.

'I came to find Timmy,' said Daisy. 'Where is he?'

Still flushed and smiling, as if he had just been left a fortune, the Professor shook his head and spread out his long fingers. 'I do not know. They were going to listen to the band. I think our friend Sir George proposed to rehearse the band. There was a great deal more shouting and many people, and I felt I wanted a rest from shouting and people for a while. So I came here.'

'Well, you seem very pleased with yourself,' Daisy remarked, not too pleasantly, for she felt he had deserted Timmy.

He smiled at her. 'I am. You see, I sent this address to my friend in London, and now there has come permission for me to go to America. My son Karl is there, a professor, and I go to him, to be a professor too. So at last my troubles are ended.'

Daisy's face cleared at once. 'That's fine. I'm glad. I expect you'll like it over there – especially with your son there too.'

'Yes – and his wife – and their two small children, my grandchildren.' He was alight with tender anticipation. Then he laughed. 'Soon then I shall be professor again, with students, with serious colleagues, a grandfather, and no longer running away from policemen and trying to play *Hoopy-Toopy-Toots* on the piano. How Karl will laugh at that! But I will play *Hoopy-Toopy-Toots* for the children.'

'Good for you! Though if you ask me,' Daisy added, with professional severity, 'it's a terrible number, and how some of these girls now get away with such numbers just beats me.'

'I saw you,' said Mrs Mitterly shyly, 'the very week I was married – I'll never forget.'

'That puts a few years on me,' cried Daisy, delighted at this recognition. Then she continued hastily: 'Mind you, I was only a kid when I made my name. Nobody'll believe how young I was. Now, Professor, I suppose Timmy's all right?'

'Yes,' said the Professor dreamily, 'I am sure he is all right and will be all right – and you too – and the beautiful Hope too and the young man who fights but is too shy. There are some days when we feel that the mysterious tides and currents in the ocean of universal being suddenly change, and with them change our destinies. I feel this is one of those days. Just as there are times when we are swept on to misery, and do not know how or why, so too there are these times, though we do not speak so much about them, when we sail on, without knowing where we are going, into happiness.'

'And I think,' said Fern solemnly, looking at him with big solemn eyes, 'that you're a lovely talker – lovely!' And she sighed, as if she knew herself to be exiled from some once-familiar world of shining talk.

'You too!' And the Professor beamed upon her. 'You too, Miss Fern, I think are being carried along, towards some happiness that you know nothing about yet.' He held up a finger. 'Perhaps this very night – it may begin.'

'Well, I'm sure,' said Mrs Mitterly, who sounded most unsure. 'Though I say it – Fern's really a very good girl – and then they ought to treat them properly – these American tricks, as she says – but if you do go out tonight, Fern, do be careful – what with Raymond and that band – not that I don't like a bit of music myself, though my husband was the one – he'd go *anywhere* for music – specially them *overtures*. Why,' she added, blinking rapidly in affectionate wonder, 'he'd have overtures from morning till night.'

There fell upon them now one of those silences rare among people who do not know each other very well, not an empty but a full silence, not separating them but drawing them together; and it happened that at this moment the clouds were lifting from the dying sun and a sudden rich gold light came flooding that corner of Pike Street, so that they sat in a warm dusk behind a golden window; and as they kept that companionable silence their minds wandered away from the present time, with its sharp signalling of pleasure and pain, and began to look over a wide, dream-like prospect of life, regarding it with that tenderness which exists, like an ultimate tide of feeling, even beyond joy and sorrow. And out of this silence came a real friendship between Daisy and Mrs Mitterly and Fern, though to this day not one of the three has ever mentioned that moment.

It was broken for them by a *thud-thud-thud*, over which, when they listened carefully, they could hear distant music. 'It's the band,' cried Mrs Mitterly, springing up. 'I do believe they're – but no, they couldn't be – yes, I'm sure they are, though – '

'Playing in the square,' announced Fern, on behalf of the family. 'We've a strike meeting too. It's nearly time for it. Perhaps the band's helping us. I'll have to go.'

'Well, really,' said Mrs Mitterly, looking wistful, hopeful, doubtful, half-decisive, nearly decisive, 'seeing that you're going – and with Raymond in the band – I'm wondering – '

'We'll all go,' said Daisy firmly. 'You too, Professor, eh?'

'Yes, for it will be my last evening, I think, in Dunbury. And I must see everything there is to see tonight.'

Daisy and the Professor left the house together, then waited outside for the other two. 'If our little Timmy hasn't turned himself by this time into a bandsman,' she said, with more worry in her manner than the words suggest, 'then God knows where I'll find him.'

'He will be found,' said the Professor calmly. 'And when you find him, perhaps you had better keep him.'

'If you mean what I think you mean,' replied Daisy tartly, 'then you've got a sauce.'

'A sauce?' The Professor looked almost startled. 'How can I have a sauce?'

'I mean – a nerve, a cheek – '

'Impudence, eh? A curious idiom. I must remember it for America – '

'You needn't, 'cos the slang's all different there. You'll have to start all over again, Professor. But what did you mean about me an' Timmy? You think he needs somebody sensible to look after him?'

'And I think you would like somebody senseless to look after. Not that Timmy is senseless, of course. But he is an artist, and I think now he could be, with encouragement, a great clown. Mrs Daisy, I think you should make him into a great clown, who would reveal the shy English people to themselves and make them laugh and be happy. Now then,' as Mrs Mitterly, who came out into the street like a conspirator entering a secret meeting, joined them with Fern, 'we will go and find everybody.'

On their way to Daisy's car, Hope had been separated from Daisy by one of those strings of youths and girls that are always to be found, making a nuisance of themselves, on these occasions. Then just as Hope was about to catch up with Daisy, she had suddenly seen a tweed coat, about twenty yards away, and had darted across to it, dodging more youths and girls, because she was certain that Roger was inside it. And though Roger had turned up at the 'Dog and Bell,' he had said nothing to her, that is, nothing that really *meant* anything; and he had disappeared again, in that maddening way he had now, after the meeting at the Guildhall. So Hope, who could no longer extract the least enjoyment out of being proud and aloof, darted across to the tweed coat, which was moving away, gave it a tug and cried: 'Roger, I'm here.'

'And I'm here, too, girlie,' said the grinning youth, who even if he had not deceived her into thinking he was Roger would still have been a horror. When she turned away in disgust and hurried back to find Daisy, this youth still didn't realise that he had been a complete mistake. When Hope found the car but no Daisy (who by this time was looking round the nearest tea-shop), the idiot was sauntering up, grin and all. She flew again, and now she remembered that she had promised to go to the Cottage Hospital and tell Uncle Fred and Dr Buckie all that had happened. So off she went, feeling rather miserable, and though Uncle Fred and Dr Buckie gave her some tea and refused to believe half she told them about Sir George and laughed a lot at the other half, and it was really a cosy and merry little party they had up there, she came away feeling forlorn and empty and dissatisfied with everything.

It was almost dusk when she returned to the market square. The band was playing; there seemed to have been some kind of meeting; and the square was thick with people, and not just youths and girls but older folks too, people of all ages. Something had certainly happened to the town. You could feel it in the very air. Dunbury really was coming to life. But unfortunately Hope, in her present mood, could not enjoy the spectacle. They seemed to her a lot of dull fools. Now and then, as she slowly moved round the edge of the square, for the crowd was thick in the centre where the band was, one or two of them would recognise her, nudge each other and point, and several young men were about to tell her that the weather had cleared up a little, but though their mouths opened no sound came out of them when they saw her stony look. Most of the people there, however, were too busy exchanging news and views or, if they were nearer the centre, towards which the girl found herself drawn, too much occupied in listening to their band to bother about her. There is a certain glum satisfaction in being solitary and melancholy where so many others – mere light-minded creatures – are beginning to enjoy themselves, but Hope soon discovered that it palled. She began to ache a bit inside. The waltz the band was thumping out, with more energy than skill, seemed utterly without gaiety. It informed her, in strict three-four time, that now, owing to her own foolishness, she had lost the only man she would ever love, and she saw herself going down the years, a grave (but handsome), aloof woman with a broken heart. 'I wonder what Hope Ollerton's story is,' she could hear them saying; and then, being a sensible young woman, told herself that just leaving them wondering didn't seem much of a life. Oh dear! Oh damn!

It was then that a good strong hand fastened itself on her arm, and she wheeled round and there, not six inches from her, was Roger. And he just grinned, and it was wonderful.

'Oh – Roger!' And she kissed him, very quickly, as if they had arranged to meet on that very spot. His grip on her arm was terrible, hurt like anything, and was wonderful. His face was crimson, and his mouth fell open, and his eyes were round and nearly popping out, and all that was wonderful too. They just stayed there, arm in arm and very close, and it was the most natural thing in the world. What really changed, most magically, was the market square and all the people in it and, indeed, all Dunbury, with the cheerful little lights coming on in all the windows overlooking the square. They were nice people, who put up with all manner of things in their own patient, cheerful fashion, trudging off to work, trudging home again, saving up hopefully for this and that, secretly wondering when the bit of magic would happen; and now, if they were waking up, not taking so many orders without question, asking for some fun of their own, then so much the better. In fact, being with them here tonight – and of course so close and happy with Roger, even though Roger hadn't yet said one word – was really an adventure, and somehow quite a wonderful adventure. But being an English adventure it was liable to be rained upon; and at this very moment down the rain came.

Instead of scattering, the crowd pressed forward, and as Hope and Roger moved with it they could hear shouts of 'What about the Market Hall?'

'But it isn't open, is it?' said Hope, as Roger pulled her along.

'No, but it soon will be,' said Roger. 'Come on. We mustn't miss this.'

The band were not playing now and must have withdrawn themselves, leaving the space they had occupied to be filled with the surging folk. The result was that Hope and Roger now found themselves much nearer the Market Hall. They could just see, between the dancing rods of rain, the entrance to the main building, which was twelve feet above the level of the square and reached by twin curved flights of stone steps. The big doors were closed, and there seemed to be several policemen up there, shouting down to the crowd, who were shouting too and moving slowly, like a rising tide of folk, up the steps. Roger and Hope and all the people near them pushed steadily forward, not angrily but quietly and cheerfully. Not that Hope herself felt quiet and cheerful; she was wildly exhilarated inside, hardly noticed the rain, which was falling heavily now; and for her the whole scene had taken on a strange magical quality, as if life itself and all the most fascinating stories and films she had ever known had somehow run into and joined one another, so that every moment was both very real and yet part of an odd enchanting dream. This might be because of Roger, and yet she could not help feeling that everybody there was under the same spell. The people in the moving crowd were quite different now. That joke about waking them up had somehow turned into something true and serious.

Roger could see better than she could, and now he reported that the police had disappeared and the people were swarming up the steps. Everybody was pushing forward again. The space in front of the big doors was now filled with people. There were tremendous shouts from up there. 'Those doors'll be bust wide open in a minute,' cried Roger, charging forward and pulling her after him.

'He's just aching to pull something down himself,' Hope said to herself, as she went bumping after him through the crowd. 'Why I ever thought he was feeble, God only knows. He's terrible really. He's frightening. I love him.'

But now, within a few yards of the steps, the crowd was too densely packed even for Roger to penetrate, and he had to be content with holding her safe and tight and heaving forward with the rest. 'Now then, boys,' roared a great voice above their heads. 'Ready! Steady! Go-o-o-o!' There was a tremendous cracking and then a cheer. The big doors had been burst open, and the crowd, cheering and cheering, was swarming into the hall. A moment later, when Hope and Roger had almost reached the left-hand flight of steps, lights came on inside the building. 'Clear those steps,' they were shouting now. 'Make way there.' And all the people surged to the left, to keep the right clear. Hope and Roger were almost swept up their steps, for the people were still pouring into the hall, but with a great effort Roger forced himself and Hope out to the side, against the dripping stone balustrade, and there he held her securely while the crowd came pushing and stumbling by to enter the hall. The chandeliers within dramatically lit a section of the scene outside, the white

faces and the uplifted shining eyes in the golden rain.
And now they knew why the steps on the right had been
kept clear. They heard the heavy beat of the drum, a
sudden cheering, and then the full glory of the marching
band. *Let the People Sing* cried the clarinets and flutes,
thundered the trombones and euphoniums. Tom Largs
was marching in front, beating time and roaring out the
words of his song, and the crowd took it up at once, so
that by the time the band was marching up the steps, two
by two, the people themselves were sending the chorus in
great gusts of sound through the rain:

> *Let the people sing,*
> *And freedom bring*
> *An end to a sad old story —*

And as these waves of song broke over her and the band
came marching up, trilling and booming, Hope felt
herself shaken by an ecstasy, and leaned back hard against
the rough wet stone and clung tight to Roger's arm, for it
seemed as if a new and greater world, some rumour of
which had already haunted her young mind, were now
growing all round her, shooting up like the magic bean-
stalk. And she did not know whether to laugh or cry, and
did a little of both, when the final pair of bandsmen,
behind the big drummer, came into view. There, enthusiastically clashing the cymbals, were Sir George Denberry-
Baxter wearing a fireman's helmet, and Timmy Tiverton
wearing no hat at all and looking like a happy half-
drowned Yorkshire terrier. When this rum pair had passed
on and the band had entered the hall, the crowd went
swarming in after them; but Roger and Hope remained
where they were, though they were pushed a little farther
from the doorway, into the corner of the entrance plat-

form, by the sheer pressure of folk. They watched the faces streaming by – and Hope thought she caught a glimpse of Daisy and the Professor going in by way of the other steps – and they listened to the band and the singing inside and sang a bit themselves. After another ten minutes or so it seemed as if the hall must have been filled, and now only a few stragglers hurried past them to join in the impromptu concert, in full triumphant swing, and to escape the rain. Hope could feel a little cold stream trickling down her back, and her shoes felt pulpy, and she just might as well have lifted her face out of a cold bath. And as there was more of Roger than there was of her, he was correspondingly wetter, and there was a cascade off the end of his nose. There they were then, standing there like idiots, wet through, with a very noisy sing-song for half the town in full swing just round the corner, and it was there and then, in this barmy situation, that they had their talk. She had imagined herself having such a talk many, many times, but never in her most ridiculous fancies had it happened like this.

'I couldn't keep away, you see,' said Roger, 'couldn't think about anybody else, of course, but I didn't say much to you because I thought you were absolutely fed up with me.'

'I was – until Sunday.'

'What happened on Sunday?' asked Roger, peering anxiously at the lovely wet face.

'It was all queer. I'd never felt like that before. Then I decided,' Hope continued, omitting any mention of her scene with the others at tea-time, 'I must have fallen badly for somebody. Then when you came in – you remember? – I knew it was you.'

'Oh, Christopher! – I can hardly believe it,' cried Roger, embracing her so fervently that the few places that had been still comparatively dry were now as damp as the rest of her. Then staring at her again, he mumbled: 'I suppose it's all right – I mean, you won't suddenly find out it's all a mistake, will you?'

'No, Roger,' she told him gravely, 'I really, truly love you.' And she held up her face.

'Well, chump, what are you going to say to me?' she demanded, after an interval.

'Oh! – well, if you really mean it' – he floundered on – 'I suppose we'd better get married, hadn't we?'

'Yes – but you're not *saying* anything. Are you going to be feeble again?'

'Feeble!' he roared. 'Don't you start talking to me like that again, girl.' And then it was as if she had been seized by a great dripping bear. Everything she had on would be ruined for ever. She could hardly breathe. People would be looking at them. It was terrible. It was heaven.

'Now, now, now!' cried a waggish voice. But the owner of it did not give Roger time to knock him down but hurried past them into the hall. He was a middle-aged man, thick-set, square-faced, solemn, with a searching, detective look about him. Once inside the hall, where the band had established itself in proper style on the platform and was now accompanying the full chorus of all the people there, he listened with some interest for a minute or two, then looked about him in that solemn searching way he had. Not five yards away, sitting at the end of a row, was a group of five, consisting of two women and a girl, a tall thin man, and a little man, who was beginning to look a trifle weary. The little man was at the very end, and now this square-faced fellow, with a triumphant glint in his man-hunting eye, edged his way round until he was within easy hailing distance of this little man and could be seen clearly as well as heard.

'Hey!'

Timmy heard it, and his heart sank as he recognised it. He looked round. Yes, the very same man, now wearing a grim smile and beckoning with a podgy finger. No use upsetting the others. Better to go quietly. He slipped out. 'All right,' he whispered miserably, 'you've won. I'll come quietly.'

'That's right,' said the thick-set bloodhound, and moved him towards the entrance. Once there he stopped and looked about him doubtfully. 'We can't talk here.'

'What do we want to talk for?' asked Timmy bitterly. He felt he never wanted to talk again. This was life – just as things were coming right, with friends and fun all round you once again, down comes misery like a ton of black bricks.

'Now what's this about?' Very sharply this, from Daisy, who had followed them out. She saw the misery in Timmy's face, then turned like a little tigress on the other man. 'Who are you? What do you want?' There they were, the three of them, in the big doorway with *D'You Ken John Peel?* going at full blast behind them.

Timmy put a trembling hand on her arm. 'It's all right, Daisy,' he muttered miserably. 'Never mind. I've – I've – been expecting this – though I did hope to be disappointed.'

'You leave this chap to me,' cried Daisy fiercely, turning on him again and fairly bristling at him.

'Now listen, listen,' the man implored them, 'don't make it too tough for me 'cos I have to rush it. And I'll admit I have to 'cos I ought to have left here last Friday but stayed on just to try and get in touch with Mr Tiverton here. Rawson's the name, and I think you'll remember it though I never had the luck to do business for you in the old days. Since then I've been in South Africa and

America. Well, I'm booking acts for a road-show – a certain twenty weeks already and it's also going on the air early in November – and I've been looking high and low for a good broad comic and couldn't find one. Wasn't looking here, of course – who would? – but happened to put in a couple of days staying with my sister on my way up north – and who did I see but Mr Tiverton here. Then on Sunday night I see him again – and – say – what an act you've got there, Mr Tiverton! It'll murder 'em. And here I've been running round an' round, and was just givin' it up when I pop in here and find you. Now don't think I'm just commission-hunting. I'm a partner in the firm that's producing the show, and what I say goes.'

Timmy tried to speak but couldn't. He only made a little bleating kind of noise.

But Daisy had not lost her tongue. 'What is this firm?' she asked suspiciously.

'Silver and Baumber,' replied Rawson, and then as he heard a gasping sound from Timmy, he added hastily: 'I know, I know! You're going to tell me they're only a provincial firm, but let me tell you Silver and Baumber have some real money to play with now and they've got me to show them a few big ideas. And you're one of them, Mr Tiverton. Don't let the fact that it's only Silver and Baumber stand in your way at all, because I'm going to offer you as good a contract as anybody in London can offer you.'

'Well, we'll see,' said Daisy firmly. 'You've got a car, eh? All right. Then come and see me in an hour's time out at the "Dog and Bell".'

'See you, eh?'

'Yes, me. I'm his manager.'

'Okay,' said Rawson, who talked exactly like an agent

and yet still contrived to look like a square-faced, stern detective. 'I could do with a drink.'

'And I,' said Timmy faintly, 'could do with a bucketful.'

Two wild and dripping figures now appeared in the light. 'I thought it was you,' said one of them, Hope. 'I recognised your voice. Isn't it wonderful? We're engaged.'

'You look drowned,' said Daisy severely. 'And if you're not careful it won't be wedding bells for you two but pneumonia. Come on, let's go home and dry ourselves and be happy. It's all right waking these people up, but I'm about tired of hearing 'em kenning John Peel. Collect the party, boys.'

'But what about Sir George?' asked Roger. 'We don't want him, but we can't leave him in the lurch.'

'He's not been left in the lurch,' replied Timmy grinning, 'he's been left in "The Bull." I told him not to wear that fireman's helmet, but he would have it – an' it did him in. So three of us took him over to "The Bull" and saw him to bed, an' God help 'em over there when he wakes up in the morning.'

'It'll do 'em good,' said Daisy. 'Now, pop off, Mr Rawson an' get your car while we collect our party. Then at the other end, all nice and comfortably, we'll talk business.'

And they did talk business. Timmy, dried and warmed and fed, waited upstairs in Daisy's little sitting-room, still wondering if there was a catch in it somewhere, but also, being a true artist, busy, too, working out a few extra details in his new act. He was tired, though, and he was glad when Daisy had insisted on handling Rawson herself. Timmy couldn't have talked terms tonight. Either he would have refused everything or accepted anything. He'd never been much of a business man, and now tonight he felt farther away from a business man than ever. A little

man, half-old, half-young, with a new act to work out (it'll
murder 'em), still bewildered and very tired.

Daisy came bustling in, a triumphant fiery particle.
'Well for all his talk he was pretty tough when we got
down to it, but they're putting a lot of money into the
show – they've got names – and the bookings are there all
right. So I didn't haggle too long. Fifty a week certain,
and after the six weeks if they gross over a thousand you
jump to sixty-five, and over fifteen hundred you get
seventy-five, and there you stay. All right?'

'Fifty – sixty-five – seventy-five!' stammered Timmy,
smiling weakly at her. 'I'd forgotten there was any money
like that. I feel I'm dreaming, Daisy.'

'Not you, duck,' she said fondly, and put a solid little
arm across his shoulder. 'I'm real, aren't I?'

'Yes, Daisy, you're real all right.' And he kissed her
gently. 'You're a pal – the best. Meeting you again – well,
you can't imagine what it's been like. Only a week last
Monday I was sitting in a park in Birchester – thinking I
was finished for good – wondering what was the easiest
way of slipping out for ever – '

'Don't let me hear you ever mention that again,' cried
Daisy, like an affectionate little thunderstorm. 'You silly –
little – oh dear!' And she sat down opposite him and
looked into the fire.

'What are you thinking?' he asked, after a long pause.

'I was thinking,' she began slowly, 'about you an' me,
Timmy. Here you are, booked up again, and in my
opinion all set for a big new success, going right up to the
top again. But you've not many real friends left. You've
no home to come back to. You've nobody to look after
you.'

'That's true. Whatever happens, it won't be the same as
it used to be. All different now. Still, I mustn't grumble.'

'Let me hear you start grumbling!' she cried indignantly. Then she looked down at the fire again. 'Then there's me. I've got this place. It's doin' well, makin' money. But I don't want it all the time, an' now it's running easily it doesn't need me all the time. An' I feel too cut off from the old life. An' I want somebody to look after.' She looked him mistily in the eyes. 'You know me, Timmy. I was a wild young devil once, an' I've been a silly woman – an' sometimes a dam' selfish one – many a time since. But I'm not a bad sort – '

'Bad sort? You're a – '

'Shut up an' let me finish or I never will. Though if you were goin' to say something nice, I could do with it, so keep it in your mind till afterwards. But I'm not a bad sort, an' I'm easier to live with an' have a lot more sense than I used to have. Well, you know what I'm like. No chicken but no damned old hen neither. Glad to put my feet up sometimes an' no treat to look at on a bright mornin', but with plenty of life an' fun in me yet. And I'm fond of you right through an' through, Timmy.'

'Well, that's grand, Daisy,' he told her, looking bewildered. 'Never heard anybody make a nicer speech. But – er – what's it all about?'

'What's it all about?' she shouted. 'What d'you think it's all about, you fat-headed little comic? I'm askin' you to marry me.'

'Oh!' He was dumbfounded.

'Yes, an' don't sit gaping there, as if you'd never heard of anybody marrying before. It's not new. There's been a hell of a lot of it. An' I'm askin' you before some peroxided, pie-faced, gold-diggin' little soubrette gets her claws into you. No, no, ducky,' she cried hastily, 'forget that. I didn't mean it. But I did mean what I said before – about us. What do you think?'

'But of course I will, Daisy,' he told her. 'And it's a marvellous idea – best I ever heard of.'

'If you don't mean that, Timmy, I'll – I'll kill you. Oh! – duckie, we'll do our best for each other, won't we?' There were voices outside. 'For God's sake! They're all comin' in now – no private life at all!'

But she forgave them and told them the news. The other engaged couple was loud in its congratulations. The Professor was delighted and kept shaking hands with both of them, bending well forward to do it and looking as if he were about to present them with a prize for the best essay.

'It is as I said it would be,' said the Professor, when they had settled down. 'We are all happy because this is one of the days, perhaps the beginning of one of those periods, when we feel that the mysterious tides and currents in the ocean of universal being suddenly change, no longer beating against our wishes but sweeping our lives forward to show us these wishes being granted. We can sail on into happiness just as we can drift and flounder into misery. As it is with individuals, so it is too, in longer periods, with communities and whole races. Now the relation between ourselves,' he continued, dropping into his lecturing manner, 'and these invisible tides and currents, this strange rhythm of good and ill fortune, is not understood at all. Astrology pretends to understand it, and this, as well as the prevalence of mere idle superstition, explains the present popularity of astrology. On the other hand, neither religion nor science – '

'You're dead right, Professor,' said Timmy cheerfully. 'By the way, Daisy, where does this tour open?'

'Didn't I tell you, duck? I meant to. You open at the good old Palace, Birchester.'

'Birchester, eh?' said Timmy thoughtfully. 'Well, I'd better take care I'm good.'

The Shapes of Sleep

Journalist Ben Sterndale is asked to track down a stolen sheet of figures, although no one will tell him what was on it. However, when a local newspaper reports a hit-and-run involving a certain philatelist, Sterndale suspects a link and finds himself plunged into mystery and mayhem. The chase takes him on a lightning tour of Germany as he tries to make sense of the stamp-collector's dying words, 'The Shapes of Sleep'.

'J. B. Priestley is the most skilful of all the writers of his generation'
Daily Telegraph